Robert Fabbri read Drama and Theatre at London University and worked in film and TV for twenty-five years. He has a life-long passion for ancient history, which inspired him to write the bestselling Vespasian series and the Alexander's Legacy series. He lives in London and Berlin.

ALEXANDER'S LEGACY

FORGING KINGDOMS

ROBERT FABBRI

CORVUS

First published in Great Britain in 2023 by Corvus,
an imprint of Atlantic Books Ltd.

Copyright © Robert Fabbri, 2023

Map and illustrations © Anja Müller

10 9 8 7 6 5 4 3 2 1

A CIP catalogue record for this book is available from the British Library.

Hardback ISBN: 978 1 83895 613 4
E-book ISBN: 978 1 83895 615 8

Corvus
An imprint of Atlantic Books Ltd
Ormond House
26–27 Boswell Street
London
WC1N 3JZ

www.atlantic-books.co.uk

FSC
www.fsc.org
MIX
Paper | Supporting
responsible forestry
FSC® C171272

To my friend and fellow author, Tim Clayton,
who introduced me to the world of the
Successors forty years ago.

SELEUKOS
THE BULL-ELEPHANT

ROXANNA
THE WILD-CAT

LYSIMACHUS
THE CRUEL

BYLAZORA
MACEDON
EPIRUS
PASSERON
PELLA
AMPHIPOLIS
TYMPHAIA
THESSALONIKE
THRACE
PYDNA
THESSALY
LEMNOS
KARDIA
BYZANTIUM
CIUS
HELLESPONTINE
PERGAMUM
LYDIA
PHRYGIA
HALYS
AMISIUS
KAPPADO
SARDIS
CORINTH
SPARTA
ATHENS
EPHESUS
CELAENAE
PISIDIA
CILICIA
CARIA
HALICARNASSUS
MESO
TARSUS
ISSUS
RHODOS
RHOSOS
CYPRUS
THAPSACUS
MARION
SALAMIS
TRIPOLIS
PAPHOS
KITION
SYRIA
BERY.TOS
DAMASCU
CYRENE
BARCA
TYROS
CYRENAICA
NILE DELTA
HIEROSPHY MA
ALEXANDRIA
GAZA
PETRA
PELUSIUM
MEMPHIS
ARABI

EGYPT

NILE

W

PTOLEMY
THE BASTARD

KASSANDROS
THE JEALOUS

A list of characters can be found on page 456.

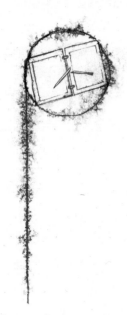

ARTONIS.
THE WIDOW.

VENGEANCE RULED ARTONIS' heart; vengeance for the execution of the man she had loved: vengeance for her husband Eumenes. Ever loyal to the Argead royal house of Macedon, Eumenes, a Greek from Kardia, had fought those who would usurp that line after Alexander, the third so named, had died in Babylon following ten glorious years of conquest.

Alexander had given the Great Ring of Macedon to Perdikkas, the chief of his bodyguards, with the words, 'To the strongest', but had neglected to say whom that might be. With Eumenes as his ally, Perdikkas had endeavoured to be that man, ruling as regent for the son delivered of Alexander's wife, the eastern wild-cat Roxanna, three months after his death, and Philip, Alexander's half-brother, a fool with the mind of a child. Perdikkas' attempt had ended with the assassin's blade. Thus, the empire had begun to split asunder as generals and governors of satrapies looked to secure what they already had with an eye to grabbing more.

Antipatros, Alexander's eighty-year-old regent in Macedon, had attempted to craft a settlement at a conference at The Three Paradises, a favoured hunting lodge of the old Persian

Achaemenid dynasty in the wooded hills above Tripolis. But this too had failed for he had not made peace with Eumenes who still upheld the right of the Argead royal house, in the persons of the babe and the fool, to rule the empire; neither had he included Olympias, Alexander's power-lusting mother, and Antipatros' greatest enemy. But crucially, the settlement failed to address the fundamental question: was the empire subject to Macedon or was Macedon a constituent part of the empire?

With the loss of his favoured son, Iollas, in battle against Eumenes, Antipatros had returned to Macedon to wither and die, leaving the field clear for a new force to stake a claim: Antigonos, the one-eyed satrap of Phrygia, a man in his sixties who had not shared the adventure in the east; he had been left behind by Alexander to complete the subjugation of Anatolia and now he surged with the ambition to prove himself the strongest. With vigour did Eumenes prosecute the war against Antigonos for he realised that with the ageing cyclops' one-remaining eye on the ultimate prize there would be no place for the Argead line in his settlement, for he wished to establish his own dynasty and ensure his precocious son, Demetrios, succeeded him.

In the west and then on into the east did the campaign roll, devastating the lands it swept through, to culminate in two great battles, each involving just shy of a hundred thousand men, on the far side of the Zagros Mountains in Media. But only one general could return to the sea from such a tumultuous struggle and that man was Antigonos, for Eumenes had been betrayed by Peucestas, satrap of Persis, and handed over to his foe. Antigonos offered to spare the Greek's life should he accede to his demands: that he should join with him and, as the champion of the Argead royal house, support the claim of Kassandros, the eldest son of Antipatros, and his new bride, Thessalonike, the half-sister of Alexander, who now ruled as regents for the boy-king in Macedon – the fool Philip having been murdered by Olympias.

Eumenes had refused.

Garrotting had been her husband's fate and Artonis wept to recall the memory. But Eumenes had left hope in that, before he died, he had worked out the implication of what was demanded of him for Antigonos' rivals vying for empire and the young Alexander: it was death, including those of Kassandros and Thessalonike.

Thus, from beyond the grave, with her help, her husband would engineer an alliance that would bring the cyclops down. To that end she had, with the aid of Seleukos, then satrap of Babylonia, escaped from the east and sought refuge with Ptolemy, the putative bastard half-brother of Alexander, who had taken Egypt. Ptolemy had enabled her to visit firstly Asander, the satrap of Caria, and then Kassandros and Thessalonike, and on to Lysimachus, satrap of Thrace, high in the north.

With her husband's warnings of Antigonos' plans delivered, Artonis had come to Pergamum to visit her elder half-sister, Barsine, the former mistress of Alexander and the mother of his illegitimate son, Herakles; and it was here her single-minded desire for vengeance had been diluted, for the boy was approaching his majority and yearned to emulate his father in his deeds – as he already did in his looks – and in this endeavour Artonis now wished to share.

And so a new scheme had entered Artonis' head, one which would further her quest for revenge and aid the cause of her nephew; for Artonis realised the surest way of preventing Antigonos from stealing the empire was to promote one who had a natural right to claim it: a youth who looked so like his father that no Macedonian would refuse him his birth-right; a youth who had been underestimated, then overlooked and then forgotten; a youth who could shake the Macedonian world and command allegiance from almost all. A youth whose success would spell Antigonos' death.

'If Herakles' claim to the throne of Macedon is accepted, all of the empire's satraps would have to swear loyalty to him, thus recognising they are subject to Macedon,' Artonis said, looking out west from a high terrace of Pergamum's royal palace. Perching on a hill thrusting precipitously up from the plain, to the height of two hundred men, the town dominated its environment for leagues around; with sheer drops on the northern, eastern and western sides, it possessed a virtually impregnable position as it could only be approached from the southern slope rising in three natural terraces, each one a line of defence. 'If they refuse, they expose themselves as rebels to what Alexander built.' She turned her dark eyes to Barsine, standing next to her. 'And from what I know of the Macedonian mind, that would be the equivalent of renouncing your identity.'

Barsine, once a lithe beauty unsurpassed who had captivated Alexander, but now, in her fiftieth year, running to homely fat in her isolation in Pergamum, looked down at her half-sister, half her age and half a head shorter than her. 'And you think Antigonos will be unable to swear that oath to my son?'

'I do; if he does, he'll be laying himself open to the charge of treason for defeating and executing my husband as he fought to defend the right of the Argead royal house.'

'Thus, leaving him no choice to refuse to pledge

allegiance and be seen as a rebel?' Barsine paused for a few moments' thought. 'What about Ptolemy and Lysimachus? They will surely want to keep their independence.'

Artonis smiled. 'Sister, as satrap of Hellespontine Phrygia our father Artabazos was forced by the Great King Artaxerxes to flee to the court of Philip of Macedon when you were a young girl; I was born there and our late sister, Artakama, was conceived in exile. But when Darius succeeded Artaxerxes he restored our father to his satrapy, as a favour to your mother's brothers. He was thereafter loyal to Darius and fought for him against Alexander, sharing his exile after the battle of Gaugamela. Alexander then rewarded him for his loyalty to Darius by appointing him the satrap of Bactria, a post he kept until his death.'

'And what's that meant to tell me?'

Artonis gestured to the brown lands far below, flecked with the last of the winter snow. 'This was his domain, a king in all but name, subject only to the King of Kings; he was only forced to flee when Artaxerxes became too high-handed and offended our father's dignity; Darius, however, was forgiving and our father served him loyally until his murder. All he wanted was to be left to rule his satrapy with little or no interference, paying annual tribute to the Great King, providing men for his armies and doing him honour as was due to his rank. That is what Ptolemy and Lysimachus will settle for should a true Argead come to the throne.'

'My son, my Herakles, ruling the empire as his father's heir; a true Argead.' The glint of ambition flashed in Barsine's eyes; but then doubt clouded them. 'Will Herakles be accepted as a true Argead? Alexander never took me as a wife whereas there's no doubt he married Roxanna; her child, the namesake of his father, is legitimate.'

'And twelve years old and a prisoner of Kassandros and Thessalonike in Amphipolis as they strut around posing as the rightful regents. No one has seen him in four years. And besides, his mother is Bactrian; you are at least half-Greek. Who would the Macedonians rather have on the throne: the whelp of an eastern wild-cat in four years' time – if, on the off-chance, Kassandros foolishly allows him to live – or Herakles now he's turning sixteen and can rule without a regent immediately?'

'I know what most would say but Kassandros and Thessalonike would opt for neither of those options. They're secure in Macedon and have Thessaly, Athens and much of Boeotia under their control; they won't give all that up without a fight.'

'Which is why I need an army, Mother.'

Artonis and Barsine turned to Herakles as he walked out onto the terrace; fair of skin and hair – worn long over his ears and down his neck – he looked at them with Alexander's eyes, one blue and one brown, mesmerising to those seeing them for the first time. He smiled, his face lighting up and radiating warmth. 'Two sisters plotting together are what I've discovered out on the terrace. Plotting, yet the subject of their machinations is excluded from their whisperings.'

Barsine held out her hand to her son. 'Then tell us what you think?'

'I think we should dine and I shall tell you the news that has just reached me from the south.'

'From whom?'

'Kleopatra.'

Barsine frowned. 'She wrote directly to you?'

Herakles did not share his mother's incredulity. 'Why

14

not? She's my father's sister and, as her nephew, I'm her eldest male relative; in a few days' time, when I become sixteen, she will be my responsibility.'

'Two whole moons ago?' Artonis said, having been apprised of the contents of the despatch from Kleopatra, currently residing just twenty-five leagues to the south in Sardis.

'Yes, the message from Ptolemy came overland to Sardis as the midwinter seas were so treacherous this year, but two moons ago he defeated Demetrios at Gaza on Egypt's border, capturing eight thousand infantry and a couple of thousand cavalry plus all his elephants; since then he's been moving north, retaking all the towns Antigonos took from him last year and, at the time of his writing to Kleopatra, he was negotiating the surrender of Tyros whilst his general, Cilles, harried Demetrios as he withdrew north.' Herakles raised his cup. 'To Ptolemy's endeavour; may it keep Antigonos' gaze drawn south.'

Artonis was less enthusiastic than Barsine in drinking the toast. *I'll not drink to the man who sent my sister to her death.*

Barsine caught the shadow pass across Artonis' face. 'Whatever you think of Ptolemy's treatment of Artakama, you must not let it get in the way of pragmatic politics: Ptolemy needs to be an ally.'

Artonis' smile was wry. 'That doesn't mean I have to drink to him.'

'No; but it does mean you should forget your hatred of him when we consider his usefulness. Artakama was your full sister but she was of my blood as well; yes, she shall be avenged but not until we no longer need Ptolemy.'

15

Artonis breathed deeply through her nose, her eyes closed, and nodded. *She's right. I need to be more mature and focus on what needs to be done now.*

'But it's not just Ptolemy who might be of use to us,' Herakles said, holding out his cup for a slave to refill. 'He gave Seleukos a thousand men and he set off across the desert with the object of retaking Babylon and reinstalling himself as the satrap.'

Artonis was incredulous. 'Taking Babylon with a thousand men?'

Herakles shrugged. 'He did it before with fewer; and besides, Pythan, Antigonos' satrap of Babylonia, was killed by Seleukos' in hand-to-hand combat at Gaza. But if he's successful...' Herakles let the thought ride.

Artonis saw the implications immediately. 'Antigonos will have to deal with Seleukos after he has dealt with Ptolemy.'

Barsine smiled. 'He's going to be very busy looking south and east for the next couple of campaigning seasons.'

Herakles lifted his cup in another toast. 'Which is why I need an army to take the west.'

Artonis raised her cup and sipped. 'I think it's time I visited Kleopatra.'

'There's no need. The other news this letter conveyed is that my aunt is on her way here to celebrate my coming of age.'

It was disguised as the wife of a merchant that Kleopatra passed the guards on the city's lower gate, down on the plain, and then made her way up the three rising levels of the south-facing hill, to the palace in the upper town, with one female slave accompanying her. 'It took all my power to convince the officer on the palace gate to call you down to identify me,' Kleopatra said, laughing at the memory. 'I think he's still shaking at the choice between what you would do to his testicles if you were brought down to the gate unnecessarily and what I would do to his testicles if I was kept waiting a moment longer.'

'I knew it was you because of your letter to Herakles,' Barsine said, coming forward to greet her guest as Artonis held back. 'We came down immediately; the officer was very pale when we arrived. But why the secrecy?' Barsine held Kleopatra's by the hands and stepped back to admire her disguise. 'You look as if you haven't had a change of clothes in a moon and a bath in two.'

'Both of which I would be grateful to remedy as soon as I may. But it was imperative that word of our meeting does not reach Antigonos' ears. I've left my women, except my body-slave, Thetima,' she indicated to her slave, a cheerful-looking buxom creature, 'back in Sardis carrying on their routine as if I were still in residence; one of them, Daphne, who can pass for me at a distance, will even dress in my clothes and walk in the gardens where Antigonos' men will see her and believe I'm still there. Here we don't have that worry as it's Lysimachus' men who still hold the town.'

Barsine grimaced. 'Yes, but for how much longer I can't say. Antigonos has appointed his own satrap of Hellespontine Phrygia, a friend of his nephew Ptolemaios by the name of Phoinix. So far, he's left us alone.'

'What happened to Lysimachus' satrap?'

'He never appointed one. Lysimachus doesn't believe in delegation; he rules by brooding threats. Now that Antigonos is going to be busy in the south and east he may venture back over the Hellespont and remove Phoinix, but it's hardly worth his while. I think he prefers to keep the ownership of Hellespontine Phrygia opaque, a buffer between him and the cyclops.'

'If the cyclops were gone, he wouldn't need a buffer.' Kleopatra kissed Barsine on the cheek and then looked at Artonis with a frown.

'My half-sister, Artonis,' Barsine said.

'Eumenes' widow?' Kleopatra conjectured, taking Artonis' hand. 'I hoped you'd be here, but I couldn't know for sure. I want to thank you for all your husband tried to do for my family, to the extent of giving his life for our cause. My deep condolences on his death, my dear.'

Artonis bowed her head, remembering Kleopatra was technically a queen, albeit of Epirus, far to the west. 'You are most gracious, lady.'

'Please, let's have no formality between us seeing as we have the same objective. We shall speak after I've had that bath you promised me, Barsine. And I want my nephew to be present.'

'You'll find it impossible to keep him away; he's becoming most assertive now he's reaching his majority.'

'That is to be expected of Alexander's blood.'

It was Artonis' favourite time of the day, the two hours after noon, when those who could afford to do so retired to their beds, as those who could not toiled out in the fields or at whatever work supported them and their families in their meagre lives. But it was not for the peace and rest she enjoyed the time, it was for the memory of this part of the day spent in the arms of her husband once he had returned to her in Susa, after almost a five-year absence fighting for the family that had raised him from obscurity. A Greek from

Kardia, Eumenes had been forced to flee after the Tyrant, Hecataeus, executed many of his family. He had ended up in the court of Philip in Pella. Although diminutive in height, the little Greek had come to the king's attention through his analytical mind and ability to distil a problem to its very essence; it was not long before Philip made Eumenes his personal secretary, a post Alexander renewed when he came to the throne after his father's assassination.

His reputation for cunning had earned him the sobriquet 'sly'; it had been well deserved, and Alexander had valued his services. So much, indeed, that Alexander had thought to give him Artonis as a bride when he had forced his officers to take Persian wives in the mass wedding at Susa. Artonis had been fifteen at the time. Most eastern women would tower over the sly little Greek, but not Artonis; she forever thanked her god Ahura Mazda for her short stature for it had caused her to be given to the best of men. Her sister, Artakama, two years her junior, had been less fortunate and had become Ptolemy's wife only to be abandoned, like most of the eastern brides, on the death of Alexander. But Eumenes had kept Artonis and thus she would always cherish his memory, especially in the heat of the afternoon.

And it was with that warm thrill of sexual recollection, despite the chill of an Anatolian winter compared to a summer in Susa and Babylon, that she sat in Barsine's private apartment, plush with rugs strewn on wooden floors and deep cushions on luxuriously upholstered couches, sipping warmed wine and listening to the woman whose views on what needed to be done were so in tune with her own it was as if they had been conferring for some time.

And it was as Kleopatra finished outlining her plans that Artonis felt at last there was the real chance of bringing down the man who executed her husband, and his son.

DEMETRIOS.
THE BESIEGER.

BEING TAKEN FOR a fool was an affront; being taken for a fool with no military experience was intolerable; Demetrios vowed to set the record straight. Yes, he had been soundly beaten by Ptolemy at the battle of Gaza, losing almost eight thousand infantry, two thousand cavalry and his entire elephant herd to the satrap of Egypt, as well as all his personal baggage. And his shame at his reversal burned within him so that he found it hard to meet the eyes of his officers as they came in, in ones and twos, with stragglers from the defeated army, to his new camp at the Three Paradises hunting lodge, in the hills above Tripolis on the northern Phoenician coast. And yes, he had barely managed to rescue his wife and children from the path of the victorious army, and so he now felt diminished in front of Phila, his spouse of ten years, for he had failed her as a husband and had put their children in jeopardy. Thus he was convinced he was less of a man in her eyes, a feeling compounded by the fact Phila was ten years his senior. He now felt as if he were a small boy in her presence; a small boy who, no matter how hard he tried, failed to give satisfaction.

This could not continue.

But it was one loss, one mistake, one piece of bad luck, which had brought him to this humiliating position and he would reverse it soon – indeed, it had to be soon as, not only did he need to shine in Phila's eyes but also he would not be able to face his father, Antigonos, when he came south from Phrygia after the snows had melted in the spring, if he had not made up for his mistake.

In the meantime, the manner of Ptolemy's general Cilles' advance north with the bulk of the Ptolemaic army's mercenaries was too provoking to be borne. With little discipline and even less scouting, Cilles was leading more of a victory procession than a military advance to scour the country for a defeated foe. And it was this casual approach that so offended Demetrios: Cilles advancing towards him as if he were a fool of no consequence; a blunderer to be laughed at and not the son of Antigonos, the greatest general of the age who had defeated Eumenes to become the one man able to hold the entire empire. And even more hurt and humiliation did he feel at the memory of Ptolemy's returning of his personal baggage and slaves, all captured along with his tent, together with lavish gifts, each of which rubbed yet more salt into a very raw wound.

And so Demetrios had sent to all the towns holding a garrison loyal to his father, ordering their commanders to leave their posts and report to him with their men at The Three Paradises immediately, for he intended to crush Cilles, capture his troops and push back south to retake all he had lost. Only then would he be able to look his father in the eye and ask forgiveness for the disaster he had presided over at Gaza. Only then would he be able to do justice to himself in his wife's bed.

Demetrios looked sidelong at Phila, yearning to unpin her high-piled auburn hair and see it fall against the pale skin of her cheeks as her green eyes fixed him with desire, but she kept her gaze firmly forward. He returned his attention to his growing army parading, for Phila's benefit, under his general Philippos' command, on manicured parkland, part of the vast area of hunting grounds making up The Three Paradises – each paradise centred around a hunting lodge of palatial proportions – hoping she would be impressed by the force he had gathered together in such a short time.

'Surely there are still too few, Husband,' Phila commented, her tone matter-of-fact. 'I'm no expert but I would say there are no more than three thousand infantry and around three or four hundred cavalry.'

Demetrios took off his helmet and rubbed a hand through his mane of raven curls; the jaw muscles on either side of his beardless face pulsed as his dark eyes hardened and he glanced back down at his wife and then, again, looked away. 'I will have to make do with what I have, Phila; pointing out the obvious is neither helpful nor pertinent. The army is what it is and with luck it will continue to grow as more men come in from the more distant garrisons.'

Phila returned her husband's hard look as barked orders brought the parade crashing to attention; but he would not meet her eye. 'Swallow your pride and send to your father for reinforcements; don't compound your mistake by trying to rectify it with inadequate resources.'

The gods protect me from women with opinions; Antipatros should have taught his daughters their place. 'My father will come south as soon as the passes are open with his army next month.'

'Then wait for him.'

Demetrios was finding it increasingly difficult to keep his temper with his wife who had, since they had been forced to flee north from Gaza, made free with her views as to what he should do, as if he knew nothing. 'Woman, I know Antipatros consulted you and valued your advice from a very young age and I'm aware your first husband, Krateros, was equally receptive to your opinions and so am I – but not in military matters.'

Phila shook her head, lowering it to hide her exasperation; she hardened her tone. 'Demetrios, this isn't a military issue, it's a pride issue. If we were discussing a military campaign, we would both agree that to launch a counter-attack with three thousand men against an army which has already defeated you once is foolhardy to say the least. The only reason you're considering it is because you dread facing your father without at least something to mitigate what happened at Gaza.'

And I need to prove myself to you. 'He'll take away my independent command.'

'You never had an independent command! He left you with Nearchos, Pythan, Philippos and Andronicus to advise you and to curb your impetuosity. But when they counselled you to fall back in the face of Ptolemy's advance, as he would never be able to prosecute a winter campaign, you overruled them. Now Pythan's dead, Andronicus is besieged in Tyros, Nearchos is scrabbling around Syria trying to find troops for you to make the same mistake with again, whilst Philippos drills an army so small I barely noticed it.'

As you barely noticed me last night. 'Perhaps, but all the while Cilles is mocking me by parading through the country as if I were not in control of it.'

'But you're not, Demetrios. You lost control of Palestine and most of Coele-Syria, with your defeat at Gaza.'

'And I will not lose Phoenicia as well,' Demetrios growled through gritted teeth.

'Then pull back, wait for your father's reinforcements and attack Cilles' parade in the spring.'

'Enough, woman! Don't push the respect I hold for you any further!' Demetrios regretted his explosion in an instant; he took a breath to calm himself and tried a more reasoned approach. 'I'll not wait until I outnumber Cilles; if I were to do that, people would say I can only win if I have more men than my opponent. I want a better reputation than that so no one will remember Gaza and I'm going to start gaining it now.' He pointed to the lines of men, their bronze helmets shining dull in winter sun, as they were subjected to the inspection of their officers. 'With these lads I'm going to defeat Cilles, capture his troops and enrol them into my army within three days.'

Phila looked at her husband as if he were an errant child caught making yet another promise he could not keep; he did not enjoy it. 'Demetrios, I've already lost one husband in battle; don't make me a widow again and deprive young Antigonos and Stratonice of a father just to satisfy your pride and vanity.' With a curt nod, Phila walked back to the sumptuous hunting lodge which had been their home since her husband's humiliation.

Demetrios turned but refrained from shouting another boastful remark after her and then cursed himself. He had been forced to marry Phila when he was sixteen, shortly after Eumenes had made her a widow with Krateros' death in battle against him. Antigonos and Antipatros had made a pact and sealed it with the marriage of their oldest children.

Demetrios still burned with shame as he recalled his father laughing at him, joking that he would not be able to manage a woman so far his senior; but he had, in the main, and she had given him a son and a daughter. Physically it had been good between them. Phila, however, read widely and used her mind, enjoying discussions that were, in general, beyond her young husband's interest or intellect, for Demetrios was enamoured of war; if he had any interest other than its pursuit it was hunting – indeed he had won the right to recline at the dinner table as a man by killing a wild boar at the age of fourteen – and so his conversation with his wife was limited. But he had always harboured the urge to impress her with what he thought, until Gaza, he excelled in; thus the defeat had been a double calamity for their relationship, as not only in his mind had he failed deeply as a man but also what conversation there had been between them had now dried up. For how could he talk strategy and tactics with her, or boast of his achievements and prowess, when all the while the spectre of his flight as a defeated general hung over them?

But you'll think differently of me when I come back with Cilles and his army. And this was something he was confident he would be able to do since hearing an intelligence report that morning concerning how the general had made camp two nights previously at Byblus, just ten leagues to the south. He looked at his small army still being subjected to the torment of a rigorous inspection. *If Cilles really is camping so carelessly then three thousand plus the cavalry will be enough; and there's still a chance that Nearchos may bring in more before we leave.* He felt confidence grow within him as he saw the path to redemption open and turned his attention to what was to come in the next couple of days, for this parade was more than just a mere inspection; it was a muster in preparation for a night attack.

The advance south had been swift as Demetrios had no baggage to slow his column down and the path his scouts had chosen through the low hills, partially cultivated with olive groves and vineyards between resin-scented coniferous woods with little undergrowth, inland from the coast, had been none too arduous. Thus it was with pleasant relief that, as the sun sank into the west to his right, Demetrios watched a two hundred and forty-strong unit of cavalry ride towards him, splashing through a slow-running stream, for he had expected to make a rendezvous with them halfway between Tripolis and Byblus – indeed, the plan depended upon it for they had been sent in advance to bait the trap which would reverse his fortunes.

'Is it all set, Philippos?' Demetrios asked his general as he brought his mount to a skidding halt, saluting at the same time.

Greying, experienced and completely loyal to Antigonos and his family, Philippos gave a jagged-tooth-baring grin, his eyes remaining cold. 'Yes, sir. Two leagues to the south, next to a small town called Myous. We set up our camp to the north of the place and then withdrew as soon as our forward patrols sighted Cilles' column – in his arrogance he'd set no scouts. We made as if we were too panicked to retrieve the supply train from our camp and pulled back as quickly as possible. His men, mostly Greek hoplites, peltasts and light cavalry, with a small core of Macedonians to stiffen them, are so ill-disciplined that as soon as they saw we'd left four dozen wagons' worth of provisions, mostly wine, they went on the rampage; it was chaos. As you predicted, they'll move no further today and with the amount of wine we left them and also with what's in the town, I doubt they'll be going far tomorrow.'

Demetrios smiled. 'We make a temporary camp here; let the lads have their evening meal and a bit of sleep and then move out at midnight.'

Dawn was breaking as Demetrios and Philippos peered down from the crest of the hill sloping down to what could in no way, even in the gloom, be called a military camp; and yet more than ten thousand men lay asleep – or comatose – around hundreds of fires glowing dim having burned low. 'Well?' Demetrios asked the leader of the scouting party as he came to lie down next to him.

'I never seen the like of it, sir,' the man replied, his breath pungent with the raw onion he was munching on. 'And I went all the way to India and back with Alexander.'

'Yes, yes, get on with it, man.' Demetrios was not in the mood to be reminded of the greater experience of others.

'Well, they ain't set no outlying pickets and the ones on the edge of the camp, if they are meant to be pickets at all, are all asleep with wineskins or vomit in their laps – or both.'

'And what's happening in the camp? Any movement?'

'I walked through, by myself, and no one challenged me. The only movement I saw was the occasional hairy-arsed veteran lifting a buttock to fart in his sleep. Hardly anyone has bothered to pitch a tent, despite it being as cold as a Scythian's quim, and those that were set up have been fallen into by staggering drunks. Only the command tent at what passes for the centre is in a respectable condition, although there're no guards outside it as you'd expect. No, it's a sham-bles, sir.'

'Get yourself and your lads something to eat; you've done well.' Demetrios, his mood buoyed, turned to Philippos next to him. 'If not now, then when?'

'I quite agree. As planned then?'

'Yes, as planned. I'll wait for you and your boys to be in position. And make the signal loud – I want them to think the gates of Hades have opened.'

And loud it was and shrill. High-pitched horn after horn rang out from the other side of the camp to be amplified by the signallers on Demetrios' side, filling their lungs and giving their all as the first glow of the rising sun hit ragged clouds above. And with this burst of cacophonic noise, three thousand troops raised their voices in jubilant battle-cries as they got to their feet and sprinted forward to wreak havoc amongst wine-sodden men thrice their number.

It was with joy that Demetrios ran forward, sword in one hand, shield in the other, both outstretched to help him balance as he tore over the rough ground. In less than a dozen heartbeats he reached the first of the sleeping foe, stirring on the ground but showing no sign of waking. On he went, leading his men further into the camp but striking no blows as yet for he had come to capture not slaughter and had given orders that none should be harmed in their sleep; only those who showed signs of resistance should be dealt with severity. It was a young man, barely out of his teens, who made that mistake and it was with pleasure Demetrios wedged his blade into his solar plexus, punching the wind and then the life from him, as around him many of his men administered similar fates to those who reacted on instinct. Kicking the rigid body and pulling his sword free, Demetrios held it and his shield in the air and, bending back, gave an animalistic cry of relief as he and his men swept through the camp incurring lessening resistance the deeper into its heart they ventured. The relief that coursed through him as the camp fell with but a whimper was almost physical, for the enemy, now surrendering in droves, kneeling on the ground with hands on sore heads, were mainly soldiers of fortune, men who cared not for whom they fought so long as their purses and bellies were full; men who would change sides rather than make the journey across the Styx. The Macedonians in Ptolemy's pay were, however, of a different nature having been settled in Egypt for more than a decade now; they had families and other ties back there and would not make reliable additions to his army. He knew that he could not keep them, but he did not care to for he had a far better use for them.

Feeling more confidence than he had since Ptolemy sprang the trap that routed his elephants as they went forward at Gaza, thus precipitating the collapse of his line of battle, Demetrios entered Cilles' command tent.

'You catch me at a disadvantage, Demetrios,' the mercenary general said as he tore a chunk off a loaf of bread and commenced to break his fast as if nothing were amiss. 'I'm just about to eat; will you join me?'

Demetrios stood, dumbfounded, unsure whether to believe his eyes and ears.

'Please, sit down,' Cilles insisted. 'I have some excellent cheese, as I'm sure you're aware; after all, it was a part of your supply train we captured.'

'You didn't capture it, Cilles; I let you have it.'

Cilles, in his fifties with a thickening waistline and sagging jowls beneath his beard, showed no emotion at this statement. 'Very clever; it's apparent that I underestimated you in more ways than one. Do sit down; I'm getting a crick in my neck looking up at you.'

'You, Cilles, will stand up! I think you'll find that'll solve the problem.' Demetrios drew his sword. 'Now!'

The elder man looked at the blade in surprise and then placed his hunk of bread down on his trencher and, pushing his chair back, stood. 'Is that better?'

Demetrios shook his head in disgust and then beckoned to the guards behind him. 'Take him away. I'll decide your fate later, Cilles.'

'Send him back to Ptolemy,' Phila said, passing her hand over her husband's chest, feeling the contours of his muscles, 'with his tent, baggage and all his officers. Return the favour he did you.'

Demetrios looked down at the hair on the crown of Phila's head, glowing in the soft lamplight of his tent, as she lay in his arms; the relief of being revitalised had calmed him and he kissed her as he breathed a satisfied sigh, confident he had performed his conjugal duties well now his confidence in his abilities had been bolstered by the previous night's events. All of the Greek mercenaries, more than eight thousand of them, had signed on with his army and his men had cheered him for the first time since the day he was now going to attempt to erase from his mind. 'I was planning on sending him to my father.'

'Why? What good would that do?'

'If I were to execute him, it could be said that I was acting above my station as I have no official position other than being my father's son. I have no satrapy, I'm just my father's commander in the south.'

Phila looked up at him. 'Why would you want to execute someone who was only doing his job?'

'Cilles and the thousand Macedonians would make a good example of what happens when we are opposed.'

'And did Ptolemy go around executing all his prisoners he captured from you? No, of course he didn't; he knows to do so would start making business personal, which would lead to far more blood-letting than is necessary. No, return them all to Ptolemy, that'll show even more magnanimity than he showed you. He just gave you back your possessions and a few officers but kept all your men, sending your Macedonians back to Egypt to settle them there as colonists. You, on the other hand, will give him a general, his officers and a thousand men with all their baggage.' She stroked his cheek; their eyes met and held. 'That would show class and flare worthy of my husband. Don't hide behind your father's justice; everyone will know that, if he were to execute them, it was you who sent them to him; it would be as if you ordered the sentence yourself. Write to your father and tell him what you mean to do so he can't accuse you of acting without his authority.'

'But the letter will take a while to get to him at this time of year and his reply won't arrive much before he does.'

'Exactly, and by then you would have sent them all back already.'

'Of course.' Demetrios smiled to himself. 'Knowing my father, he'll claim when I consulted him he readily gave the plan his blessing.'

'Let him; but who would care, as that would be admitting it was your idea he blessed. No, you use this opportunity, this well-deserved victory, to create yourself a reputation for the big gesture. Turn yourself into a soldier's soldier; one who fights hard, who is as implacable in defeat as he is generous in triumph. Do that and the wound of Gaza, which was deep, I know, Husband, for I could see your suffering under the torment of self-doubt both in your eyes, which would not meet mine, and in your absence from my bed, will start to heal. In time the memory will fade but you won't erase it by soaking your reputation with needless blood. Boost it instead with a flamboyant act: show yourself better than even Ptolemy by allowing his Macedonians to go home. It's a luxury he denied your Macedonians, and it would make news all over the empire which will be talked about far more than a minor skirmish in the desert.'

'Minor?'

'Well, where is Gaza anyway? I'd never heard of it before last year.'

Demetrios smiled and pulled Phila close to kiss her once more. 'And you'll be seeing it again this year; that I promise. My father will be here within two moons and then we'll drive south together and take back all Ptolemy has seized and then more.'

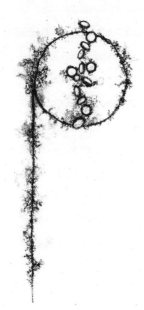

PTOLEMY.
THE BASTARD.

'I F WHAT WE hear from inside Tyros is true, Andronicus has very few followers left prepared to back his policy of resistance and refusing our bribes,' Lycortas, Ptolemy's steward and master of information, informed him as he reclined in a steaming copper bath set in the middle of his tent. Thais, his mistress of many years, scrubbed the ingrained dust from his broad shoulders and massaged them with experienced fingers.

Ptolemy paused for a couple of grunts of satisfaction and then ground his head in a circle so his neck clicked, before returning his concentration to his steward, giving him a questioning look.

Lycortas, bald and rotund, standing before his master in a floor-length white robe with his arms folded and hands disappearing into flared sleeves, shrugged. 'Two days at the most, I should guess.'

Ptolemy transformed his countenance into one of shocked surprise. 'Guess, Lycortas? That is so unlike you; I can't remember the last time I witnessed one of your guesses.' He turned to Thais. 'Can you recall a Lycortas guess, my love? Do you think we made a note of it? I hope so; I'll have a look when we get back to Alexandria. It must be in a very small book somewhere called "Things that rarely happen twice". Yes, we must look that out. Do you happen to know where it might be, Lycortas?'

'In your library next to your copy of "Things that rarely happen thrice", I would guess.'

Ptolemy laughed and held out his cup for a very attractive and sparsely clad slave-girl to refill. 'Very good, my friend, very good.' Again, he turned to Thais. 'Did you notice that? Lycortas made a rare foray into humour on the same day as he had a guess. We really must make a note of the date.' He toasted Lycortas and then took a healthy sip of wine. 'And how else are you going to amaze us today?'

Lycortas kept his expression neutral. 'An agent in Corinth has reported there's been some contact between Kleopatra and Polyperchon, although what has been discussed I'm afraid he didn't know.'

'Polyperchon? That's a name that hasn't troubled my ears for a while,' Ptolemy mused as he contemplated the re-emergence of the nonentity whom Antipatros, on his deathbed, had named as his successor as regent of Macedon, overlooking his own son, Kassandros. Forever a follower and never a leader, Polyperchon's tenure had been a dismal failure and he had soon passed the Great Ring of Macedon on to Olympias. Kassandros' execution of Alexander's mother, his sworn enemy, had meant the injustice, as he saw it, of his father's actions had been redressed for he now held the ring. 'Is he still skulking around the isthmus clutching at the skirts of his widowed daughter-in-law?'

'The redoubtable Cratesipolis, as formidable Penelope is affectionately known by her people, still manages to retain her independence despite Kassandros' control of Athens and Ptolemaios' control of Euboea and the mainland south of Thessaly and east of Aetolia for Antigonos. With Sparta remaining neutral to her south, the isthmus is a strong defensive position.'

'Defensive, yes; but she and Polyperchon are in no position to attack whether or not her people refer to her as the Conqueror of Cities. So, what does Kleopatra want with the nonentity?'

'It is rumoured, although there has been no proof, Kleopatra travelled to Pergamum last month.' Lycortas let the statement stand for his master to work out the implications. He was not disappointed.

'Did she now? I don't suppose it was just for a nice lady-like gossip with Barsine and Artonis that she went to the effort of avoiding Antigonos' guards. I assume Artonis is still there.'

'She is.'

'Remind me, how old is Herakles?'

'He was sixteen last month.'

'How very convenient; and I suppose Kleopatra just happened to decide that she wished to attend her nephew's birthday celebrations. I don't suppose his potential was discussed at all whilst she was there.'

'Nor did they discuss the fact that, should he attempt to achieve his potential, he would need an army,' Thais added, as she worked on Ptolemy's right shoulder.

'Ah.' Ptolemy removed his mistress's hands, turning to her. 'Do you think that was what the mission was for?'

'What other reason could there be? Think about it. You've done a great job in baiting Antigonos; with Cilles still pressing Demetrios north and occupying towns as he advances, Antigonos has to come south as soon as the passes are clear, which they will be very soon. Cilles will pull back, leading Antigonos and his puppy ever further south until he rejoins us here and we withdraw to Pelusium together, concentrating Antigonos' mind on us, thus buying Seleukos time to secure Babylon. Antigonos will then have to decide whether to attempt an invasion of Egypt or just look silly sitting in Gaza.'

'With my new friends the Nabatean Arabs picking at his very long supply lines whichever option he chooses.'

'Money very well spent, my love.'

'Indeed,' Lycortas agreed.

'Yes, I thought so,' Ptolemy concurred. 'It will come as a nasty surprise for our resinated cyclops when those demons come ululating out of the desert to bite him in that arse he's forever going on about.'

Thais smiled. 'And soon we should all be getting news of Seleukos' progress in the east, which, if it's good for us and bad for Antigonos, will cause him to head east skirting around the desert – again with your new Nabatean friends making a nuisance of themselves – to try to remove what would become a very severe headache for him if not dealt with immediately.'

'Busy for two years, all in all,' Ptolemy mused.

'At least.'

'Plenty of time for someone to put Herakles on the throne of Macedon.'

'If they have an army.'

'But even with an army they would have to defeat and kill Kassandros; Polyperchon and Cratesipolis don't have more than ten thousand men.'

Thais resumed her massage. 'No, they don't. However, Polyperchon has always had very good relations with the Aetolians and could take his army through their territory, reinforcing it as he goes, up to his clan-lands on the Macedonian–Eperiot border where he would garner further support, and invade Macedon from the west.'

Ptolemy did some mental arithmetic. 'Twenty thousand men at the most. That still wouldn't be enough to defeat Kassandros.' And then it hit him. 'Unless Lysimachus comes in from the east at the same time.'

'Yes, or Ptolemaios invades from the south.'

'Ptolemaios? But if Herakles takes the throne, his uncle's position becomes untenable. He would either have to submit or be seen for what he really is: an attempted usurper.'

Lycortas cleared his throat.

'What is it?' Ptolemy asked.

'I've heard it said that Ptolemaios is very displeased that Demetrios has taken his place as Antigonos' second-in-command after all the service that he has rendered him.'

'Have you now? How interesting.'

'Especially after Gaza.'

'Yes, I imagine especially after Gaza. It must be very galling for the talented older nephew to be overtaken by the impetuous young son.'

'Very galling, indeed.'

'Do you know if Kleopatra has sent a mission to Ptolemaios, Lycortas?'

'That was my first thought when I heard of her contact with Polyperchon. I'm endeavouring to find out.'

Ptolemy stood, splashing water over his steward's robe, and held out his arms for slaves to rub him dry with linen towels. 'Lysimachus, however, is busy with his Scythians at the moment; they've made another foray across the Istros.'

'A large bribe will make them go away for a season or two,' Thais said.

'Yes, I might even help raise the money myself.'

Thais shooed the girls away and took over their work. 'That would be even more money very well spent, my love.'

Ptolemy closed his eyes as Thais worked the linen towels over his body with unhurried and pleasing thoroughness. 'Was there anything else, Lycortas?'

'I've already gone, lord, and shall tell the guards you shouldn't be disturbed for a good while.'

But Ptolemy did not hear as he gave himself up, once again, to the talents of the highest-paid courtesan in the world, albeit one with but a single client.

'It proved to be a very good guess, Lycortas,' Ptolemy observed as the gates of Tyros opened to the sound of massed horns, and a group of soldiers began to make their way along the eight hundred paces of the mole Alexander had constructed during his siege of the city twenty-one years previously. 'Perhaps you ought to try guessing more often.'

'My nerves couldn't take it, lord; they require certainty and all the joys it brings.'

'Certainty you now have, Lycortas; our work here is done.'

'One thing still intrigues me, lord: why did Andronicus, who only transferred his allegiance to Antigonos after Antipatros' death, prove so loyal to the cyclops? He could be a very wealthy man by now.'

'It will be the first thing I ask him,' Ptolemy said as it became clear the man in question was being led in manacles in the midst of the soldiers.

Andronicus had no doubt as to the answer to Ptolemy's question. 'Because, unlike some men whom I could mention,' he replied, looking around at his escort, 'I believe when you give your loyalty to someone it should be death and not gold which severs the tie. I served Alexander all through his conquest and on his death I went north to find Krateros whom I considered to be the right man to hold the Great Ring of Macedon until the king came of age. After his death in battle against Eumenes I transferred my allegiance to the Greek as he fought for the Argead royal house. But when he too was defeated and then executed, I made my way west to Antipatros as he was the legitimate regent and therefore had the right to wear the ring. But when he died and passed it on to the nonentity, Polyperchon, I couldn't give him my loyalty, so I went to Antigonos as I considered him to be the man with the strength to hold the empire together.'

'And now you fall into my hands a far poorer man than you would be if you didn't have such high principles.'

Andronicus, tall, muscular and black-bearded with eyes equally dark, gestured to the men around him. 'Rich like these traitors?'

'You're lucky we let you live,' one of the group hissed.

'You left me alive because you know Ptolemy is a man of honour and doesn't take kindly to men murdering their superiors.'

A man of honour? That's a reputation I didn't know I had. I should capitalise on it. 'Very true.' Ptolemy looked at the mutineers, almost four dozen of them, filthy from three months of siege. 'You would have been dead had you killed him but instead you will be well paid for handing him over to me.'

There were murmurings of relief and approval at this news.

'I will also take you all into my service and send you back to Egypt as colonists who owe me military service.'

Again this met with approval.

40

Ptolemy turned back to Andronicus. 'And so, you are my prisoner, but you need not be. If I guarantee you'll not face Antigonos or Demetrios across the battlefield, would that satisfy your honour enough to join with me?'

Andronicus had no hesitation. 'It would, lord.'

'Excellent.' Ptolemy smiled benignly at the mutineers. 'You'll be pleased to know that I'm giving you your old commander back, gentlemen. Andronicus will be in charge of taking you back to Egypt. I'm sure you'll have a very pleasant journey.'

The look of horror passing across the men's faces caused Ptolemy's smile to widen. 'Whilst I'm grateful for your treachery I can in no way condone it. Macedonians should be better than that; don't you agree, Andronicus?'

'I do, lord; and I shall have ample opportunity to remind these gentlemen just how a Macedonian soldier is expected to behave on the march south; a march I think we might make in record time.'

'Then the sooner you get started the better.'

It was as Andronicus led the bedraggled garrison of Tyros south and Ptolemy replaced it with his own men and gave Lagus, his seventeen-year-old son with Thais, command of the twenty triremes berthed in the harbour, that another bedraggled column appeared in the north. As Ptolemy, with Thais and Lagus at his side, watched its approach from high on a tall tower above the citadel of Tyros he cursed himself for having made a stupid decision.

'Who are they, Father?' Lagus asked as Ptolemy swore under his breath.

'Cilles and what's left of his army. I should have brought my brother, Menelaus, over from Cyprus rather than give the job to a mercenary,' he said as he turned and made his way down the spiral steps. 'The situation in Cyprus was settled after Gaza, as the various kings of the island could see who was the dominant force on the mainland. Menelaus could have been spared to press my advantage and harry Demetrios north and then this setback would not have happened. Now, though...' He let the thought fade.

But Thais knew his mind well enough. 'Now any one of the twelve kings will look at this evident defeat and think, when you withdraw back to Egypt in the face of Antigonos' advance, it's through weakness, having lost a battle, and not as a strategy for buying time for Seleukos.'

'And Antigonos will send men and gold to encourage those thoughts and I'll be forced to send more troops to Cyprus which I would rather have securing Egypt's border. And all because I entrusted a mercenary general with a job I should have given to my brother. I wonder what his excuse will be.'

'They came out of the night, infiltrating the camp before we could do anything,' Cilles said as he stood before Ptolemy in the audience chamber overlooking the port. 'We had no choice but to surrender.' Cilles rubbed the small of his back and looked at Thais and Lycortas seated on either side of Ptolemy and then glanced around the chamber.

'You won't find any other chairs here, Cilles,' Ptolemy snapped, 'and even if there were I wouldn't be inviting you to sit. Look at me!'

Cilles raised reluctant, bloodshot eyes to Ptolemy but failed to hold the gaze.

'They infiltrated the camp before you could do anything? Where were the outlying pickets and the perimeter guards whilst this infiltration was going on? Had you not set any?'

'Well, yes, I had, of course.'

'Then why wasn't the alarm raised?'

'Well, because...'

'Because what?'

'Well, because it was just before dawn and they were, well...'

'Asleep?'

'Yes.'

'All of them? You had a force of nigh on ten thousand so at least three hundred would have been on guard or picket duty and you're telling me that all three hundred were asleep?'

'Well, not exactly asleep; they were...'

'If they weren't exactly asleep and yet they missed this infiltration of the entire camp, what were they, Cilles? And I warn you, I'm a very forgiving person, but my benevolence will not stretch to someone who has lied to me. The truth, Cilles!'

It was with great difficulty that the mercenary finally managed to mutter: 'They were drunk.'

Ptolemy leaned forward in his chair. 'They were what? I'm sorry, Cilles, I didn't quite catch that.'

'Drunk, lord; they were drunk.'

'Drunk? What do you mean, they were drunk?'

'I mean they had all drunk far more wine than was good for them.'

'I know what the definition of being drunk is, you idiot. What I want to know is how ten thousand men got hold of enough wine to drink themselves insensible.'

Cilles hung his head, shaking it slowly.

'Cilles, at the moment your life is worth next to nothing. Where did the wine come from?'

'We captured Demetrios' supply train.'

'Captured, as in fought a battle and beat off the guards?'

Cilles was crumbling, his breath becoming ragged. 'No, the guards rode off before we reached it.'

'Left it in other words; they left it, didn't they?'

'Well, yes, I suppose you could look at it that way.'

'I *do* look at it that way, Cilles. They left all that wine so you would drink yourselves into oblivion and they could capture all your men. Did you notice they weren't interested in slaughtering you? Did you? No, Demetrios didn't want a victory because he doesn't have the men to follow it up but you've just gifted them to him. How many signed up with him?'

'Eight thousand.' The reply was barely audible.

'It was more than eight thousand, lord,' Lycortas said. 'I've been through the numbers. Just under a thousand Macedonians came back with this,' he gestured at Cilles and then shrugged, 'this idiot; and, as you rightly pointed out, he had nigh on ten thousand in his force. According to one of his officers – all of whom have been returned along with their baggage – a couple of hundred were killed trying to resist the infiltration, so it would seem that Demetrios has just gained more than eight and a half thousand mercenaries.'

'Five hundred more than I managed to get off him after Gaza. Because of your ineptitude, Cilles, you have lost me everything I gained after defeating Demetrios as well as signalling to the kings of Cyprus that it might be time to switch sides. You've been taking my pay for a couple of years now and have grown rich by me; but no longer. You are dismissed and I forbid you to enter Egypt ever again.'

Cilles blinked as he took in the implications; his mouth fell open and his eyes widened. 'But, but,' he spluttered, 'my family, my money... what will I do?'

'Should you have any honour and take your own life, your family will receive all your wealth deposited in Egypt and I will ensure your children have a future. Should you not then I assume they will just fall slowly into beggary – unless, of course, your wife and daughters decide to prostitute themselves; who knows, perhaps your sons might join them and start a family business. Now go!'

Cilles could not even summon the energy for a final look of hatred at his former master who had just condemned him; resigned and beaten down, he turned and sloped off.

'If the consequences of what he's done weren't so drastic I would have thoroughly enjoyed that.'

'Well, *I* did, my love.' Thais reached out and squeezed Ptolemy's arm. 'You are so forgiving; it makes me very proud. Many's the man who would have nailed him up or perched him on a sharpened stake, but no, you allow him suicide if he so chooses. That is admirable, Ptolemy. Admirable.'

'Yes, I must harden myself or I'll be seen as a soft touch and have everyone taking advantage of my forgiving and generous nature.'

'And what about the Macedonians Demetrios sent back with him?' Lycortas asked. 'Are they going to see some of that forgiving and generous nature?'

'They most certainly are not.'

'You have shamed me, you have shamed yourselves and you have shamed Macedon and Egypt,' Ptolemy declaimed to the thousand Macedonians formed in rigid lines on the parade ground outside the siege camp in what had once been the old city of Tyros before Alexander pulled it down to use the stone and bricks to build his mole across to the new island city. 'To be so drunk as to allow an enemy to capture your camp with hardly a blow struck is a disgrace none of you will ever live down.'

A low groan emanated from the men and many fell to their knees, holding out their hands towards Ptolemy, beseeching his forgiveness.

Ptolemy made a grand gesture, left palm outstretched towards the parade, right arm above his head, forefinger to the sky. 'No! Do not seek mercy. If I were to pardon you, what message would it send out to the thousands of other Macedonians in my service?'

And the low moan grew to a rumble and then a cry as all were now on their knees, pleading with their lord.

'Do not beg!' Ptolemy shouted above the growing noise. 'Nothing can wash away the shame.'

'Blood can!' came a shout.

'Yes, blood!' another cried. 'We will cleanse ourselves with our own blood.'

And this was what Ptolemy had been hoping for as he was loath to lose a thousand good men; thirty, or so, however, would not be too damaging. He let the clamour grow ever more desperate until he was sure that each man would submit to the process to come and then raised his arms for quiet. It was quick in coming as all were anxious to hear his decision.

'Very well; you have appealed to my forgiving nature and I shall not deny you. Each file of sixteen will give one man up for punishment. They will draw lots; half will receive fifty lashes, the other half will lose their heads. Now go and decide who will be delivered up.'

As the parade watched in sombre silence the thirty-one men who had been lucky enough to draw the lash being tied to stakes lined along its frontage, a sleek undecked *lembus* came out of the north, its forty oarsmen pulling hard and strong, on a windless, spring-like day. Ptolemy watched the vessel approach and dock as the knots were secured and the punishment detail marched out to wait, two men behind each miscreant, bearing coiled whips. *A messenger; old news or new news, I wonder. Either way, a message from the north means the campaign season has begun.* Ptolemy drew his attention away from the man disembarking with Mercury-like haste and nodded to the officer overseeing punishment. The first whips cracked.

'You're a bit late if you've come to tell me of Cilles' ignoble defeat in Myous,' Ptolemy told the messenger as Lagus brought him up from the harbour to report. The crack of the fiftieth and final lashes died, leaving silence over the proceedings. 'I'm just dealing with it.' Ptolemy indicated to the whipped men now being untied and falling to the ground.

The man looked at Ptolemy confused. 'I've come from Tarsus, lord; we'd not heard of that when I left.'

'If you've come from Tarsus then I don't need to hear your news; I can guess.' He signalled to the officer commanding the punishment detail; the thirty-one who had drawn death were brought forward. 'Antigonos has come across the Taurus Mountains and will soon be joining up with Demetrios; is that correct?'

The man failed to hide his surprise. 'Yes, lord. How did you know?'

Ptolemy nodded to the punishment detail officer to push the condemned men to their knees. 'It was always going to be the first news of the new campaigning season. Antigonos is not a man to waste time. You've done well, thank you. Lagus, make sure his ship is resupplied.'

'Yes, Father.'

'And get your flotilla ready to leave; tell the garrison to start loading their gear onto your ships; they'll go south with you when Demetrios' column comes into view.' Dismissing his son and the messenger, Ptolemy turned to Thais as the first head rolled to the ground in an explosion of blood. 'Well, my love, apart from this unpleasant incident, it was an agreeable little sojourn in Syria. It's now time to go home, leaving as little as possible for our resinated friend to occupy.'

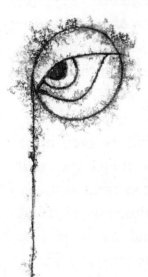

ANTIGONOS.
THE ONE-EYED.

'WHERE IS HE?' Antigonos bellowed, leaping from his horse and running up the steps of Demetrios' headquarters, the royal hunting lodge at The Three Paradises. 'Where's my son?'

Such was his ferocity as he ascended two at a time, his one-remaining eye glaring at the guards, that none dared meet his cyclopic gaze.

'Demetrios!' he yelled again as his twenty-man escort of Companion Cavalry, left behind in his haste to complete the final thousand paces of the journey, clattered through the gate, their horses blown. But Antigonos did not care that his bodyguard had been remiss in their charge of protecting his person, in his desire to find his son. Again he roared out his name, causing terror to all within earshot, for at seventy-two, his beard full and grey and his face dominated by the puckered scar in his left eye-socket, weeping clear red fluid, he was a fearsome, tall and broad figure of ever-widening girth to stand before. None could tell by his tone whether he had come to berate Demetrios for his debacle at Gaza or congratulate him for his recent success at Myous, and no one was going to stop to find out.

No one, that was, except for Demetrios.

The high-ceilinged main hall of the building echoed to Antigonos' roars even after his son had stepped through a door, twice his height, from the suite with stunning views over the undulating parkland he and Phila occupied. 'Father?'

There he is, the cocky little shit. 'Come here!' It was with amusement that Antigonos noticed the nervousness in his son as he obeyed the summons. *He thinks I'm angry with him.* He smiled – at least his face attempted a sort of single-eyed grimace that was mainly beard and scar – and held out his arms. *I forget my appearance; I'm still his age in my mind.* 'Come here, my boy.' He clasped his son into an embrace that would have rendered him unconscious when he was a lad. 'My arse, I'm proud of you.' After a couple of slaps across the shoulders which would leave bruises for a few days, Antigonos released Demetrios and held him at arm's length to admire him. 'You took a thrashing but you didn't whimper and run and hide; no, my boy, you made up for your mistake and replenished what you lost. My rancid arse, that was fine work. Fine work!'

Demetrios, a thumb's width shorter than his father and in far better physical condition, managed a smile, despite feeling battered by his display of paternal affection. 'Thank you, Father; I did what I needed so I could face you and ask forgiveness for Gaza. Nearchos, Pythan, Andronicus and Philippos all advised me to withdraw as Ptolemy wouldn't be able to supply a winter campaign with his sizable army and I ignored them.'

'Of course you did, you impetuous little rogue. I brought you up to do things like that; you were always far too arrogant to take advice. Well, my boy, I owe Ptolemy a big favour: he gave you a spanking you'll never forget and then was kind enough to replace the troops you lost to him after you'd had enough time to contemplate the error of your ways. He's a good man, apart from the fact he's a complete and utter bastard who will soon come to realise the difference between besting barely bearded boys in battle and a resinated cyclops who's been gutting men since his early teens. Oh, yes, he'll soon find out the difference and I'm here to show him.' He looked at the hurt pride on his son's face. 'No offence intended, of course.'

It was without much conviction that Demetrios expressed that none had been taken.

'Come, my boy, let's have a look at your new army.'

'The bulk of my army should be here around the same time as the fleet in four or five days,' Antigonos said as he watched the newly signed Greek mercenaries form up at short notice. 'Hieronymus and Athenaios are bringing them through the pass.'

'Hieronymus?' Demetrios could not hide his surprise. 'I thought he was concentrating on writing the history of the events, not taking an active part in them.'

'He enjoys reminding himself of his more martial years with Alexander.' Antigonos chuckled. 'Which proves my theory that there is no better life than the military one and the only true release from that love is death on the battle-field. Just look at the number of lads we've sent home or settled on new lands with a hefty payoff who've then come clamouring to rejoin within a couple of harvests. No, Hieronymus is no different, despite all the writing he does; once tasted, life in the field can't be beaten.'

And that had been true for Antigonos all his life since, as a contemporary of Philip, the second of that name to be king of Macedon, he had shared his adolescence first as a royal page and then as a loyal follower on Philip's ascension to the throne after the deaths of his two elder brothers, Alexandros and Perdikkas. Philip had been an expansionist king; having modernised the army by the introduction of the sixteen-foot-long *sarissa*, or pike, held in two hands underarm, and deepening the formation to sixteen-man files rather than the standard eight-man file used by hoplites wielding a long, one-handed, thrusting-spear overarm. He had created a military machine that could vanquish all before it. Illyria, Thrace, Thessaly and Greece all were eventually made subject to Macedon, and Antigonos had played a major part in the conquest culminating in the defeat of Athens and its allies at the battle of Chaeronea – losing his eye in the process. Rising first to the command of a *syntagma* of two hundred and fifty-six men – sixteen files of sixteen men – until he was made a *strategeos* commanding a *taxis* – six syntagma totalling fifteen hundred men – he was never happier than in the heat of combat in the front line of the phalanx. Many battles did he fight shoulder to shoulder with his close friend Philotas and each one he had loved, for war was a great thing, the only thing worth living for in Antigonos' mind – at least it had been until he had succumbed to high ambition.

No longer now did he make war for war's sake; no, it was ambition which now drove him to make it for he had resolved to be 'the strongest' to whom Alexander had said the Great Ring of Macedon should go, and, as the mercenaries began to go through their evolutions and drills, he put his arm around his son's shoulders and gave him a squeeze, for now he believed the boy was showing the true signs of one to whom he would be able to leave his kingdom.

Over the winter in Celaenae, his capital in Phrygia, with his wife, Stratonice, he had made his plans: he would forge the empire Alexander had seized into one kingdom and his son would carry on the dynasty he founded.

'They'll do, my boy,' Antigonos said as the exercises came to a close. 'We'll head south as soon as the whole force is assembled and supplied. I've sent word to Nearchos to follow us down the coast with as many men as he can get as we'll need every one.'

And it was within eight days that the great army, nearly fifty thousand strong, marched south, supported by a fleet of over a hundred vessels commanded by Dioscurides, the brother of Ptolemaios, come down from its winter quarters in the Sea of Marmara. Along the coast from Tripolis to Byblus Antigonos led them, and then to Berytus and on to Sidon – finding no garrisons holding the ports against them – to arrive at last at Tyros; and here, as he had done two years previously, did Antigonos encounter resistance.

'I don't want to waste another year laying siege to the place again,' Antigonos growled, as he stood with his senior generals looking at the high walls that had been strengthened since the last time the city fell; on the mole connecting the island city to the mainland were the remains of his siege lines.

'Then don't, Father,' Demetrios advised and then pointed to the fleet, half a league out to sea. 'This time we've got the ships to blockade it. Give orders for Dioscurides to lock off the harbour, and send a force to occupy the siege lines and Tyros will be no threat in our rear.'

Antigonos nodded. 'Yes, you're right; if we keep them contained, our supply lines will remain secure as we head south into Egypt. But as insurance, I'll send agents to Cyprus and see what loyalty I can buy now that Ptolemy is being seen as retreating. If I can control the sea between the island and the mainland then Tyros being in Ptolemy's hands is even less of a threat.'

Demetrios smiled. 'Those petty kings love the winning side's gold.'

Antigonos turned to Athenaios and Hieronymus. 'We'll leave a thousand men to secure the mole and tell Dioscurides to have a squadron of the fleet blockading both harbours. Make the arrangements; we'll move on tomorrow at first light.'

And thus with the decision made they ventured south, this time along Ptolemy's line of retreat to find he had left a trail of destruction in his wake: forts destroyed, fields burned and town walls pulled down.

'You have to admire the man's confidence,' Antigonos said, looking at the destruction of the wall connecting Gaza and its separate port. 'He's leaving me nothing to fall back on. He believes he's going to beat me.'

Demetrios did not comment as he was looking inland to the site of his defeat a mere five months previously; a defeat he did not like to bring to mind. Gazing on the ground upon which it was fought it was impossible to forget. Sitting on his horse Demetrios tried to draw his eyes away from the field, still scattered with the detritus of defeat. Just as he managed to look away distant movement registered; he frowned and turned back, squinting to better see against the glare. 'Father!'

'Hmm, what is it?'

'Look.' Demetrios pointed east into the desert.

Antigonos shaded his eyes, scanning the horizon. And

then he saw it: a cloud of dust moving north. But the cloud was not caused by the wind for it had a source at its head. 'Horsemen,' he muttered.

'And look there, Father.'

Antigonos followed his son's finger as it tracked south. Another cloud. 'This one is heading south. My arse, that's no coincidence; Ptolemy's sending me a warning to turn back. They're not just horsemen, they've got camels as well. Nabateans – Ptolemy must have made a deal with them to harry our supply lines. You can see what they're doing, they're showing me they can get around us to the north and south using the desert; a camel in the desert can keep going much longer than a horse. Forget Tyros; these bastards will be far more threatening.' Antigonos drew a deep breath and glanced between the two fast-moving units of horsemen and camel-riders. 'Well, my boy. We can't move into Egypt before we've dealt with them.'

'It's called Petra,' Athenaios said, 'because of the big stone around which all the chieftains of the Nabatean clans meet to bring their grievances to their king – I would believe Malichus to be his name as the last couple have also borne that name and they're a very traditional people.' Athenaios regarded Antigonos, Demetrios and Hieronymus to make sure he had their attention; satisfied, he drew in the sand with a stick. 'We're here at Gaza, so The Stone is about thirty-five leagues to the south-east, here.' He marked the spot. 'To get there we go due east to the Salt Sea to the south of Hierosolyma and then head south; between the sea and The Stone is desert so we would have to take all our water with us when we set out from Gaza; we can't drink the Salt Sea water and only the Nabateans know the locations of their cisterns.'

'Why don't we try to capture a few and make them talk?' Antigonos asked.

Athenaios shook his head. 'Even if we could get one alive, you would have about as much chance of extracting any information out of them as I have of pulling a talent of silver out of my arse.'

Antigonos, always one for an anal analogy, chuckled. 'And how do you know so much about Nabateans, Athenaios?'

'Alexander asked me to find out about them when he was planning his invasion of Arabia; I journeyed extensively, including visiting The Stone.'

'I'd be most interested to see any notes you might have,' Hieronymus said.

'I'll look them out for you when I get back.' Athenaios returned his attention to his map, drawing what seemed to be a hare with two thin ears of unequal size to the south of The Stone. 'This is the sea that borders the east coast of Egypt; as you can see, the shorter of these inlets comes to about fifteen leagues of The Stone. Every year at about this time a large group of Nabateans journeys down to the sea to trade with the spice and incense merchants who come by ship from the east, from India and beyond. When they do, for safety, they leave their families together at The Stone under the protection of just a few men, no more than five hundred, looking after five thousand, maybe more.'

Antigonos' eye widened. 'Five thousand, maybe more? That's a lot of hostages to choose from.'

Athenaios nodded. 'But first we've got to get there, across the desert avoiding the patrols keeping an eye on our movements, as we have seen, then fight a battle and then bring back the hostages again through hostile terrain crawling with camel-fuckers.'

56

'Well, if anyone can do it, you can. How many men would you need?'

'Four thousand light infantry as the main force, fast moving and enough to fend off attacks by their cavalry patrols, and then say five hundred cavalry to act as scouts.'

'Why not take all cavalry?' Demetrios asked.

'We'd need too much water for the horses, and besides, the column will have to travel at the speed of the pack animals, preferably camels, carrying the extra water we will need. Light infantry can do that as well as carrying a spare skin of water. For the way back we'll refill the skins from the cisterns and wells around The Stone of which there are many.'

Antigonos looked at the rudimentary map, wiping the drop of clear liquid forming beneath his scar, and then pointed to the hare-shaped sea. 'You say that borders the east coast of Egypt?'

'Yes, lord.' Athenaios pointed to the longer ear. 'The tip of that inlet is twenty leagues south of Pelusium and twenty east of Memphis.'

That is the most interesting fact I've heard for a long time. I wonder how much attention Ptolemy takes of the sea to his south. 'Are there trees on that coast?'

Athenaois' expression showed he knew exactly what Antigonos was implying. 'I'm afraid not, lord; at least, not enough to build sufficient ships to bring an army up behind Ptolemy.'

Antigonos grunted in frustration.

'Besides,' Athenaios said, 'just to get an army to the coast to board the ships, should it be possible to construct them there, would be murderous. I was with Alexander when we crossed the Gedrosian Desert on the way back from India and I can promise you the army was in no fit state to fight for a couple of moons after we arrived in Persis.'

'Well, it was just a thought.' Antigonos swallowed his disappointment. 'We'll just have to go in the front door once you've got enough hostages to bring the Nabateans over to us, Athenaios. You'll have everything you need; when can you leave?'

Athenaios shrugged. 'It'll take a couple of days to fill the skins we need so let us say nightfall in three nights' time. Travelling at night we should avoid their patrols.'

'And what will we do whilst we wait for Athenaios to come back?' Demetrios asked Antigonos as the last of the column disappeared into the gloom.

Antigonos turned and walked back through Gaza's east gate. 'We play politics. Never assume the course of action you're about to undertake is going to be successful; there should always be a plan you can fall back on.'

'And what would that be?'

'Peace.'

Demetrios looked at his father as if he had just caught him tupping Phila. 'Peace!'

Antigonos chuckled. 'Not peace with everyone, just peace with Kassandros and Lysimachus. I mean to isolate Ptolemy if I'm unable to invade Egypt and to do so I need to open negotiations with Kassandros and Lysimachus. To that end I've written to my nephew Ptolemaios in Greece to get him to approach Kassandros, and to Phoinix in Hellespontine Phrygia to have him do the same with Lysimachus. I've asked them to send ambassadors to me to negotiate the terms. They won't be here for at least three months by which time I'll know whether I want peace with them or, if I've got Egypt, whether I will demand their total surrender and acceptance of me as their overlord.' He looked sideways at his son. 'Or, for want of a better word, king.'

'Lord?' a voice said as Antigonos and Demetrios approached the palace.

A figure was awaiting them at the bottom of the steps.

'Nearchos!' Antigonos said as his features became clear. 'When did you arrive?'

'As you were seeing the column off. I've brought another two thousand men, mainly garrison troops; also some five hundred mercenary hoplites and three hundred mercenary cavalry are following me under the command of Ptolemy's mercenary general, Cilles, who has come over to us.'

'Cilles, the one Demetrios hoodwinked?'

'Yes, lord, the same. I placed him in charge of the unit as a test of his character.'

'Can we trust him?'

'His family and wealth are in Egypt and he can't get there without our defeating Ptolemy; I think his interests lie with ours.'

'Excellent. Well met, my friend; I've got a job for you involving ships, you'll love it.'

'Indeed, Antigonos, I'm sure I will. For my part, I bring both good news and bad from the east.'

Antigonos closed his eye and nodded, knowing, at least in part, what he was going to hear. 'Seleukos has succeeded in taking Babylon with his tiny army?'

'Yes.'

'How did he slip past the garrison at Thapsacus?'

'He didn't. The Nabateans guided him straight across the desert.'

'Did they? I'll not forget that favour. So, what's the good news?'

'Nikanor, your satrap of Media, neighbouring Babylonia, wrote to me in Thapsacus to say he's moving against him with a substantial force. Seleukos won't be able to resist with the meagre resources at his command. Nikanor promises that by midsummer Seleukos will be dead.'

SELEUKOS.
THE BULL-ELEPHANT.

SELEUKOS' INTENSE DARK eyes peered from either side of a thin, prominent nose, bisecting an angular face that could have been the model for many an ancient hero's bust, just as his body could have been a replica of a statue of Herakles. 'With Polyarchos' thousand men from the garrison of Sittace on the Tigris and the two thousand who were here, in Babylon, under Diphilos' command in the Southern Citadel, plus those of Teutamus' men in the Main Citadel who survived and didn't need to be relieved of their heads, all added to those I brought with me, I estimate I must have in the region of five thousand troops at my disposal.'

'Five thousand four hundred and eighty-two, lord,' Patrokles, his governor of Babylon, replied, standing opposite him and laying a papyrus scroll down on the table between them.

Seleukos took up the scroll and ran his eyes down the list written on it: despite the elation and pride he still felt at recapturing the city in hard-fought, street to street combat the numbers dampened his spirit. 'I'm grateful for your meticulousness, Patrokles; but however accurate your figures, I think we can both accept the number is simply not enough to repel an attack by Antigonos.'

Patrokles nodded and ran a hand through thin, patchy hair, prematurely grey; sallow-skinned and hollow-eyed from his four years, at Antigonos' behest, in a dungeon beneath the Main Citadel, beyond the Ishtar Gate, as punishment for his aiding Seleukos' escape from Babylon. Now he had renewed his allegiance to Seleukos as he held a personal score to settle. 'Not enough to repel him, let alone kill the bastard.'

Seleukos rubbed the back of his muscular neck, considering his position, drawing himself up to his full and impressive height, a full head taller than Patrokles. Numbers were his primary concern, numbers of men under arms and not a triumphant celebration of his return to Babylon; that would have to wait until he was secure in his possession. It was one thing to have retaken the city he loved but, Seleukos knew, it would be a far harder affair to hold onto it should he fail to enlist sufficient troops to fight for him. Antigonos would never let him keep what he considered to be rightfully his without a fight; and Seleukos expected that fight very soon now the snows in the north were melting. 'And there are no more garrisons in the satrapy?'

'I'm afraid not; and the locals make terrible soldiers. Apparently, after Antigonos left Pythan and Teutamus in command here – while I was languishing amongst the rats and filth of the dungeons – they tried forming a civic militia to bulk up their forces, as the cyclops had stripped the east of its men when he returned to the west, leaving Babylon with just a couple of thousand. But it was hopeless: the locals were shambolic, couldn't parade in straight lines, either ran away or lay down when practising receiving a charge and then spent an inordinate amount of time buggering each other.'

Seleukos sighed; he was well aware of the reputation of the population he ruled over: traders and pleasure-seekers rather than soldiers. 'Nebuchadnezzar would be ashamed if he only knew what had happened to his people. Well, my friend, I'll send out word that I'm employing mercenaries on very generous terms; more I cannot do. So, drill the soldiers we have and keep them sharp whilst I put thought to the problem.'

'The trouble is that Babylonia was never an important major military territory in Achaemenid times and Alexander did nothing to change that. I need to take satrapies like Susiana which has a big standing garrison because of the treasury there, or India on the eastern border which has to guard against incursions from across the Indus – but without men I'm unable do something like that.' Seleukos threw a pebble into the rectangular fish pond and watched the ripples grow as the fish, orange and golden, darted away from the impact.

'Forge an alliance with one or two of the eastern satraps,' Apama, his wife of twelve years and mother to his three children, suggested, looking up at her husband, towering head and shoulders over her – and she had been considered tall in her native Sogdia.

'They're all Antigonos' men, put in place by him, or confirmed by him in their position, when he made his eastern settlement after defeating Eumenes.' He sucked the air through his teeth. 'No; what have I to offer them to tempt them away from Antigonos? They know he'll come back east soon and his objective will be my defeat and execution. I can quite understand why they wouldn't want to join me in being a target for the cyclops.' He put an arm around his wife as they strolled around the Courtyard of Water in the summer palace. Two thousand paces north of the Ishtar Gate and set in parkland at the point where the outer city wall leaves the Euphrates on its way south-east before returning west and rejoining the river to the south of the city, it had been a royal residence for centuries. Cool and full of delight, the courtyard was a favourite place for Seleukos and Apama to take their exercise together away from the fetid, humid air of the city whose rankness grew by the day as spring progressed now that the equinox had passed. *I'll not lose all this a second time.* He glanced down at his brown-skinned beauty, her eyes heavily kohled in the eastern fashion, the only part of her face showing as she was veiled due to the presence of half a dozen guards. *I'll not be able to look her in the eye if we have to flee with the children again. I need some luck, or, at least, someone to make a mistake.*

It was not luck, however, but a Paktha merchant who changed Seleukos' fortunes as he sought an audience with the present ruler of Babylon upon his arrival by ship from the north.

'It's always good to see you, Babrak,' Seleukos said, genuinely meaning it as the Paktha was always a valuable source of information garnered from travelling the length and breadth of the empire in eternal trade.

Dark-skinned, hook-nosed and with sunken but twinkling dark eyes darting out from beneath a white headdress, Babrak inclined his head, one hand across his chest and grinned, exposing red-stained teeth. 'Great lord, I am always humbled by your generosity to me.' His eyes flicked to the weighty purse that, with studied nonchalance,

Seleukos placed on the table between them next to a pitcher and two cups.

'Please sit, and pour yourself a sherbet.'

'Ah, the noble sherbet, you are too good to me, lord; I've been many months in the west where, as you know, for some unaccountable reason, they choose to live without its refreshing qualities. I myself tried to import it a few years back and there was so little interest I was forced to give up the effort after a couple of seasons.' He poured himself a frothing measure and took a sip, closing his eyes with pleasure. 'As delightful on the tongue as a much-desired boy's first kiss.'

'Yes, well, I'll take your word for it, Babrak.' Seleukos took a sip of his drink without noticing the same effect as his guest. 'I haven't seen you since you were in Alexandria before we defeated Demetrios at Gaza.'

'And what a great victory that was, sire; yours and the great Ptolemy's praises are bruited by all good people.'

'Don't exaggerate, Babrak; I don't suppose any of Demetrios' or Antigonos' supporters are bruiting, as you put it. And when you saw either one of them on your recent travels, I'm sure you expressed your sympathies for their setback.'

Babrak bowed his head but refrained from comment.

'Now, tell me: was Antigonos making plans to come east when you left?'

'No, lord; at least not according to Nearchos, with whom I dined at Thapsacus, before I took ship to come downriver. He's been scouring Syria and Assyria for troops to make up what Demetrios lost at your most famous of victories. He was expecting Antigonos to come over the Taurus Mountains as soon as the snows melted and join up with his son to retake Ptolemy's gains in Coele-Syria and Palestine and then launch an attack on Egypt itself.'

Seleukos' eyes widened at the news. 'He wasn't planning on coming east?'

'No, great lord, his gaze was focused on Ptolemy as an admirer's eyes are on the buttocks of the boy he desires: fixed so that nothing can distract them.'

'I'm pleased to hear it; that sounds very focused indeed.'

'Indeed, it is, noble lord, believe me.'

The man's obsessed. 'Oh, I do, Babrak, be of no doubt on that point. And what of Ptolemy?'

'The last I heard was a rumour that Demetrios had defeated one of his generals in a night attack with the small number of men still available to him; apparently, he captured seven or eight thousand mercenaries who subsequently signed up with him, but Nearchos didn't know for sure if this was a fact. But I would say a flicker of truth always exists in a rumour like that.'

Seleukos tapped the arm of his chair in thought. *That would be very convenient, Ptolemy being put on the back foot, forced to retreat, with Demetrios and the resinated cyclops following him up.* 'Have you heard how Ptolemy's negotiations with the Nabateans went?'

Babrak took a regretful glance at the purse. 'Alas, lord, I cannot be of service on that point. Although what may be of interest to you is that Nearchos had been in contact with Nikanor, the satrap of Media. This he didn't tell me personally, obviously; he would be foolish to divulge such information to the likes of me. No, I came to find out about it as my cousin arrived in Thapsacus at the same time, having travelled from Ecbatana. He said that a messenger from Nearchos had arrived there shortly after the turning of the year and that it caused Nikanor to send out orders summoning the army from its winter quarters as soon as the weather improved enough for it to muster at Ecbatana ready for a campaign. I would say, Nikanor has been told to deal with you, noble lord.'

Seleukos pushed the purse across to Babrak, considering it money very well spent.

'Assuming the weather had improved sufficiently by the spring equinox for the muster, that was, what, twenty days ago?' Seleukos looked for confirmation around the gathering of his five most senior officers, four Macedonians and a Sogdian, in his study overlooking the Courtyard of Water. The fresh smell of early blossom and the tinkle of a gentle water feature came in through an open window.

'Twenty-two, lord,' Patrokles said.

'Twenty-two days.' Seleukos regarded Diphilos, once loyal to Antigonos but who had surrendered to Seleukos upon his return and had kept his command of the Southern Citadel. 'You must have had contact with Nikanor whilst you served Pythan when he was satrap, Diphilos; what do you know of the strength of the Median army?'

Diphilos shrugged. 'I've never been there, lord.'

'I have, lord,' the youngest man in the meeting said; blond and clean-shaven, he reminded Seleukos very much of Alexander.

'Yes; where, Polyarchos?'

'Sittace, where I was garrison commander, is only ten days' travel from Ecbatana by horse in the fair-weather months; I made the journey a few times. Nikanor doesn't have much in the way of infantry, no more than seven thousand all told, assuming he were to leave reasonable garrisons on the frontiers with Armenia and the kingdom of the Albanii to the north. His main strength is in cavalry; at least five thousand.'

'Twelve thousand men is still three times what I can expect to put into the field if I leave a garrison here.'

'Plus, he may well get contingents from Euagoros, satrap of Persis, and Aspeisas of Susiana; both appointed, along with Nikanor, by Antigonos,' said Euteles, Teutamus' replacement as commander of the Main Citadel; pallid like Patrokles, he too had suffered four years' incarceration until Seleukos had liberated him having killed Teutamus. 'Euagoros is Nikanor's cousin, and Aspeisas, stuck between the two of them, is keen not to upset either one as that would result in his making two enemies.'

Seleukos looked at Patrokles, who nodded his agreement with the assessment. 'Bringing another two or three thousand each, potentially?'

'Potentially more,' Euteles said, his voice flat with gloom.

Seleukos caught the pessimism. *This is where I have to lead and win or abandon all hope of keeping Babylonia.* He looked to the fifth of his officers, bearded and betrousered, reeking of horse-sweat and with wild hair protruding from under a leather cap matching his jacket. 'Azanes, take your Sogdian cavalry directly east along the road towards Susa; cross the Tigris and get as close to the city as you can without alerting them to your presence. I want to know if any force is moving north along the Royal Road to link up with Nikanor as he comes towards us. Report to me in Sittace; I'll be there with the army by the next full moon.' He smiled inwardly at the look of astonishment on the faces of the four Macedonian officers.

'What army?' Patrokles asked.

'The army of Babylon, all three thousand of them; the army that Nikanor is going to believe has run away. I want to be ready to march after the festival of Bel Marduk in two days' time so that I leave with the blessing of Babylon's guardian god upon me.'

With his knees becoming increasingly weak the higher he climbed, Seleukos followed Naramsin, the chief priest of Bel Marduk, up the steps climbing the side of the first level, ninety paces square, of the Etemenanki, the Temple of the Foundation of Heaven and Earth, the Ziggurat dedicated to Bel Marduk. Behind him followed Apama with their three children: Antiochus, now twelve, Archaeus, aged ten, and the younger Apama, now nine. Below them the large area surrounding the edifice was crammed with the citizens of Babylon, thousands of them, all here to pay homage to their guardian god and to see the man who now ruled over them perform his sacred duties.

But Seleukos did not wish to look down for it was a long drop, a drop which made his knees feel weak and gave him an illogical desire to cast himself down into it. And yet he had to keep climbing for it was expected of him to sacrifice at the altar atop the building made of four levels, each progressively smaller than the last, tiled with vivid blue, green and yellow ceramics in the Babylonian style depicting the god in many forms and linked by precipitous steps. It was, therefore, a relief to him that work on its reconstruction had ceased during his absence and it was still only half the height it should be. *Do I really want to resume its reconstruction and doom myself to going even higher in the coming years?* He risked a quick glance down to his right and felt his head begin to swirl; he knew the answer from a personal

69

level but politically it would be wise to continue the rebuilding that Alexander had originally ordered – but then had countermanded just before his death – for it linked Seleukos' name with the great man and it ensured that the priests of Bel Marduk, a powerful organisation in the city, would be vocal in their support for him. And he knew that he would soon be in need of that support.

Up the second and third levels he climbed, these thankfully stepped in so that the drop was no longer sheer – but still terrifying nonetheless – as the droning dirge of the priests, a couple of hundred voices in all, rose and fell in their praise to the god. The priests walked behind his family, following the procession up the countless steps, their heads with their tall cylindrical hats nodding up and down.

Upon reaching the altar on the fourth level Seleukos was treated to the spectacular sight that was the entirety of Babylon, both the Old Town, and then the New over on the west bank of the Euphrates, a wide, brown, sluggish ribbon dividing the city. Set at almost the exact centre of Babylon the Etemenanki was now, once again, the tallest building in a city crammed with habitations. And yet the outer walls encompassed parks and gardens, watered by the extensive irrigation canals, making the view both urban and pastoral, its colours, its smells and its sounds both natural and manmade. And then to the north and the south, along both banks of the river, stretched a green fertile belt of farmland, as far as the eye could see, whose produce fed the ravenous mouth of this ancient city.

With his equilibrium restored by the almost aerial view of the city he had won for the second time, and putting his fear of heights from his mind, Seleukos concentrated on his religious duties and the despatch of the two black bulls that had somehow – and he made a mental note to ask how – been coaxed or dragged up to the altar.

He had learned the form of words by rote, so the foreign prayers slipped from his tongue as the sacrifices were prepared, blessed and then offered, to the audible religious awe of the crowds below. With the ceremony complete and the auspices taken and pronounced excellent – news that was quickly communicated through the crowd by well-placed priestly acolytes – Seleukos turned to the crowd, raising his arms and eyes in the air, and cried his thanks to Bel Marduk for bringing him home. It was a popular sentiment for the acclamation rose like a wave. He beckoned Apama to stand next to him and bring their children, and together they stood, as a family, to receive the adulation of the city.

'You were generous to them during the short time you ruled,' Apama said, clasping her husband's hand, 'a lesson Pythan and Teutamus evidently didn't benefit from. If we can defend it, we'll be safe here.'

'And you and the children will be safe here whilst I go and find the means to defend it, my love.' He pulled her hand up to kiss it, drawing a huge cheer from the crowd.

'We're not to come with you?'

'Not yet; Patrokles will watch over you. If all goes well, I'll call for you and the children as I move east. I have no intention of returning until I have an army that can defend the city from an attack from the west and have defeated Antigonos' allies in the east.'

Apama looked up at her husband, concern in her eyes. 'But what happens if we're attacked before you've achieved all that?'

'We will be, Apama, I can assure you of that.'

71

'But then we'll lose Babylon for sure.'

'Not all of it. I'll make sure there are enough men and supplies for Euteles in the Main Citadel to hold out for a year whilst Patrokles conducts a guerrilla war in the surrounding country, keeping them busy until I come back.'

Apama looked down at the crowd still cheering them below. 'What about the people?'

Seleukos gestured to Naramsin. 'That's where the priests of Bel Marduk will play their part: the city is worth little without the people and so I'll make sure the people aren't here when either Antigonos or Demetrios arrive.'

The priest smiled, inclining his head. 'The will of Bel Marduk is that you should triumph, lord, and we will guide the people in accordance with it.'

'I'm thankful, Naramsin.'

Again, the priest inclined his head. 'Bel Marduk has also provided a weapon which will help you defeat the foe.'

'A weapon?'

'Yes, lord, twenty of them to be precise. Come and see.'

It was with an open mouth and wide eyes that Seleukos surveyed the twenty chariots hidden beneath the Temple of Bel Marduk. 'How long have you known about these, Naramsin?'

'Just recently, during the rebuilding, the door to the chamber was discovered,' the priest replied, indicating to the half a dozen slaves bearing torches to go deeper into the room so as to light it better.

Seleukos looked in wonder at the chariots; he had heard tell of them being used by the Achaemenid dynasty in the past but never had he seen one. Solidly built, with an almost square platform with high sides to protect the driver, the chariot rode on two wheels and it was these wheels that were its primary weapon: protruding from each hub was a double-edged blade, curved like a scythe that, revolving at speed, would take the legs off any standing against it. More blades attached to the yoke, designed for four horses, made the chariots a terror to face.

'But of what practical use are they?' Seleukos asked, seeing the major flaw in the concept. 'It's a suicide mission to charge the enemy in one of these.'

'If death is better than life, you would be willing to drive one, should the wage be freedom were you lucky enough to survive.'

'Slaves?'

'Yes, lord.'

'But we never use slaves in our armies;, only Illyrians take their slaves to war with them and expect them to fight.'

'I will see them trained, lord. When the population leaves Babylon, I'll send some of my brethren with the chariots with us and whilst they're in the wilderness they'll teach slaves to drive the machines – slaves who are willing to risk all for the slim chance of survival and freedom.'

Seleukos looked over the scythed chariots again, nodding to himself as he contemplated the deadliness of the weapon. 'You do that, Naramsin; I look forward to seeing the expressions on Antigonos' and Demetrius' faces when they have twenty of these hurtling towards them.'

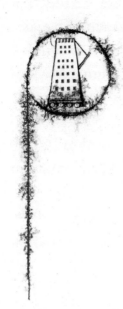

DEMETRIOS.
THE BESIEGER.

'IS THAT ALL that remains of you?' Demetrios stared aghast at the ragged group of no more than fifty horsemen recently arrived in his camp on the edge of the desert ten leagues due east of Gaza.

Sunburnt with lips peeling and eyes in a permanent squint, the men looked back at him, exhausted. 'We think so, lord,' one replied, his voice rough and weak.

'What about Athenaios?'

The man shook his head. 'We've seen no one else since the ambush.'

'Ambush?'

'They came out of the south as we were coming back from The Stone. They used the glare of the midday sun; we didn't see them until it was too late.'

'Who?'

'The Nabateans, lord.'

'The Nabateans are meant to be down at the Southern Sea, trading with the spice fleets.'

'Well, they came back, lord.'

'What happened?'

'There's not much to say. We got to The Stone in five

days and easily overcame the small force they had left to guard their women and children. Some got away and fled to a virtually impregnable position high on top of sheer cliffs with only a goat track as access, but that didn't bother Athenaios as we already had seven hundred hostages; so, we left them where they were, on their cliffs, and headed back north to the Salt Sea.' The man shrugged. 'Halfway there they fell on us seemingly out of nowhere; they waited for the sun to be at its height and then took us in the rear using the heat-haze as cover. There were thousands of them, many riding camels; their stench spooked our horses who panicked – and that was that. Those who tried to surrender were hacked to death; the rest died fighting. How we got away the gods alone know; we just put our heads down and drove our mounts without mercy. I think by that time the Nabateans were busy slaughtering the infantry who had been herding their families. I wouldn't like to think how they died.'

'How long ago was this?'

'Twelve days ago, lord. We were hiding out for a few days, waiting for the chance to make it back here without being seen.'

Demetrios did a quick calculation. *If I were to leave tomorrow, they could be at least eighteen days to the south. There's no way I can catch them. But we can't move south against Ptolemy unless we have some hold over them.* He looked back at the spokesman. 'What's your name, soldier?'

'Mantias, lord.'

'You've done well, Mantias. Get your men back to Gaza and rested and fed and then report to me when I get back in a couple of days. I'll need you as my guide when we go back to teach those camel-fuckers a lesson.'

'Yes, but not for a while,' Antigonos said, before downing a cup of resinated wine in one long draught; he was sitting, enjoying his midday meal, in the shade of a tavern's awning on the quay of Gaza's port, to the west of the ancient city, watching a squadron of a dozen ships gliding in through the harbour mouth. Gulls circled the new arrivals, cawing and soaring through the warm air, in the hope of titbits cast overboard.

'A while?' Demetrios looked down at his father, astounded. 'A while? What's a while?'

'A while is however long I say it is.' Antigonos' one eye glinted with amusement at the look of outrage on his son's face; he took a grilled sardine from the pile on a plate before him and bit it in two.

'But we should go immediately.'

'Why?' Antigonos asked, crunching his fish, head, bones and all.

'Well, because the sooner we defeat the Nabateans the sooner we can take Ptolemy.'

'I agree; but if we've learned anything from the loss of almost five thousand men in the desert, it is that we are vulnerable out there; but for the Nabateans it's their home. If I send you back now with even more men, as you're suggesting, I'll not only lose another few thousand lads but I'll lose a son as well. Your brother may be growing fast and showing a precocious talent, as you did at sixteen, but it's you, not Philippos, upon whom I rely.'

Demetrios turned away to look out over the port as the last of the squadron Antigonos had come to meet slipped in whilst the first few, with much shouted nauticalese, hurled ropes to dock-hands on the quays to be secured at their moorings. 'I can do it, Father,' he said through gritted teeth, 'I can teach those bastards a lesson.'

'You *think* you can do it, Son; and that is entirely different. But look at the facts: Athenaios and most of his men are dead. It was a mistake to send them, as I did, to raid and snatch hostages. This time I shall take a different approach. Malichus, the King of the Nabateans, sent a message complaining about the raid.'

'When did he do that?'

'It arrived the day before yesterday.'

'You didn't say anything to me.'

'You were still out on patrol so I'm telling you now you're back. He objected in very strong terms to the raid, saying he had never done anything aggressive against me.'

'Apart from threatening our flank, at Ptolemy's behest, should we attempt to move south?'

'In diplomacy it is sometimes best not to mention the more perfidious characteristics of the party with whom one is negotiating; it can lead to an awkward situation. I sent a message back condemning Athenaios for overstepping his orders, apologising to Malichus for the harm he did, stating that I had sent him to negotiate and not fight and requesting we have a meeting at the earliest opportunity to discuss a peace agreement between us.' Antigonos signalled his son to join him. 'Come and sit down; have a cup of wine and some of these fish. There's another matter to discuss which came up whilst you were away.' He patted the table and then indicated to a chair opposite him. 'Come on.'

Demetrios paused. 'Are we really going to let those men go unavenged?'

'My boy, what choice do I have? It was a mistake, my mistake, to send them in the first place. I underestimated the Nabateans' ability to use their environment to their advantage, thinking the desert was a shit place for everyone. It's my miscalculation based on the fact that whilst we were out in the east we never came across any tribe in any of the deserts we crossed who could best us.'

'The Cossaei?'

'The Cossaei don't live in the desert; they live in the Zagros Mountains.'

'Which is, to all intents and purposes, a desert; it's a wilderness that can kill you. They nearly did, raiding our foraging parties and picking off stragglers.'

'Look, I'm not going to argue with you the finer points of habitat. When I receive a reply from Malichus agreeing to talks it will be you who goes; you'll go with a proper force big enough to dissuade Malichus from any treachery and to convince him of the fact that he would be better off siding with us as we are much closer to his precious Stone than Ptolemy.'

Demetrios considered his father for a few moments and then nodded his consent. 'Very well, Father, we'll wait.' He pulled out the chair and sat. 'Well?'

'Well, what?'

'Well, you said there was another matter we had to discuss.'

'Yes, there is.' Antigonos poured two cups of wine and pushed one across to his son and then set the jug down next to a scroll, pointing to it. 'It's family business.'

'Oh, yes?' Demetrios took a sip and suppressed a wince. 'It's always quantity over quality with you, Father, isn't it? You're probably the richest man in the world and yet you always seem to have the roughest wine.'

'This is what most of the lads drink. If it's good enough for them it's good enough for me; besides, I'm used to it. Just because you're becoming a pampered pleasure-seeker with a penchant for what you consider to be the finer things in life is no reason for me to change the way I live. Now, drink your wine, stop moaning and listen to me.'

Demetrios eyed his cup but took it no closer to his mouth. 'Go on, then.'

Antigonos picked up the scroll, unravelled it and perused it without much interest as he evidently knew the contents. 'I've kept Aristodemus in Greece as my eyes and ears since he is so good at using my gold to sow discord amongst my enemies – and, when it suits my purpose, my allies – so when I wrote to Ptolemaios and Phoinix to look into the possibility of a peace deal I also wrote to Aristodemus, telling him to keep an eye on the negotiations; one wouldn't want them getting on too well, after all.'

'Quite.' Demetrios succumbed to a grilled fish.

'Well, Aristodemus writes to report trouble between your cousins Ptolemaios and Telesphorus. Apparently Telesphorus has taken exception to the fact that I asked Ptolemaios to approach Kassandros.'

'They were always jealous of each other.'

'True. But it seems he's rebelled, sold the ships I'd given him to help Ptolemaios subdue Greece and has hired a mercenary army, taken the region of Elis in the western Peloponnese and put a garrison in its Main Citadel of Kyllini.'

Demetrios saw the implication immediately as he licked his fingers. 'Has he made advances to Cratesipolis and Polyperchon in the isthmus?'

Antigonos beamed at his son. 'Good lad, I knew you'd understand. Aristodemus said that there is no evidence of that but he's looking into it. However, what he did find out was there has been contact between Kleopatra and Polyperchon and his daughter-in-law.'

'What does she want with him?'

'A good question and one made even more pertinent by the fact there's a rumour, and it is nothing more than a rumour, that Kleopatra travelled to Pergamum towards the end of the winter, at the time of a very significant date.'

Demetrios wracked his brain but could come up with nothing of relevance. 'Tell me.'

'Herakles was sixteen three months ago.'

'Ah.'

'Ah indeed.' Antigonos reached for another fish. 'Kleopatra will, of course, deny going to Pergamum – and my guards in Sardis will swear she never left the city otherwise they would have informed me – and she will also deny any contact with Polyperchon.'

'Which leaves us where?'

'It leaves us, once again, exposed on too many fronts. Thank the gods Nikanor is dealing with Seleukos for the moment. But if there is some sort of alliance between Telesphorus and Polyperchon and his amazon daughter-in-law and, somehow, they get Herakles as a figurehead, it could be very inconvenient for us.'

'It would be more inconvenient for Kassandros and Thessalonike, surely? Herakles would have to be placed on the throne of Macedon to have any chance of legitimacy.'

'I agree. But looking into a future where that were to happen?'

That would make us either subordinates or rebels. 'I see the problem. You'll have to send Ptolemaios against his cousin, won't you?'

Antigonos nodded and then drained his cup. 'Yes, I'm afraid that's the conclusion I've come to. Aristodemus will take over the negotiations with Kassandros so Ptolemaios can take his army and bottle up Polyperchon in his enclave of Corinth and Sykion and then head west to beat some sense into Telesphorus.'

'Don't you want him to kill him?'

'Perhaps it would be for the best.' Antigonos shrugged. 'But he is my late younger brother's son; it would be a shame. In the meantime, all we can do is wait and react to the news as it comes in. Speaking of which...' He waved at Nearchos as he made his way down the gangway from his newly arrived ship. 'I've got wine and fish here, my friend.'

Nearchos winced and shook his head, having drained his cup. 'You wouldn't get worse in a dockside brothel on the south coast of Crete; and I should know, I come from there.'

'Not you as well, Nearchos?' Antigonos took another swig, savouring it. 'This is good, honest, resinated wine.'

'Thank the gods it's resinated.'

Demetrios put down his unfinished cup. 'Yes, at least it's one of those things because it's neither honest nor good – nor wine, for that matter.'

Chuckling, Antigonos poured himself another cup, emptying the jug. 'Your loss, gentlemen. Now, tell me what Ptolemy's up to, Nearchos. Did you manage to sneak a look at his defences?'

'I didn't need to sneak,' Nearchos said, risking another sip. 'Ptolemy invited me for a tour.'

Antigonos spluttered a mouthful of wine. 'He did what?'

'He saw the squadron standing well out to sea off Pelusium and sent a ship out to us under a branch of truce to ask me if I wouldn't be more comfortable with my feet on dry land where, he assured me, I would get a much better view of what I had evidently come to look at.'

'And you went?'

Nearchos looked confused. 'Of course I did. You wanted me to find out about Ptolemy's defences and his strength in men and ships; how better to do it than be given a tour by the man himself and his lovely mistress, Thais?'

Antigonos shook his head. 'My arse, he's got a nerve; you have to hand it to him. Well, tell me then; you've had the tour.'

'Ptolemy says to tell you he's very comfortable and to thank you very much for sending someone to enquire.' Nearchos suppressed a grin.

'My rancid arse, Nearchos; are you enjoying this?'

'Not at all, I'm just relaying a message,' Nearchos replied, choosing a fish. 'He says his granaries are full, he has all the fresh water he needs and he gives his men meat once every three days, all forty thousand of them.'

'Forty thousand?'

'I thought it was an exaggeration until he took me to the south of Pelusium where he has a couple more camps. He keeps his elephants there.'

'His elephants! My arse they are! They're *my* elephants that *he* stole.'

'He thought you might be of that opinion and he asked me to assure you that he's taking very good care of them so do not concern yourself about the beasts.' Nearchos disguised his smile by chewing on his fish.

Demetrius failed to hide his amusement, despite the fact that it was his mistakes which had led to Ptolemy's acquisition of the herd.

'Don't you smirk, boy!' his father growled. 'I should send you down there to get them back single-handed.'

'Father, can't you see Ptolemy's just goading you and he's,' he pointed sideways at Nearchos who was smiling into his beard despite a full mouth, 'playing along because he always got on well with the bastard and enjoys his sense of humour?'

Antigonos' eye glared at the Cretan. 'Well, you shouldn't; you're on my side.'

'I can still enjoy a joke with an old friend.'

'But not at my expense. How many ships does he have?'

'He showed me over a hundred at Pelusium and promised there would be more soon, should you ever solve the Nabatean problem and manage to move south.'

'What does he know about my dealings with the Nabateans?'

It was at this point that Demetrios wondered if Nearchos was about to go too far for he could see exactly what had happened.

Nearchos put his cup down. 'Ptolemy sends his apologies; he didn't mean for all those men to be killed when he warned the Nabateans you were mounting an expedition. He thought getting them to curtail their trade with the spice fleets on the Southern Sea coast and hurry back north would just scare Athenaios off.'

'He did what?' Antigonos could no longer contain himself; he jumped to his feet, his cup hurtling onto the bow of Nearchos' moored ship, splintering into scores of fragments. 'That bastard! That arse-groping, cock-riding, sperm-guzzling bastard. How the fuck did he know to warn the camel-fuckers? Who fucking told him?' Antigonos grabbed Nearchos by the collar of his tunic and hauled him up. 'Did you tell him? Did you? Seeing as you seem to be so matey with him, I wouldn't put it past you.'

Nearchos gripped Antigonos' wrist as he stood facing him. 'Calm down. What would you prefer I do – not tell you what he said? Of course he was going to find out; nothing goes on in each other's camps that isn't reported, seeing as there's so much coming and going. And it doesn't take long to get a message by camel from Pelusium to the Southern Sea coast. But Ptolemy was genuinely sorry Malichus had taken your raid so personally as to kill almost five thousand men. He is, after all, first and foremost, as he wished me to point out, a Macedonian and doesn't take kindly to too many good Macedonian lads – or even Greeks, including Cretans, for that matter, as he was gracious enough to add in my presence – being killed by camel-botherers; and he sends his apologies.'

'Well, he can shove his apologies up his arse.'

'And he promises next time he warns Malichus of your coming he will also tell him not to kill too many, otherwise he will have him to deal with.'

Demetrios leaped from his chair as Antigonos hurled the table, cartwheeling, against the wall of the tavern, inchoate with rage. 'Calm down, Father. Calm! Nearchos is only the messenger.' He gave the Cretan a sidelong glance. 'Granted, he seemed to get the correct nuances and stresses to the speech as if it were Ptolemy delivering it himself. But Ptolemy said all this just to provoke that very same reaction.'

'I'll rip his balls off, stuff them up his arse and make Thais suck them out. We're going south tomorrow.'

'Father, that's just the reaction he wants. He wants you to be triggered into doing something rash.'

'Well, he's managed it.'

'Then control yourself because there is no way we're going south if he's got all that waiting for us. I can now see the wisdom of your strategy of isolating him by making peace with Kassandros and Lysimachus. When Ptolemy realises that he has no allies, he might be far more open to reason and negotiation.'

Antigonos fumed; a deep growl rumbled in his throat. 'I suppose you're right, my boy; it's obvious that, against those numbers, invading Egypt would be far too risky at the moment. You can deal with the Nabateans meanwhile; leave once you've got everything you need. We can still inspire the fear of the gods into Malichus without waiting for his reply, as his helping both Ptolemy and Seleukos is reason enough for me to crush him.'

SELEUKOS.
THE BULL-ELEPHANT.

'A CROSS THE RIVER to the north, about ten leagues away, is Opis,' Polyarchos said, pointing into the heat-hazed distance. 'It's where the canal the Babylonians dug from the Euphrates joins the Tigris.'

Seleukos looked out from the walls of Sittace over the fertile fields to either side of the mud-brown course of the Tigris, supporting so much life. Villages abounded and farms and homesteads dotted the landscape; the fact there were two towns of prominence so close to each other, one either side of the river, demonstrated what a prosperous part of his satrapy this area was. *And defensible; at least far more so than Babylon where the rivers are much further apart.* He turned and looked west. 'How far is it to the Euphrates, would you say, Polyarchos?'

'Ten leagues. We're at their closest point to one another, which is why the canal was dug here. Nebuchadnezzar also built a wall between the rivers in order to defend Babylonia from the Medes after they defeated the Assyrians and took their capital, Nineveh, thus threatening Babylonia from the north.'

'Did he now? How very wise of him; pointless having two mighty rivers defending your east and west flanks if an army can just come down between them from the north.' Again, Seleukos looked at the surroundings, contemplating the beauty of the site as a defensive position and the abundance that was evidently produced by the area; he let his thought wander. *Is Babylon really in the right place? A city here where the rivers are at their closest and connected by a canal and where an army could stop an invading force half as big again would surely be far more advantageous.* He sniffed the air, a light and cool breeze. *And it's so much fresher than Babylon where there is hardly ever a wind unless it's a storm.* He allowed himself a few more moments' thought before returning to the matter in hand and gazed at the northern arm of the Zagros Mountains just visible on the eastern horizon. 'I assume that, with the weather set fair here, the pass must be open by now, Polyarchos?'

'Definitely, lord; summer is fast approaching. Nikanor will be moving through the mountains by now – if he's coming.'

Seleukos shaded his eyes as he stared across the Tigris; along its near bank barges, boats and ships were being assembled in preparation to ferry his men across the water. 'Oh, he's coming all right. You can be sure of that. The question is, how many of his friends is he bringing with him?'

'We saw nothing,' Azanes reported as he arrived at Sittace the following day, having been ferried across the Tigris, leaving his three hundred followers to camp on the eastern bank. 'There was no military movement on the road between Babylon and Susa and no column of troops has left Susa since last summer, according to the farmers living close to the road. Nor was there any sign or rumour of a force coming north from Persis as we picked up the Royal Road at Susa and followed it north along the Cheaspes River through the foothills of the Zagros; we left the road, turning west as the river veers east. There was nothing, lord, just travellers and merchants; we saw Babrak's caravan two days from Susa and he reported nought of interest. If any force has headed north from Persis to Media then it has used the eastern route on the far side of the mountain range.'

'That would mean getting to Ecbatana before Nikanor left; they must have travelled before the snows melted,' Polyarchos said.

Seleukos shrugged. 'Eumenes and Antigonos fought a whole campaign during the winter, including two pitched battles involving over one hundred thousand men in each.' He stared again in the direction whence his foe would come. 'We will assume the worst: that Euagoros has gone to his cousin's aid and therefore there's an army of nine to ten thousand infantry and seven to eight thousand cavalry on its way here and Aspeisas is either bringing a strong force north to join up with them or is making his own attack on Babylon. That's what we have to deal with.'

'And we're going to face them with our three thousand infantry, three hundred Sogdian horse-archers and your hundred Companion Cavalry?' Polyarchos looked incredulous.

'On the contrary, Nikanor's going to face us; but he won't know until it's too late.' Leaving Polyarchos neither any wiser nor more encouraged, Seleukos turned and walked away along the walls. He looked back over his shoulder and resisted the urge to wink. 'Have the men ready to move across the river at dawn tomorrow.'

It had been an easy operation getting his army across the river; but only, Seleukos reflected, because it was such a meagre force. So meagre was it, fewer than sixty vessels were needed for the crossing and these had struggled against the current to keep pace with the army as it had marched north to Opis where the road to Ecbatana, the canal between the two rivers and Nebuchadnezzar's wall all met. *The obvious place for me to meet an army coming from the east; Nikanor won't be at all surprised to see me here.* And he was relieved to have made it to the Tigris before the arrival of Nikanor; indeed, he had hurried so it would be thus, having left Patrokles in command of two thousand men to garrison Babylon should Aspeisas hear of his movement and launch an attack in his absence. Speed had been essential and speed had brought him to a place where he could, he hoped, make the enemy's numbers count for nothing. *Just as Demetrios did.*

Seleukos looked towards the wall of Opis, less than a thousand paces away, and then smiled at his officers. 'We make camp here, gentlemen. Polyarchos, I'll leave that to you; keep it basic, as I expect we are going to want to depart in a hurry. And see the river transports are all drawn up on the bank and ready for a swift retreat. Oh, and seize any boats in Opis' harbour; we don't want to make it easy for Nikanor.'

With a salute and a quizzical look Polyarchos went about his task.

'Diphilos, set up a strong perimeter,' Seleukos ordered. 'I want none of the lads going into the town to whore and drink. Make sure they know that and then hang the first couple stupid enough to try as an example to the others. I want strict discipline; it's vital for what I have in mind.'

'And what is that, lord?'

'Beating Nikanor, of course. Send Azanes to me as soon as he comes back in.'

'He's about ten leagues away by now,' the Sogdian reported as dusk fell, 'or thereabouts. We sighted him at noon, fifteen leagues off, and then turned around immediately and headed back here. Your estimate is correct: seven thousand infantry and five thousand cavalry, split evenly between heavy and light; all javelin armed.'

'Did you let them see you?'

'Yes, some of their light cavalry came after us but we easily outran them.'

'Good.' Seleukos digested the information. 'If they're making camp ten leagues from here, their scouts could arrive by midday and the main column in the late afternoon.'

'There were no scouts, lord.'

'No scouts?'

Azanes shook his head, his long, wild beard waving across his chest. 'None; at least none we saw.'

'I hope that'll change now he's spotted you. We need to show a bit of resistance; and by we, I mean you and your lads.'

Azanes grinned. 'And we're looking forward to it. We haven't fought mounted since Gaza.'

Seleukos slapped the Sogdian on the shoulder. 'Tomorrow afternoon you'll get your chance.'

*

And it was shortly after noon the following day that the dust cloud Seleukos had been expecting appeared on the eastern horizon. 'Have the men finished their midday meal, Polyarchos?' he asked, although he knew the answer from the sweet smell of grilled mutton and river perch in the air.

'Yes, lord.'

Seleukos looked back at the camp. *This is going to take careful timing.* 'Have the men pack their kit but leave the tents up. They should get all their possessions onto the boats and then we'll get them to form up as if we're going to face the enemy.'

'Are we?'

'Yes, for a few moments it will certainly look like we have every intention of doing so. And then...'

'And then what?'

'And then I'll give the order for the lads to break formation and head for the boats in a mad dash.'

'What about the tents?'

'Oh, I think a few tents are a small price to pay for what I'm going to achieve. Have Azanes report to me when his horse-boys are mounted.'

It was as the dark shadow under the dust cloud resolved into tiny figures on horseback that Seleukos unleashed Azanes and his three hundred Sogdian horse-archers; his small phalanx stood, with light troops screening it, in front of the camp. *Every man's no doubt wondering what their general's thinking of.* Seleukos smiled inwardly.

Over the dry ground the Sogdians thundered towards the oncoming foe, their horsemanship prodigious, controlling their beasts with their knees, their feet hanging loose, bow in left hand and an arrow ready for nocking in the right.

Seleukos sat on his horse, at the head of his hundred Companion Cavalry, behind the right flank of his small formation ready to make the biggest gamble of his life. If it failed, he was lost – he had, should that occur, left Patrokles with orders to take Apama and the children and escape Babylon by ship and try to make his way to Ptolemy as he, Seleukos, would be dead. If it worked… *Well, if it works, who knows what it could lead to?*

A dark shadow rose from the Sogdians as they let fly their first volley. Seleukos drew a deep breath, realising he had been holding it for a long time. Another shadow rose from the speeding formation momentarily and then another as volley after volley was loosed, the third still rising in the air as the first slammed down into the approaching cavalry now at a full gallop. Seleukos squinted and was rewarded with the sight, a thousand paces away, of small figures tumbling to the ground and horses rearing as another three hundred projectiles rained down upon them; and then another. *Between four and five hundred of them, I should guess; less by the time they get here.*

As they released their fourth volley, Azanes' men split down the middle, swerving to the left and right, using nought but their legs for control as they drew another arrow from their quivers and nocked it, aimed and released in one fluid movement in less time than it took Seleukos to draw a single breath. Back they now raced, the horsemen from the east, with the Median cavalry chasing after them, waving their javelins in impotent rage and leaving their dead and wounded in the blood-soaked dust behind them.

'Steady, lads!' Seleukos shouted to his infantry formation as the Sogdians drew the Medes on. 'Stay steady; horses won't charge into infantry bristling with pike-tips.'

And this everyone who had served in a phalanx was well aware of. And it was a balm to soothe jagged nerves as the enemy came on.

'Present!' he shouted as the cavalry came within five hundred paces.

A wave flooded across the formation of the phalanx as pikes were lowered, the first five ranks to the horizontal; the eleven rear ones at progressively raised angles to act as deflectors to incoming missiles.

'Light infantry, disperse!'

The screen of skirmishers raced away to either side revealing the phalanx, as three hundred paces out, then two and then one, were the Sogdians, becoming more terrifying with every galloped pace until with less than thirty before they would have collided with their own front line, they wheeled, again left and right, skimming along the glistening, polished iron of the pikes, ululating as they thundered by, to reveal the chasing Medes, drawn into the trap by a desire for revenge; the line of steady infantry, behind a bristling hedge of iron, shocked them into a skidding pull up and a hasty turn. Equine limbs strained as momentum pressed down on them, so sudden were their heads pulled back by yanked reins; their bodies collided and buffeted as they were hauled around by horsemen desperate to avoid almost certain death. Round they went, many throwing their riders or crashing to the ground in twisted-limbed agony, their bestial cries and shrieks grating on the ear and the dust they raised stinging on the eye. But turn they did, for the most part, leaving just shy of three dozen writhing on the ground, the remainder a disordered shambles as they attempted to ride away from terror so suddenly revealed.

'Now!' Seleukos shouted, waving his lance above his head and urging his Companions on as he kicked his stallion forward. 'Now!' he cried with urgency for this was his opportunity to set the bait which would make his next tactical move seem plausible. 'Now!' he yelled again, feeling the joy of battle surge within him as he led one hundred heavy lancers into the unprotected rear of more than four times their number; forward he went with hope quickening his heart.

And behind him his Companions roared their support, following his lead, fanning out to either side so that Seleukos became the point of a wedge. On they sped, their mounts stretching their legs as they were given their heads, accelerating into the charge, their objective struggling to make headway such was the confusion within their ranks; a few streamed away, extracting themselves from the press of their comrades as panic grew with the war-cries of the Companions penetrating their ears.

Forward Seleukos thrust his arm, his sleek-bladed weapon clasped fast in fist, as he stretched his torso low along his mount's neck to get maximum reach; beside him, half a length back on either side his two cover-men did the same. It was with a jolt, shuddering his shoulder, that the lance point rammed into the spine of a shrieking Mede, his high headdress flying off as his back arched and his arms flailed in the air. Almost instantaneously his cover-men struck and then those outside them, along the line as the wedge carved its way into the disordered cavalry's unprotected rear. Such was their close proximity none could manoeuvre to face the attack and they fell from their horses, blood spurting from dishonourable wounds in their backs, to be trampled beneath the pounding hooves of their comrades' panicking beasts.

With glee did Seleukos push forward, his arm working back and forth, stabbing his lance blindly into the compressed mass of enemy flesh, for he knew the first stage of his plan had succeeded. On and on he pushed his stallion with his Companions to either side pressing their advantage as the momentum of the wedge ground the opposition to a pulp, mangled beneath thrashing equine limbs.

And then they were through, exploding out of what was left of the enemy formation as those who could broke away to flee back towards the main column of the army, just visible as a dark line a league or so away.

'Let them go,' Seleukos shouted, pulling on the reins, watching a good two hundred, perhaps half of the surviving Medes, gallop away as their remaining comrades slithered from their mounts either in death or in an attempt to kneel on the ground in surrender. 'Take prisoners, lads, and spare the wounded. You may be fighting alongside these men some day; let's show there are no hard feelings.'

It was a scene of carnage that greeted Seleukos as he looked back; each of his hundred Companions must have skewered at least one man, many two and some three for there was a carpet of dead thrown over the ground along the front line of the phalanx. But that was not what pleased him most, for he would rather not have killed so many men who could have joined his ranks; what brought him greatest pleasure were the cheers rising from the pikemen, the sixteen-foot-long sarissas punching into the air as they saluted their cavalry and the man who had led them. Not being one to waste an opportunity to garner praise, Seleukos rode towards his cheering men and raised both arms in acknowledgement.

For some time, he indulged the ovation before gesturing for silence; as it became manifest, he turned and pointed to the oncoming army. 'Macedonians, before us is an army from the east. Yes, there may well be old comrades, Macedonian and Greek, amongst their number, but, nevertheless, they are an eastern army intent upon our destruction. But we will not let them achieve that aim, will we?'

The response was deafening, their blood up.

'But we are too few to take them head on; they outnumber us by five or six to one. But do not fear, for I have worked out a way to beat them. Soon I will give you an order that, I pray to Ares, god of war, I will never give again. Trust me, for it is a way to confuse the enemy and lull him into false security. We will wait here as the column advances and then, as we see the size of the force compared to our own, I shall give that order for the one and only time you follow me.'

'Fall back! Fall back to the boats! Back to the boats!' Seleukos shouted as the front of Nikanor's column, no more than a thousand paces away, began to fan out to form line of battle, giving a true indication of the numbers within it. 'Back! Back across the river!'

And back Seleukos' troops ran, just as they had been told, in a fine impression of men, fearful of what stands before them, seeking the safety of flight. Back they went in haphazard disorder, fleeing through the still-standing tents in the camp to the boats lined along the riverbank as the sun westered and glowed deep golden on their helms. And into the vessels they piled as Azanes took his Sogdians and the Companion Cavalry, along with Seleukos' stallion, south along the eastern bank. Not long did it take for the little army to embark; by the time Nikanor's men had advanced to the edge of the camp the last of the craft had pushed out into the river, towards the setting sun, leaving no other river transport available on the east bank.

Downriver they floated, keeping to the west bank, letting the current draw them on at its slow, unhurried pace and leaving Nikanor's army in control of their camp, their celebratory cheers drifting on a light night-breeze.

A league they went until Seleukos gave the order to strike out for the east bank. As he stepped ashore, he heard the whicker of soft-snorting horses. 'Were you followed?' he asked Azanes as the Sogdian materialised in the gloom.

'No. I had a couple of my men watching Nikanor and they've just reported in: the army pitched camp and then settled down to their evening meal. They've set a perimeter guard, but not a very strong one; my boys should be able to slit their throats without them noticing.'

Seleukos smiled in the darkness. 'I imagine they will notice; but as long as they notice quietly, I don't mind. Get your horse-boys fed, Azanes; we'll move north as soon as the lads have disembarked and had something to eat.'

It was a cold supper Seleukos allowed his men, for the lighting of fires was forbidden. Stealth was the watchword as it was by stealth that Seleukos gambled he could overcome five or six times his number.

With just swords and shields, their pikes and other weapons left at the landing point, the little army marched back north, covering the league in an hour to arrive at Nikanor's camp soon after midnight. With their advance screened by the Sogdians none were aware of their presence as they moved into position close to the sleeping foe.

All along the southern perimeter of the camp Azanes' men ranged as they searched for the men charged with ensuring the safety of their slumbering comrades; with a sliced throat and a hand clasped over their mouths, did the guards die; knives ripping open flesh with brutal force. Not a sound was made as the Sogdians stripped away the protective line in the darkness, leaving the camp exposed and unsuspecting.

'Diphilos will take his men to the left, circling around and preventing any escape to the north. Polyarchos will do the same to the right whilst I head for the command tent at the centre with Azanes' archers covering my flanks. And remember, gentlemen, keep as quiet as you can until the alarm sounds or my signaller blows his horn as we get to the centre of the camp, and then make as much noise as ten times your number – we have to terrify them into surrender. Oh, and try not to kill too many, bearing in mind these men are going to be comrades soon.'

With muttered assurances, the officers crept off to their commands, and Seleukos returned to his dismounted Companions, muffling their gear and readying themselves for an infiltration by stealth into the heart of the enemy.

There was little point in delay and thus, with a fast-beating pulse, Seleukos moved forward at the crouch, his head low and his hands brushing the ground ahead of him, checking for rocks and other hazards. On he went, his speed growing as he moved closer to the camp, its low-burning fires providing a little light.

Past the first tents he led his men, standing upright and forcing himself to walk now with a measured pace as if he had every right to be there, his Companions following his lead, but none noticed their passing for all were asleep in their tents, oblivious to the fact the army they thought they had seen run away that very afternoon had re-crossed the river and was now amongst them.

Deeper into the camp Seleukos travelled as his men fanned out behind him; following them were light infantry and peltasts, blades at the ready for the moment the shouting began. And it was from his right the first sound of alarm was raised; it was quickly suppressed by a knife in the throat, the gurgling crescendo being only too recognisable. Stealth was no longer the issue now; it was speed. Into a sprint Seleukos went, the large command tents at the centre of the camp looming before him, great shadows against a dim firelight glow. As the guards on the tents sprang alert, Seleukos and his comrades were upon them, their swords thrusting low, under their breastplates to slice into groins. Down they went, their screams ringing loud. Through the tent entrance, Seleukos pushed; his objective Nikanor or his cousin, Euagoros, or, indeed any other high-ranking officer. Now horns rent the night air, and shouts and roars rose from his men as they swooped down on their prey still coming to their senses after the grogginess of sleep.

It was an instinctive reaction to duck; the javelin whistled over his head by no more than a thumb's breadth; he hurled himself forward as his assailant, half-naked, charged him with his sword raised. Down came the blade, ringing onto his parrying weapon, causing his forearm and bicep to bulge with the strain. Into dark eyes bulging with effort Seleukos looked as he forced the sword away from him and up. He gave a quick glance to his left, enough to distract his attacker who followed the look, his eyes bulging even further as Seleukos' knee rammed up between his legs. Downward pressure on his weapon ceased; grabbing the man's wrist with his left hand, Seleukos brought his sword down to slash across his enemy's face, opening his cheek and slicing deep into his lower jaw. Blood slopped down his front as he pushed the staggering opponent back and followed with a punch of his blade into the unprotected midriff as, around him, his comrades subdued resistance from four other men in a frenzy of violence, showered with gore.

It was quickly over.

'No one else in here, lord,' one of his Companions reported, having searched the tent.

Seleukos looked at his victim, lying with glassy eyes staring at the roof; he did not recognise him from his time serving with Antigonos during the campaign against Eumenes. 'Any idea who this is?'

The man shook his head; blood dripped from his clean-shaven chin. 'No, lord, I've never seen him before, or, indeed, any of them,' he said, looking at the other corpses.

'No matter. Come.' Seleukos headed for the exit.

Outside the violence had subsided as the men so brutally woken from their sleep had failed to mount a solid defence; down they went to their knees, if, indeed, they had even managed to get to their feet, such had been the speed of the attack and the thoroughness of the infiltration.

With haste, weapons were collected and the prisoners rounded up, secured in groups of eight with ropes around the neck.

Polyarchos strode up to Seleukos, grinning and his right forearm dark with blood. 'I give you joy of your victory, lord; we must have captured over ten thousand of them.'

Seleukos acknowledged the salutation and then pointed to the command tent and the bodies being dragged out. 'Is any of them Nikanor or Euagoros?'

Polyarchos shook his head after a quick perusal. 'I don't

know what Euagoros looks like, but certainly none of them is Nikanor.'

'Get me a prisoner who might be able to identify them.'

It was not a prisoner who made the identification as the sun rose in the east, but a mercenary commander newly signed into Seleukos' pay. 'That's Euagoros, lord,' the man said, his accent the lilting speech of far-off New Greece in southern Italy as he pointed to Seleukos' blood-smeared opponent lying rigid, the slash across his jaw exposing his teeth in a macabre grin. 'You won't find Nikanor here, though. He spent the night as a guest of the elders of Opis.' The mercenary looked towards the dawn. 'He'll be long gone by now.'

Seleukos swore under his breath. 'Now I'll have to follow him.'

'But at least you now have the men, lord,' Polyarchos reminded him.

And that thought calmed Seleukos as he looked around the camp; all through it prisoners were being untied, having taken their oath to Seleukos, for it mattered not to them whom they served as long as they were paid, and paid well and regularly. Seleukos would soon be able to afford to pay them very well indeed for with them he was heading south to Susa and the royal treasury therein. *And once I have that under my control, I'll look to the east and settle with Nikanor before either Antigonos or his pup come to try to wrest Babylon from me.*

DEMETRIOS.
THE BESIEGER.

IT HAD TAKEN longer than Demetrios had wished to get the four thousand infantry and a similar number of cavalry together and still leave Gaza secure against a surprise attack from Ptolemy – a serious consideration seeing as his information about the last raid into the Nabateans' territory had been so accurate. And then the time it had taken to provision the expedition in order to be self-sufficient for fifteen days had also added to the delay; thus it was eleven days later that Demetrios sat on his horse next to Hieronymus, looking in amazement at the Salt Sea. It was not the sea itself, remarkable though it was, that caught his attention: it was an area along the southern shore that fascinated him.

'What is it?' he asked, looking at the almost black, viscous substance that oozed from the ground. All around, men, stripped almost naked, worked with wooden spades collecting the stuff in reed baskets.

Hieronymus dismounted and knelt to sniff the ground whence it oozed. 'I've not seen it before although I have heard of an oily black substance that hardens when cold and melts in the heat. Apparently, it was used in the mortar between the bricks in the walls of Babylon. This must be it.'

Demetrios turned to Mantias. 'Have you seen this before?'

'Yes, but I don't know its name, lord,' his guide replied. 'But it seems to be of value as each time I've passed this place men are harvesting it and then they send it south.'

'South? To the Nabateans?'

'I assume so; although what they would want with it, I don't know.'

Demetrios looked again at the workmen, black with the sticky slime. 'Well, we shall find out.'

Leaving the southern tip of the Salt Sea behind, Demetrios led his men into an unremitting desert of crags, ravines and sharp hills above whose rough floor no clouds formed, leaving the sun to burn down onto already scalding stone adding heated misery to the parched column. But Demetrios took no notice of his men's discomfort for he ignored his own growing distress, telling himself it was but a three-day journey to The Stone and the sooner it were done the better.

And so, with a pause for a couple of hours during the full heat of the day, Demetrios pressed on, following where Mantias led until, on the evening of the third day, they passed through a narrow passage between two towering red-rock peaks into a bowl surrounded by scraggy hills on all sides. Demetrios blinked a few times unable to believe his eyes for what he saw within the bowl: nothing. There was no man nor beast nor dwelling to be seen; nothing but scrub and rock. Apart from the occasional call of an unknown bird there was silence.

'I had at least expected to see some sign of habitation,' Demetrios said to Mantias. 'Some evidence, perhaps, that a great many people live here.'

'But they don't, lord. This is where they gather for festivals and meetings of the clans. They would have moved their families and flocks long before we arrived had they been here in the first place.'

'Then how do we threaten them?'

Mantias pointed to a large monolith set at the centre of the bowl. 'That is sacred to them.'

Demetrios smiled. 'Yes, that should do it.'

Just how the monolith had come to be there, Demetrios could not tell; it was old, that was certain, for there were symbols engraved on it which were worn to almost invisibility through age. Ten times the height of a man and thrice the circumference, it was of a stone that did not match the type prevalent nearby. 'Who brought it here, I wonder,' Demetrios mused.

Mantias shrugged. 'But it's here.'

'And very useful that it is.' He turned to Hieronymus. 'Organise a party with ropes, wedges, hammers and levers. I want this thing ready to topple by the end of the day.'

The historian was shocked. 'You're not really thinking of destroying this, are you?'

'Why not? Well, at least I want to look as though I'm going to destroy it to get their attention.'

Small figures standing on the skyline, high above the bowl, appeared as the first of the ropes were lassoed around the top of the monolith. More and more came as the work continued. In a circle around the sacred stone the cavalry stood formed up, with the infantry, mainly archers, acting as a screen; Demetrios was taking no chances of sharing Athenaios' fate.

As the sun fell into the west and long shadows engulfed the bowl, a single horn sounded, echoing mournful tones off the rock, slowly fading into the distance. Again, it sounded and then again. On the third call, Demetrios halted the work. 'Get your lads to stand away, Hieronymus. Everyone is to pull back now.'

As The Stone was cleared of men, Demetrios looked around; the heights above the bowl were now teaming with people, men, women and children, standing in silence, their numbers growing with every heartbeat.

It was another horn, a deeper call, which announced the arrival of a small party, mounted on camels, through a narrow pass at the northern rim.

'Let them approach!' Demetrios shouted as they drew closer showing no fear of the archers aiming at them. 'Lower your weapons and let them through.'

Demetrios stood before the monolith as the group approached, one foot on a rock, his forearm resting on his thigh, watching the leader, a man in his mid- to late forties in long, flowing white robes and a wound, white headdress, contrasting sharply with his full black beard and matching eyes; any skin visible was the colour of ancient wood.

'Demetrios, my friend,' the man said as he brought his camel to a halt, 'I welcome you to the heart of my realm.' With a couple of taps of the goad and a pull of the reins, his camel knelt on its front legs and then lowered the rear two so the man could dismount. 'I am Malichus, the King of the Nabateans, and you and your men are most welcome to spend the night here under my protection.'

It was as much as Demetrios could do to keep a straight face at Malichus' audacity in implying he and his men needed protection. 'And you are welcome to share a meal with me in my camp,' he replied with as much grace as possible.

Fires lit the rock surrounding the bowl with faint flickers of orange and gold, giving the scene an eerie quality amplified with the constant drone of many voices, whose soft echo rebounded around the camp.

Demetrios cut a leg from the lamb roasting on the spit and, placing it on a trencher, offered it to his guest.

Malichus' dark eyes twinkled with mirth in the firelight. 'You are very generous to offer me such a tender morsel of the beast which I presented to you. Had I not ordered one of my flocks to be slaughtered I believe we would have been eating dried meat and stale bread.'

Demetrios returned the smile, finding the king's humour infectious. 'I think it was the least you could have done seeing as I could have given the order for your death at any time during your approach.'

Malichus waved the thought away with a chuckle. 'You know perfectly well that, had you done so, none of you would have left here alive and I – or my heir – would have been richer by three of four thousand horses. No, my friend, you didn't spare my life, I spared yours.'

Demetrios' smile transformed into a laugh at the absurdity of the notion. 'And just why did you do that? Was it because if you had offered any violence, I would have given the order for your sacred stone to be toppled?'

Malichus looked over his shoulder at the monolith that still wore its ropes, dangling loose down its sides. 'Egypt would have sent me another one, had you done so.'

'Egypt?'

'Yes. It was Egypt who sent our ancestors that stone as a

sign of friendship when we harried the Sea Peoples who settled along the coast, having invaded Egypt and been beaten off hundreds of years ago. The Philistines we called them in Aramaic. But enough of history and down to practical business: I spared your lives because Ptolemy asked me to – told me to, even.'

'Ptolemy?'

'Do you always repeat what has just been said? Yes, Ptolemy. He was upset I killed so many of his fellow countrymen repelling your last raid, even though they were his enemies – you have strange customs I can never quite get used to. Anyway, Ptolemy asked me to make peace with you and give you hostages and gifts, which I am very happy to do. So, to make up for the seven hundred hostages I took back from you I will present you with seven hundred camels.'

Demetrios stared at the king, unable to understand his motivation. 'But if Ptolemy wants you to make peace with me then what threat is there to the east that would prevent us from marching on him in Egypt?'

Malichus picked a piece of well-cooked meat from his leg of lamb and chewed on it with obvious pleasure before licking his fingers. 'The fact is there is nothing to stop you, except Ptolemy judges you may have more serious priorities now.'

'What does Ptolemy know about my priorities?'

'Oh, he knows much. Tomorrow you should return to your father and you will find news will soon come from the east that has changed the situation entirely.'

'Nonsense. How can Ptolemy possibly know what news is going to come before it arrives?'

'What you must remember is that Ptolemy gets his news from the east from us, straight across the desert.'

'Just as you took Seleukos straight across the desert.'

'Exactly so.'

'We still have a score to settle with you on that account.'

Malichus shrugged as if it were a matter of little import. 'It was a favour to Ptolemy and I do a lot of business with him. Two or three times a month, I send a caravan with bitumen from the Salt Sea to Egypt – they use it for embalming, you see, and they pay well – with it goes the most up-to-date news from the east. You, on the other hand, have to wait for it to travel up the Euphrates, over into Syria and then down the coast to Gaza. By the time you or your father has heard what Seleukos is up to, Ptolemy has known for half a moon.'

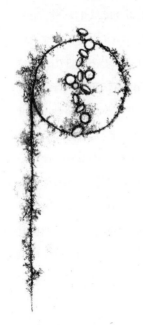

PTOLEMY.
THE BASTARD.

INEVITABLY, PTOLEMY KNEW from bitter experience, bad news would always sour a pleasurable situation; and this was no exception. His leading of Nearchos on a personal tour of his defences around Pelusium, now that he had fallen back to the Nile Delta in the face of Antigonos' advance, had amused him, especially as he had been able to share the enjoyment with his old friend and comrade of imagining the look on the resinated cyclops' face when Nearchos recounted his visit and Ptolemy's exact words accompanying it; just because they were on different sides in this war did not mean they could not enjoy a joke together. This pleasing incident had been followed by the equally pleasing news from Ophellas, his governor in Cyrenaica, that the Carthaginian general, Hanno, had won a decisive victory over Agathocles, the Tyrant of Syracuse, at the Himera River in Sicilia. Agathocles was now under siege in Syracuse, a city so well defended it would take the Carthaginians months, if not years, to take it, thus ensuring there would be no threat on his western borders for some time to come. This would give him ample time to complete the construction of the three ports he had commissioned on the coast closest to Sicilia, one of which he would name after himself, another after his most recent wife, Berenice, who had just delivered him a second daughter, Philotera, and the third after their first child, Arsinoe. Disappointed to have been presented with a second daughter, he was now contemplating working on begetting a son with Berenice when he returned to Alexandria, thus ridding himself of what was becoming a growing problem in his dynastic planning. It was an undertaking he would take seriously; nevertheless, he would thoroughly enjoy himself during what he would ensure would be an intense process.

'It was all looking so good and all going so well,' he bemoaned to Thais as they walked the walls of Pelusium in the lessening heat of late afternoon sun, admiring the strength of the army of Egypt encamped outside the town and the fleet at anchor in the distance out to sea – the harbour itself being full of transport ships. 'Seleukos planning to set off east against Nikanor was wonderful news: whether he wins or loses – and we should be hearing soon, one way or the other – it will distract Antigonos' attention away from us. And then what with Carthage and Syracuse keeping each other amused and Nearchos explaining to the cyclops how well Egypt is defended plus Antigonos' failure to overcome Malichus' threat on his flank, I was looking forward to a peaceful couple of years building my position here and in Cyprus and Cyrenaica. And then this.' He pointed accusingly with his thumb over his shoulder at his steward, Lycortas, following him, seemingly gliding as all leg movement was hidden under his long white robe. 'I should have his bowels removed and wrapped around his neck for spoiling my day in such a manner.'

110

'Indeed, lord,' Lycortas agreed, 'it is no more than I deserve and I marvel at your forgiving nature in allowing my copious viscera to remain within me. It is not so many years ago that the rulers of Egypt would have had the messenger's entire family, village even, relieved of their innards for bearing such ill tidings.'

'But the news would not have changed, would it, Lycortas,' Thais pointed out, 'no matter how many coils of colons were wrapped around people's necks?'

'Alas, no, mistress, unfortunately the disembowelment of messengers has never proven to be an effective antidote for bad news. As far as I'm aware the only thing it changes is the messenger's mind as to the wisdom of his bringing the news in the first place; if, indeed, he is still capable of reasoned thought with someone else's hands rummaging around his insides.'

'Yes, Lycortas, you make a good point.' Ptolemy scratched the back of his neck, prickling with summer heat despite the westering of the sun. 'But how should I act on this news?'

'I should have thought it was obvious,' Thais said, her voice reprimanding. 'If Kassandros and Lysimachus are both prepared to engage in Antigonos' offer of peace and their representatives really are travelling to his camp with Aristodemus, there can be only one outcome should the talks be successful, and I wouldn't wager against them being so as it would be in the interests of all three.'

Gloom fell upon Ptolemy. 'Antigonos will be free to concentrate all his energy on me and Seleukos at the same time.'

'Exactly; therefore, you have to make him an even more tempting offer.'

'Which is?'

Thais looked at him, disappointment in her eyes, and linked her arm through his. 'If you can't think of something so obvious then I don't see why I should help you.'

Ptolemy sighed, his gloom deepening. 'Why is it that you always make me feel as if I'm a student who is a constant disappointment to his grammaticus?'

She gave him her most severe expression of exasperation. 'Ptolemy, did you not just complain that Kassandros and Lysimachus entering into peace talks with Antigonos will mean you won't have the couple of years you were looking forward to for building up your position in Cyprus and Cyrenaica?'

Ptolemy frowned. 'I believe I said something along those lines.'

'And why will Kassandros and Lysimachus making peace with Antigonos have that inconvenient effect?'

'Because it will free him from concerns in the north and the west thus allowing him to concentrate on me.'

'Ah, well done, you remembered that part. But what about the other detail: the one about Seleukos?'

Ptolemy felt his impatience rising. 'Antigonos can concentrate on me *and* Seleukos if he has peace with... wait.' His impatience disappeared as the strategy took root in his mind. He smiled at his mistress. 'Of course; you're a very clever girl. I throw Seleukos to him. The cyclops knows if he loses the east then his wealth and military power will be greatly reduced and therefore it would make sense for him to deal with Seleukos' threat before he tries to overcome me.'

'I knew you'd get there in the end.'

'I'm afraid I'm still lagging far behind,' Lycortas said.

It was now Ptolemy's turn to be the disappointed grammaticus as he turned to his steward. 'Oh, Lycortas, if only you had paid more attention in your cunning-strategy and advanced duplicity lessons when you were younger, you might not be so behind now.'

'Indeed, lord; it is to my lasting regret that I... oh, I see.' Lycortas' pudgy face unfolded into a smile. 'That would be very hard on Seleukos, would it not?'

Ptolemy pursed his lips. 'To make myself feel better I'll send him a few thousand men across the desert before any agreement with Antigonos is made; a negotiation like this can be spun out for quite some time. Send a message to Malichus to make the arrangements for their passage when the next bitumen caravan returns, Lycortas.'

'Indeed, lord. And might I ask one question?'

'You may, but I'd hazard that, as you do so, the answer will come to you.'

Lycortas did not even begin to ask his question; instead, he put both hands to his chest and looked at Ptolemy, his expression turning from horror to pleading. 'No, lord, not me surely?'

Ptolemy put a hand on Lycortas' shoulder and squeezed it in sympathy. 'I'm sorry, old friend, but this will make up for your bringing me the bad news in the first place, and besides, you are the best person to go to Antigonos and negotiate my inclusion in his peace proposal. I shall write to him immediately.'

It was but a matter of five days until Antigonos' reply came back from Gaza agreeing the embassy headed by Lycortas with instructions for it to be in Tyros four days after the next new moon but suggesting grave doubts as to the likelihood of successful talks. The reply also coincided with the arrival of the latest bitumen caravan from the Nabateans which brought the news of Seleukos' victory over Nikanor on the Tigris and his intention to move south to Susa.

'You see, Lycortas,' Ptolemy said, his voice brimming with good humour as he saw his steward aboard the ship that would bear him north, 'our Titanesque friend has just made your job infinitely easier. I would imagine this news will reach Antigonos' ears soon after your arrival in Tyros, having gone the long way around the desert, and you'll suddenly find him very anxious to strike a deal. You know what to ask for?'

'He should renounce any claim to Egypt and Cyprus and recognise your rule of Cyrenaica and in return you will renounce your claim on Gaza and the lands to its north.'

'Quite; but there's one more clause that I wish to have included, and that is all four of us – Antigonos, Kassandros, Lysimachus and myself – will pledge to uphold the autonomy of the Greek cities as we've all done before, three years ago.'

'He will ask why it needs to be restated.'

'Say I won't sign the agreement without it as I want to reassure the Greek cities in Cyrenaica they still possess some autonomy.'

'But the last time you did so they took it literally and rebelled.'

'And I doubt they will again, seeing as I had all the leading citizens involved in the rebellion executed. No, Lycortas, this measure will be my way out of the agreement when the time comes. You don't really think I'm going to completely abandon Seleukos, do you?'

'I had wondered, lord.'

'Well, stop wondering. Have you given the caravan-master the letter requesting passage for two thousand cavalry and three thousand infantry across the desert to Babylon?'

'Yes, lord.'

'So, what does that tell you?'

'You don't intend to completely abandon Seleukos.'

'You and I know that, but Antigonos must not.'

'I shall ensure the cyclops remains completely unaware of your good faith and thoroughly convinced of your duplicity, lord.'

'I have great belief in your ability to promote my reputation as a disloyal bastard.'

Lycortas bowed his head, his arms crossed with his hands tucked into his flared sleeves. 'Lord, your actions make it easy for me to convince people so.'

'Lycortas, you are a true friend.'

And thus it was in a relaxed state of mind that Ptolemy returned to Alexandria and turned his attention to Berenice and the need for a son from her; a task he set to immediately upon his arrival.

'I'm not complaining, Ptolemy, not in the slightest,' Berenice said, holding his face in her hands and leaning down to kiss the sweat glistening on his brow, 'but why are you in such a rush to have another son when you already have Ptolemy, Meleager and Menelaus, with Eurydice? As much as I want to give you a son – and I do hope it will be soon, believe me – I fail to see the urgency; for two days now since your return and you summoning me to your rooms you've given me no rest.' She kissed his lips, lowering her body so that her nipples brushed his chest as she rocked back and forth, riding him to a return to full arousal. 'Not that I'm not grateful for all the practice, obviously, but won't you upset Thais and Eurydice by showing me all this attention?'

'Thais is never jealous, and besides, she understands exactly the necessity of my having a son with you as soon as possible. And as for Eurydice, her behaviour is the root of all this.'

Berenice paused her gyrations and looked down at him, curious. 'What do you mean?'

Ptolemy reached down to her hips and set them in motion once more. 'Her uncontrollable jealousy of you after I decided – at Thais' suggestion – to marry you led to her always trying to undermine you and attempting to set herself up as the dominant female in the palace. Her constant complaining and petty sniping has had a detrimental effect on her children to the extent I can now barely look at that little brat, Ptolemy, who at the age of ten is capable only of satisfying a rather vicious streak of cruelty by torturing slaves if he can't get hold of his younger siblings. Meleager, therefore, is turning out to be as hideously contrary and spiteful as his brother. I don't hold out much hope for Menelaus either, as the last time I ventured into the nursery the little beast bit me and then started screaming as if it had been *me* trying to take a chunk out of *him*. Needless to say, I clipped the brute about the ears and made a mental note not to go anywhere near the little fiend again unless he has a muzzle fitted. As for what is soon to slither from Eurydice's womb in a month or so, may Serapis preserve us from it. No, I'm afraid the harsh truth of the matter is I got the bad choice out of Antipatros' three daughters. From all accounts, Phila is the level-headed, intelligent one and she's been wasted on that puppy Demetrios; I haven't heard any rumours of Lysimachus complaining about Nicaea, and apparently, she's cheerfully delivered a son and two daughters to him without managing to upset everyone she comes

116

into contact with. Considering what a dour and vicious man Lysimachus is it's a miracle she remains so good-humoured in her cheerless northern fastness. Imagine Eurydice up there surrounded by mountains and savages.' Ptolemy found it easy to do so and a fine and heart-warming vision it briefly was until Berenice's growing vigour brought him back to the matter in hand and, taking a firmer grip on her hips, he ground her down and round on his groin repeatedly with slowly increasing thrusts.

'What difference will my bearing you a son make?' Berenice asked as soon as her breathing had slowed to somewhere near normal after the conclusion of the bout.

Ptolemy took a while to rouse from the near-sleep stupor he enjoyed falling into after an active spell of satisfactory sex. 'Hmm? What?'

'How would a son of mine solve your problem?'

He opened his eyes and looked at his newest wife, gazing into her hazel eyes. In her late twenties, tall and slender, with smooth pale skin, long dark thick hair and lithe limbs, Berenice was a woman of extraordinary beauty, and he thanked Thais for having the foresight to persuade him to marry her – not that he had needed much persuasion – and the gods for endowing his mistress with such a fine analytical mind. 'A son of yours, should he be brought up in a way that makes him an acceptable human being, would be the perfect answer to my problem because he would become my heir.'

Berenice's eyes widened and Ptolemy noted, with relief, it was through surprise not ambition. 'You would pass over your older sons?'

'Of course. Even if I were married to Thais, Lagus, although he's almost eighteen, would not be a possible heir

117

as he lacks the royal blood you bring, or even the noble blood flowing in Eurydice. I'm thinking about a dynasty that's going to last for generations; a son of a courtesan is not going to be in nearly such a strong position as the son of the daughter of Alexander's regent or the son of the daughter of a princess.' He tapped the tip of her nose. 'You. The trouble is Eurydice's sons will be so unsuited to power that my dream of a dynasty won't survive them; therefore, it has to be your son who will inherit my crown – once I've taken it when the time is right, that is. And so you have to promise me the boy will be brought up well through his formative years in order that I can start moulding him to follow in my footsteps when he's seven or eight.'

Berenice laughed. 'And why should it just be my responsibility to see him well formed? Surely, it's down to both parents?'

'I have never been a great one for the nursery; it's a woman's realm. You choose the nurses, and between you you'll form the child into something I'll be able to train for kingship and to hold the kingdom I've forged here. But he needs to be born soon seeing as I'm fifty-seven; and whilst I fully intend to live well into my eighties, one can never know.'

Berenice laughed again, causing Ptolemy to smile such was its clarity and joy. 'I'll do that for you, Ptolemy; to see my child supplant Eurydice's after all the sleights she has shown me will be a reason in itself, but to make you happy and to help you to secure your legacy would be a greater prize.' She rested her head on his shoulder and, cupping his chin with her hand, eased his head towards her to kiss his cheek. 'I suppose we had better carry on trying if he has to be born as soon as possible.'

Ptolemy closed his eyes and gave himself up once again to the pleasures of conceiving a child.

Exhausted by his exertions over the past couple of days, Ptolemy stretched his arms straight out before him, palms up at ninety degrees, and, with rigid control of his muscles, went down onto one knee, lowering his hands so that his fists rested on the floor of his terrace. Overlooking, from the east, the Great Harbour of Alexandria, now divided into two by the completion of the Heptastadion, the mole linking the Pharos Island to the mainland, it was here he exercised soon after dawn each day so as to survey the progress of the city conjured by Alexander from a small fishing village and nurtured by Ptolemy since his claiming of Egypt, thirteen years previously. Few construction sites now littered the waterfront as the commercial and military harbours, to either side of the mole, were almost complete, but in the city beyond both public works – Ptolemy's pet projects, including the Serapeum – and private building continued apace as the population of the nascent city grew with each passing season. Buoyed by how well the city had progressed in his absence, and by the fact his palace was nearing completion, Ptolemy contemplated his next step and cast his eyes onto the newly formed peninsula of Pharos and smiled. *Soon, no more than a few years; when the city is full grown, that'll be the time.*

With renewed vigour he continued his exercise as, directly below the terrace in the royal harbour, the palace's small private port shielded from public gaze by a curtain wall, his personal galley, a majestic Five, sleek, quick and seaworthy in rough weather, was being prepared for him. Now midsummer had passed and his reinforcements to

Seleukos were ready to make their journey across the desert, he had little else to do other than await news from the peace conference that should have convened in Tyros. And so, to pass the time, he had decided to take Berenice on a river cruise down to Memphis to pay his respects to the embalmed corpse of Alexander, hoping that upon his return Berenice would be sure of her pregnancy and he would learn of Antigonos falling into his trap.

But, before he went, he had two issues to deal with: one waited for him, along with his breakfast, in his suite, whilst the other would be with him shortly after. He completed the ancient set of movements, with which the people he now ruled had greeted the rising of the sun each morning for thousands of years, tipped a bucket of cold water over his head and then went inside rubbing himself down with a linen towel and humming the battle paean of Macedon such was his good mood.

'"Great happiness is not lasting among mortals."'

'Euripides may have a point there, Archias,' Ptolemy said without taking the towel from his face, 'but who is to say I'm a mere mortal?'

Archias the Exile-Hunter's round, boyish face, crowned by rich brown curls, broke into a radiant grin as he tore a loaf of bread, discarding half back into the bread basket. 'I'm overwhelmed to be in the presence of a deity, especially so early in the morning.'

Ptolemy threw the towel to the floor and, picking up a tunic draped across a chair, slipped it over his head. 'And I'm overwhelmed to be in the presence of a tragic actor turned murderous assassin at any time of the day. I trust you and your little friends have been gainfully employed since I last required your services.'

Archias inclined his head. 'Your man in Cyrene has had a tolerable amount of work for us.'

'Ophellas? What did he want?'

'I never discuss my commissions.'

'I'm sure, but if I find out that any of my spies in Ophellas' administration has turned up without his throat intact I shall not be pleased with you at all; it's hard enough to keep a check on what he's doing as it is.'

'"Life is unending struggle."'

'And don't make it harder for me.' Ptolemy sat, picked up the half-loaf from the basket and ripped a chunk off. 'But for now, Archias, you can make my life easier for me.'

'I live to serve you.'

'No, you don't; you live to serve anyone who'll pay you.' Ptolemy wagged a finger at the assassin. 'And don't forget we all know that. I still haven't forgiven you for killing Asander for Antigonos' gold. And don't insult either of us by continuing to deny it; Asander died in mysterious circumstances and you were in Halicarnassus at the same time. With you, Archias, there is no such thing as coincidence. So now I'm going to get you to equal the score between Antigonos and me. I've recently heard from an emissary, currently in Tyros—'

'Lycortas.'

'How did you know?'

Archias took a sip of his wine and savoured it. 'Because had Lycortas been here he wouldn't have allowed your slave to serve me such a good vintage.'

'Yes, well, yours and Lycortas' petty squabbles are your own affair. Anyway, Lycortas wrote that soon after his arrival in Tyros a certain Cilles joined with Antigonos.'

'The mercenary general who let his troops get drunk?' Archias said through a mouthful of bread and olives.

'Who let *my* troops get drunk; yes, the very same. Just why Antigonos wishes to employ such a useless man, I don't know, unless it's for his knowledge of my forces.'

'Perhaps you should let it be, as he could prove as helpful to you as he is unhelpful to Antigonos.'

'Don't you have a literary quote on the subject?'

'Not one that springs immediately to mind.'

'You disappoint me.'

'"You are not alone in sorrow; it is the mortal's lot."'

'I said disappoint, not sorrow; that was just a cheap way of getting a Sophocles quotation in. But enough of this; you know perfectly well what I expect of you.'

'The price?'

'A talent in gold for you and a talent shared between your seven foul-smelling Thracian pets upon receipt of the man's head.'

'Done.' Archias took a full draught of wine, burped and then got to his feet, wiping his mouth with the back of his hand. 'I'd better get going then.'

'"I advise do not delay."'

'Indeed, but Euripides used that quotation in relation to young men fathering children.'

'Then perhaps I was talking to myself.' Ptolemy waved Archias away and set to his breakfast in the most jovial of moods.

It was in the same excellent humour that Ptolemy entered the audience chamber on the floor below his suite. 'Ah, Lagus, my boy,' he said, seeing his eldest son waiting for him, leaning against one of the painted marble columns lining the room's four walls, 'are you packed and ready to go?'

'Yes, Father,' Lagus said, coming towards his father, 'and I'm thoroughly looking forward to it. Thanks for giving me the opportunity.'

'Excellent.' He opened his arms to embrace his son, slapping him in a manly fashion on the shoulders. 'And remember, this is your first command but take the advice of your officers, all of whom are professionals with far more experience than a seventeen-year-old.'

'Yes, Father.'

'Travel fast, trust the Nabateans' judgement and, when you get there, tell Seleukos to trust me and not believe what he hears; it's not what it seems.'

SELEUKOS.
THE BULL-ELEPHANT.

S USA HAD PROVED a far easier
prospect this time around. On the
last occasion Seleukos laid siege to
the city, over four years previously, he
had been set up to fail by his then master, Antigonos:
deprived of sufficient troops, Seleukos had been made to
look a fool in a deliberate ploy by the cyclops to lessen his
standing in the eyes of the army thus weakening him and,
therefore, making his removal from Babylon so much the
easier. The strategy had worked and Seleukos had fled to
the west with no more than fifty followers. But now he was
back and behind him was an army of more than fifteen
thousand men. The gates of Susa had been opened by the
garrison commander after only a month, once Seleukos
had convinced Aspeisas, Antigonos' appointment as
satrap, that neither the cyclops, his son nor Nikanor were
coming to relieve him; he had died on his own sword as
Seleukos rode through the gates, making his way directly
to the treasury.

'That was a sensible decision, Xenophilus,' Seleukos said
to the warden of the treasury after he too had opened the
gates to the citadel in which was housed the wealth of the

east, 'one you shall find me grateful for, even though you've betrayed Antigonos to whom you owe your position.'

Xenophilus, a balding man in his early fifties, running to fat after fourteen years as the warden of the royal treasury of Susa – an appointment he held from Alexander – looked solemn and lowered his eyes. 'I'm well aware of that, lord; however, the east is in need of a strong power if we are to avoid constant war between the satrapies. Since Antigonos went back west, all the satraps have seen themselves as independent kings; it will only be a matter of time before there's war between them and whoever wishes to win that war would want the contents of the treasury here. I even had to keep the citadel closed to Aspeisas as he would have stolen everything being a low, undeserving cheat. I would rather it went to a man of honour than a petty despot.'

Seleukos hid his amusement at the thought he was any different from any other man seeking power. *He seems very anxious to ingratiate himself; perhaps he's trying to get me to reinstate him even though he's proved himself disloyal.* 'That is far sighted of you, Xenophilus. Now, if you wouldn't mind, my wife has newly arrived from Babylon and we would very much like a tour of my new-found wealth.'

It gave Seleukos much pleasure to watch the expression in Apama's eyes as Xenophilus guided them through the torchlit, smoky corridors of the Susa treasury, past room after room loaded with crates containing coinage, jewels, bullion and precious objects all of either gold or silver. Even though Antigonos had all but emptied it four years before, it had since been restocked by the tribute of the east. Never had he seen so much wealth in one place; he could only imagine what his Sogdian beauty made of the display worth more than the entire wealth of her homeland put together. 'Take anything you want, Apama,' he said, putting an arm around her shoulders, drawing her close and kissing the corner of her temple, the only piece of flesh left exposed by her veil.

Apama glanced up at him, dark eyes full of love and hope. 'This is going to make the difference, isn't it, Seleukos?'

'I believe so, my love; with this I can buy an army big enough to face Antigonos and then secure the eastern satrapies and carve ourselves a kingdom we can defend. With this we can take half the empire.' He turned to Xenophilus. 'Have you an inventory of everything here?'

'I have, lord.'

'And what is the total weight?'

'Seven hundred and twenty-three talents of gold, one thousand two hundred and eight talents of silver and then fifty-three talents of assorted gems, including diamonds, rubies, sapphires and emeralds and some lesser stones.'

Seleukos had to check himself from giving a whistle of amazement. 'That is indeed a fortune.'

'You wish for me to arrange for its transfer to Babylon, lord?'

Seleukos looked at the warden with incredulous eyes. 'And why would I possibly wish for you to do that?'

Xenophilus looked confused. 'Well, lord, surely you would want all this safely with you in Babylon.'

'And who said I'm going back to Babylon?'

'Well, I assumed—'

'It's not your place to assume, Xenophilus; your job is to keep this safe for me whilst I take Persis and Media.'

*

It was, therefore, to that end that Seleukos found himself at the head of a deep valley in the foothills of the Zagros Mountains to the north of Susa. With an escort of five hundred cavalry – Azanes with his Sogdians and two hundred heavy lancers – as well as the same number of light infantry, Seleukos had come to use a small fraction of his new-found wealth – two crates on a mule-drawn cart – to do what Antigonos had failed to do when he made the journey north from Susa to Ecbatana: pay the Cossaei for their protection. Seleukos had been a part of that ill-fated march through the rough country of the Zagros; terrain known intimately by the tribe living there. Antigonos' army had suffered at their hands in attritional guerrilla warfare which had cost the lives of hundreds of men and damaged the morale of the entire army; such was the extent of the army's losses that a mutiny, when they reached the safety of Ecbatana, had only just been averted by the generous gifts of cash which had depleted Antigonos' resources to a dangerous degree. But this was a mistake Seleukos was not going to make as he planned his campaign against Media and Persis as, for it to be a success, he would need to be able to pass to the west and to the east of the mountain range as well as send troops through the middle. Full mobility in the entire area was what he would need in order to bring a swift conclusion to the campaign.

'They're approaching,' Azanes said, pointing with one hand and shading his eyes with the other, peering down into the valley through which snaked a rushing mountain stream, its banks and bed strewn with boulders. 'No more than twenty men; all mounted.'

Seleukos followed the direction of the Sogdian's finger. After a couple of moments, he became aware of movement about a thousand paces away, but so well did the men and their mounts blend into the surroundings he found it hard to pick out individual figures. 'I'll take your word for it, Azanes; your eyes are evidently far better than mine.'

The Sogdian tapped his quiver. 'You should take up the bow, lord; it keeps them sharp.'

And the truth of that statement became apparent when the grey-bearded, sunken-eyed chieftain, who held sway over the rough interior of the Zagros Range, approached with an escort of just eighteen men only becoming discernible at a hundred paces. Wearing baggy black trousers tucked into sturdy boots and woollen, short-sleeved tunics of off-white with black stripes of varying widths running down from black collars, and topped with black, rimless felt hats, the party presented an outlandishly uniform spectacle. The holsters holding their bows and the quivers full of arrows were also of the same monochrome colour scheme, which, along with the ponies' grey, dun and beige hues, meant they blended in with their surroundings even as they stood before Seleukos, no more than twenty paces away.

Well aware of the prickliness of such men, especially when they considered themselves to be on sovereign territory, Seleukos decided it would be politic to make the first move, sacrificing dignity for good manners. He bowed his head, brushing his forehead with his right hand as he extended it to the Cossaei chieftain as he had been told to do by Xenophilus who knew their customs. 'Noble Spinates, it pleases me that we meet in peace. May you have many sons and may they beget only males.'

Yellowed teeth appeared in Spinates' beard as he grinned at the correct form of address. 'It pleases me too, Seleukos, that we meet in peace. May you have many sons and may they beget only males.' His Greek was good, if somewhat accented.

Well, we seem to be off to a good start. He dismounted, knowing Spinates would feel himself to be in the superior position being left in the saddle for longer. 'Shall we break our bread together?'

At this Spinates laughed and threw a remark over his shoulder which caused his followers to join his mirth as they too dismounted. With an extravagant leap, one that would have been remarkable even in a younger man, Spinates swung his legs behind him and vaulted from his horse. 'We shall break bread together, my friend.'

'I like you,' Spinates said, leaning over and slapping Seleukos on the shoulder. 'You are the first Macedonian to have shown me respect. The Achaemenid kings would always pay me and my fathers before me for the privilege of crossing our lands when they moved their court north to Ecbatana to escape the heat of a southern summer; and then they would pay again for the privilege as they went back south for the winter. It was a fair price we asked and no more than they could afford. But they are gone now and who has taken their place? Macedonians! First there was Alexander who, after the death of Hephaestion, tried to drown his grief in our blood.' Spinates' sunken dark eyes burned with rage at the memory. 'Thousands of my people did he kill, including many of my family; three sons I lost during that campaign.'

Seleukos shook his head, sighing at the injustice of it, feeling it best not to mention his part in Alexander's assuaging of his grief.

'And then Antigonos refused to even reply to my request to meet in peace as he took his army across my lands without my agreement. Such disrespect deserved my enmity. Hundreds of his men fell to my warriors; and those who made the mistake of surrendering rather than dying with honour were impaled.'

'Yes, I heard the tales.' *Better not admit that I witnessed them at first hand; lines of men set writhing on stakes to either side of the column as the resinated cyclops led us on, refusing all advice to pay the Cossaei's price.* 'Such discourtesy on Antigonos' part was unforgivable and his men paid the price for his arrogance. I'm told that by the time they reached Ecbatana they refused to take orders, so deep was the terror you had instilled in them.'

The laugh was long and guttural; Spinates' eyes watered. 'That's what happens when I am not shown the respect due to me. We have lived independently here for hundreds of generations; we call none our master and no man tells us when to come or when to go.'

'And no man shall, Spinates,' Seleukos asserted in his most solemn tone. 'I am now the master of Babylon and Susa and by this time next year I shall also be the master of Ecbatana and Persepolis, and although my domain will surround yours, I shall respect your independence.' He motioned to a couple of Companions to bring forward the cart. 'This is a sign of my good faith in this matter. Come and see.' He got to his feet and stroked the flank of the nearest mule as the cart drew up. 'Open the crates,' he ordered the guards as Spinates came eagerly to his side.

It was with an expression of incredulity that the Cossaei chieftain gazed down into the glittering contents of the two crates, for within was contained more wealth than he had seen since the fall of the Achaemenid kings.

'Is that the respect you deserve, Spinates?'

Spinates controlled himself, standing up straight rather than drooling into the treasure. 'It is a very generous testament, Seleukos.'

'It is what you shall receive each year, my friend. And in return what will you give me?'

Spinates was in no doubt. 'You shall have access over my lands. Any man who travels in your name will not be molested nor be required to pay a toll. On this I give my word.'

'Very good, my friend. However, there's one more little thing I'd like you to do for me.'

Spinates looked at the treasure and then back at Seleukos. 'Name it.'

'Keep me informed of people who aren't in my pay who cross your lands. People who would perhaps mean me harm. People who support Antigonos, for example.'

At the mention of the cyclops' name Spinates spat a thin stream of saliva onto the ground. 'If I find anyone who serves that dishonourable man in my lands, they will end up living out their final hours on a stake.'

'That is a noble sentiment, my friend, very noble, although perhaps a little wasteful. I would much rather you send them to me along with whatever messages might be found on their person. You would be doing me a great service in helping me to monitor Antigonos' communications.'

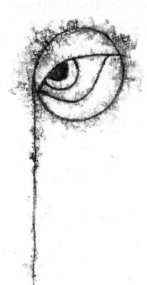

ANTIGONOS.
THE ONE-EYED.

'PTOLEMAIOS HAS PERSUADED his cousin to end his rebellion and pay off his mercenaries,' Aristodemus informed Antigonos upon his arrival in Tyros. 'Telesphorus asks your forgiveness and pledges his allegiance.'

Antigonos could not quite believe what he had just heard. 'My fetid arse! The treacherous little shit asks what?'

A tall and slender, balding man with quick cunning eyes and thin lips bedded in a grey beard, Aristodemus bowed his head and made a graceful gesture of restraint with one hand. 'He humbly asks for your forgiveness, lord.'

'That's what I thought you said, except without the humble bit. He can be as humble as he likes sitting over there in Greece, thinking I'll forgive him just because he happens to be my late brother's child, but what's the fucking use of asking humbly for forgiveness if I can't look him in the eyes and see how fucking humble the bastard really is? For all I know, my arse is humbler than Telesphorus.'

'Indeed, lord, for all you know it may well be if you were unable to see Telesphorus face to face, not that you can look your arse in the eye, er... well, you know what I mean.

Anyway, it's to that end Telesphorus has travelled with me and Gelon, Kassandros' ambassador, to ask forgiveness personally and humbly. He just wanted me to inform you of his remorse before he appears before you as a penitent.'

'So I won't bite his balls off at the sight of him, eh?'

'So that you will know just how repentant he is when he comes before you.'

Antigonos grunted and kicked at a footstool so it flew clean out of the open window of his study, high in Tyros' palace – a cry from the courtyard below indicated an unfortunate hit. 'Well, keep him wherever he is and put a guard on him so he has to stay in his room and has time to think on his treachery. I'll make him sweat whilst I talk with Gelon and Ptolemy's man.' Antigonos shook his head at the thought of having to deal with the smooth-talking Lycortas again. *The last time I would've sent him back without his balls; but I'm sure he's lost them.* 'What about Lysimachus' emissary? There's been no sight of him yet; did he come with you too?'

'No, lord; Gelon will speak for both Kassandros and Lysimachus.'

Antigonos, again, could not quite believe his ears. 'Are you saying their interests are completely aligned?'

Aristodemus shrugged. 'It would seem that way. Ptolemaios had the initial meeting with Kassandros and Thessalonike just to the south of Pydna on the border between Macedon and Thessaly. They were immediately receptive to the idea of peace with you but wanted to consult with Lysimachus, hence the delay in our arriving here. They didn't wish for Lysimachus to believe they were going behind his back as you know what a suspicious and vindictive man he can be.'

'Can be? Is.'

'Is, indeed, lord. Thessalonike travelled to Thrace and conferred with Lysimachus very successfully, it would seem, as he gave her full authority to negotiate for him, thus they sent only one emissary between them.'

Antigonos' eye gleamed with amusement. 'What did she do to him to persuade Lysimachus, probably the most untrusting man I know, to negotiate on his behalf? I would like to have seen Kassandros' face when she came back and told him that.'

'I don't think he would've been unduly worried as she is – or was at the time – heavily pregnant with their third child, which must have been whelped by now.'

'How any woman could bring herself to bear just a single child for Kassandros never fails to amaze me, but to do it three times is beyond reason. And then as for calling the eldest two Philip and Alexander, who does he think he is?'

Aristodemus had not got to be so high in Antigonos' favour by sheltering him from the truth. 'He thinks he is going to be king of Macedon one day and thus he's producing royal-sounding progeny; note how he hasn't named a brat after himself as Kassandros is not a royal name. I would wager the latest one will be called Antipatros just to lay claim to the regency as well.'

'If he thinks he can take Macedon as his kingdom then the pockmarked little toad is going to be sadly disappointed. He still holds the king in Amphipolis and the young Alexander is thirteen; does Kassandros have the balls to kill him? Because I surely wouldn't. He got away with killing Olympias but that was because he gave her to the families of her victims, thus he could hide behind other people's vengeance. But killing the heir to Alexander himself?' *Although I wish he would summon up the courage.*

Aristodemus considered the question for a few moments. 'In my opinion Kassandros and Thessalonike are well on their way to being secure in Macedon.'

'Until I push them out.'

'If you manage to, Antigonos.'

'What are you saying?'

'I'm saying the reality of the situation at the moment is that dynasties are being created. Kassandros has Macedon along with Athens, Thessaly and Epirus closely allied, as well as an evident understanding with Lysimachus as they are both negotiating with you together, so despite Ptolemaios being in control of the rest of Greece, down to the isthmus and Polyperchon's territory, Kassandros has a very secure position, as does Lysimachus in Thrace.' The Greek paused to gauge his master's current receptivity to hard truths. 'As does Ptolemy.'

'That's because of his fucking Arabs! They offered peace and gave my boy seven hundred camels, according to his last despatch, as if that's going to make me trust the slippery bastards; and they still pick at my supply lines. My arse! I lost a couple of score of good lads in the last month and I've still got seven hundred fucking camels coming my way! What the fuck am I meant to do with seven hundred camels? And don't give me the obvious answer; I'm not a Nabatean!'

Aristodemus raised both palms, pacifying the explosive temper. 'But let's face it, lord: the reality is four kingdoms are being forged.' He pointed through the window to the east. 'The question is: what news of Seleukos? Is he forging a fifth?'

135

This thought brought Antigonos back to the matter in hand. 'Call Gelon and Lycortas; it's time to dictate the peace. The sooner it's done the sooner I can deal with our Titanesque friend and put Ptolemy in his place.'

'Both Kassandros and Lysimachus are very keen for a state of peace to reign throughout the empire,' Gelon declared; grossly overweight and ludicrously undersized so that he resembled a weighted pig's bladder used for gymnastic training, he stood before Antigonos in Tyros' main agora which was packed with officers from Antigonos' army. 'And indeed, it was Kassandros who made the first move to Ptolemaios suggesting a conference.'

That's an interesting slant on things, Antigonos mused as the ridiculous man continued with a speech that would be as long as it was unnecessary: *it would be he, Antigonos, who would set the terms and not the two weaker parties. Ptolemaios didn't mention a mission from Kassandros and Thessalonike in his report to me; he said he made contact with them. Is he hiding things from me? I'll need to get to the truth of that.*

'Thank you, Gelon,' Antigonos said, when it was finally his turn to speak, 'for putting the case for peace between us so forcefully and succinctly. Before I hear from Ptolemy's ambassador, I'll lay out my terms for Macedon and Thrace. I agree to recognise Kassandros and Lysimachus in their spheres of influence and, in return for a promise of non-aggression on my part, demand that Kassandros, whom I name commander-in-chief of Europe – *not satrap, regent or ruler* – leaves my nephew Ptolemaios to build his strength in Greece, recognising his hegemony over all the land between Thessaly and the isthmus, with the exception of

Athens. Kassandros is free to deal with Epirus and the Illyrian tribes as he wishes as I have no claim on either. As for Lysimachus, I thank him for his valiant work in keeping out the threat to us all of the barbarian tribes to the north and am most happy to contribute a modest sum to his ongoing building of fortifications along the Istros. I name him general in the north; in return I ask he desists in meddling in Hellespontine Phrygia and recognises the satrapy as being under my control through Phoinix who is my appointee. Should those terms be acceptable to you, Gelon, and your two masters – *and mistress, more to the point* – recognise me as the overlord of Asia and Africa, and be willing to consult me on matters appertaining to Europe, then you may consider there to be a state of peace between us.'

Gelon puffed himself up, his cheeks bulging with self-importance. 'That is the wish of both Kassandros and Lysimachus: peace on those terms.'

Antigonos glanced at Aristodemus next to him; the Greek nodded. Satisfied, Antigonos looked around the packed agora. 'Did you hear that, soldiers of Macedon? We have a basis for peace. What say you?'

It was loud and unanimous; at least from the soldiers it was – they cheered the announcement with gusto, their voices ringing out in celebration of the thought of the empire coming together. But there was one present who did not share everyone's joy. Lycortas got to his feet and stood before Antigonos, his arms crossed and his hands hidden in his flared sleeves, waiting for the noise to die down. By degrees it did as more and more of the jubilant officers noticed him waiting to speak.

Silence soon fell.

'Yes, Lycortas,' Antigonos said, looking forward to slapping the steward down.

'Lord Antigonos,' Lycortas said, bringing his eyes up to meet the cyclopic glare. 'The agreement is unacceptable.'

Antigonos' smile was ice. 'Oh, is it, Lycortas? And just why would you consider an agreement that has nothing to do with you unacceptable?'

Lycortas held the gaze. 'Because my master, Ptolemy, is the overlord of Africa. He controls Egypt and Cyrenaica and has influence in the lands to the west as far as Carthage. Your territory, Lord Antigonos, ends at Gaza, which, I believe I am right in saying, is Asia. My question is: how can you consider yourself overlord of lands you do not control?'

The ice cracked, revealing fury beneath. Antigonos jumped to his feet and thrust an accusatory finger at the steward. 'You dare to come here and tell me what I am overlord of and what I'm not? An effete eunuch such as yourself making judgements on me! I'd have your balls, if you had any, for that. I am master of the whole empire and everyone should either understand that or they will be made to understand it; even your precious Ptolemy.'

Lycortas stood silent as Antigonos fumed at him.

Red-faced, his chest heaving, Antigonos continued to point at Lycortas, his finger shaking. 'Well, what have you to say, eunuch?'

Lycortas did his best surprised face. 'Did you mean me, lord? If so, you are very much mistaken as, last time I checked, which wasn't that long ago, I was still the proud possessor of a full set of testicles. But that is neither here nor there. What is pertinent to my assertion is Ptolemy remains in Egypt and doesn't recognise you as his overlord. However, as an equal, he has sent me here to negotiate peace between you both.'

'Peace! Why should I want peace with Ptolemy when I have just made peace with Kassandros and Lysimachus? Now I don't have to look behind me, I can concentrate on going forward despite your master's treacherous Nabatean friends.'

'I don't believe that would be a wise move, Antigonos. I think accepting Ptolemy's offer of peace would be the sensible course of action in your position.'

The cyclopic eye narrowed; a clear, red fluid flowed from the empty socket next to it. Antigonos took a step forward. 'What do you know that I don't?'

Lycortas stood his ground and indicated to all the officers filling the agora. 'I know that to keep an army of this size in the field you need the wealth of the entire empire. Now, if you accept that Egypt is closed to you—'

'Which I do not.'

Lycortas held up a hand. 'To put it another way: if you accept that to gain the wealth of Egypt you might have to concentrate all your strength in this direction for a good while – which is the reason you made peace with Kassandros and Lysimachus as you have just asserted – then what happens if the east, and, more importantly, the treasury at Susa fall into another's hands?'

'Seleukos, you mean?'

'Indeed.'

'Nonsense. Nikanor, the satrap of Media, is dealing with him along with an alliance of other eastern satraps loyal to me.'

'How long since you've had a message from him?'

Antigonos paused. *Longer than I can remember. Nearchos was the last person who had contact with Nikanor and that*

was a couple of months ago. I need to make this private.
Antigonos composed himself. 'I had a message from him a few days ago telling me his campaign against Seleukos was proceeding as planned. This meeting is over.' As he turned to walk away, he muttered to Aristodemus: 'Have the eunuch brought to my study; and find Nearchos too.'

'So, you've heard nothing,' Lycortas said, 'judging by the brazen lie you've just told.'

'Don't accuse me of lying,' Antigonos snarled, spinning round from the view over the harbour out of his study window.

'Well, what you said was not the truth. The truth is Seleukos defeated Nikanor on the Tigris and captured his entire force, but you haven't heard that yet. However, Ptolemy has as the news came across the desert directly to Egypt. Also, Seleukos has taken control of the roads to the north so no messages can come through from Media. You are cut off from your eastern army. You don't know what's happening. You don't know whether Seleukos has taken Susa yet and already has control of the wealth of the east. Not knowing that, do you really not wish to make peace with Ptolemy?'

Antigonos stared at Lycortas and then looked at Nearchos. 'Well? What do you think? I've been concentrating on the Nabateans and negotiations with Kassandros and Lysimachus and so haven't given much thought to Nikanor as I assumed he'd make easy prey of Seleukos and his tiny army.'

'But we still haven't heard from him,' Nearchos said. 'And none of the messengers I've sent out have returned yet. But it's impossible Seleukos could have defeated Nikanor; he must be just leading him on a chase.'

'He was inspired by what your son Demetrios did, Lord Antigonos,' Lycortas said. 'He attacked at night and captured the camp with very little loss. Nikanor escaped but his cousin Euagoros was killed. Seleukos signed on most of his men and the last information I had was that he was on his way to Susa; with that army, he has probably taken it by now. Unless you act soon, you've lost the east. It would take your whole force to perhaps defeat Ptolemy or half of it to keep Ptolemy in check whilst the other half wins back what you have just lost. Can you take that gamble, Antigonos? Ptolemy offers you not just peace; he offers you time as well.'

Antigonos restrained his desire to strangle Ptolemy's smooth-talking steward, his fists bunching and his arm muscles tense. 'Get out!'

Lycortas responded immediately.

Antigonos turned on Aristodemus. 'Get Demetrios back here to Tyros, now!'

'I told you, Father,' Demetrios said upon his arrival the following day, 'Malichus said the bad news would come from the east, but when it didn't come after a month, I thought the greasy bastard was just bluffing.'

Antigonos looked at his son morosely. 'So did I; but if what Lycortas says is true then we must act upon it, otherwise our dreams of controlling the whole empire are dead and we'll become just another family trying to forge a kingdom out of its wreckage.'

'I'll go, Father.'

Antigonos squeezed his son's shoulder. 'Good lad. I'll give you fifteen thousand men; that should be more than ample to take Babylon and then retake Susa if necessary. Oh, and I'll give you Telesphorus as well. He can prove just

141

how sorry he is in the field with you; if there is the slightest doubt about his loyalty, you know what to do.'

Demetrios nodded. 'Yes, Father.'

'And you can keep Cilles to command your mercenaries. How's he been doing for you? I hope you keep reminding him of all that wine you left for his men.'

Demetrios' eyes widened. 'Haven't you heard, Father?'

'Evidently not as I seem to be the last to hear anything!'

'Cilles has disappeared; he hasn't been seen for five days now.'

Antigonos dismissed the news. 'Drunk, no doubt. Now go and work out what you need and we'll talk later. Send Aristodemus in as you go.' Antigonos poured himself a large measure of resinated wine; he did not bother with the water. 'Well, old friend,' he said as Aristodemus came into his study, 'am I doing the right thing?'

'Yes; if there's the slightest chance of losing the east then that must be thwarted.'

Antigonos nodded and sat back in his chair, his cup in both hands. 'Go with Lycortas back to Egypt and negotiate the details with Ptolemy in person. Make it a peace that could last at least a year, until the end of next summer, by which time Demetrios should be back.'

'I will, lord.' Aristodemus paused and looked at his master. 'May I ask what your plans are until then?'

Antigonos downed the remains of his wine. 'I'm going to use the peace I've just negotiated to foment trouble between Lysimachus and Kassandros.'

KASSANDROS.
THE JEALOUS.

HIS WIFE WAS right, that much was obvious to Kassandros; but just because Thessalonike advised a bold course – radical even – did not mean he necessarily had the stomach to see it through. Moreover, even if he did steel himself into ordering the deed, did he have the strength and latent popularity to survive the opprobrium that would come with such a move? The answer, he had to admit, was no – or at best, not yet.

Yes, he had despised Alexander with all his being for the many humiliations he had heaped upon him through his life, not least leaving him behind on the greatest adventure of the age – not that he would have wanted to go as his innate cowardice would have, inevitably, been exposed for all to see. But publicly left behind he had been and thus forced to endure the sniggering of women behind his back and the scorn of discharged veterans returning home. And so, he had avenged that shame with the woman's weapon of poison in Babylon, thirteen years previously; a deed his father, Antipatros, had refused to acknowledge up until his death. But that crime had been a personal score-settling, as had the execution of Alexander's mother, Olympias. The pleasure he had felt watching her being gradually stoned to death by the families of her victims in her brief but deadly assumption of the regency of Macedon had almost made up for the desecration of his kin's graves and the murder of his step-mother and young half-siblings the harpy had instigated. Almost, but not quite: the sight of his father's and brother's bones – as well as those of scores of ancestors – exposed to the elements still burned in his heart and even the image of the bloodied and broken corpse of the perpetrator of that outrage did not assuage the raw hatred he felt for her.

And it had been the same feeling he had harboured for the rest of Alexander's family: he had rejoiced when Olympias had murdered his fool of a half-brother and his wife, Adea, Alexander's niece. The news of Cynane's death, the mother of Adea and Alexander's half-sister, came as a pleasing surprise, and then the fact that Alexander's full sister, Kleopatra, was restricted to a cloistered life in Sardis was of no cause for concern to him other than it would make it harder to send assassins should he choose to do so.

His hatred of Alexander was such that he had once come across a statue of him and had almost broken down as its shadow fell upon him, shaking uncontrollably as his loathing – and yes, he could now admit it to himself, his fear – had overwhelmed him.

But suddenly his world had changed: he had been smitten by love with a force so strong and swift it had transcended the barriers of his hate, for it had been Thessalonike, the second half-sister of Alexander, who had captivated him. And, despite his pinched, avianesque face, his lanky, thin-chested, stooping body and his limp, she had consented to be his wife – although, he had realised, it had suited her ambition as much as his desire – and had now borne him three sons, Alexander's nephews.

And thus, it had not surprised him when she had made the suggestion.

Suggestion? In fact, it was closer to being an order.

Kassandros looked sideways at Thessalonike, with her golden hair piled high, save for a ringlet falling to either side of a milk-skinned face jewelled with sapphire eyes, and felt his unsteady heart leap even more than when she had made her suggestion just moments ago. 'Now?'

Thessalonike stared directly ahead as they progressed in regal state from the throne room in the royal palace of Pella, Macedon's capital. 'If not now, when? Gelon's negotiations have brought the peace we desired: Antigonos has recognised us as sovereign in Macedon and rather pompously appointed you commander-in-chief of Europe. The peace means you have no threat from Ptolemaios down south, which now leaves you free to conduct your overdue campaign against the Dardani and take the army into Paeonia as a show of force to keep the local chieftains in their place and punish them for their constant raiding. Lysimachus has everything he wants and will keep his eyes on the Istros and continue with building his defences along the river. Now, therefore, as the cyclops fights to retain the east, is the perfect time.' She paused as the double doors of the chamber were pushed open on goose-fatted hinges and they progressed, footsteps echoing, into the main hall of the palace, guards snapping to attention as they passed. Colonnaded and brightly painted with scenes from the *Iliad*, illuminated by shafts of sunlight piercing down from high windows, the hall felt cool after the late-summer fug of a packed throne room listening to Gelon's report. 'Let us face it, Kassandros, what Ptolemy did in joining the peace process is force Antigonos to admit there are four separate entities to the empire in order to give him time to prevent the birth of a fifth. He has admitted that kingdoms have been forged by recognising ours, Lysimachus' and Ptolemy's areas of influence as Gelon reported the cyclops putting it. Now, if we admit that kingdoms have been forged, it is only a matter of time before someone claims a crown; and once one makes that move then we can all do so – but it can only happen after you have done what only you can do.'

Kassandros swallowed, his throat dry. 'I know, Thessalonike.'

'Then give the order; or better still, let me travel to Amphipolis and watch Roxanna's face as I order the death of her and her son.'

And that was the dilemma Kassandros now faced: since Gelon, fresh from Tyros, had finished briefing them on the peace concluded with Antigonos, not two hundred heartbeats ago, Thessalonike had proposed he should immediately effect the deed they had both prepared for: the assassination of Alexander, the fourth of that name to be king of Macedon; the son of the greatest – in most people's eyes – Macedonian ever to have lived. And he, Kassandros, was going to be the man to take responsibility for this huge step. He looked again at his wife from the corner of his eyes; she held her countenance expressionless. *She knows if this were to go wrong and the opprobrium of the Macedonian world falls upon me, she will still be safe as she has the sacred blood in her veins and not on her hands. Whereas I...* He did not want to admit it to himself but it rang in his head nevertheless: he was from

146

lesser stock. And what was more, he was only tolerated by the people of Macedon because of the love they bore for his wife whose resemblance to her half-brother was palpable. *Has she been playing me all along to get to this moment only to throw me to my enemies, denouncing me as the murderer of Alexander's heir and then rule by herself as his half-sister and mother to his nephews?* Again, he sneaked a quick look at her and, again, she gave nothing away. *And yet she says she's willing to go and order the deaths herself; is that the act of one who would betray me?*

Kassandros shook his head as he struggled with the issue, for, in his old self, he would have simply negated it by having his wife executed along with the boy and his mother, and any man who found fault with that would share their fate in a slower manner. No, it was a problem and it was the only problem that he was unable to share with Thessalonike, obviously, for she would give the same answer whatever her true feelings. *She will just tell me not to be so ridiculous and get on with it.* Uncertain how to proceed, he took his wife's arm, now they had crossed the expanse of the main hall and were about to mount the stairs to the first floor. 'Come, Wife, let's retire for a while and then afterwards I'll think on it. I'll make the decision when I return from the Dardani campaign.'

'Why wait so long?'

'Because if I am to order the murder of Alexander's son, the manner of my return will have a great impact on my ability to weather the consequences of the deed.'

It had been a quick campaign thus far and one in which Kassandros excelled as there had been little actual fighting and that had been left to his twin half-brothers, Philip and

Pleistarchos. Kassandros had learned long since that any exposure to danger resulted in an uncontrollable urge to flee and the loss of control of his bladder. Three years previously he had led from the front in a night attack to open the gates of Corinth from the inside. That had proved to be more than he was able to bear and he had collapsed in a sobbing wreck, with urine gushing down his legs; fortunately, darkness and the arrival of supporting cavalry had masked that humiliation. He had, therefore, been able to boast to Thessalonike afterwards that he had led the attack which had taken the city and also counter some of the rumours within the ranks that he was shy of a fight.

But today was to be the second occasion he would lead from the front for today Kassandros would take Bylazora on the Axius River, the largest town in Paeonia, commanding the pass from Dardania into Macedon through the Scardus Mountains. With this move Kassandros hoped to show himself to be a concerned and caring ruler of Macedon, as the Dardani, an Illyrian tribe, had not been a part of the peace he had negotiated with Glaucias, the king of the largest conglomeration of Illyrian tribes, and thus constantly raided the farmsteads of the northern part of the country.

With his heart rate climbing, Kassandros looked left and right along the front line of his army as it formed ready for an assault of the town walls, crumbling with age and no more than the height of two men; those closest to him punched fists into the air and cheered. 'The men seem to be enthusiastic,' he observed to his half-brother Philip as the younger man drew his horse up next to him in a flurry of dust.

'They're anxious to have a proper fight,' Philip replied with a grin. 'Chasing raiding parties who disappear at the first sign of trouble is not the most satisfying of exercises. Besides, Bylazora will be a great addition to Macedon's defence and the lads understand that; many of them are from the uplands; good, hard hill-country boys who love nothing better than an honest toe to toe.'

He always has such an affinity with the men; it makes him popular. Too popular. 'Are we ready?'

'My lads are ready and with a hundred scaling ladders between them they're also very happy.'

'And your brother?'

'Almost. Pleistarchos is still forming up the left flank.'

'What's taking him so long?'

Philip shrugged, obviously unwilling to tell tales on his twin brother, though they both knew that Pleistarchos was both accident-prone and slow; identical though they might be in looks, the twins were of completely different temperaments.

'Tell him to get a move on; I want to start the assault before the elders change their minds and open the gates for us. If we wait much longer, looking down at the size of our army might make them overcome their hatred enough to be sensible.'

Philip tutted. 'We can't have that; especially when you're going to lead the assault.'

Kassandros' pinched face soured even further. 'What do you mean by that remark?'

'I mean you're going to lead the assault.'

'And what's so remarkable about that?'

'Nothing; it's just the lads don't often see you in the field and they appreciate it when their leaders share their jeopardy.'

Kassandros stared hard into Philip's eyes but saw no sign of accusation within. *I know he suspects my cowardice but he's never implied he knows about it to me in any way. It's just my terror of being exposed makes me suspect that everyone knows.* 'And today I fully intend to do so.'

'Good luck, Brother,' Philip said, turning his mount to speed back to his command.

'And to you,' Kassandros replied, wondering if he was doing the right thing knowing just how careful he would have to be to keep himself out of harm's way whilst seeming to be at the head of the escalade. *Why am I doing this?* It was the hundredth time he had asked himself that question since he had made the decision the previous day, whilst reconnoitring the ancient walls, and the answer had always been the same: because if he was to go through with what his wife had urged, he needed the full respect and support of the army, and Bylazora, with its low, crumbling, ancient walls, gave him the opportunity to put himself at the head of that army without placing himself into gut-wrenching, bladder-emptying danger. Or, at least, so he hoped.

And so it was with a knotted stomach that Kassandros dismounted and handed his stallion to a slave to be taken to the rear; an assault on a town was no place for cavalry and he was certainly not going to draw attention to himself by leading it on horseback.

With palms moist and heart pumping, he steadied himself, retying his helmet strap and then taking longer than necessary to heft his shield and draw his sword. But no amount of fiddling could delay the inevitable, and if Kassandros was to take any kudos away from this affair he had to be seen to lead from the front and so, therefore, to the front he needed to go. With bile rising in his throat, he stepped beyond the front rank, walked a further ten paces and turned to face his army, ten thousand strong, mainly javelin-armed heavy infantry and light archers; with a show of eagerness, he raised his sword in the air. 'Follow me, men of Macedon!' he yelled, his voice thin and reedy in his tight throat. 'Follow me to Bylazora and vie with me to be the first upon the walls!' He punched his weapon skywards as a cheer rose from the troops, a cheer of genuine enthusiasm for what he had said; a cheer of men prepared to follow him and vie with him to be first into the town. And vie with him he prayed they would for he would not hinder their progress.

Drawing a deep breath, he nodded to his signaller, hoping the fear was not showing in his eyes. As if in slow motion, the man brought his horn to his lips and with the blast of three notes the assault was under way. It was down to him, Kassandros knew, to take the first steps however much it went against every fibre of his being to move any closer to the danger that lined the walls five hundred paces off. But forward he went, hoping that any shaking of his legs would be construed as a part of his limp, the result of a failed boar hunt soon after the death of his father – another reminder of his inadequacies as, having never killed a boar in the hunt, he had yet to earn the right to recline at the dinner table and was obliged to sit upright as if he were a boy or a woman. But that was, for now, the least of his worries as, with his eyes rooted firmly on his feet, he forced one after the other to take a pace forward, each feeling as if it were filled with lead, all the time horribly aware that he was at the head of ten thousand men all looking to him for leadership. *Be strong and get through this today and you'll be secure enough never to have to face battle from the front again. It's the manner of your return to Pella that'll ensure that.*

The manner of his return: that was what he had to focus on as, through the files of the heavy infantry, light archers streamed, flowing past Kassandros and spreading out into dispersed order, nocking arrows as they went. Hundreds of them flooded to the front of the formation as, from the walls, the first volley rose, a grey stain dirtying the sky, to fall amongst the advancing skirmishers. With interest, they returned the arrow storm as the first screams of the wounded within their ranks pierced Kassandros' ears causing his panic to rise. He lifted his eyes from the ground, forcing himself to look ahead as another dark wave of missiles slammed into the screening infantry, thumping a score or more back, arms spreading wide and heads rolling to land in a crumpled heap on the ground. And over the corpses Kassandros was forced to step as the advance continued and the main body of infantry came within range of the defenders.

With tears forming in his eyes, Kassandros lifted his shield over his head; he sobbed with each hollow impact as the deadly hail now focused on the real threat to the walls: the assault troops with him at their head. But forward he still forced himself, knowing that to fail would cost him everything and so, for the one and only time in his life, he would not let himself be conquered by the shaming urge to run weeping and hide.

And on he went, his men grimly following in his footsteps, their minds concentrating on their own dangers and not on the constant trail of urine now seeping down their general's legs. Heavy grew the volleys raining in on them as they came within the lee of the defences and the screening infantry streamed back down the files as the defenders unleashed their hand-held weapons. It was now he had to muster everything within him to stay still. It was now, as the ladder-bearers rushed forward to the base of the wall, comrades holding their shields over them against the javelins and rocks pounding down from above. It was now, as the heavy infantry launched their javelins in return up at the defenders until the archers, falling back behind them, turned and recommenced releasing their shafts. Down did the defenders duck behind the parapet as up did the ladders arc to slam onto the stone, and Kassandros knew that the moment had come, the moment that would define the remainder of his life: if he failed in this moment, his life would be forfeit, whether it was this day or in the months to come; for, to lay claim to the kingdom he had forged, by murdering its rightful heir, he would need to return to Pella a hero at the head of this army. Anything less and he would be unable to withstand the hatred that would come from his murder of the great Alexander's son.

With a shriek, tight and strained, Kassandros stepped forward, pulling a veteran off the first rung of a ladder, and placed his foot there instead. With another gush of urine he began to climb, shield above his head and eyes squeezed shut, sword fisted, pushing down on the rungs with his wrist as his legs, thighs straining, propelled him up with the file-leader he had replaced following close behind him. To either side along the wall other file-leaders were making the same journey as archers shot over their heads to keep the defenders down; but as the assault neared the parapet the strafing paused for fear of hitting their own. It took but a moment for the defenders, wild-bearded and matted-haired, to realise the implication of the pause; up they leaped, swords punching forward, as the first wave of their attackers crested the parapet. Into shields and faces, honed blades slashed and stabbed as violence turned from remote to hand-to-hand. Now Kassandros had passed a point he had never reached before: he was in contact with the enemy. With vomit spraying from his mouth and nostrils, and moisture blinding his eyes, he leaned hard against his shield as he pushed it over the parapet; feeling the juddering impact of a direct thrust, he heaved against it for fear of being cast back onto the weapons of those following behind or waiting below.

With no option for survival other than forward progress, Kassandros put all his weight against his board as he hurled himself from the last rung of the ladder; with an ear-shattering explosion, an iron spear-point burst through his shield, slicing, to the bone, the flesh on the left of his forehead, almost to the temple. He screamed, spraying vomit over the weapon and the wood in which it was embedded. Now did he succumb to panic as blood poured from the wound, clouding his vision and filling his senses with its iron tang; his arms flailed at the same moment as the man below him heaved his shoulder against his buttocks, propelling him up and over the wall, his sword slashing at random across the bridge of a defender's nose, taking his eyes, his howl one of agony and terror. Over did Kassandros roll, dislodging the spear from his shield, as he landed on the thrashing, blinded man with the next in line on the ladder leaping onto the parapet before hurling himself forward to crash into a defender, pulling back his arm for a downward thrust into Kassandros' neck. It was the act of a cornered animal that drove Kassandros up to his knees, his shield cracking into the shin of a raging, snarling warrior with his hands at the throat of the file-leader to his left. With a yelp of pain as the bone fractured, the man jumped back, releasing his grip and then falling, his leg buckling under him, onto Kassandros' shoulder as he continued to rise; such was his momentum he sent the man somersaulting over him to fly, screaming, onto the crush below. But of this Kassandros was oblivious as he blindly surged forward, a wild boar on the charge, in his attempt to get anywhere that was not a cauldron of violence; anywhere but where he was. And so, in his abject terror, he became a thing of uncontrolled force, unstoppable as he ploughed through the defenders, skittling them over, plunging them down into the street running behind the wall, as his men ran in his wake, cheering as they followed their general on what seemed to be an orgy of destruction.

He came to his senses leaning against a column in the agora, hyperventilating, as his troops cheered their victory and the general who had led them over the wall and through the town. With blank eyes he looked around, unable to register what was happening as tears rolled down his cheeks, blending with and hidden by the blood still oozing from his forehead. He looked down at his arms, gory and with filth clinging to them, to see his shield was missing but his sword was still clasped tight. Below, his knees were grazed and bleeding. His right leg was without its greave and sandal; in their place were smears of faeces – his own, he had no doubt. Enough of his consciousness had returned to warn him not to do what he most desired and fall to his knees, sobbing with relief and thanking each and every god for preserving his most precious of lives. He managed to stay upright, staring blankly around him as slowly it dawned that he must have, somehow, achieved what he had set out to do for there was admiration in the eyes of the men surrounding him.

He tried to thank them but his voice was lost and his breaths too frequent for coherent speech and so he raised his arms in the air and threw his head back to roar at the sky, amazed he still lived. With a wild grin engraved across his face, he brought his gaze back down to meet familiar eyes. It took a few moments before he said: 'Philip?'

'No, Kassandros, it's Pleistarchos,' his half-brother replied; equally as bloody and caked in filth, the twin did not have the air of a victor.

And then Kassandros knew; he did not need to see the face of the body carried on a makeshift stretcher behind Pleistarchos. 'Philip?'

Tears rolled down Pleistarchos' cheeks and he lowered his head, his shoulders shaking.

It was almost a relief for Kassandros to be given the excuse to do what he really needed to: drop to his knees and let out all his trapped tension in a long wail, a wail that was seen as manly grief for a beloved younger half-brother, a wail none of the soldiers around him would have been embarrassed by had it been their kin they were mourning.

And thus, with heaving chest, Kassandros cried his relief: not only had he survived the most reckless deed of his life, but with that deed he would now feel secure of the army's support for they had seen him, finally, in battle and, to their eyes, he had not shied; in fact, judging by their faces, it had been the complete reverse. He sobbed, his head low, his tears flowing free; but they were not tears for Philip; they were not tears of grief and mourning for his heart was now brimming with joy.

Now he would be able to be the man Thessalonike wanted him to be, for now he was unafraid to do what she had asked. Now he would order the deaths of the young Alexander and his mother, Roxanna.

ROXANNA.
THE WILD-CAT.

'To your right!' Roxanna shouted, pointing at a watermelon skewered onto a pole the height of a man.

Nocking an arrow, her son, Alexander, the boy-king of Macedon, swung his body in the saddle, bracing himself with his thighs and knees gripping his mount's flanks, and released the arrow in one swift, fluid motion; as a right-handed bowman it was the hardest shot to get away from the back of a horse. It missed.

'Half a pace to the left and a hand's breadth high,' Roxanna said, twitching the reins of her galloping mare, easing it left and racing away from the target. 'Now behind you, now!'

With a grin of sheer pleasure, Alexander swiped an arrow from his quiver as he twisted round to the easier left side, pulling back the bowstring, his thumb brushing his chin, and released with barely a pause; straight and true the arrow flew to thump, juddering, into the post, a hand's width below the target. He cursed as he reloaded, his long blond hair streaming in the wind, and sent another shaft flying directly through the melon now almost fifty paces away.

'Good shot,' Roxanna said, pulling up her mount. 'That's enough for today; go to the kitchens and get yourself something to eat.'

'Later, Mother. Just one more round first,' Alexander shouted, riding on, across the parkland, at full gallop.

Roxanna smiled, her heart full of pride for the son she had once been prepared to abandon; a son she had, if she was honest, seen as a tool and not as a joy. That was now in the past for, as they had shared their captivity in a walled estate just outside of Amphipolis, Roxanna had surprised herself with the discovery of a maternal instinct within her, manifesting itself in the desire to teach the child.

It had taken a year to persuade her gaoler, Glaucias, to request his superior, Atarrhias, to transfer them from the fortress in the city to a country estate where at least she could have her son the king educated in the manly pursuits of riding, hunting and weapon-craft; it had been impossible for Atarrhias to refuse such a reasonable request from the mother of the King of Macedon. It had been an act of mercy for the boy had been inconsolable after their move from Pydna for he could no longer spend his days gazing out to sea in a half-trance. Glaucias had undertaken to make the request after a year of the boy doing nothing more than lying in bed – or on the floor if he was forced to get up – and his health had deteriorated to the point that Glaucias had worried for his own safety should Alexander die. Although the request had been granted, a plea for the boy to have royal pages of his own age for company, as had every King of Macedon since the Argead line began, was refused; in their stead came a score of guards patrolling mainly outside the walls to deter not only any escape but also any attempt at a rescue;

but none had come for, Roxanna could but assume, the world had forgotten them.

And so, she had settled down to making the best of her restricted life and nursed her son out of his despair, finally getting him to take a walk in the open air six months after they had arrived on the estate. Once that step had been taken it was not long before he had been persuaded onto the back of a pony. All Roxanna had of any use to teach her son was her skill at horsemanship and archery, honed growing up with many brothers in the uplands of her native Bactria, far to the east, in the days before Alexander had claimed her for a wife. Hence, with careful nurturing, in gradual stages, Alexander had flourished so that now, three and a half years since moving to the estate, he was almost a normal boy of thirteen.

Almost. Where he differed markedly was how he clung to his mother. This had been a surprise to Roxanna as she had never showed the child any love, thinking of him solely as a route to power, a weapon to be used to get the influence and status she deserved. But as she had coaxed him out of his despair and back into the world, he had come to rely on her as the only person with whom he could have normal contact; he had no friends of his age – or, indeed, of any age, as the hunting-master and weapons-master were cautious of becoming too involved with him for fear of their loyalty to Kassandros and Thessalonike coming into question. There were many guards to report back any conversation deemed to be too close or sympathetic.

Thus, Roxanna had come to be the last thing she had expected to be when she had been given by her father, Oxyartes, in marriage to Alexander: she had become a full-time mother; and to her surprise she had started to enjoy it.

'Just the one,' she shouted after Alexander as he sped away on another circuit of the field around the single-storey villa encompassed within the walls, twice the height of a man, surrounding the estate. But he did not hear as he released a shot at the first of the half dozen targets spread out at hundred-pace intervals.

It was with pride that Roxanna watched the arrow pierce the target as, to the west, the sun dipped towards the horizon, lengthening shadows and bathing her face in warm, golden light. She sighed; that she, a queen, and her son, the king, should be treated thus, confined and silenced, was intolerable but they were still alive and that at least must count for something. Surely, they were of some use to Kassandros and his bitch-wife Thessalonike if they had been spared? What was the point in keeping them alive in seclusion when they could as easily be murdered without anyone knowing? This thought gave Roxanna hope, for she knew that if she were Thessalonike, she would have had them poisoned years ago – indeed, it would have been the only sensible thing to do.

She followed her son's progress as he moved onto the third target leaving an arrow in the second; it was as he nocked, ready to release, that something caught the corner of her eye. She turned to glimpse the top of a head peering over the wall. She stared at it for a brief moment before it disappeared to be replaced with a spearhead rising up, reflecting the orange glow of the sun from its polished blade; there it stayed for a couple of heartbeats, waving to and fro, long enough for her to register its meaning. Her heart jumped as hope soared within her. It was not the spear itself which gave her the first surge of optimism she had felt since being dragged before Kassandros outside Pydna, it

161

was what was attached to it: the outspread wings of an eagle. She knew then she must gather her son and make ready, for it was the symbol of her tribe. It now seemed she had not been forgotten after all; indeed, her father must have been plotting all along to get her back, for, without doubt, this was a warning of an attempted rescue and she must stand prepared to play her part.

Gesturing to Alexander to follow her back inside, she hurried to the main door, handing her horse to one of the few slaves in the compound. If she was to do what she intended, speed was of the essence. No, not speed, but haste; well-managed haste. She must not let her euphoria show and give a clue to the guards that something was amiss by acting out of the ordinary.

Drawing a long breath to calm herself and conceal her haste from the two guards on the door, Roxanna hurried with as much decorum as possible, head held high, eyes meeting no others, the leather soles of her riding boots clicking on the marble as she went along the echoing corridor down the centre of the villa, with rooms off to either side. The smell of the guards' evening meal – mutton and herb stew – being prepared in the kitchens covered the corridor's normal musty odour. Again, she passed another guard, and then another at the entrance to her quarters; once more she slowed her pace and breathing as she opened the door to the suite she shared with her son.

No personal slave was she allowed, which at this moment was a blessing for she now had complete privacy. Hurrying to her bedroom, she knelt and pushed an arm under the bed, pulling out a small hessian sack that clanked as it slid.

She emptied the contents on the floor: a small copper pot, a set of scales, a mortar and pestle, a couple of vials the length and breadth of a thumb, one full of thick liquid, two bags of seeds, one bag of leaves and one of dried berries and a small nugget of a hard substance, light brown in hue. *It's all I need other than water and fire.*

The last two items were quickly found and soon the pot was suspended over a fire set on the small altar in the corner of her bedroom at which she nightly prayed to all the gods of Bactria, and beyond, to hold their hands over her and her son and release them from their prison. Today, it seemed, her prayers had been answered.

As the water came to the boil, she measured out her ingredients, the recipe known by heart for it was one of the first her mother had taught her; of all the potions she could brew, this was the most lethal. That she had managed to get the ingredients and equipment together over the three years she had been on the estate had been a triumph of surreptitious bribery, with the last few pieces of jewellery remaining to her, of the very few slaves on the compound who could come and go. But over time she had managed and, once the final piece fell into place at the end of the previous year, she had settled down to await her opportunity, for she knew she would only be able to brew the potion once. Now was that time.

'What are you doing, Mother?' Alexander asked as he came into the room, wiping the dust from his face with a cloth.

'Making a way out of here for us,' Roxanna replied, eyes fixed upon her task of crushing dried berries, once red in colour, beneath her pestle, grinding them to a powder. 'Get anything you want to take with you; a thick cloak and sturdy boots.'

Alexander's young, olive-skinned face creased into a quizzical countenance and he pointed to his mother's brew.

163

'Even if you could make enough to poison all the guards, it would be impossible to administer it to every one of them.'

'I don't need to.'

The puzzlement increased. 'What's brought this on, Mother?'

Roxanna raised her eyes and met his, her face illumined by the glow from her small fire as the light faded outside. 'I saw a sign just now: two eagle's wings nailed to a spear; it's the emblem of my tribe, our tribe, and my father's banner. Somewhere beyond the compound there are men waiting to rescue us; it'll be tonight as to wait would increase the chances of capture.' She tipped the contents of the mortar into the steaming pot, and then followed the viscous liquid in the vials. Immediately the room was filled with a pungent, sour smell that brought back happy memories of her as a girl, with her mother, brewing potions which they would use to eliminate entire families from rival clans, ensuring her father Oxyartes stayed the all-powerful chieftain of Bactria. 'Go, Alexander, and get the cloak and boots along with anything else you might need that won't slow us down and then come back as soon as you're ready; I've an important task for you.'

It was the leaves which went in next followed by the nugget, crumbled thinly, so grains dissolved almost instantaneously as they hit the bubbling liquid. Stirring slowly first one way and then the other, Roxanna chanted under her breath, pouring all her inner energy – hatred, vindictiveness and jealousy – into her potion as its strength grew with every curse.

The seeds completed it; Roxanna added wood to the fire, bringing up the temperature so the potion boiled with intensity, producing brown oily bubbles on its surface. Still she stirred, and still she chanted her curses as the liquid thickened and the steam grew more pungent.

'I'm ready, Mother,' Alexander said, coming back into the room.

Roxanna looked up and perused her son in the flickering light: he had chosen a dark tunic and cloak and a pair of leather trousers as worn in her homeland – a land Alexander might yet get to see. 'Good boy.' Turning her attention back to her potion, she lifted the pot from the flame, her hands protected by thick cloths, and tipped its contents into the vials.

Stoppering them, she placed them into the hessian bag and handed it to her son. 'The kitchen slaves give you things to eat if you ask them, don't they?'

Alexander nodded.

'Go and ask for something and then tip at least one of the vials into whatever they're cooking for the guards' evening meal. Be quick and be careful. And leave your cloak here.'

Alexander unslung the garment and turned to go; he paused and then returned to give his mother a hug, resting his head on her shoulder. 'I understand what's at stake.' He kissed her cheek before running from the room.

Still in her riding trousers and boots, Roxanna slipped a leather jerkin over her short tunic and then fastened a thick belt around her waist. Again, she rummaged under the bed to retrieve two knives in their scabbards, attached to the inside of the frame, and wedged them into her belt at the small of her back.

Now all she could do was wait.

She went to the window and pulled back the drape, outside it was now dark apart from a couple of torches to the left, either side of the main door; it was a moonless night, a night well chosen for an attempted escape. The lack of moon dispelled any last doubts she had about whether she had been imagining things or placing too much emphasis on what she thought she had seen. Very shortly dark shadows would slip over the wall and the most important and desperate exploit of her life would begin and its success rested on her thirteen-year-old son.

For what seemed like an age did she stand, peering into the dark, hoping to see a movement flit through deep shadow, but there was nothing out there, just the call of an owl and another night-bird, a hollow-sounding clicking, that she could not identify – unless… *But that's it, surely? I know all the sounds of the night here and that was out of place.* And then it struck her as a memory came back from her childhood. *They're using an eastern bird call so that I know they are coming.*

She stepped back from the window as she heard the door to her suite open; Alexander rushed in.

'Well?' Roxanna asked.

The boy nodded, tears welling. 'I did it, both vials, whilst pretending to taste the stew.'

Roxanna took Alexander's chin in one hand and looked into his moist eyes. 'And so what's the matter, then?'

Alexander shook his head, losing her grip.

'Tell me.'

'It's nothing; it's stupid.'

'What is?'

'The kitchen slaves were always kind to me.'

'So?'

'So, I've just killed them; they're bound to eat the remains of that stew.'

'What of it?' Roxanna's eyes flamed; she grabbed her son's chin again, squeezing it, her knuckles white. 'You are the King of Macedon; how much more is your life worth than that of a slave? They should be honoured that their worthless existence has come to some good in the end. Now dry your eyes and tie on your cloak. I've already heard their signal. Is the first shift of guards eating yet?'

Alexander steeled himself, standing straight, and nodded. 'They were already in the mess when I left.'

And that was all she could do, for, after what would happen to the first shift, she was sure that the second would not be eating the same fare. She pulled one of the knives from her belt and handed it to her son. 'It may come to this.'

Alexander took the weapon and freed the blade to test its keenness. 'The guard on our door?'

Roxanna smiled at his willingness, his weakness forgotten. 'No, I'll take him as soon as we hear the first shouts.'

And they did not take long in coming; a warning shout, abruptly curtailed, sounded from the direction of the main entrance.

'They're here,' Roxanna said, moving through the darkened room towards the door. She pulled her knife free and lay her hand on the door handle, placing her ear to the wood, listening. Outside the guard called to his comrade further up the corridor; another scream rang out. Roxanna yanked open the door and pounced out, blade extended high, causing the surprised guard to turn to her; she was the last thing he saw as the honed iron tip punched into his right eye. His roar of agony reached a crescendo as Roxanna rolled her wrist to shred the brain; limp, he went down, the knife pulling free with a release of suction and a squirt of blood and matter slopping to the marble floor. 'Come!' she called back to her son as, from the other end of the corridor, came the sound of close combat. Glancing behind to check

Alexander was following, Roxanna sprinted towards the fight as the second guard came running towards her, sword drawn, whooshing the small fires burning in sconces as he came. To her left she dodged, as the man thrust his blade at her throat, to crash her shoulder into the wall, leaving her right foot trailing. The weight of his shin hitting hers brought a cry from her gorge; over they both went, she straight down whilst the guard clattered along the floor, sliding to a halt between her and her son. Despite the pain she pushed herself up, her knife still fisted, and turned to her opponent; he got to his knees, looking directly at Alexander who had paused in the doorway.

'Here!' she screamed, to get the man's attention as she leaped forward.

He turned and, seeing Roxanna about to strike, swung his sword in an arc, forcing her to jump back, tucking her stomach in and flinging her arms up. Using the momentum of the stroke, the guard sprang to his feet, slashing at her; again, she retreated, narrowly avoiding the hissing blade and knowing that to try to parry it with just her knife would cost her hand.

Now he was up, his face set in a hate-filled snarl, eyes burning in the light from the sconces. Two more steps back she took, going into a crouch, ready for his attack, as behind her the sound of hand-to-hand fighting raged, a cacophony of metallic clashes and harsh voices made harsher by the hollow echo. And then he sprang forward, both feet leaving the ground, his blade pulled back next to his ear, left arm extended in balance, straight at Roxanna. To her right she went this time, her footing slipping on the marble, such was her haste, as the tip of the blade flashed towards her; a hand's breadth from her face it pulled back, as did the guard's whole body with his left hand now grasping a small arm clasped around his throat. Alexander's knife slammed down into the side of his neck at the same instant as an arrow shuddered into his chest, punching him over to crash to the floor, cushioned by his attacker. With a shriek, Roxanna grabbed the dead guard's arm and hauled him off her son. Winded, gasping for breath, Alexander lay for a few moments as footsteps rushed towards them from behind.

'We go!' a voice shouted. 'Quick!'

It took a heartbeat for Roxanna to recognise her native tongue, a language she only used with her son. Immediately it galvanised her; she pulled Alexander up, still struggling for breath. 'Take him,' she ordered the first of her rescuers whose smell preceded him.

Dark of skin and beard, with a leather cap crammed over a mane of hair, the warrior took the boy, slinging him over his shoulder, before pushing Roxanna in front of him as he turned to make his way back down the corridor.

With pounding heart and ragged breath, Roxanna ran; at least a dozen of her countrymen surrounded her with more lying on the ground, tangled with the bodies of her erstwhile guards; no sound of reinforcements came from the direction of the kitchens and the mess. *I've played my part.*

Out into the night they pelted; with the torches by the doors now extinguished there was no light by which to see and Roxanna grasped the arm of the man carrying her son. On they ran with no sound of pursuit until the wall was reached; with a few moments taken in orienting themselves, the rope used for ingress was found. Up went the first man to sit astride the wall as Alexander was handed to him. With powerful arms, he hauled the boy up and over and then leaned down to lower him close enough to the ground before letting go. It was Roxanna's turn next; she eschewed all help and walked up the wall, hand over fist on the rope, hooking her leg over and then jumping down to land next to Alexander. He clung to her as she held him in her arms and kissed his cheek as the Bactrians, one by one, landed beside them.

'Come,' the leader whispered. 'Our horses are close by. We have far to go.'

At a crouch he led them on through the night, stumbling on the rough ground; Alexander close behind him and then Roxanna with the rest of the rescue party spread out to either side, invisible almost in the gloom. Two, three hundred paces, Roxanna could not be sure, they went, feeling their way as if blind, their breathing the only way they could tell another's whereabouts. As they entered a copse, making their steps even more treacherous, a soft, equine, flaccid-lipped snort indicated their proximity to their mounts. The leader made the night-bird clicking sound that Roxanna had heard earlier and paused, awaiting a reply. None came; again, he tried his signal, but still there was no response. For a third time he blew the call but the sequence of clicks and clucks was clipped by a hollow thump. Back he fell and, although Roxanna could not see the detail, she knew he had been hit by an arrow, shot through the dark, guided by his sound.

'Run!' she cried as another unseen missile hissed by; a curse behind her bearing witness to a hit. Back she turned, grabbing Alexander by the arm, to run blindly away from the perceived threat as shafts breezed by from the invisible foe.

It was with a flicker of sparks that the first torch was lit, breaking through the night, sending unwanted light to discover the crouched forms of her rescuers. And then another flared, and another. And now javelins joined the arrows in their assault of the men from the east. Roxanna threw herself to the ground, her arm over Alexander, as the Bactrians released return shots into the night with little hope of contact for their assailants stayed beyond the growing ring of fire.

As she looked up two of her rescuers were punched back, bows flung up into the night, to crash onto the ground, lifeless, as the strafing of their position grew in intensity.

'Surrender and you might live,' a voice shouted from the night.

Hope died within her as Roxanna recognised the voice of her gaoler, Glaucias. *How did he know?* Around her, she was aware of the surviving Bactrians sheltering behind the trunks of trees with those caught in the open crawling along the ground to find similar safety. But, following a pause of twenty heartbeats after the demand for surrender, a hiss, a thump and an explosion of breath proved that nowhere was safe.

'Come, Alexander,' Roxanna whispered. 'They might kill their rightful king, but if they do get us so be it; it's better than being taken prisoner again. We run deeper into the wood.'

Alexander nodded, his eyes determined in the weak torchlight.

'Now!' Roxanna leaped to her feet, her son close behind her, and darted away towards the darkest patch she could see. But a dozen paces was all she managed before light flashed across her inner eye, her head was pounded back and she collapsed to the ground screaming to her gods with her last speck of consciousness.

*

That her hands were tied behind her was the first thing Roxanna became aware of as she slid out of a dark and empty dream; that and the throbbing in her head. She pulled at her bonds, but they held fast, cutting into her wrists, before opening her eyes; the sight froze her for it was the same that had greeted her every morning for the last three and a half years: the ceiling of her bedroom. She was back; she was a prisoner again.

Despair grew for she knew now she would never be allowed the relative freedom they had enjoyed on the estate again, not after the escape attempt, not after poisoning half of her guards; no, those brief hours between seeing the spear and being caught were the closest she would ever get to freedom again in her life. The only question now was: how long would that life last?

Drifting in and out of sleep, she did not know how much time had passed before she was dragged from the bed by firm, but not rough, hands.

'Where are you taking me?' Roxanna asked the officer commanding the two guards manhandling her.

'Thessalonike has summoned you.'

'To Pella?'

'No, to the next room.'

And there she was, Thessalonike, seated in the main room of Roxanna's suite as she was pushed through the door from her bedroom. Kneeling before her was Alexander, his hands, too, bound behind him.

Kneeling! The king kneeling to her?

'Bring her here,' Thessalonike said, her voice imperious and her manner cold. 'Bring the eastern bitch before me on her knees.'

Down Roxanna was thrust and then dragged along the

172

floor to be left next to her son, her eyes facing down to the floor.

'Look at me!'

Roxanna took no notice of Thessalonike's command.

'Look at me!'

'You will not address a queen thus,' Roxanna said, her voice weak but clear.

'Glaucias, pull her head back.'

Roxanna did not resist the savage tug on her hair.

'That's better.' Thessalonike's smile did not thaw the ice in her eyes. 'I want to see your face when I tell you it's over; your time has come, Roxanna.'

Roxanna glanced at her son beside her.

Alexander looked back with the visage of one who knew he was dead. 'Don't fight it, Mother; don't give her the satisfaction.'

'He's a wise boy,' Thessalonike observed. 'It's such a shame he's not destined to be king.'

'He *is* king!' Roxanna all but screamed.

Thessalonike looked down at her, enjoying her frustration. 'Well, perhaps; but not for very much longer. And you were so close to escaping too, weren't you, my dear? So close. Do you know what gave you away?'

Roxanna did not want to know and made no reply.

'It was Glaucias who spotted it. You see, he's served in Bactria and he knows the sound of their night-finch and he found it very odd hearing it last night so he stopped the first shift of guards from eating and led them out to patrol in the direction of that eastern sound. It was just as well he did as after you had been caught and the guards went for their meal they found all the kitchen slaves lying dead. Tut, tut, Roxanna; you and your potions.' Thessalonike shook her head in exaggerated exasperation. 'But that was the last you will brew. But first you will watch your son die. Glaucias, if you please.'

Roxanna turned in panic to see her gaoler, still a fit man in his fifties, walk from behind her, a leather garrotte dangling from his right hand. With his left he pulled Alexander's head back.

'I'm ready, Mother,' Alexander said as the leather was passed around his throat. 'I never expected to live once I realised who I was. How could I have when my father gave his empire to the strongest? What chance did he give me?'

Glaucias slipped a short wooden rod into the loop and twisted, tightening the leather. Alexander's eyes bulged. Roxanna turned to her captor. 'Thessalonike, no! No, please, I beg you!'

Thessalonike sighed then signalled with her hand.

Two arrows shuddered into Alexander's chest; the boy convulsed and fell back on the floor as Glaucias let go his grip.

Roxanna screamed as the life left her son and then rounded on her tormentor. 'He was your nephew, Thessalonike; your blood. And he was your king!'

THESSALONIKE.
THE HALF-SISTER.

'**H**E WAS MY rival,' Thessalonike said, triumph on her face, her eyes ice-cold, blue and beauteous, as she looked down at the lifeless body of Alexander, the fourth so named of Macedon. *Dead, finally; and in a manner that can be explained away.*

'You'll never get away with murdering the king, you bitch!' Roxanna's voice was strangled; tears sprang as she spat at Thessalonike's feet.

'No, perhaps not; it would have been difficult, I grant you, even after Kassandros managed to make himself so popular with the army. But now, thanks to your father – I would assume, as it must have been him who sent the rescue – we haven't murdered him. Look at the arrows.'

Roxanna turned her head to her son with obvious reluctance. After a moment her tear-glazed eyes widened.

'Yes,' Thessalonike crooned, 'Bactrian arrows.' She clicked her fingers. The two guards who had made the shots came forward; they had compact Bactrian bows in their hands. 'Shot with Bactrian bows. And I have a score of dead Bactrians to go with them who were obviously sent as an assassination squad; but, by whom? Well, I can only suppose it must have been Antigonos, seeing as he controls the eastern satrapies.' Her face, now, was all innocence; such beauty could surely never lie. 'Yes, I know they're only nominally under his control but the good people of Macedon, grieving for their young king, so tragically taken from them by barbarians, won't know that, nor would they care if they did. And I shall lead them in their mourning whilst displaying the bodies and weapons of his assassins; that'll all make for a good display in Amphipolis.'

'You'll never get away with it.'

'What's it to you, Roxanna? You'll be dead.' Thessalonike clapped her hands; the door out to the corridor opened and a slave came in with a bowl; he laid it on the low table Roxanna used for dining.

'You have a choice,' Thessalonike continued once she had read in Roxanna's eyes that she had realised what the bowl contained. 'You can either take your own life with that potion you brewed yesterday – a grieving mother unable to live without her murdered child – in which case I will grant you funeral rites along with your son. Or I can have you hacked to death in front of me and have your body parts scattered for the wolves. Either way you will be dead before the sun's moved noticeably in the sky.'

Roxanna looked down at her son again, tears now streaming down her face; grief flooding through her. 'Why should that bother me? What reason do I have to live for now? No, Thessalonike, you've won and I only have myself to blame: had I not acted so haughtily towards you when we first met then, perhaps, we might have been friends and could have fought Olympias together; but I thought you were just her maidservant and treated you thus.'

Thessalonike resisted the urge to laugh. 'We would never have been friends or allies, Roxanna; there can be only one queen in Macedon and I intend it to be me. Now, make your choice before I order Glaucias to start with your eyes.'

Roxanna leant down and kissed Alexander's lips and then turned to Glaucias. 'Untie me.'

He looked at his mistress; Thessalonike nodded. With a flick of his knife Roxanna was free. She took her son in one arm and pulled at the arrows; they were stuck firm so short had been the range of the shots. A wail of frustration rose from deep within her being and she hugged Alexander's corpse close to her, covering his face with tears and kisses.

'That will do,' Thessalonike said, gesturing to Glaucias.

The gaoler pulled his charge to her feet, still hugging the body of her son, and disentangled her from it. As Alexander slipped to the floor all fight, life, hope and will left Roxanna and she physically sagged, her head bowed. Glaucias led her to the table where her final meal awaited.

It was a sight Thessalonike revelled in: the total subjugation of the once proud and vicious eastern wild-cat reduced to a sobbing wreck to be led, unresisting, by the arm wherever she was told to go. It was a triumph she had longed for but never thought she would see. *Utterly defeated; how very pleasing.* 'Now eat!' Thessalonike ordered as Glaucias placed a spoon in Roxanna's hand.

Roxanna looked at the implement as if struggling to realise its purpose, tears still flowing and low moans rumbling in her throat.

'Eat!'

The suddenness of the shout seemed to penetrate Roxanna's consciousness, and with a mechanical movement, she pushed the spoon into the mush of stew. She did not pause; pulling a spoonful up, she lowered her head at the same time and putting it in her mouth swallowed with barely a chew.

This she repeated again and then again and Thessalonike shook her head in grudging respect as Roxanna finished the bowl. *She knows the pain that awaits her; she's witnessed it in others often enough.*

And the pain was not long in coming. It hit Roxanna first in the stomach; over she went, falling onto the floor, her arms clutching her midriff and her eyes widening, throat tightening.

'Is that how Alexander's other two wives began their death dance, Roxanna?' Thessalonike asked. 'What were their names? Stateira and Parysatis, wasn't it? I heard about that; very nasty. You threw their bodies down a well, according to the slave who witnessed it. They're still there I would have thought. You'll be better off than them.'

With a jerk and then a massive convulsion, vomit sprayed from Roxanna's mouth, flying high into the air, splattering down onto the table and the floor around it. Another jet surged from her and then her body relaxed, her chest heaving and the moan changed from one of grief to pain.

'How many others did you make go through this in your time? Fifty? A hundred? Two hundred, perhaps? Oh well, it doesn't matter now.' Thessalonike stood and walked across to Roxanna as she lay on the ground, her chest heaving in the desperate attempt to suck in air through a constricting throat. 'I've always thought poison must be a nasty way to die; I see now I was right.'

Roxanna's eyes bulged as they stared up at her, her head shaking to and fro as the ability to breathe was finally denied her; puce she went in her final moments, puce and bloated around the cheeks; and then with a suddenness that amazed Thessalonike, she was still; her eyes glazed.

'Not nice; not nice at all,' Thessalonike said, prodding the body with her foot. 'That she should have died like this is a testament to justice.'

'That she should have died like this is a testament to her loyalty.' Thessalonike looked around the nearest faces of the huge crowd, in the newly constructed agora of the city named after her; thousands surrounded the dais from which she had announced the distressing events of two days previously. All held sorrow in their eyes. 'She could not bear to live once her son, our king, the young Alexander, had been taken from her! Taken!' She pointed to the pile of corpses at the foot of the dais. 'Taken by these vile creatures. Trouser-wearing barbarians!'

Thessalonike paused to let that sink in. The fact Alexander and his mother were both in trousers at the time of their death was quietly forgotten as each was now in their finest Macedonian attire. 'Barbarian assassins sent from the east!' Thessalonike favoured the crowd with her finest look of outrage. 'And who sent this filth to take our king from us? Who, I ask you? Who?' It was an interesting question, not because she did not know the answer, or, at least, *her* answer; it was interesting because she wanted to know whether her answer had travelled to Thessalonike from Amphipolis where she had announced the deaths and displayed the bodies and the evidence, the day before.

And she was not disappointed.

'Antigonos!' a couple of voices in the crowd shouted.

'Yes, Antigonos,' another joined in.

'He controls the east,' somebody else pointed out.

179

'Yes, and oi were in Bactria, and them there's Bactrians,' a veteran said, pointing at the offending corpses with his one-remaining arm. 'So, it must have been the resinated cyclops.'

'Yes, it was Antigonos,' another confirmed. 'He took our king from us because he wants to take the crown himself.'

'Never!'

'Where was he when we was in India?'

Thessalonike allowed the railing against the cyclops to carry on until indignation at his actions was turning into outright hatred, before raising her arms demanding quiet. 'You may be right, citizens of Thessalonike, and I, as your patron, shall listen to what you say. But at the moment we have a peace agreement with Antigonos and I would be loath to tear that agreement up without firm proof it was him. But I promise you, if evidence is found that he did indeed send these assassins then we shall pursue him and exact our vengeance. He will pay for the death of our king; that I can promise you.'

And that promise she made in every major town she passed through on her way back to Pella with the bodies of Alexander and his mother and their assassins. 'And the best part about it, Kassandros,' she told her husband as they met on the palace steps upon her return to the capital, 'is they believe it; the people believe Antigonos did it, not us. It hasn't even occurred to most of them that we wanted Alexander dead more than the resinated cyclops. They hear the stories of his victories out in the east and believe he wants to take the whole empire for himself. They don't understand that all we want is Macedon and Greece. And with Alexander removed and no blame attached to us soon we will be able to achieve it.'

'So, my heroics at Bylazora were all for nothing, were they?' Kassandros did not look overly pleased.

Thessalonike took her husband's arm and, turning him, led him back through the great double doors into the high-ceilinged entrance hall. 'Do you regret it?'

'I regret having to do it when actually I didn't have to. I would rather not have nearly died; I still have dreams.'

'But you didn't die and they are only dreams; what's more, you conquered your fear and led men over the wall. No one can ever accuse you of being a coward again.'

Kassandros turned on his wife, rage in his eyes. 'Who ever said I was a coward? Who?'

Thessalonike smiled and stroked his face. 'Oh, Kassandros, do you think I don't know you? Do you think I don't know what you yourself know? We're both aware you are, how shall I put it, less than willing to enter a fight and totally unwilling to be in the front line.' She saw his avian-esque face changing from its usual pallid shade to blood-tinged fury; she clamped her hand over his mouth. 'Don't try to deny it and keep your temper. It's done. You overcame your fears and pushed through your cowardice to be the first on the walls. No one can ever take that away from you; and just because it now seems like you didn't need to do it, as we can present ourselves as being clean of Alexander's blood, doesn't mean that you shouldn't have done it. Do you imagine we'll never have to fight another battle to keep our positions secure?'

Kassandros squeezed his eyes shut and pulled her hand from his mouth, taking a deep breath through his nose, calming himself. 'You're right, of course, my love; I am a coward and I have always known it, right from a very young age.'

'No, you *were* a coward, Kassandros; now you're not and the whole army knows it because the ten thousand men whom you led at Bylazora witnessed your deeds, and their reports have spread to all corners of the country. Now, when you lead the army into battle you can let others do the dangerous stuff whilst you direct the fight; no one will think badly of you because they know when you must fight you do and you do it bravely. Now come, let's go and see our children and then you can show me just how pleased you are that I'm back, before we leave for Aegae tomorrow to bury the brat.'

It had been a mournful two days, journeying from Pella to the royal burial ground at Aegae. The roads had been lined with folk, both from town and country, grieving for their young king so tragically taken from them. And they wept and called out his name as he passed, on a high bier, in a royal purple tunic and cloak and crowned in a delicate, gold-leaf crown of oak leaves and acorns that shimmered in the sun as it shivered with the rumbling movement of the carriage bearing the king.

Thessalonike, her face ever sombre, glowed within herself for she and her husband were able to present themselves as true mourners for her beloved nephew and also show their generosity in granting royal rights to the boy's mother who followed him on a lesser bier. *Fortune has favoured us; there can no longer be any obstacle between us and the crown.*

With this pleasing thought in mind she watched as Alexander's body was consumed by the fire blazing up through the stacks of oil-soaked wood of his pyre. And still she remained sombre in countenance but joyful in spirit as Kassandros delivered the young king's eulogy extolling his many virtues, virtues which would have made him the greatest of kings had he not been so cruelly cut down by the agents of Antigonos. He assured the mourners that those who had been responsible for the king's safety and had failed in their duty had paid with their lives, as Glaucias and his surviving men who were responsible for this sad state of affairs had been executed.

And cannot now contradict our version of events. Thessalonike had ordered the executions as she left Amphipolis as a precaution: she did not want blackmailers to come calling just when she and Kassandros were so close to achieving their ambition. Throughout the ceremony she played her part, taking Alexander's funerary crown of oak leaves and acorns into the tomb and laying it on the silver urn containing the ashes as Kassandros adorned the tomb with weapons, luxurious clothing and precious tableware. In a final act of hypocrisy, she and her husband laid a cloak of royal purple around the base of the urn bestowing upon him in death the kingship they had denied him in life. Her duty complete, Thessalonike turned to the crowd with tears flowing free as the marble door to the tomb was closed for the last time, ending the brief life of the son of Macedon's greatest king; and all wept with her.

With the funeral over, Thessalonike and Kassandros travelled in haste back to Pella, anxious to commence the last stage of their journey to royalty. It was as they entered the entrance hall of the palace that their steward approached them. 'There is a messenger from Ptolemaios waiting for you, lord. He wishes to see you as soon as possible.'

'Ptolemaios?' Kassandros repeated in surprise.

'Have him sent to the audience chamber,' Thessalonike ordered, feeling uneasy about the development as things had been going so well. 'We'll see him immediately.'

And it was with a sinking heart that Thessalonike saw the serious expression on the messenger's face as he was shown into the chamber. 'Well?' she asked. 'What is it that's so urgent we have neither washed nor changed after our journey?'

'My lady, lord, in view of the fact that, with your peace agreement with his uncle, you are now allies, Ptolemaios asked me to give you this.' He took a scroll from its case, proffering it, unsure as to whom he should offer it.

Thessalonike took it, unravelled it and began to read. The good humour of the past few days evaporated immediately. *Just when we were unopposed and so close, this happens.*

'What is it?' Kassandros asked, concerned at his wife's expression.

She handed him the scroll. 'Polyperchon has marched to Aetolia and is supplementing his army there with a view to invading Macedon.'

Kassandros scoffed. 'With what reason? Who would support him against us?'

'No one if he were on his own, but he's not. Alexander's bastard, Herakles, is with the nonentity.'

POLYPERCHON.
THE GREY.

NOW HE COULD arrest his slow slide into obscurity; now he could become more than just his daughter-in-law's general commanding a few thousand men along the isthmus with just Corinth and Sykion under their control, for now he had a position entitling him to respect; now he was the general commanding the king's European army. Now Polyperchon was once again a man to be reckoned with.

'Yes, my lord king,' Polyperchon said, bowing his head in response to Herakles' command, 'I shall see to it immediately. I already have dozens of foraging parties out collecting supplies for the winter, but making provision for a further two thousand cavalry joining us from Athens will be challenging; yet I am up to the challenge.'

'See to it you are, general,' Herakles said, turning his horse and walking it away from the army's morning muster, a routine Polyperchon insisted upon – there could never be enough inspections in the military life. 'And report your progress to me when I return from my hunt later this afternoon.'

'Indeed, my lord king.' Polyperchon saluted in a stiff, parade-ground fashion as Herakles rode towards a group of his companions – once Polyperchon's men – armed with hunting spears and nets; standing rigid for a few moments Polyperchon then ordered the dismissal and to strike camp and to prepare to march, did an about turn and marched himself off at double time as if he were taking himself for extra fatigues along with the two hundred and twenty-three defaulters found wanting this morning. This was soldiering at its best: parades, inspections, dealing with supplies, listing provisions, ordering the distribution of rations and kit, checking and double-checking requisition orders and everything else that was part and parcel of a well-run military machine on the march. For Polyperchon was a master of detail, a consummate second-in-command who rated a soldier by the neatness and completeness of his kit and not by his ability to fight – for a well turned-out man was, obviously, a ferocious fighter.

It was with a warm feeling of contentment that Polyperchon set about his new task for there was nothing more satisfying than receiving and executing orders and to receive them from a king once more was a relief; finally, he could be sure he was on the side of right for how could the King of Macedon be wrong? Not that Herakles was officially the king as he had yet to take Macedon, but since his arrival in Greece from Pergamum, in secret, three months previously, Polyperchon had addressed him as 'lord king' for, in doing so, it made him feel an important part of the Macedonian hierarchy. The fact that it had been Alexander's full sister, Kleopatra – through an agent – who had negotiated his support of Herakles had shown just how highly he was considered by that hierarchy.

And now, here he was, at the head of an army approaching twenty thousand in strength, marching through Aetolia, in secret, having taken the western road from Corinth along the northern coast of the Peloponnese and crossing the Gulf of Corinth at Erineus, landing on the sparsely inhabited coast of Aetolia. He planned to head north to Tymphaia, his clan's country, on the borders of Epirus and Macedon, to raise more troops over the winter from the locals loyal to him. When he was ready and his army fully supplied and immaculately turned out, he would invade Macedon from the west in the spring, defeat Kassandros and place Herakles on the throne. And his reward would be the position of general commanding the army of Europe; an impressive title, one that would command respect throughout Macedon. Yes, fortune had favoured him and plucked him from the obscurity into which he had slumped since the death of his son, Alexandros.

There was, however, one complication: the presence of Herakles' mother, Barsine, and her half-sister, Artonis. It was they who were the force behind Herakles' claim to the throne and, therefore, it was Barsine and Artonis who ruled. Having served under, first, Adea, the wife of the fool king Philip, and then under Olympias, and having had a less than harmonious relationship with his daughter-in-law, Penelope – who had advised him against the venture – Polyperchon found it hard to be comfortable in the presence of strong, domineering women, finding himself, well, dominated; unfortunately for him he was in their presence every day and had to endure their opinions on the way he commanded the army, calling into question his methods and priorities.

And it was to this end, once more, that Polyperchon assumed he had been summoned to Barsine's tent as soon as the morning muster was complete and the army was readying itself for the day's march. As the shouts of the officer barked and horns sounded the dismissal, Polyperchon marched with purpose towards Barsine's tent next to the king's at the centre of the camp.

With a sharp nod of the head as he removed his helmet, he acknowledged the crisp salutes of the two guards on the entrance as they stepped aside to let him pass.

'There you are, general,' Barsine said, sitting at her breakfast table, peeling an apple and not looking up; the rest of the tent was empty having already been stowed in preparation for the march. 'How was your morning terrorisation of the men? Did you put a satisfactory number on fatigues? I do hope so.'

Polyperchon had learned to ignore jibes such as this, as defending his practices often resulted in uncalled for and, frankly, incomprehensible mirth from Barsine. He bowed his head to her and acknowledged Artonis, sitting beside her, with a nod. 'You sent for me, my lady.'

Barsine looked up from her apple and smiled. 'I did, general; you're quite right.' She indicated to a chair opposite her. 'Please sit down. And help yourself to wine or fruit juice.' Wary at being treated with a degree of cordiality, Polyperchon did as he was asked, literally, thinking he had to make a choice between the two options; choosing the juice and sipping at it whilst waiting for Barsine to finish peeling and quartering her apple. He rubbed his bald head and looked at her with rheumy eyes gazing from a wizened face looking every bit of his seventy-three years.

'Still fresh,' Barsine said as she chewed on her first mouthful.

'I'm pleased to hear it. I believe we had a good apple harvest this year.'

'But the secret is to keep them fresh after the harvest.' Barsine gave him a significant look as she took another bite.

Confused as to what was really going on, Polyperchon looked to Artonis but received no help from that quarter.

Barsine pressed on with her incomprehensible line of thought. 'I'm talking about keeping things fresh, Polyperchon; fresh? You know what fresh is?'

'Of course I do.'

'Either you use something when it is fresh or you preserve that thing so it stays fresh until you wish to utilise it; would you not agree?'

What have I done now? She only says 'would you not agree' when she's leading me into a trap. 'Most things are better fresh, yes.'

'Then why have you been sitting on intelligence, keeping it to yourself and not sharing it with me?'

Steely eyes bored into Polyperchon; he fought hard to keep still and not squirm. 'What intelligence would that be?'

'Oh, so you've more than one piece of information that you're keeping from me, have you? In which case you'd better start listing them, beginning with what Ptolemaios is up to.'

'Ptolemaios?'

'Yes, Antigonos' nephew; the one who controls Euboea and most of eastern Greece except Athens.'

'What about Ptolemaios?'

Barsine put her apple down and looked at Polyperchon for a moment, frowning. 'You really don't know?'

'I don't think so.'

Barsine looked to her half-sister. 'Artonis found out about it; tell him, my dear.'

Artonis leaned back in her chair and placed her fore-arms on the table. 'Did one of your spies not report to you that Ptolemaios had written to Kassandros and his wife last month?'

'Yes, but he didn't know what the letter contained; only that he'd sent it.'

Barsine closed her eyes, exasperated. 'And you thought it was of no significance and it wasn't worth passing on to me?'

'People write letters every day.'

'No, they don't! At least not Ptolemaios and certainly not to Kassandros and Thessalonike. Why would he be writing to them at all, do you think?'

'I don't know.'

'And it didn't occur to you to think upon the problem, to realise it was a problem, even, and perhaps inform me?'

'Why should it have been a problem?'

'Oh, Polyperchon, where do I start?' Barsine shook her head, her eyes clouded by disappointment. 'Artonis, *you* ask him, I can't bear to.'

'What else happened a month ago; just over a month ago, in fact?'

It took a moment for Polyperchon to put aside the insult and then to see where this was going. 'We set out from Corinth.'

'Well done.' Barsine clapped her hands.

Artonis pressed on. 'And when did your spy report Ptolemaios wrote to Kassandros and Thessalonike?'

'Hmm, about ten days ago.'

'No, I mean when did the letter go, not when did your man arrive here to tell you about it.'

'The new moon after we marched.'

'At what time of day did he leave?'

'I believe the messenger is reported to have left at dawn.'

'In other words, at first light four days after we marched Ptolemaios sent a message to Macedon.'

'Yes, I suppose so.'

'How long does it take a ship to sail from the isthmus to Ptolemaios' base on Euboea?'

'Two days at the most.'

Barsine's impatience was now apparent. 'So, one day for the spy to get to his ship after he saw whatever it was that he needed to report to his master; two days for him to get to Ptolemaios and then the message leaves the first thing the following day. Might you be able to hazard a guess as to the contents of that message?'

Polyperchon swallowed; he could feel his temperature rising. 'That we were marching north with an army into Aetolia?'

'Well done, you're finally there. Now explain to me why I had to wait until now to find out, not from you but from Artonis?'

Polyperchon shrugged. 'I didn't think it important.' He paused in thought. 'How did Artonis find out?'

'The same way as you found out about the letter: a spy.'

'A spy?' Polyperchon looked at Artonis, outraged. 'You're spying on me?'

'My sister and I keep our eyes on everyone in the army.'

'It would seem we have to,' Barsine observed, 'seeing as you can't tell what is relevant and what isn't. Shall we just say, for sake of argument, that everything is relevant and I need to be informed as soon as possible?'

Polyperchon knew contrition, although humiliating, was the best policy. 'Yes, my lady; I'm sorry, you're right. Still,

Kassandros and Thessalonike would have found out one way or another that we were on our way north.'

Barsine's look of disappointment deepened. 'Oh, Polyperchon; oh dear.'

What have I done now?

'You really don't understand the significance of the letter, do you?'

'They know we're coming and probably have a good idea of our numbers.'

'And what about the fact that Ptolemaios wrote to them in the first place? Doesn't that tell you anything?'

'Ptolemaios is their ally.'

'Obviously, but more than that, he's turned against his uncle.'

'Antigonos?'

'He only has one, so yes.'

'How do you know?'

Barsine sighed and tapped her right little finger with her left forefinger. 'Firstly, Kassandros and Thessalonike have a peace treaty with Antigonos at the moment and yet he has done nothing to disrupt our plans to invade Macedon, which he must know about by know – *he's* not stupid. He neither tried to intercept us crossing from Asia nor prevent Herakles and me from joining with you once we landed. Nor did he write to Kassandros warning him about our deal with you; I would have known about the letter either from my spies in his camp or in Pella or from Kleopatra's. Therefore, one can only conclude that our attempting to kill Kassandros and place Herakles on the throne suits Antigonos' interests – at least in the short to medium term. In the long term he needs both Herakles and Kassandros dead, so, he must reason, why not let one of them kill the other thus leaving less dirty work for him. Ptolemaios, however, in writing to Kassandros and Thessalonike has picked a side, something his uncle was very careful not to do.'

She tapped the ring finger. 'Secondly, Kleopatra wrote to me to say that Phoinix, the satrap of Hellespontine Phrygia, has recently rebelled against Antigonos. Phoinix is Ptolemaios' friend and there has been a more than usual amount of correspondence between them recently.'

She tapped her middle finger. 'Thirdly, with Demetrios out in the east trying to regain Babylon from Seleukos, Antigonos is running out of generals he can trust. Telesphorus has barely been forgiven for his rebellion last year and is now serving on Demetrios' staff where a close eye can be kept on him. Dioscurides, the other nephew, is commanding the northern fleet whilst Nearchos commands the southern one. Hieronymus has been left in charge of this strange business collecting a black substance from the Salt Sea to disrupt the Nabateans' trade in it, which leaves young Philippos, Antigonos' youngest son, now seventeen, but no match for Ptolemaios. Perhaps Antigonos could send him against Phoinix if he had sufficient advisors, but against someone as experienced as Ptolemaios it would be an unnecessary risk. So now is the perfect time for him.'

She tapped her forefinger. 'Fourthly and finally, it makes sense for Ptolemaios to form an alliance with Pella: neither of them are strong enough to resist Antigonos on their own – especially if one has damaged himself by destroying the other. Therefore, an alliance makes sense and how better to approach it, from Ptolemaios' point of view, than by warning Kassandros of a claimant to the throne he wishes to make his own.' Barsine raised her eyebrows at Polyperchon. 'Are those enough reasons for you?'

Polyperchon's head was spinning; politics and intrigue were worlds apart from lists and rosters. 'I think so.'

'But the most important fact, the one that draws it all together, is the fact which you kept from me for ten days, which is: Ptolemaios wrote to Kassandros and Thessalonike in the first place. Think about it.' Barsine paused for a moment to allow him to do so. 'When you send scouts out, which direction do you favour?'

'Well, north of course, that's the direction from which any opposition from Kassandros would come.' And then the full weight of what he had missed hit Polyperchon; once more he felt small and dominated by these women. He turned from one to the other; their mirthless smiles broadened as they registered his understanding. 'Oh.'

'"Oh" is one way of putting it,' Artonis said.

'"Oh fuck" is another,' Barsine continued. 'East is where the first threat will come from; east from Ptolemaios showing Kassandros and Thessalonike just how good a friend he could be to them and how it would be much better for all of them if he were left alone in his portion of Greece to look after their southern flank for them. East, Polyperchon, that's the direction in which you should look.'

And it was from the east that the first report of foraging parties and scouts going missing did come, with five of the former and three of the latter failing to report in as the column halted for a brief midday meal. Concerned but not yet dismayed, Polyperchon sent out a couple of search parties; neither returned within the two-hour time limit he had set them.

And then the first of the stragglers came in, bloodied and exhausted. 'We never saw them,' one file-leader said, his voice croaking despite the water he took regular draughts of. 'Euboeans and Boeotians, judging by their accents, although what they're doing this far west, I don't know.'

'It's not your business to know,' Polyperchon snapped, drawing pitying looks from Barsine and Artonis for his ineptitude at dealing with a brave survivor. 'Are you sure about the accents?'

'I am, sir; as I lay playing dead, I heard them moving around me finishing off the wounded. How they missed me, I don't know.'

Barsine put a hand on his shoulder. 'You've done well, soldier. I shall see you rewarded; my physician will take care of you. You can go.'

'It might just be freebooters,' Polyperchon suggested more in hope than in certainty.

Barsine turned on him. 'Polyperchon, don't compound your mistake with stupidity. It is Ptolemaios' men and had we known about this possibility ten days ago we could have sent a force east to stop them. Instead, they are here amongst us and disrupting our supplies.'

'Mother!'

They turned to see Herakles riding up with his hunting companions, their horses almost blown; his eyes, one blue, one brown, were full of concern as he dismounted. 'Mother, the hills to the east of us are swarming with cavalry. We just escaped with our lives!'

It was at that moment Polyperchon knew he would have to find a good defensive position and await whatever Ptolemaios had sent against him, probing all the while to find out the exact nature of the threat. 'We retreat to high ground and wait for them to come to us.'

Barsine regarded her general with a mixture of disbelief and disgust as if he had soiled himself and was quite content to stand there allowing the ordure to run down his legs. 'And how long do we wait? A day, a moon, a year, ten years? No, you fool, we have to press on keeping a strong screen to the east and pray to the gods we can get to Tymphaia and the relative safety of your clan's lands. Do you understand, Polyperchon?'

Once again humiliated and dominated. A weak 'Yes' was all he could manage.

'Good.' Barsine turned away. 'Herakles, Artonis, come with me; we have urgent business to discuss.'

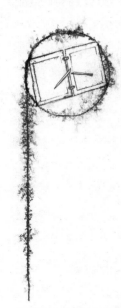

ARTONIS.
THE WIDOW.

'WHAT HAVE WE done?' Barsine bemoaned as soon as they were out of Polyperchon's earshot as the shouts of officers signalled the end of the meal break. 'The man's incompetent.'

'Worse than that,' Artonis said, 'he's also a fool.'

'Then why did you choose him?' Herakles asked, accusation in his tone.

Barsine rounded on her son. 'Because he was the only general in Europe with an army who would have had any self-interest in seeing you on the throne; in that respect he was and still is the perfect choice. The trouble is he's an incompetent fool.'

'Then replace him.'

'With whom?' Barsine pointed at her son. 'You? You who've spent every day of the march going out hunting with your new friends? Do you know more than half a dozen of the officers' names? No, of course you don't, but perhaps it's time you did start to get to know them. I've indulged you for this long because I know how little hunting you got in Pergamum; but from now on you're a soldier not a huntsman. Understand?'

'As the king it is my right to please myself,' Herakles said, his eyes locked with his mother in a war of wills.

'You are not king yet; and if you think of nothing but pleasure, you may never be.'

The tension between mother and son lasted a few moments before Herakles gave the faintest of nods. 'Perhaps you may have a point: I shall make more time for military affairs.' He turned and walked away, back towards his waiting companions.

Artonis was surprised by the contrition he showed, however small. Since his arrival in Greece, Herakles had displayed little interest in martial affairs, preferring, instead, to explore his new-found freedom now he was out of the confines of Pergamum, where, although free to come and go within the city, it was understood he was not free to wander far from it. And so, upon arrival in Corinth he had wasted no time in collecting together a group of young men with whom to hunt. For days did they disappear into the hills whilst the army was mustered, supplied and equipped in a very pedantic but ultimately successful manner by Polyperchon, and Herakles learned nothing from it. *And now he isn't even nearly in a position whereby he could command the army without a lot of help; and Polyperchon is the wrong man to advise him and there are no other officers who could step up to the task.* With a sickening realisation as to what it may come to, Artonis took Barsine's arm and led her through the men as they formed column again. 'We need a new general.'

'Yes, we do,' Barsine said, her voice one of regret. 'We've made a huge error of judgement.'

'No, Barsine, he was our sole option because of his army; now we've got the men, but we don't have the right man leading them. However, for the moment he will serve his purpose, provided he can get us to his homeland safely. Once we're there we'll still need him to attract more troops to our numbers, but when we move into Macedon – which we know now won't be a surprise – will we need him then? Or will that be the time to bring another general forward?'

Barsine thought for a moment. 'Who?'

'I don't know, but I do know someone who could help us; someone who owes us for a great wrong done to our family.'

Barsine's eyes widened. 'Ptolemy?'

'Yes, we ruled him out before because he had no presence in Greece; but now we have an army, he may be able to provide us with a general.'

'Why stop at just a general? He owes us enough for Artakama's death to send a force to keep Ptolemaios busy whilst his general leads us into Macedon. He may have a peace treaty with Antigonos but he hasn't got one with his rebellious nephew.'

A smile of comprehension spread by degrees across Artonis' face; she squeezed her sister's arm. 'Yes, that would do it.'

'I'll write to him immediately.'

'No, Sister; it needs more than a letter. I shall leave at once.'

And thus did Artonis set out upon a journey she had never expected to make before the time came for her to claim her vengeance on the man responsible for Artakama's death; it was not as a bringer of death she travelled but, rather, as a supplicant. South, she rode at speed, escorted by the companions Herakles had hunted with, and so taking the temptation to neglect his duties away from the future king.

Riding to the limits of their mounts' endurance, they reached the Gulf of Corinth in three days. Dressed as travellers, they attracted no attention as they hired a ferryman in Naupactus to take them and their horses across the water. Once back on the northern coast of the Peloponnese they covered the sixty leagues to Sykion along the rough coastal road in a little over two days to find Cratesipolis, or Penelope, had left a few days before for Corinth. It was in that city they caught up with her six days after the scheme had come to Artonis' mind and it was with much amusement that Penelope heard Artonis' plan.

'I told you my father-in-law was worse than a man short; but did you listen? No, because you weren't looking at him but at his army, like some sailor who takes no notice of a whore's face because he's only interested in what's between her legs. And now you see just how old he is and how his pedantry gets worse with age. No, Artonis, you've found out the hard way that Polyperchon should have been put out to stud a while ago, although I doubt he'd be any good at that as he'd spend more time making sure the mares could parade in straight lines and their twats were in pristine condition, rather than doing something constructive with them; not that I think he could get it up any more. I would imagine it's been a while since he had any thoughts in that direction unless he gets an order, checked and cross-checked, to consider the act. No, Artonis, you do need my help; I'm just surprised it's taken you this long to see through the old phoney. What do you want from me – a ship, I assume?'

'Yes, along with gold, a physician and a female slave.'

'I'm sure that can all be arranged; however, I think it would be better if you sailed from Corinth's western port and go back through the Gulf and then down the west coast of the Peloponnese and then on to Crete and from there cross to Cyrenaica, approaching Egypt from the west.'

'Why, surely it's a more hazardous crossing?'

'It is; but for two reasons it would be better. Firstly, you'll avoid Antigonos' fleets; I don't suppose he'll be too kind to you should you fall into his hands. And secondly, I've heard that Agathocles, the Tyrant of Syracuse, has recently escaped from the Carthaginian siege of his city and has landed in Africa with an army, intent on taking the war to Carthage; with Demetrios away in the east and Antigonos concerned with Ptolemaios and Phoinix in the north, there's a fair chance you'll find Ptolemy looking to his western defences should Agathocles' war spread. He's been building three new ports on the west coast of Cyrenaica to counter the threat from Syracuse; I'd say the expense of the venture has been justified by the Tyrant's recent actions.'

And so, taking Penelope's advice, Artonis sailed west and south; at least, the ship sailed west and south as Artonis lay, wracked by the curse of sea sickness to the point of delirium whilst the physician provided by Penelope watched over her and the slave-girl sponged her face, cleaned up the vomit and helped her on the rare occasions she had to relieve herself in a bucket.

For four days did she suffer in the daylight hours, nights being spent ashore, before striking out for the crossing to Crete, hoved-to in darkened waters overnight. The relief of one night ashore in Crete was soon forgotten before the mountainous island dropped below the horizon, with the three full days and two nights for the crossing to Africa a blur of bile-retching distress.

She was barely conscious when stretchered off the ship at Apollonia, Cyrene's port below the city towering on the hill above, and she was still oblivious to her surroundings as she was taken back aboard the vessel on the news, from Ophellas, the governor of the province, that Ptolemy was indeed in Cyrenaica but on the west coast inspecting the new port of Berenice. It was in a sweat-soaked delirium that she hauled herself from her cabin upon arrival in the new port; it was two days before she could present herself to the man she held responsible for her sister's death.

'I must say, I am surprised to see you, Artonis,' Ptolemy said, looking at her with an amused twinkle in his eye as she was brought before him on his great Five, moored in Berenice's new harbour of gleaming stone and freshly treated wood as yet undamaged by the wind, rain and brine. 'I had heard you'd threatened all sorts of violence towards me for what happened to Artakama; you haven't got a knife concealed in your skirts, or grains of poison under the stones of one of your rings, have you?'

Artonis did not trust herself to play along with the banter. 'I've come for your help, Ptolemy.'

'Help?' Ptolemy was genuinely bemused. 'Why should I help you? Archias the Exile-Hunter told me in exact detail what you planned for me, and it wasn't at all nice. I'm not responsible for Artakama's death; it's whoever gave away the position of the fleet you should be applying your honed blade to, not me.'

'You should never have sent her away in the first place,' Artonis all but shouted, regretting the outburst before it was even complete. *Now I'll never bend him to my will.*

'I sent her away because I have two wives and a mistress and, therefore, a precarious domestic situation which I didn't need exacerbated by the addition of yet another wife. But I'm not here to justify myself to you. What do you want?'

Artonis steeled herself. 'I want to borrow one of your generals.'

Ptolemy leaned forward in his seat, straining to see whether he had heard correctly. 'You want to borrow what?'

'One of your generals; preferably one who can perform better than Polyperchon.'

'Ah, of course.' He turned to a group of officers awaiting the conclusion of the interview standing on the deck behind him. 'Did you hear that, gentlemen? This lady wishes to borrow one of you. Andronicus, do you think you would make a better general than Polyperchon?'

At the front of the group, a tall and broad officer, black-bearded and dark-eyed, grimaced an attempt at a smile. 'I might be better at tactics, lord, but there is no way that I could compete with his pedantry.'

Amusement at his observation was shared by all his companions and Ptolemy, who turned his attention back to Artonis. 'I heard you were trying to put Herakles on the throne of Macedon. Kleopatra wrote me a very nice letter asking if I would help; I declined of course as I couldn't see what was in it for me other than annoying Kassandros. I was most amused when I heard that the redoubtable Polyperchon had taken up the bastard's mantle. I remember Thais saying to me: "that's how to guarantee not getting the thing done", or words to that effect. I gather she was correct in her assessment?'

'Yes; he has no imagination and—'

'Spends most of his time inspecting the troops?' Ptolemy grinned. 'I'm sorry, finishing people's sentences for them was a habit of your late husband; it irritated everyone he talked to. I do apologise, it won't happen again.'

Artonis felt a pang within her at the mention of Eumenes' foible; he claimed to do it because he found the Macedonian military mind to be a lumbering thing and she had loved him for it. 'Yes, his inspections are excruciating. But the point is that we, Barsine and I, don't see how such a relic can defeat Kassandros now that he has been made aware of our coming.'

'You should have thought about that before you asked him.'

'Who else could we have turned to?'

'Who else indeed? Ptolemaios might have been an interesting choice.'

'We thought that, as Antigonos' nephew, he was a part of the peace treaty with Kassandros.'

'As well as Lysimachus and me; but since when has a peace treaty ever been an obstacle to making war? Ptolemaios has been very unhappy about the way Antigonos has been promoting Demetrios and Philippos at the expense of himself and the other two nephews; in fact, they all have, Telesphorus' little rebellion being a case in point.'

Artonis lowered her eyes. 'Well, we didn't approach him and now we regret it; he informed Kassandros and Thessalonike of our planned invasion; we were going to Macedon through Aetolia and then coming in from the west.'

'Sensible.' Ptolemy frowned, thinking. 'Ptolemaios wrote to Kassandros and Thessalonike?'

'Yes; we saw the significance of that too. At least, Barsine and I did; it completely passed Polyperchon by.'

Ptolemy laughed. 'I'm sure it did. So Ptolemaios is breaking from Antigonos and plans to ally himself with Macedon? Interesting.'

'Yes, and that's the other thing we would ask of you—'

'Is to send a fleet to Greece to distract Ptolemaios.' Ptolemy held up his hand. 'I'm sorry; I promised I wouldn't do that again.'

'That's all right; it's always good to be reminded of Eumenes. But, yes, you're right. We need him distracted.'

'Whilst you put Herakles on the throne? Hmmm.' Ptolemy's eyes narrowed as he calculated; he stood, a decision made. 'Do you know what, Artonis? You can have Andronicus.' He turned to the general. 'I think your strained relationship with Ophellas could do with a break, don't you, Andronicus?'

Andronicus' eyes gave nothing away.

'Good then, that's settled,' Ptolemy said, beaming and turning back to Artonis. 'I'm minded to do this for you because now I can see what I could get out of it: Demetrios has been in Babylonia for long enough and I've had the time to secure the defences of Cyrenaica; I think the peace treaty has served its purpose and it's time I started to play with my fleet again. An attack on Caria and an attempt to take Halicarnassus followed by a probe into Euboea will help you, me and Seleukos. You, because it will distract Ptolemaios; me, because it will expose Ptolemaios as a traitor to Antigonos; and Seleukos, because, that being the case, Antigonos will have no choice but to recall Demetrios from Babylonia.'

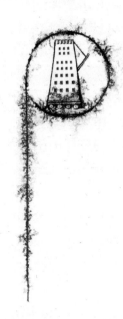

DEMETRIOS.
THE BESIEGER.

T HERE HAD BEEN no one there, no one in the city except the priests of Bel Marduk. Babylon had been evacuated. Granted, the garrisons in the Main Citadel beyond the Ishtar Gate and the Southern Citadel within the city walls remained but they had locked themselves in. And yes, his men had come across the occasional grey-beard, cripple or one of the gibbering, left behind out of practicality, but the rest of the population had vanished. There had been no sighting of them in the surrounding countryside despite extensive scouting, and no news of their passing as all the farms and homesteads had been abandoned too, their livestock taken and crops harvested or destroyed. Demetrios had simply walked into Babylon unopposed and taken control of it all bar the two citadels whose defenders – between three and four thousand in each, Demetrios soon learned through a couple of deserters – had been intent upon resisting him. But that had been the least of his concerns as, without a population, the city was no more than an empty shell of no value, for what was it now other than a collection of deserted buildings populated by stray cats and dogs and human dregs? It was strategically of little importance now, as with no wealth emanating from it, it became just another piece of land no different from any other area of scrub in this semi-barren environment. Its only value was as a billet for his army and Demetrios had made full use of the facilities and had replanted the fields on either side of the river. But before his agricultural endeavours came to fruition, his army of fifteen thousand infantry and four thousand cavalry had to be provisioned by foraging parties ranging far and wide.

And then the guerrilla raids had started, striking at the foragers as well as Demetrios' lines of communication back to the west along the Euphrates, burning vessels sailing south downriver with vital supplies. At first, they had been a mere annoyance but gradually they had become a real threat to the survival of the army and a drain upon its morale. It was not long before he discovered the effort was being led not by Seleukos himself, due to his continued absence out in the east, but by Patrokles, Seleukos' loyal governor of Babylon. It was, therefore, with a growing sense of urgency that Demetrios hunted the shadows doing such damage to his army; but most of all he wanted Patrokles.

'What do you mean you've lost his trail?' Demetrios had to rein himself back from shouting at his cousin as Telesphorus reported to him at his headquarters in the summer palace.

Ten years Demetrios' senior and with the same luxuriant head of raven curls, Telesphorus did not like his kinsman's tone. 'I mean that because of his excellent scouting, Patrokles had advanced warning of our coming and so crossed the Euphrates, heading west out into the desert where he can survive due to his Nabatean friends showing him the location of their wells and cisterns. We can't follow him there, even though it's winter; we lose too many men every time we venture into the desert.'

'Have you left a force to watch for when he emerges and tries to cross the river again?'

'Of course I have; don't treat me as if I were an idiot!'

Demetrios squared up to his cousin. 'You'll not talk to me like that, Telesphorus. One word from me, questioning your loyalty to my father, and you'd be a dead man after what you did in Greece.'

'What I did in Greece? No. My rebellion was caused by you, little cousin; by you managing to lose to Ptolemy at Gaza, thus proving what I'd always contended since you came of age: Antigonos had bypassed me – and Ptolemaios and Dioscurides, for that matter – and over-promoted you. Capturing a few thousand drunks in a night attack doesn't make you a competent general, Demetrios, and I can see now, from the mess we're in, I really do have a point.'

'What do you mean?'

'You not being able to see it adds weight to my argument. Why are we still stuck here in Babylon with winter almost past, when your orders were to deal with Seleukos who remains on the far side of the Zagros Mountains fighting Nikanor? Surely our nineteen thousand men would be better joining with Nikanor and helping to defeat Seleukos in the field, not running around chasing groups of well-organised guerrillas who can do far more damage to us than we ever could to them because they know the land and can disappear? Why is that, Demetrios, why?'

Demetrios slammed a hand, palm down, onto a table. 'Because my father told me to take Babylon and there still remain two large garrisons in the citadels and I intend to remove them.'

'Leave them there. What harm can they do locked up in their fortresses, one of which is outside the main city walls?'

'They're not confined to their fortresses; as you well know, they've managed to burn down the last four siege towers we've made just as they were ready to go into action.'

'If we're not here, they can burn whatever they like.'

'If we're not here, they can retake the city, and if we were to leave a garrison to prevent that happening, it would need to be in the region of seven or eight thousand men, nearly half the army. We would never get anywhere near joining with Nikanor with eleven or twelve thousand. Seleukos would hear of our movements and cut us to pieces out in the open.'

'Then let them have the city; what is Babylon worth with no one living here? We can retake it once we've dealt with Seleukos.'

'I'll not lose Babylon, now that I've taken it.'

'You walked in, Demetrios, you didn't take it. You've never really taken anything except your father's patronage and lessons in arrogance; oh, and, er, seven hundred camels from the Nabateans. No, sorry, they were a present, weren't they?' Telesphorus grabbed Demetrios' wrist as he drew his knife, clamping it in a grip of iron. 'It hurts, the truth, doesn't it?'

Demetrios strained against his cousin, his face coming close, their noses almost touching. 'I should kill you!'

'No, you shouldn't; you should take my advice.'

He's right, the bastard. I've let matters slide here and lost the focus on what I was really supposed to do. I'm letting my father down – again. He strained for another couple of moments and then relaxed. 'I can't lose Babylon.'

'So, basically, we're not using nineteen thousand troops to their full advantage because we're afraid of six or seven thousand men retaking a city with no inhabitants should we go to do what we really came for? You see, Demetrios, this is the mess we're in and you've not got the experience to get us out of it.'

'And you have?' Demetrios regretted the question as soon as it was out.

'That's not what's in question; it's not about what I'm going to do. Your father placed you in command so the question is: what are *you* going to do?'

Demetrios clenched his right fist around the dagger's hilt, his arm muscles tensing, but refrained from striking his cousin as he knew he was right. *That's exactly my problem: I can't see a way around it.* He sheathed his blade, breathing deep to calm himself, and walked to the open window to look out over the hunting grounds of rolling parkland that once belonged to the kings and then satraps of Babylon and were now Macedon's. 'If we can take one of the citadels when the new siege towers are ready then we would only need to leave four thousand men here; with fifteen thousand we'd have a good chance of joining with Nikanor and defeating Seleukos. That would do it.'

'It would.'

'And we need to do it quickly.'

'Then what are we doing standing here admiring the view?'

Gods, this man is annoying; but mainly because he's right.

With a renewed sense of urgency, Demetrios concentrated all his efforts on the Southern Citadel, leaving just a holding force at the Main Citadel to prevent a sortie. To avoid them sharing the same fate as the first four attempts, he had the two new siege towers built far away from the citadel close to the Ziggurat. Day and night they were worked upon, taking the wood from the abandoned houses all through the central quarter of the city, leaving them open to the elements. Up the Processional Way under the cover of darkness, towards the walls of their target, they were rolled upon completion, ready for the assault that would begin in the small hours of the morning.

'Seleukos took the Main Citadel with under a thousand men the first time he came to the city,' Demetrios said to Archelaos who would command the second tower, the first being under Demetrios' care. 'If we can't take the smaller Southern Citadel with four times that number then... well.' *Then perhaps Telesphorus is right and my father has over-promoted me; I have no choice but to prove his faith in me justified and show Telesphorus my worth is more than his – or at least his equal.*

Through the pre-dawn air came the regular pace of thousands of feet making double time, as the assault troops – Macedonians for Demetrios' tower, and Greek merce-naries for the other – made their way along the Processional Way to form up, ready to enter the great beasts of siege warfare, rising to the height of eight men, as they were thrust up against the citadel's eastern wall. Behind them came the archers who would keep a withering hail of arrows strafing the battlements as the towers were positioned and their human cargo delivered.

In final preparation, water was sprayed onto the leather lining of the front- and side-facing walls, soaking them to act as a dampener for the fire that would surely be hurled at it.

With a nod of his head and a clap on the shoulder, Demetrios wished his fellow commander good luck – they would both be first to race across the bridges as they slammed down onto the parapet. He joined Telesphorus waiting at the head of the Macedonians. 'On the wall, I'll take the left and you go right to link up with Archelaos.'

'Good luck, Cousin.'

Demetrios heard no sarcasm in Telesphorus' tone nor saw it in his eyes. 'You too, Cousin.' Raising his arm, Demetrios punched the air and his signaller raised his horn to his lips; thrice he blew the same high-pitched note. Archers readied their bows. Torches flared, lighting up the gloom so the path the towers would navigate for the final fifty paces of their journey was visible, surprise being no longer an issue. With a huge groan of exertion, the men pushing the wooden behemoths bent their backs to the task; the wooden wheels rolled forward at a slow but inexorable pace. With a roar of command, five hundred archers released, aiming at the top of the parapet; but none had dared to poke a head over to look down for all knew exactly what would occur should they do so. Besides, there was nothing the defenders could do at this range to slow the great engines rolling towards them; that would come later. Instead, they contented themselves with letting their archers shoot blindly up in the air from behind the walls to very little effect.

Now was the time Demetrios had to show his quality, now he would lead his men to victory – a small victory perhaps, but one which would pave the way for a far greater result in that he would regain the east for his father and with it he would earn what he now realised he lacked: the respect of the older members of his family. And so, he looked back at the men following him, lined up four abreast, ready to pound up the flights of wooden steps within the towers as they neared their destination, and then to surge across the bridge to overwhelm the defence upon the wall. Closer did the towers come, all the time gaining speed as momentum grew and all the time did the archers keep up their storm of missiles, keeping the defenders down. Again, he raised his arm in the air, this time with a spear clamped in his fist. His heart raced as he shouted: 'With me, men of Macedon. With me!'

With less than ten paces to go before the wall, Demetrios raced forward, leaping up into the tower and then taking the first flight of steps two at a time, his followers pounding after him, their footsteps echoing around the wooden chamber encasing them, growing more thunderous the higher they went as scores more men surged up behind them. On and up, Demetrios raced, his legs working, muscles straining as he turned from one flight onto the next, the tower shaking with the combined rumble of its wheels and the din of so many men coursing within it.

Then a new sound joined the cacophony of assault: irregular thumps now beat against the leather-clad front and side faces of the tower. *Fire arrows, we must be close if their archers are risking raising their heads above the parapet.* As the thought went through his mind, Demetrios arrived at the holding floor at the summit of the stairs; ahead was the ramp, hauled horizontal, its four-man crew standing ready by two pulleys to lower it upon his command. To a narrow slit in the wood, he placed his eye; the wall was less than five paces away, its length now filled with defenders, heavy infantry, crouching, their round shields, bristling with shafts, interlocked to protect the archers behind them as they thumped hails of burning missiles into the two tapered towers. As he looked, the tower halted whilst behind him the holding floor filled and the reverberation of hundreds of footsteps died as the stairs below became crowded.

All was set. To wait was to hand the enemy more time to fire the towers.

He glanced at Telesphorus, who grinned a mixture of exaltation and terror. 'Now!' Demetrios shouted to the bridge-crew.

Restraining bolts were pulled from the pulleys and, with a nod between them, the crew kicked at the ramp, dislodging it from the vertical so that gravity took over. Down it swung, ropes running swift through the pulleys. Demetrios' foot was on it an instant before it crashed onto the parapet; his shield raised before him, his spear poised, he leaped across the bridge even as it still shook from the impact, his men in his wake, their footsteps vibrating the wood. Stasis bringing instant death, Demetrios hurled himself at the nearest defender, his feet jumping high as his spear thrust low, an inchoate battle-cry rising in his gorge, his cloak billowing out behind; scraping over the rim of the man's shield, the spear-tip cracked into his teeth and then on down his throat; blood exploded either side of the haft, sloping over Demetrios' arm as he followed through the thrust, bursting the tip out through the back of his victim's neck as he flopped back, spinal cord severed, collapsing onto stone. Landing with one foot on the corpse's chest, Demetrios heaved his weapon loose as support pressed to either shoulder, shields to the fore, spears thrusting overarm and the weight of men behind pushed them on. A line of shields, four abreast, Demetrios and his companions formed, the honed blades of their spears flashing above, jabbing at all exposed flesh; they pressed forward, clearing the way as the ferocity of their assault drove all before them. With the sure knowledge that his military reputation rested upon success out here in the east, Demetrios did not hold back, letting violence pour from him, merciless and implacable. Never again was he going to stand accused of being over-promoted; he would repay his father's faith in him, even if it was based on nepotism. He would take the Southern Citadel, seal off the Main Citadel beyond the gates with a small garrison and then take the war east to Seleukos and, with Nikanor's army, crush the man who would steal the east from his family.

With gore now spattering both arms and legs as he waded through freshly reaped dead, Demetrios' resolve did not falter; none could stand against him such was the extremity of his savagery. Not for one moment did Demetrios pause for breath, never did he hesitate in striking a blow and each blow struck was at the utmost of his strength and brutality. With his comrades to either side doing little more than deflecting slashes and stabs aimed at him, Demetrios forced his way to the first set of stone steps leading down into the citadel's parade ground. With a sharp crack of his shield he thrust a defender standing at its head back into the man below him, dislodging both to tumble onto unforgiving stone. Down a step did he advance and then another, his shield raised as his comrades, just to his rear, held theirs to either side and over him, protecting him from flicking arrows, hissing in through the gloom. Another three steps of descent and still none dared to come against him; two more steps and still the defenders quavered. Like a god he felt, all-powerful and unassailable. Still shafts thumped into his shield and those of his comrades but they were just long-range shots; no one dared approach for a closer encounter.

'Toe to toe!' he shouted, shaking his spear at the men backing away from him. 'Toe to toe!'

The strafing lessened as more and more assault troops from the second tower, now overwhelmed by fire arrows and ablaze, stood on the walls looking down into the parade ground and others descended further sets of steps, some with violence, others, like Demetrios, unopposed. The defenders looked up at the weight of men now standing over them and groaned as they had nowhere to retreat to.

'Toe to toe!' Demetrios shouted again but still did the opposition back off, their eyes shifting from him to one another to gauge whether any of their number wished to take on this blood-spattered vision risen from the depths of Hades.

The combat on other sets of steps faded as Demetrios neared the foot of his, his opponents backing away at his pace. Silence fell over the parade ground, the many faces of the defenders illumined by the flickering bronze light of the burning tower.

'Toe to toe!' Demetrios bellowed, his voice cracking with the strain, as he stepped onto the flagstone of the parade ground. As his words echoed around the wall and then died, the first clink of metal hitting stone replaced them; and then another and another until it became a deluge of iron discarded. And as they threw their weapons down so did they shed their shields and kneel in submission, heads bowed.

Disappointment and frustration coursed within Demetrios for still he wished to slice the life from his foes; he threw his spear away in disgust and lashed out with a boot at the nearest man, the man who had refused his challenge on the steps, sending him sprawling onto his back. 'Maggots,' he growled and then repeated himself at full bellow: 'Maggots!'

Demetrios looked around. 'Archelaos!'

'I'm here, lord.' His second-in-command appeared from the other side of the parade ground, shoving kneeling prisoners aside as he made his way through the crowd; Telesphorus followed.

Demetrios barely registered the blood covering Archelaos' face and arms, his whole body in fact. 'Round them up and kill any who would rather not sign up with me.'

'Many of us would gladly sign with you again, lord,' came a voice from the crowd.

Demetrios turned in the direction of the words studying the faces slowly becoming clearer as the dawn sun rose in the east. 'Who said that?'

A veteran of many winters stood, his speckled beard full on his face in the manner of Alexander's father, Philip, and his own father, Antigonos. 'I did, lord. Straton is my name. I served your father and then I served you. At least a quarter of the lads here did the same.'

It was then that Demetrios registered that most men had the full beard so prevalent before Alexander made shaving fashionable. *Most of them are above fifty; many in their sixties.* 'You served me? Where?'

'Gaza, lord. We were among the seven thousand captured by Ptolemy.'

'What are you doing here then?'

'Ptolemy sent reinforcements to Seleukos across the desert, five thousand in all, including a thousand of us older sweats he captured at Gaza.'

Ptolemy sent his older, less trustworthy troops as a gift to Seleukos and Seleukos used them for garrison work, thus freeing up better-quality men for the field; that makes complete sense. I would have done the same. 'And you would fight for me again, despite what happened at Gaza?'

'We would, lord; and for your father.'

This sentiment was endorsed by a growl of agreement and much nodding of heads, many of which remained bowed.

'If you knew it was me coming over the walls, why did you resist me? Indeed, why didn't you just open your gates months ago when I first arrived?'

Straton could no longer meet Demetrios' eyes. 'Seleukos made us swear that we would resist until you had made it onto the walls; with our blood we swore and on the lives of our women and children. What man would break that oath?'

None, Demetrios admitted to himself and then smiled. *Except, perhaps my father.* 'Well, you can hold your oaths fulfilled and can rejoin me with a clear conscience. See to it, Archelaos.' Suddenly exhausted, Demetrios turned away, wishing only to drink a jug of wine and then lie down.

'That was an impressive display, Demetrios,' Telesphorus said, coming up behind him. 'I must have hit a raw nerve to have made you so reckless in wanting to take on a whole garrison single-handed. Daddy would be proud of you.'

'Fuck off, Telesphorus.' Demetrios swung around to face his cousin. 'I did what every good general does: lead from the front and force victory.'

'Exactly what I would have done; but I'd have done it a couple of months ago. Still, better late than never. The question now is: how quickly will you link up with Nikanor now spring is upon us?'

And so, it was with an urgency brought on by a desire to prove to himself, as much as to Telesphorus and his father, that he was worthy of independent command through ability and not just through blood, that Demetrios readied his army for the forthcoming campaign. Strong patrols were sent out in all directions. Ships cruised the river in squadrons to keep Patrokles and his guerrilla army at arm's length so the vicinity of Babylon and the river was clear of their threat as the force was provisioned mainly by ships sent further up- or downstream to areas unaffected by the mass exodus from Babylon. As the days grew longer and the weather hotter the Main Citadel was circumvallated and a garrison of four thousand set to guard it. Bit by bit the column was readied for its venture east.

Demetrios stood on a terrace of the summer palace admiring his army, fifteen thousand strong now, forming up to the east of the outer city wall as the pack animals and wagon train assembled ready, waiting for him to give the order to march. It was with a feeling of wellbeing that he reflected on his achievement and his ambition, but it was not without some grudging gratitude to Telesphorus for his harsh but true highlighting of his failures, forcing himself to face up to the fact that the arrogance of youth was not suffi-cient to counter the reality of responsibility.

With this realisation and a new determination to listen to advice more carefully, Demetrios found himself amused by the irony that had he taken the advice of Nearchos and Andronicus before Gaza and withdrawn, forcing Ptolemy into an unsustainable winter campaign, he would never have lost the battle; thus he would not have embarked upon the course that had forced him to confront his false assumptions of his precocious talent and the innate ability of his blood. *Father was right when he said he should thank Ptolemy for whipping me; every young puppy needs at least one good hiding.*

Footsteps coming out onto the terrace drew him away from his revelation of self-knowledge; he turned to see Telesphorus. 'Why aren't you with the army?'

Telesphorus pointed a thumb over his shoulder to a man waiting at the terrace doors. 'That man has just arrived by ship from your father. He came looking for you at the muster and so I thought I'd bring him up to you as I'm curious as to why Antigonos is writing to you.'

Demetrios clicked his fingers and the messenger came forward. 'When did you leave my father?'

'Two days before the last new moon, lord,' the man replied, holding out a scroll case.

'Wait inside as there will probably be a reply.' Demetrios dismissed the man with a wave and then opened the case, tipping its contents into his hand. Unrolling it, he scanned the script, his lips moving with the words; as he read his face lengthened.

'What is it?' Telesphorus asked.

Demetrios handed him the scroll. 'Ptolemy has broken the peace and has launched a fleet from Cyprus and landed in Caria. Phoinix, the satrap of Hellespontine Phrygia, is in rebellion and Father has sent my younger brother Philippos against him.'

Telesphorus looked up in shock. 'But he's barely seventeen.'

'I'm sure Father will send some wise heads with him.'

'But will he listen to them?'

'We shall find out. But the worst news is that Ptolemaios has made a formal alliance with Kassandros and, to make

220

matters worse, our other cousin, Dioscurides, has not been heard of for a month; he and his fleet have completely disappeared. We're ordered back west.' Demetrios looked with regret at the force mustering out on the plain. 'Seleukos is going to have to wait.'

SELEUKOS.
THE BULL-ELEPHANT.

SELEUKOS HAD BEEN enjoying himself. With Antigonos' appointee as satrap of Persis dead at Seleukos' hand, and the satrap of Susiana dead by his own, the previous autumn had been one of steady progress through both satrapies, establishing his power by taking the oaths of the local headmen and petty lords and then wintering in Persepolis – or what there was left of it after Thais had induced a drunk Alexander and his even drunker Companions to burn down most of the royal palace all those years ago. He had been comfortable enough over the cold months; Apama had kept him warm. But what he had most enjoyed was his complete evacuation of the entire population of Babylon and its environs by marching them to Susiana where they had been temporarily settled in camps centred on the main towns of the satrapy in order to spread the burden of such an influx. 'What's the use of an empty city?' he had asked Apama. 'Demetrios will either have to come east to find the people, in which case Patrokles will make his life impossible by harrying his supply lines and killing his foragers, or he stays in Babylon trying to remove my garrisons which are a lot better manned then when I took the city. And besides, it's good practice for the population: they'll have to get used to moving as they won't be staying in Babylon after I've founded Seleucia on the Tigris and transplanted them there.'

Seleukos' amusement had been great when he heard from his frequent reports from the city that Demetrios seemed to be doing a mixture of those two possibilities, neither very well, thereby managing to achieve nothing at all. 'Inexperienced, arrogant pup,' he confided in Apama. 'He should have learned from his whipping at Gaza that decisive action is always better than a half-hearted approach. Had he sent his cavalry forward instead of trying to sneak them around our right flank, he would have discovered the elephant traps before the elephants did and it might have been a different day. Still, hopefully he'll never learn.'

And so, confident that he would not be troubled by his young opponent too early in the season, Seleukos had set out north to Media with the intention of dealing with Nikanor and the ragtag army he had managed to patch together from garrison troops, eastern warlords fighting for the promise of ridiculous sums of money, which would, like as not, never be paid, and the dregs of Media's and Parthia's armies, plus some freebooters on the side.

At least, that is what the army looked to be comprised of as he sat on his stallion surveying the shambolic host attempting to find some sort of order atop the exact same hill, in Paraetacene, that he had stood upon with Antigonos when they managed to catch Eumenes as he tried to cross the plain to the fertile lands of Gabiene. Eumenes had won the day from the same position as Seleukos now occupied. 'The battle went on into the night and ended by mutual consent, but we had suffered by far the greater number of casualties,' Seleukos explained to his eldest son, Antiochus, sitting beside him. 'However, Eumenes' men's desire – mainly the Silver Shields and the Hypaspists – to catch up with their baggage train, which had been sent ahead, meant Antigonos had the honour of camping on the battlefield and Eumenes had to send to him to negotiate for his dead.'

'So Antigonos claimed victory?' Antiochus asked.

'He did, but we all knew it was Eumenes' really. Antigonos never likes to talk about that battle as he knows Eumenes bested him.' He looked down at his fourteen-year-old son. 'I fought on the wrong side that day, Antiochus. I went to parley with Eumenes on Antigonos' behalf and the sly little Greek offered me a chance to come over to him; I said no because I couldn't imagine taking orders from a Greek, and a not very tall Greek at that. It was a mistake.'

'What makes you say that, Father?'

Seleukos looked back up the hill and contemplated the army now beginning its descent. 'Had I joined Eumenes and come over to him during the battle I think it would have made the difference and Antigonos would have been routed. That being the case, Eumenes would have been in a far stronger position at the battle of Gabiene the following year and Peucestas would not have felt the need to play both sides and eventually take his men from the field thereby guaranteeing the resinated cyclops his victory. Eumenes would have won instead and we wouldn't be here now; we'd still be back in Babylon as loyal subjects to whichever of the kings Eumenes decided to place on the throne. All in all, a far better state of affairs.'

'But you would just be one satrap out of many, Father,' Antiochus pointed out. 'However, if you win this battle you'll control Babylonia, Susiana, Persis and Media; that's a kingdom.'

'Almost, Son, almost. But first we've got to win it and the way Nikanor's coming down that hill will make it reasonably simple.'

'Why is he coming down the hill in the first place?'

'He wants to fight and he knows I'm not stupid enough to come up to him, and, besides, he thinks the terrain on the plain is better suited to his heavy cavalry and horse-archers, of which, by the looks of it, he has plenty. But, thanks to Ptolemy sending those reinforcements, our phalanx outnumbers his by almost four thousand. I'll play to that strength and try to counteract his superior cavalry numbers.' Seleukos studied the approaching host in silence for a few moments before coming to a decision and grunting with satisfaction. 'Come, Son, it's time we took our places. And remember, you stay at the rear of my Companions; I want you to taste the charge but not the combat; soon you'll be ready, but not just yet.'

The boy was about to protest, then, seeing the steel in his father's eyes, turned his horse away.

Seleukos watched his son go and then glanced back at the oncoming army before ordering his signaller to call 'officers assemble'; he was ready to relay a few adjustments to his battle orders to the men in whom he would place his trust.

There was, in truth, not much Seleukos needed to adjust: he had drawn up his army with a firm plan in mind, for he knew this ground well. He had raced to reach it; moreover, he had timed his arrival so it would have looked to Nikanor as if he had tried but failed to climb the hill and face him on the high ground rather than cede the advantage of the slope to his opponent. This had been his plan ever since his spies had informed him of Nikanor's intention to come south, early in the year, from Ecbatana, Media's capital, keeping to the east of the Zagros Mountains, and take the fight into Persis where, he hoped, the local warlords would support him. Seleukos had rushed north at the news and had allowed his scouts to be seen by the enemy, thus drawing Nikanor towards him as a fish on a hook; now he stood in the very place he had intended to.

Although he had a little over half the fifty thousand troops Eumenes had commanded five years previously, he planned to do roughly the same: occupying the low hills to his left with light infantry, mainly archers; the heavy cavalry, with the Sogdian horse-archers for support – on the left rather than the right as Nikanor would expect – would then link them with the phalanx in the centre with the peltasts on its left flank and the light infantry screening its frontage. His light cavalry including the rest of his horse-archers he had placed on the extreme right. *I'll not make Eumenes' mistake of being unable to counter Antigonos' eastern cavalry. I'll win this in the centre, just as he did, if I can keep my flanks secure. But then I'll do what Eumenes failed to do in order to secure complete victory. Who would have thought I would learn a lesson in tactics from the sly little Greek?*

And so Seleukos rode back to inspect his troops lined up a thousand paces on from the foot of the hill so that any advantage of momentum would have been swallowed by the march across the dusty, rough ground of the plain. As his officers reported their readiness to him, and received any final instructions, astride his stallion at the head of his Companion Cavalry and Azanes' Sogdians, on the left flank of the phalanx, Seleukos watched the enemy host move out onto the flatter ground. Confidence grew within him, for, although the forces were of roughly equal size – he with more infantry, Nikanor with superior horse – his army, as his officers were showing, was ready to act as a unit whereas Nikanor's was clearly a collection of glory-hunting chieftains supporting a phalanx that was having trouble keeping a straight frontage. He shook his head at the shambolic display. *They're more use to me alive than dead.* A decision made, he turned to Azanes. 'Get me a branch of truce; I'm going to see if we can stop this and achieve my objective without being obliged to massacre a lot of decent Macedonian lads and useful Greek mercenaries.'

With the branch of truce held high, Seleukos rode forward with Azanes on his shaggy pony and half a dozen of his shaggier men, to within a couple of hundred paces of the hill. Down the eastern army came, the light cavalry on either flank leading, steadying their mounts, pulling back on the reins to prevent them from picking up too much momentum and tangling their legs. Behind them on the right flank came their heavy comrades from Media and Parthia, men born to the saddle, armed with both bows and javelins. And then in the centre, falling behind as they struggled with the gradient, came the block of heavy infantry, both Greek and Macedonian, screened by light troops.

'If we were to attack as they reach the bottom, they would be so disorganised we'd break them with one charge,' Azanes observed, watching the frontage of the phalanx undulate as the pace of each man varied with the changing terrain.

Seleukos slapped a horsefly from the back of his neck. 'It's tempting but I think it would be best if we try to settle this without a massacre. These men are of far more use to me alive and serving in my army than being feasted upon by vultures.'

Azanes shrugged in a way that implied, judging by what he was observing, he was not convinced and then brought his hand up to shield his eyes, looking at the enemy's right. 'Sogdians!'

Seleukos followed his gaze: leading the cavalry down were troops dressed just like Azanes with trousers, a quilted jacket and brimless leather caps with long flaps, tied under the chin or left loose, pulled down over a mane of wild hair. 'Do you know them?'

'Maybe. I'll see when they come closer.'

They're all related out in the east. Seleukos offered a quiet prayer to Ares, the god of war, that it would be so. The descent continued and the first units made it onto level ground, advancing another hundred paces before halting and forming up in an effort to get a semblance of order into their ranks. From their midst came a small party, in similar number to Seleukos' parley escort, made up of easterners with a Macedonian in their midst. *So Nikanor is willing to talk; that, at least, is something.*

With twenty paces between the two groups, Nikanor pulled his horse up. 'Do you wish to surrender, Seleukos?' he asked, amused at his own wit; a big man, almost equal in height to Seleukos if not in muscle, he was twice his age, a contemporary of Antigonos and thus was bearded in the older fashion.

Seleukos dismissed the suggestion with a curt wave. 'I've come to see if we can avoid bloodshed; there is no need for this confrontation. I hold the east and Antigonos will not get it back from me.'

'I hear Demetrios has Babylon.'

'He has the empty buildings, but I have the people. The buildings are meaningless on their own.'

'He'll come east to get the people.'

'He doesn't have the men: he's only brought nineteen thousand with him and he would have to leave at least a third of them in Babylon to counter the two garrisons I've left there. Even if he manages to defeat one of them, he still couldn't come against me with more than fifteen thousand; ten thousand less than I can muster. So, what's it to be, Nikanor: do we fight or will you see sense and realise that I am the new power in the east?'

'What's in it for me?'

'Swear an oath of allegiance to me and you keep your satrapy.'

'I keep it if I win today.'

'But you won't, Nikanor; not against me with an army which is willing to fight for my cause because they know I hold the best hope for uniting the east in peace.'

Nikanor laughed. 'My army knows Antigonos is the best hope for uniting the *entire empire* in peace, Seleukos. No, you need to do better than that. I'll not waste time bandying words with you; if you're not thinking of surrendering then we've nothing more to say to each other.' With that he turned his horse and accelerated away, back to his army as it continued to form line.

'Fool!' Seleukos shouted after him but the word was lost under the bellows of the officers and the blare of countless horns. 'Well, that was a waste of time.'

'It wasn't, lord,' Azanes said, 'it was very productive.'

Seleukos turned to the Sogdian. 'You knew one of his escort?'

'I did; a cousin.'

'Naturally. And?'

'And he will join us.'

'What makes you think so? You didn't utter a word.'

'We spoke with our eyes and small movements of the head and hands. I trust him.'

Seleukos looked at the parley party as they rejoined the army and then turned his horse away. 'Let's hope that is so.'

And it was with that hope Seleukos ordered the immediate advance of his army before the enemy had had time to properly deploy for, having chosen to parley rather than strike when Nikanor was at his most vulnerable, there was no sense in allowing him more of a chance than he already had.

To the sound of massed horns, the phalanx, almost ten thousand strong, rumbled forward, the screening light infantry out beyond it; peltasts protecting the lumbering beast's left flank with Azanes' horse-archers keeping pace next to them as their heavy counterparts – Macedonians, Greeks, Thessalians, Thracians and Persians – came along behind with Seleukos at their head, now clasping a lance in his fist. Out on the right, the rest of the light cavalry began their gyrations, taking care of the infantry's unshielded flank, swirling back and forth, disrupting the enemy, countering and feinting, drawing their more numerous opponents away from their objective.

With his orders already distributed and his officers briefed, the plan being simple – engage the phalanx as soon as possible, pushing them back, refuse the right wing and then he would counter Nikanor's heavy cavalry with his own on the left, looking for an opening to exploit and so complete what Eumenes failed to do – Seleukos felt himself to be in control of the day. It was with a smile that he witnessed the first of the volleys from the infantry archers rise to the overcast sky and then dip and plunge, bringing death to the heavy infantry below. But just as they released, so did the opposition, the air soon filling with fast-moving dark clouds that hissed as they passed. But he took his mind from the phalanx and its screen, for whatever happened in the centre was now beyond his control; he concentrated upon what was occurring directly to his front now that Nikanor's army was on the move. Beyond Azanes' Sogdians – now galloping forward to begin their revolutions – Seleukos could make out the gaudy colours of the banners of the Medes and Parthians. *Break them and their phalanx's unshielded flank is exposed.* He glanced to his right: both phalanxes had opened ranks to allow their light infantry to retire in advance of contact. *Hit them hard, lads; disorder them and we'll do the rest.*

From behind the Medes and Persians, a small stream of light cavalry now came out to chase away the Sogdians, to clear the path for a massed cavalry attack, proving Seleukos' guess correct: Nikanor had expected him to have placed his cavalry on the right and had therefore positioned most of his light cavalry on that wing to negate them; but here Seleukos was with his lancers and allied heavy cavalry facing the Medes and Parthians, the best troops in Nikanor's army. *But not nearly of the same quality as my cavalry.*

Like flocks of starlings the light cavalry swirled, back and forth, releasing as they approached, turning and then falling back, never letting the enemy close enough to do any damage in return and raising dust so that soon clear vision was difficult, sometimes impossible. But sound still carried through the thick air and the battle-cries of massed formations of infantry rang out as the two phalanxes clashed toe to toe.

The clamour of combat now dominated the field as nigh on twenty thousand men struggled together lunging honed iron blades of pike and thrusting-spear at throat and face, stabbing and jabbing as they paced forward. Rear ranks heaved with shoulders on the backs of the men before them, pushing them on to clash shield to shield with the foe. Too close now for spears and pikes, the front ranks resorted to a scrimmage, neither side wishing to cause too much unnecessary death to one-time comrades who, by a quirk of fortune, happened to be ranged against them, as the supporting ranks still jabbed over their shoulders or between their hips. But it was the weight that began to count in Seleukos' men's favour as, to make up a similar frontage to the greater-sized opposition formation, Nikanor had been forced to keep his Greek hoplites in their eight-man-deep formation rather than doubling them to replicate the sixteen-man files of Macedonian pikemen; and it was the Macedonian pikemen who made up the majority of Seleukos' phalanx. And forward they edged, slow at first as they overcame the initial inertia of hitting their opponents' shield wall, but soon, with resounding groans at each concerted heave, foot went before foot and ground was gained. And as they advanced, the second and third ranks concentrated on despatching the wounded, mercy not extending to old comrades who could punch a blade up into the groin as they were straddled.

Ululations rose, coming nearer; Seleukos peered into the dust of the light cavalry skirmish before him, squinting as he tried to make sense of the shadows he saw; with sudden urgency, he raised his lance, signalling to all the officers of his cavalry wing to ready their men for from the cloud came Azanes, pell-mell, at the head of his ululating men.

'Go now, Seleukos! Now! We'll circle around.'

There was no time to evaluate the call, only to know that Azanes had served him and Apama – his compatriot

– loyally for more than five years now. In the confusion of the battlefield the risk of not taking such advice outweighed the danger that his Sogdian commander might have done the reverse of the deal he had claimed to have made with his cousin.

His course was clear, and besides, with his phalanx going forward with their peltasts' support on their flank, the cavalry needed to keep pace so that a tempting gap would not open up. 'Forward! Forward, men of Macedon!' he cried to his Companions to either side of him. 'Forward with me!' With his weapon raised high, Seleukos kicked his stallion into a walk and then accelerated into a trot before lowering his lance and urging the beast into a canter, pulling ahead of his wingmen to either side; they closed together a fraction, creating the sharpened point of a wedge of which he was now the tip. He did not look behind him to check whether the rest of the heavy cavalry units were following his Companions; he trusted their officers and, besides, there was little need as the dust from his men's advance plumed above them obscuring all following. Into the unknown he led his Companions, trusting on the word of an easterner; but never once did he doubt Azanes, never once did he consider turning back as the speed of the charge increased and the thunder of hooves and the roar of his men filled his senses.

It was sudden and heart-stopping, but inevitable, the emergence of the enemy from the dust: one moment eddying cloud, the next a dark line of shadow and then an instant later the solid forms of men intent upon dealing death. Out, as far as he could reach, did Seleukos extend the tip of his lance, leaning along his mount's neck, keeping low as the javelins flashed by, no more than a blur, there one moment and gone the next. But the lack of visibility took away the initial advantage enjoyed by javelin-armed cavalry over those with only the lance: the speed of the reveal had given them time only for one volley before contact – and contact was sudden. Seleukos crashed between two Medes, his lance punching back the first as if he had been jerked from behind by an invisible rope, his high helmet staying motionless in the air for an instant as his head was whipped from under it. Knees scraped along the rumps of the two enemy horses as Seleukos' stallion thrust himself between them, snapping at them and then at the beasts in the second rank, as Seleukos yanked his lance free from his skewered victim.

Back he leaned, clinging onto the reins as his mount reared, its front legs lashing into the muzzle of the beast before it, causing it to shy to its left and crash into its neighbour, half-dislodging its rider. Down Seleukos stabbed his lance, down into the man as he fell from the saddle, to catch him at the base of the neck, his blade slicing through soft flesh, unleashing an explosion of arterial blood shooting up the weapon's haft. Screaming, the man disappeared beneath the trampling hooves of his own mount, his weight snapping Seleukos' lance. With an instinctive flick of the wrist, born of years of training, Seleukos spun the remains of the broken haft to bring the butt-spike to bear, slashing it horizontally, to crack into the arm of a Mede thrusting a sword at his left wingman, shattering it. But such was the force of the blow, the makeshift weapon shot from his grip, the blood coating it giving little or no grip. Cursing and reaching down for his sword, Seleukos felt the heat of a keen blade slicing his upper arm as he drew the weapon from its scabbard; his hand tensed with the sudden searing pain and then opened, losing its grip on the hilt for it to fall into the churning earth below. Disarmed and wounded, Seleukos pulled on the reins with his left hand, rearing up his stallion to act as the only weapon at his disposal. Snorting with bestial battle-joy, the creature thrashed its forelegs to crack down onto the shoulder of a Mede taking his chance with the thrust of his short spear to make a name for himself by killing the enemy commander. With a cry he grabbed his crushed shoulder, his weapon falling away, as his comrade behind him hurled his spear into the unprotected belly of the stallion. With an equine shriek that pierced even the din of battle, the great beast looked to the sky, its tongue lolling from the side of its mouth as its legs stretched up and apart as if appealing to the god of warhorses to reverse his decision and grant it life. But the god was deaf to the power of the stallion's roared plea and the spear lodged firm. With the last remaining strength left within it, the dying animal pushed up with its back legs, hurling itself forward onto the man who had delivered the mortal blow, landing its full weight onto his head, pressing him down to snap his spine as his mount buckled beneath the assault, falling away in a flurry of thrashing limbs and a cacophony of bestial protests. Still clinging to his fading warhorse as it went down, Seleukos pulled his legs up, so he knelt on the beast's rump as it slumped to the ground, hitting it with the full force of its great mass, punching the spear further in, to lie, panting in diminishing breaths, as its eyes rolled white in their sockets.

With a dive, Seleukos got between the legs of the dying horse, allowing the body to provide some sort of protection as his wingmen held their mounts steady, lashing out with their lances at all who came near. Grabbing the shaft of the spear that had done for his stallion, Seleukos pulled at it, causing a final spasm of pain to pass through the animal, its legs kicking Seleukos behind the knees and sending him onto his back, the fall drawing the spear from the belly of the beast. Up, immediately, he came, blood-dripping weapon pointing towards the enemy as still his wingmen stood over him, their mounts stamping as they turned this way and that. But there was no new surge of attackers coming at them in their weakened position; where there should have been a dozen men all competing for the right to strip the general of his armour and high-plumed helm there were but two or three and they were turning and kicking their mounts away; not directly so but, rather, at an angle to Seleukos' left. And away they flew as another sound came to his ear, a sound he had heard just recently: the ululations of the Sogdians. But the noise was coming from the wrong direction to be Azanes and his men, unless they had gone all the way around the cavalry struggle and taken the Medes and Parthians in the rear, from completely the opposite direction. He knew now what to expect. 'These Sogdians are our friends!' he shouted to his wingmen. 'Shout it on so all the lads know. The Sogdians are our friends!'

And the cry went up as the cavalry disengaged from the fleeing Medes and Parthians all along the line. The Sogdians were coming and they were their friends. Through the dust the wild figures on their small and shaggy steppe ponies appeared, galloping fast; chasing their prey, they veered away in the direction the Medes still fled, picking off many of the routers with prodigious bowmanship.

And as he watched them go, the dust cleared to his right and the phalanx became visible with his men surging forward to push their enemies back to the base of the hill. *Now I can trap their phalanx between mine and the hill,*

which is why I came here; but I need to stop a massacre other-
wise all this would've gained me very little. 'Get me a horse!'
he shouted to his wingmen. It took but a few moments to
bring the mount of one of the few of his men to have fallen
in the charge.

Freshly mounted and with orders to follow him sent to the
cavalry units along the line now disengaged due to the rout of
the Medes and Persians, Seleukos urged his new horse
forward, leading his cavalry past the peltasts covering the
phalanx's flank and then skirting around the infantry battle
to climb the hill behind it just as the rear ranks of Nikanor's
phalanx were pushed back onto its base. Higher Seleukos led
his Companions, with the Thracians, Thessalians, Persians
and Greeks following, higher so they looked down upon the
two vast blocks of men still locked in mortal struggle on the
plain below. But a vast block of men with pikes or spears
bristling along its frontage may be confident in receiving a
cavalry charge to the fore, but when already engaged in a
bitter struggle with a more numerous foe and thus unable to
turn and face an enemy forming up to its rear – and upon
higher ground to boot – its confidence vanishes as quickly as
the news of the threat spreads.

Onto their knees the men of the great phalanx of the
eastern army fell, as Seleukos led his cavalry along their
length a hundred paces above them on the hill. Nothing
remained to support them, the Medes and Parthians
having been chased from the field, attacked from behind by
their treacherous erstwhile allies the Sogdians, under the
command of Azanes' cousin; and on the other flank the
light cavalry skirmishing an irrelevance that would not
sway the battle one way or another. No, they saw no alternative for they did not have the honour of Media or Parthia

as a burning issue in their hearts; their concern was life and pay, with preferably enough of the latter to make the former as pleasant as possible, something that being trampled underfoot by a wall of horses charging downhill was not going to facilitate.

The killing stopped and Seleukos breathed deep with relief for he knew most of the men now cowering in surrender had done honour to themselves in resisting the superior force for so long and would become an integral component of his burgeoning army. He urged his mount forward, down the hill, towards the kneeling men, at least eight or nine thousand of them he estimated, now he could see them all together. Halting thirty paces from them, he held up his right hand, palm out. *This is how you should have ended it, Eumenes; you could have got your cavalry behind and then it would have all been over.*

Silence fell.

'You have fought bravely, men of Macedon and Greece, and I offer you your lives. Join me in making peace in the east and you shall receive the same conditions as my men, without prejudice. Join me and we shall bring the satrapies from Babylonia to India together in peace. There will be land for all who want it and garrison duty for those who prefer to remain under arms.'

'He lies!' came a shout from above him. 'He lies, for it's not peace he wants, it's a kingdom.'

Seleukos looked back to see Nikanor at the hill's summit with no more than a hundred cavalry; physically he presented no threat but his words could still wound. *Especially if they're the truth. I should counter them with equal truths.* He pointed to his enemy. 'That man is Antigonos' creature, and even before both the kings were murdered,

Antigonos desired the empire for himself. Many of you were here in this very place when he faced Eumenes; you were aware that Eumenes fought for the kings and Antigonos fought for himself; himself, not the Argead royal house, not for Macedon, but himself. But I will hold the east for that royal house of Macedon, for whoever takes the throne!' *It might even be me.* 'Join me!'

The cheer was unanimous from the defeated troops; their vanquishers joined with them and the front ranks embraced even as they stood among the dead. On the light cavalry wing the skirmishing had ceased as both sides realised who had won the day and the easterners prepared to swop masters or scurry back home. Over the other flank the dust had settled and Seleukos could make out Azanes and his cousin with at least a thousand Sogdians behind them, making their way back towards him with half their number again of captured Medes and Parthians.

'Will they fight for you too, Father?' Antiochus asked, bringing his horse to a halt next to his father.

'I think so,' Seleukos replied, smiling at his son. 'If they want to live, that is.'

'And what about Nikanor?'

Seleukos looked back up the hill; Nikanor was there no more. 'I'll deal with him next year, after I've taken back Babylon and defeated the huge army Antigonos is bound to send against me; but at least I've got the men to do so now, thanks to Ptolemy.' He looked down on the army he had now amassed: including his garrisons at all the major cities and Babylon, he calculated that he could now put upwards of forty thousand men in the field, even after he sent back the five thousand Ptolemy had lent him. Those five thousand had made the difference in that he was able to leave the older and less reliable troops as garrisons and use his best in the field. 'Yes, Antiochus, we've got a lot to be grateful to Ptolemy for. I just hope he doesn't try to extract too high a price for his generosity.'

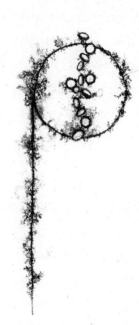

PTOLEMY.
THE BASTARD.

PTOLEMY, TOO, HAD been enjoying himself – although, in truth, rarely did he not. But the opening of the campaigning season had been a triumph to relish. He had left Ophellas, his governor of Cyrenaica, with adequate men to keep his western border safe from any incursion by Agathocles, as the Tyrant of Syracuse had taken his war against Carthage to Africa and had managed to inflict a stunning victory over them in their homeland. Then Ptolemy had taken his fleet north; Phaselis, Xanthos, Kaunos, Iasos and Myndos, as well as scores of smaller towns along the Lycian and Karian coasts, had all fallen to him as he progressed west, coming up from Cyprus. It was not that he had even had to try very hard: none had been taken by storm, nor, indeed, had he laid siege to any. In fact, he did not think he had lost a single man during the whole campaign – apart from a few unfortunates who had received summary justice at the hands of fathers, husbands and brothers of women they had raped; the luckier ones had died of their injuries. He winced at the thought of what the survivors would endure for the rest of their lives, but despite the grotesqueness of the genital mutilations, he had not sought out the perpetrators: it was good his men knew that if they went too far despoiling a town that had given itself up willingly, there would be no sympathy from him. And they all had surrendered without a fight, for Ptolemy had been using his new favourite method of paying the faction within the town not in power – generally the democrats – to open the gates and reward them for their treachery by allowing them to massacre their political opponents – normally the oligarchic faction supported by Antigonos. He had found it a very satisfying way of doing business, having learned it from Kassandros' campaign in the Peloponnese a few years previously. 'And the best thing about it is,' he had explained to his son, Lagus, after he had sent Archias the Exile-Hunter into Phaselis, the first time he attempted the ploy, 'is that you don't have to pay them very much at all as they're so keen on revenge nothing else matters to them. It's perfect, really. I shall congratulate Kassandros on it when I see him – if I do see the pimply little toad; although, in truth, I hope I'm spared that dubious pleasure.'

'I'm sure it's been done before, Father. Many times, I would have thought, with all the wars there have been.'

'I'm sure it has; but my history was never so good. Anyway, it was Kassandros who's recently revived the old custom.'

But that old custom was not going to work in this case, he realised as he and Lagus listened to the Exile-Hunter's report upon return from yet another well-paid foray into one of Antigonos' cities in an attempt to subvert those with a grievance. 'You mean to say the democratic faction met with Antigonos' oligarchic supporters and told them what you'd offered them to open the gates.'

'They did; and we only just escaped with our lives. "When death is near, no one wants to die."'

'Yes, well, we all know that Euripides has a good point there. But it gets us no further. If they have found a common cause – loyalty to their city,' he shook his head at such an outlandish thought for Greeks of opposite political persuasions, 'then I'm just going to have to lay siege to Halicarnassus.'

'Is it worth the effort, Father?' Lagus asked, looking out over the huge port city crowned with the tomb of King Mausolus and a theatre that would have been impressive in itself had it not been dwarfed by such an edifice basking in warm spring sun. 'After all, it took Alexander months to break in.'

Ptolemy waved the statement away. 'That in itself is no argument against the endeavour.' Pausing for thought, he looked around his environs at what had been Alexander's main camp during the siege, twenty-three years before, on the coast to the south-east of the harbour; grunting in agreement with himself, Ptolemy came to a course of action in his head. *Of course, those would be the logical steps to take, and both strands will need time.* 'The real question is: why should I go to all that effort when I know I won't have the time to succeed because my Nabatean friends have told me Demetrios left Babylon a month ago and I'll have to withdraw when he arrives with a fleet?'

'"Prepared for the present, ready for the future,"' Archias quoted.

Lagus looked at his father, clearly nonplussed. 'It makes no sense to me at all.'

'Of course not; that's because you're thinking the taking of Halicarnassus is an end in itself, which clearly it isn't, seeing that, if I were to take it, I wouldn't hold it for long; as, indeed, is true with the rest of the towns that have come over to me. But I've known that all along; this campaign has only ever been a diversion. It would have been nice to have had Halicarnassus betrayed to me if only to have the democratic faction massacre all of Antigonos' supporters; but he'll take the place back soon enough and execute all those who killed his chums. So apart from the population being a few hundred lighter nothing would have changed.'

Lagus was clearly growing impatient with his father's opaqueness. 'Just explain it to us, Father.'

'The objective is to keep Antigonos busy and scatter his forces all over the place. He's got Philippos fighting Phoinix in Hellespontine Phrygia, Demetrios is dashing back from Babylon in order to deal with me, having completed only half his task, whilst Antigonos himself remains in Tyros intriguing with the petty kings on Cyprus and wondering what Ptolemaios is doing with Kassandros and where Dioscurides is and whether or not he has to find a way to bring his nephews to heel. He's already stretched. So what better usage of my time would there be other than to stretch him further by pretending to be interested in taking Halicarnassus and using that time,' Ptolemy turned a benign smile onto Archias, 'to have our exile-hunting friend here persuade Ptolemaios that, if he wants to turn against his uncle, I'm a far better prospect than Kassandros. Whilst you're over there, go to see the fair Cratesipolis and convince her – although I doubt that will be too hard – that, seeing as her father-in-law is still sitting on Macedon's western border doing nothing, for some unaccountable reason, she might well benefit from my protection from the vengeance Kassandros will take once he's neutralised the nonentity and killed Herakles; which, if my arrangement with Andronicus works out and he plays his part, is a foregone conclusion.'

Archias returned Ptolemy's smile, equally benign. 'That sounds to me to be a very expensive couple of months.'

Ptolemy placed a hand on Archias' shoulder and looked at him in mock wonder. 'As expensive as only you and your little Thracian chums can make it; the normal rate, plus a talent in silver for you and one for your charming friends to split, if you're successful.'

Archias placed his hand on Ptolemy's shoulder and gazed back with an equal sense of wonder. 'Your generosity is a source of deep joy to me; of course, it shall be the normal rate plus a talent in gold for me and for my associates for *each* successful negotiation.'

Ptolemy laughed. 'You know, one day, my friend, I'm going to be forced to have you executed.'

'That would only happen if someone doesn't again pay me to assassinate you first. Next time I might not tell you about the offer, thereby giving you the chance to outbid the client by a single drachma.'

Ptolemy's mirth increased, although, in truth, he did not like to be reminded of Agathocles' attempt to have Archias assassinate him even though the Exile-Hunter had been honest with him about the contract and allowed him to buy him out. 'If you were to take that contract, who would you find to pay you the huge sums of money that I do?'

'If you were to execute me, who would you find to do all those little chores that keep your life so tidy?'

'Indeed, my friend. And for an extra payment, I would like you to slip into Athens to take my reply to Demetrius of Phaleron's letter. I'll have it ready for when you leave tomorrow.'

'"O glorious Athens! Violet-crowned, worthy of a song."'

'Well, you can sing it later, out of my earshot. Pindar has a lot to answer for.'

'And much to enjoy in his language.'

'If you say so. Now, go and get drunk or watch your Thracian friends play with their pet sheep or whatever it is you do for entertainment.' Ptolemy indulged the exaggerated bow and smiled as he watched Archias walk away along the beach, through the camp that would soon become siege lines.

'Do you think he'll be successful?' Lagus asked as soon as the Exile-Hunter was out of earshot.

'Hmm?' Ptolemy blinked and turned to his son. 'He might be; it would be nice if he were. But the main objective is: if it's known I'm in negotiations with Ptolemaios it may well bring his brother, Dioscurides, out from wherever he's hiding and give me a chance to make a deal with him.' Ptolemy put an arm around Lagus and led him back towards his tent at the centre of the camp. 'And Dioscurides, my boy, has a fleet.'

'One can always use another fleet.'

Ptolemy chuckled. 'I can see I've taught you well. Yes, indeed that's true but what's even more to the point is Antigonos will have one fleet less.'

'So, we lay siege to Halicarnassus and pretend to be busy here whilst all the time our focus is on destabilising Antigonos' position in Greece both on land and sea.'

'Yes, Lagus, but when you say we, that doesn't include you.'

Lagus looked sideways at his father in alarm. 'You're not going to send me back to my mother in Egypt, are you?'

'Certainly not, seeing as Thais will be coming here very soon; indeed, she is probably already on her way. No, my boy, you're going to go and do what every good son should do for his father.'

'What's that?'

'Find him a new wife.'

'But you've got three already, if you include my mother.'

'What did you say about fleets?'

'One can always use another one.'

'And sometimes it's the same with wives – at least it should be but sometimes they can be more trouble than they're worth. Anyway, this one should be well worth it.' He clapped Lagus on the back as the guards on the tent snapped to attention at their approach. 'Tomorrow, I want you to leave for Sardis and meet with Kleopatra, delivering a letter from me to her, asking if she feels she's finally ready to take a new husband.'

'And the best thing about it is,' Ptolemy told Thais shortly after her arrival, 'it was my idea for once; you never even thought of it.'

'Oh, didn't I?' Thais shot Ptolemy the withering look that she reserved for his more special moments of stupidity; she contemplated Ptolemy's scheme for a few moments as they made their way around the siege lines on a tour of inspection. 'You seriously think I've completely forgotten the existence of Alexander's full sister who has been residing in Sardis since her marriage to Perdikkas was called off when he managed to get himself assassinated by his own officers?'

Ptolemy did not like the way the conversation headed. 'Well, we haven't discussed the matter since Perdikkas was killed.'

'And with good reason, Ptolemy: we didn't want to make a play for the empire as we'd both decided Egypt was quite enough for our needs and, thus, I advised you to marry Eurydike and then Berenice.'

'And good advice that was – even if Eurydike does have a habit of making people's lives more difficult than they really ought to be.'

'And what makes you think the situation has changed enough to warrant you making a move that everyone will see as an attempt to make yourself king over the whole empire? The next Alexander.'

'But that's not my intention.'

'What is your intention then? Just to add to your collection of wives? Because, if it is, I could suggest more than a few far less dangerous candidates.'

Ptolemy stopped to inspect the digging of the final stretch of trench from the end of the hills upon which a good part of the city lay to the shore; it was more to straighten the arguments for his decision in his head rather than for a military interest. With a few words of encouragement to the soldiers sweating at the bottom of the trench, Ptolemy turned back to his mistress. 'I need to counteract Kassandros' marriage to Thessalonike; he will always claim to be the legitimate heir to Alexander because he's married his half-sister and fathered his nephews.'

'Kleopatra is forty-seven, Ptolemy; you have about as much chance of fathering a child on her as you have on Lycortas – although, I grant you, the experience will probably be more to your liking with her.'

'I've no intention of having a child with her, even if it were possible; nor do I intend to make a bid for the empire, which, as you rightly implied, would be madness. No, my dearest, I'm making advances towards Kleopatra because if I've got her then no one else can have her; and, if I have her, then Kassandros cannot claim to be the most senior in our alliance against Antigonos.'

'I thought he was still adhering to the terms of the peace treaty with Antigonos, which, as we can all see,' Thais indicated to the army digging in around Halicarnassus, 'you quite evidently are not.'

'Antigonos broke the terms of the agreement first by not respecting the autonomy of Greek cities and imposing garrisons on them.'

Thais smiled and took Ptolemy's arm, her mood softening. 'Not that you could give a Bactrian's wet fart for Greek autonomy.'

'Of course I do, that's why I insisted the clause was put in the peace agreement.'

'So you could accuse Antigonos of breaking it as soon as it suited you; I know, Ptolemy, I thought it was very clever too. In fact, I suggested it, if memory serves.'

Ptolemy smiled down at her and squeezed her hand resting in the crook of his arm. 'Do you know what, I think you might be right. Anyway, Kassandros has already angered the cyclops by making his own private agreement with Ptolemaios, recognising his areas of influence south of Thessaly and on Euboea; the cyclops won't like that as it implies Ptolemaios is independent of him.'

'So you're suggesting the peace treaty is now over between Kassandros and Antigonos?'

'To all intents and purposes, yes. It's just a matter of time before it becomes obvious.'

'And when it does and Kassandros comes to you to suggest another alliance against Antigonos, you want to be able to deal with him on equal terms.'

'I'm far more than his equal.'

'But he doesn't accept that.'

'Exactly. So I think the point is when he does come to me and he sees I'm married to the full sister of Alexander rather than a mere half-sister, he won't feel like he should have the dominant position in the relationship.'

'But don't forget, since his murder of the young Alexander, he's in a position to claim the throne of Macedon; he could come as a king – if he manages to deal with Herakles, that is.'

'Which is why I lent Andronicus to Artonis.'

'But you know perfectly well Polyperchon doesn't stand a chance against Kassandros, even with Andronicus' help.'

'Who said Andronicus was necessarily helping?'

Thais thought for a moment and then looked at Ptolemy with a smile of dawning understanding and a conspiratorial twinkle in her eyes. 'You're getting to be as sly as Eumenes.'

'I did admire our late undersized Greek friend, yes, I'll admit it. I think you'll agree that no one needs the complication of another king, now we've managed to rid ourselves of the last two incumbents. However, it always looks good if one is seen to be supporting the Argead royal house. The reason I sent Andronicus was to look as if I was helping Herakles, but the effect will be quite the opposite as it will help me.'

'In that it'll make Herakles go away, in a manner of speaking?'

'In a manner of speaking, yes; but I can't be seen to be responsible. No one wants a king with Alexander's blood running in his veins sitting in Pella, not me nor Antigonos, Kassandros, Lysimachus or Seleukos; that would be far too inconvenient for all of us. Did you notice how silent everyone was when Kassandros had the boy killed? It was a relief to us and we all admired the pimply toad for having the balls to do it; Antigonos hardly bothered to refute the accusation that he was responsible seeing as we all knew he wasn't. Well, through Andronicus I'm going to ensure the pimply toad and the fading nonentity both share the opprobrium for spilling yet more of Alexander's blood and no one will even suspect I did anything but try to help Herakles.'

'How will you do it?'

'You'll have to wait and see.' Ptolemy looked – and felt – particularly pleased with himself. 'And then, with the fool Philip, the young Alexander and Herakles all out of the way there will be crowns to claim. Who's going to do it first and with what authority?' Ptolemy looked sideways at his mistress. 'Now do you see?'

'Kleopatra,' Thais declared and then walked on in silence as she considered Ptolemy's train of thought. 'You're wrong and you're right,' she announced eventually.

'Thank you for that vote of confidence.'

'What I mean is, you don't need Kleopatra, but it would be better if *you* had her and not someone else.'

'Exactly.

'Do you think she'd be content with just Egypt?'

'Do you think she's content with just Sardis?'

'That's a good point.'

'And I'd love to see Kassandros' face when he hears the news.'

KASSANDROS.
THE JEALOUS.

I T WAS NOT going as smoothly as he and Thessalonike had hoped – that much was for sure. There were, according to his agents amongst the nobility and discharged veterans, whisperings about the circumstances of Alexander's death, whisperings about how convenient it had been for Kassandros and his wife – although some argued it was just as convenient for Antigonos, the man who had purportedly sent the killers. But many of the nobility in Macedon, and much of the common soldiery now retired back to their smallholdings, had been east with Alexander's father, and thus knew the difference between the eastern tribes they had fought and subdued. It was, therefore, something of an eyebrow-raiser that Bactrians should have been used for the assassination of the boy and his mother, seeing as Roxanna was herself a Bactrian – granted, her father, Oxyartes, was now satrap of Paropamisadae, out on the border with India, but by blood he was Bactrian. Why, therefore, would Bactrians be sent to kill Oxyartes' daughter and grandson? The answer was obvious: it was not an assassination but, rather, a rescue attempt sent by

Roxanna's father; an attempt that had been foiled and then used to cover up a foul double murder.

And there was nothing that Kassandros could do to curb these whispers, for to deny them was to imply that they were a credible version of events, but to ignore them allowed them to spread and grow with exaggeration.

'And if I were to execute anyone whom I believe has been spreading these false rumours, that's almost like admitting there is some truth to them,' Kassandros complained to Thessalonike as they stood on the terrace of the new palace in the harbour town bearing her name, looking out over the bay at a great Five swiftly approaching from the south with an escort of half a dozen triremes. Sails hoisted and oars spread, the vessels glided across a smooth sea glistering bronze with late afternoon sun, as gulls circled around them, their calls carried on a warm breeze.

'But there is truth to them, Kassandros,' Thessalonike reminded him. 'The Bactrians did come to rescue the boy and his mother and they had been – most likely – sent by her father, and we did intercept them, kill them and then blame them for the deaths of Alexander and Roxanna.'

'I know! But that was meant to be kept a secret; we had all the guards and slaves executed so no one but us knows what really happened and yet the rumours persist.'

'Let them,' Thessalonike said, taking his hand as it lay on the balustrade. 'They're only rumours and they can never be substantiated for there is no one left alive who knows the truth other than you and me.'

Kassandros' avianesque face seemed to droop more than usual as his sulk about the unfairness of the world deepened.

'Besides, Kassandros,' Thessalonike said in a cheerful tone that she hoped would raise his sagging spirits, 'think of the positive things: Ptolemaios is arriving to negotiate an alliance which will bring peace to all of Greece above the isthmus, leaving us free to oppose Polyperchon with our full strength should he ever pluck up enough courage to cross the border and invade.'

But, in truth, that did not restore Kassandros' mood as the ageing nonentity and his bastard pretender had been sitting in his clan-lands of Tymphaea since their arrival at the end of the previous campaigning season, seven months ago. Kassandros had left his general, Crateuas, with twelve thousand men to watch over them but they had done nothing since the snows had melted. According to spies, Polyperchon had spent the winter recruiting, training and having far too many inspections for good morale, although, since the arrival of a new general the pace of things had begun to accelerate and the invasion looked to be imminent. Just who this newly arrived general was Crateuas' spies had been unable to say as, since his arrival, security had been tightened and none had made it out of the enemy camp, which now had the heads of those suspected of passing information to the enemy decorating its gates.

It was, therefore, crucial that this alliance with Ptolemaios should be completed soon so Kassandros could take a much larger force west to join Crateuas and face the incoming army together. This could only be achieved by knowing his southern border was secure and watched over by a friendly Ptolemaios rather than open to attack by him as soon as he moved against Polyperchon. And thus, with Antigonos' eyes distracted by Ptolemy's antics in Karia and Lycia, Kassandros and Thessalonike had decided to take advantage of Ptolemaios' friendly gesture of warning them of Herakles' claim and his planned invasion with Polyperchon, and open negotiations.

'You have my respect, Kassandros,' Ptolemaios said as he was shown into the audience chamber of the new palace; bright with fresh whitewash, and still smelling of cut timber and drying plaster, the room was in as pristine a condition as it would ever enjoy. 'And my respect to you too, Thessalonike.' A muscular man in his mid-thirties, and with a strong family likeness to his uncle, but minus the beard and plus the second eye, Ptolemaios strode down the centre of the chamber, passing a round table set with three chairs, his leather soles clacking on smooth marble as he approached his hosts seated on a dais at the far end beneath a window looking out to sea.

'We thank you, Ptolemaios,' Kassandros replied, trying his utmost to sound weighty and statesmanlike as he looked down on his guest. 'We've put a lot of planning and gold into the new city and intend to make it the wonder of Macedon.'

Ptolemaios looked momentarily confused and then smiled. 'No, you mistake me, Kassandros; that was not what I meant, although I do admire the city.' He bowed his head to Thessalonike. 'Not least because it shares its name with so fair a jewel.'

'You are very kind, Ptolemaios,' Thessalonike said, standing and putting her hand out to Kassandros for him to rise too. 'Come, there is a table set; we shall sit around it, all at the same level.'

Kassandros took Thessalonike's hand and, in an attempt to regain the initiative from his wife, quickly descended the dais, thus leading her. 'You are welcome here, Ptolemaios; I hope we can conclude a treaty advantageous to the two of... three of us. Please, be seated.' He indicated to one of the three chairs around the table and then made a show of seating Thessalonike in the second before taking the third for himself. He clapped his hands; slaves came scuttling in with wine and fruit.

'To our joint endeavour,' Kassandros said, raising his cup as the slaves departed. 'Peace in Europe.'

Ptolemaios inclined his head in agreement. 'Peace in Europe, which will be much easier now; it is for that you have my respect as I mentioned on my arrival. It took a lot of courage to kill Alexander and his wild-cat of a mother, but it needed to be done.'

Kassandros felt the blood drain from his already pale face. 'Alexander and Roxanna were killed by assassins.'

'Sent by my uncle, yes, I heard the story you put around: Bactrians killing the half-Bactrian king.' Ptolemaios waved the thought away as if it were a mere trifle. 'That will do for the farmers and shepherds, if they even care, but don't expect me to believe that.'

'But it's what happened.'

'Please, Kassandros, don't insult my intelligence. If you want folk to believe that's what really happened, all well and good, but don't try to feed me the same meagre fare as you do your people. It's important that we're honest with each other. You killed the young Alexander and I applaud you for that; it needed to be done and I would hazard that my uncle, as well as Ptolemy and Lysimachus, take the same view – judging by their silence on the matter. Yes, Antigonos denied that he sent assassins – as well he should, seeing as he didn't – but it was a disinterested protest and he did not turn the accusation back on you, an act, or lack of it, that speaks volumes.'

Kassandros looked in horror at his guest. *I can't let him pressure me into admitting this; I've always publicly denied involvement in Alexander's death and so if I admit to his son's then I will have no name left in Macedon.* 'But it must have been Antigonos who sent the assassins; who else has access to the east?'

'Well, Seleukos for a start, if the current rumours are true: he's expanding his territory east. But that is not the point. Alexander is dead, there is no king unless you count the bastard, Herakles, but I don't think he'll last long, not with Polyperchon, despite Ptolemy sending Andronicus to aid his cause.'

Thessalonike leaned forward. 'Andronicus? Antigonos' former commander of Tyros?'

'The very same. He went over to Ptolemy after the fall of Tyros soon after Gaza, on condition that he would never have to serve against Antigonos or Demetrios. Since then he has been in Cyrenaica. Artonis managed to get to Ptolemy and persuade him that they needed a more proactive general than Polyperchon; so, he sent Andronicus.'

Thessalonike nodded. 'Yes, a perfect choice: Andronicus won't be facing either of his former masters.' She frowned in puzzlement. 'But why would Ptolemy be interested in helping Herakles to the throne?'

Ptolemaios agreed. 'Yes, I wondered that. Seeing as Olympias and you have just rid us of two kings, why suddenly produce a third?'

This was too much for Kassandros. 'We did not kill Alexander!'

'My dear, calm yourself,' Thessalonike said, putting a hand on his arm. 'We know we didn't kill Alexander.'

Kassandros pointed at Ptolemaios. 'But he keeps on insisting that we did.'

Ptolemaios sighed. 'Look, if we can't be honest with one another then how can we make an equitable deal? Please, stop this act and tell me the motivation behind it. I need to know what you're thinking if I am to come to an agreement with you: do you plan to make yourself king?' His gaze strayed to Thessalonike. 'And queen. And if so when and of what?'

Thessalonike tightened her grip on her husband's arm, warning him to keep his already frayed temper. 'Assuming we were responsible for Alexander's death – which we weren't – what difference would it make to what we do or don't plan to do?'

Ptolemaios sat back in his chair, his elbows resting on the arms, his cup in both hands, contemplating them. 'Thessalonike, everyone with any sense knew that the young Alexander would never make his majority; it would have taken too much away from too many people. You see, now he's dead, one of two things could happen: either one person,' he paused and inclined his head, 'or two, perhaps, could claim his position and attempt to rule over the entire empire – and you being of Alexander's blood and Kassandros being the son of Alexander's regent are well placed to make that claim – in which case the wars will continue. I think we can all agree that no one, other than yourselves, would be very keen on that scenario. The other scenario is the empire splits and is forged into separate kingdoms. Now, if that's what you're planning, will you take Macedon and Thessaly or will you consider yourselves sovereign over all Greece, and if that is the case, where does that leave me? Do you see the problem?'

Kassandros could restrain himself no longer. 'It's none of your business what we plan to do! You're here to make a treaty with us.'

Ptolemaios smiled over his cup. 'Oh, but it *is* my business, Kassandros; I have Euboea and most of Greece from Thessaly down to the isthmus; if you plan to make yourself king of everything north of my lands then that's fine by me, but if you're thinking of declaring yourself ruler over my territory as well, then we have a serious problem. For what's the point of my turning against my uncle in order to become independent if I only end up in a situation whereby you claim authority over my territory?'

Kassandros broke from Thessalonike's grip and thumped the table with the palm of his hand. 'Macedon is mine!' Again, he thumped. 'Greece is mine!' And again. 'All of it!'

Thessalonike entwined her fingers through his. 'Calm yourself, my dear. Ptolemaios is absolutely right to bring this up now; he does, after all, have a great interest in Greece. I'm sure we can come to an accommodation with him.'

Ptolemaios took a sip of wine. 'That's why I've come in person: to see your eyes as you tell me what your plans are. And I just saw the determination in Kassandros' when he claimed all of Greece.' He placed his cup down in a manner contrasting with Kassandros' treatment of the table, and pushed back his chair. 'Thank you for being so open with me; I believe we now all know where we stand.'

'Where are you going?' Kassandros demanded.

'Back to Euboea, of course. There's nothing more to say between us.'

'But our treaty?'

'What treaty? The one where I agree not to attack you whilst you go and deal with Polyperchon – who I warned you about as an expression of good faith – and then, when that's done and Herakles is dead, you declare yourself to be my king and come south with a huge army to prove it? That treaty? Do you think I'm an idiot?' He turned to go.

'Ptolemaios,' Thessalonike called after him, 'you're making a mistake. Only we can guarantee your autonomy here in Greece.'

Ptolemaios looked over his shoulder. 'Autonomy is not independence. And that is not true, Thessalonike: I've already had a more than generous offer of support and full independence. So, don't worry about me.'

'Who from?' Kassandros shouted.

'That's for you to find out. Oh, and don't try to interfere with me leaving; my ships have orders to set fire to the port if I am delayed. If you look out the window, I think you'll see I'm in earnest.'

Kassandros and Thessalonike both turned and mounted the dais to better see: through the window Ptolemaios' squadron could be observed; on the deck of each ship a brazier burned. Men stood around each one roasting meat on skewers; bows and fire arrows wrapped in cloth lay on the deck at their feet.

Kassandros turned to see Ptolemaios disappear out of the door, his escort surrounding him.

'Well, that did not go at all well, did it, Husband?' Thessalonike said through clenched teeth.

Kassandros looked at his wife, glaring at him, and flinched. 'Don't blame me, Thessalonike.'

'Who else is to blame, eh? You're the one who declared in no uncertain terms, even using the table as a drum to emphasise the point, that you were going to claim sovereignty over Macedon and Greece thus making an alliance with us pointless from Ptolemaios' point of view. And now he doesn't trust us in the slightest; he's gone and there will be nothing we can do to change his mind. And all because you couldn't keep your temper.'

'But he kept on accusing us of killing Alexander.'

'Which, if you will only recollect, we did.' Thessalonike

took a deep breath to calm herself before sitting back down on her raised chair and tapping the seat of her husband's, next to her; Kassandros did as he was asked. 'Ptolemaios isn't stupid; of course he's worked out it was us who killed Alexander and Roxanna, and so what? We needed him, so let him think whatever he likes. Now, though, we have to keep a force in the east of the country bigger than we would like, just in case Ptolemaios and his new friend decide to take advantage of our absence and make a foray north.'

Kassandros' anger was still smouldering. 'Who is this new friend?'

Thessalonike looked at her husband in surprise and then shook her head, disappointed. 'Oh, Kassandros, you really aren't having a good day, are you?'

She's laughing at me.

'And no, I'm not laughing at you, whatever you might think. You've let your temper overpower your ability to think logically. If Ptolemaios has made a break with his father to become independent, and he was worried that we plan to claim all of Greece, then who is the only person who could protect him?'

I've been stupid; she's right: my temper got the better of me and needlessly so. What does it really matter what Ptolemaios thinks so long as he's our ally? Kassandros sighed. *Too late.* He took his wife's hands and squeezed them. 'I'm sorry; I've made things a lot harder for us now. It's Ptolemy he's gone to, isn't it?'

'I'd wager it is, seeing as he has superiority at sea over Antigonos; a foothold in Greece would be very tempting for him.'

'What do we do?'

'Do? We do the only thing we can do. We can't risk

taking sufficient troops west to face Polyperchon, or, more to the point, Andronicus, so if we can't defeat them, I would say the only thing to do is neutralise them. You and I need to speak to Polyperchon.'

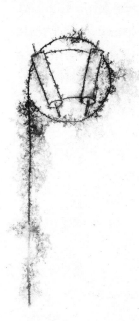

POLYPERCHON.
THE GREY.

INTOLERABLE. *HIS INTERFERENCE is just intolerable.* Polyperchon had found that word going round and round his head ever since the unexpected arrival of Andronicus and his insistence on spending more of the winter months in fitness training and drill and less in make and mend and inspections. He had wondered where Artonis had gone when she disappeared so suddenly and that was the humiliating answer. *I have a position as commander-in-chief of the king's European army and this man is trying to undermine me. Women are trying to undermine me. How can I ever get the army ready for a campaign if my authority is being forever undermined?* And upon that question he had brooded, his mood growing blacker and his temper shorter as the men he had recruited from his family's heartland, on the Macedonian border with Epirus, were moulded by Andronicus into the sort of soldiers he entirely disapproved of: coarse fighters with no respect for pristine kit and immaculate turnout. And all the time Andronicus had taken every opportunity to mock him and, worse still, encouraged the king, Herakles himself, to do so too.

263

And yet there was little he could do as the king seemed to be in support of this approach and now spent most of his time with Andronicus, learning his bad habits, whereas before Artonis' disappearance Herakles would be out hunting through the hours of daylight, taking little notice of the day to day running of the army. It was upon his return in the evening that Polyperchon could regale him with all his lists and take him on a tour of the fatigue parties of miscreants who had failed inspection in the minutest of ways.

But now a line had been crossed and he felt the dignity of his position compromised. He turned his eyes on the cause of his woes. 'You're wrong, Andronicus. Wrong. How can we advance until we know the exact position of the enemy?'

Andronicus looked at the wizened general in surprise. 'But we do know where Crateuas is: he's twenty leagues from here to the east, on the far bank of the Haliacmon River with an army of fifteen thousand, waiting – with knees trembling, no doubt – for us to come at him with our twenty-three thousand.'

'But where is Kassandros? That's what we don't know. We shouldn't move until—'

'Until Kassandros has brought up enough reinforcements to outnumber us? We shouldn't move until he's ready? Is that what you're saying?'

Humiliation again as this got a laugh from all in the room. 'No, I mean we need to know whether he's coming to join Crateuas or whether Crateuas is going to fall back before us and lead us into an ambush.'

Andronicus looked towards Herakles, reclining between himself and Polyperchon. 'What's your view, lord king?'

Herakles licked the lamb fat from his fingers, deliberately postponing his answer.

He's creating a silence to make his words even more devastating.

'Cowering here when the road to Pella is open is the strategy of an old man with no balls and little brain.' Herakles turned to Polyperchon. 'And I mean that figuratively, not personally.' He then turned back to Andronicus and included his mother, Artonis and the other half dozen officers sharing the evening meal with him. 'The route to Pella is along the Haliacmon valley to Alorus and then north, thus avoiding the coast road. We've wasted enough time; we go now and defeat Crateuas and then deal with Kassandros as he comes the opposite way down the valley. Take them one at a time.' He smiled at Polyperchon; it had none of the warmth he had known when they had first met. 'We will make scouting our priority, far and wide on both sides of the valley as well as before and behind; we'll know of any ambushes well in advance, so don't be frightened, Polyperchon.'

They were sniggering now; most of them without the decency to place their hands in front of their mouths, Polyperchon noted as he looked around for support. There was none. 'Very well, my lord king, we will advance and attempt to defeat Crateuas as we cross the Haliacmon without giving him the chance to withdraw.'

Herakles' smile was frozen on his face. 'Very good, Polyperchon; but I have one correction to make. We *will* defeat Crateuas, not *attempt* to defeat him. Do I make myself clear? Andronicus, do you have any difficulty understanding that?'

'None at all, my lord king. We will leave tomorrow and be at the Haliacmon by the following day, which we will cross with the rafts and boats we've had assembled there and then we'll defeat Crateuas.'

I assembled them, not 'we'.

Herakles' eyes stayed on Polyperchon. 'There, you see; that's the sort of decisive leadership I expect.'

'Indeed, lord king; but I only advocate caution because I want to be sure your victory is certain and absolute.'

'Certain and absolute victory is a fine objective for any general, Polyperchon, and I commend you for it; however, there is a third word that goes with "certain" and "absolute" and that's "immediate". Try to remember it.'

Polyperchon dipped his fingers in a bowl of water, shaking them dry; he had had enough of this. 'My lord king, excuse me; if we're to march tomorrow then I've much work to do before dawn, we have a river crossing to make and everyone must know their place to make it a success.'

'Indeed, my dear general. I would not keep you from your lists.'

It was to the sound of more sniggering that Polyperchon left the room; it was to the sound of raucous laughter that he made his way to his study.

Although technically wholly within Macedon's territory, the Haliacmon River was the practical border between Macedon and Polyperchon's homeland of Tymphaea, the buffer between the two kingdoms of Macedon and Epirus. The river was already fifty paces wide, even this far upstream; a formidable task for any army to cross. But it was better to cross now than follow it downstream as it widened, and besides, Polyperchon had found a perfect place where the hills fell away from the river leaving open space, with gentle banks, where the army could embark and disembark. For Polyperchon it was an exercise in logistics that fully absorbed him, for an orderly river crossing was a thing of beauty in his mind and he had striven all night, since the army's arrival at the Haliacmon, to affect it to the best of his ability from the moment he had sent the assault troops across to seize a bridgehead shortly before midnight.

Now, as the dawn sun rose behind the mountains to the east, he looked back to the west bank at the hundreds of craft, just visible in the gloom, being loaded with men and horses, each one attached to a rope spanning the river, rigged overnight. Much had gone into the planning and so far the operation had gone smoothly. The assault troops, commanded by Andronicus, had created a perimeter long enough to encompass the landing area and deep enough to accommodate the first wave now embarking over on the opposite bank. But there was now an urgency developing, growing more critical with each degree the sun rose, for during the night only infantry had been transported across as, in Polyperchon's experience, horses tended to be spooked travelling on river craft in the hours of darkness. But now with the operation no longer a secret, he needed light cavalry on this side of the river to scout for signs of the enemy, for soon the army would be at its most vulnerable: split in half with a fair proportion mid-river.

'Get them moving, now!' Polyperchon bellowed across to the officer in charge of the embarkation. 'There's enough light for the horses to see!'

If his shouting did anything to speed up matters it was hardly evident, and the long queues leading to each of the ropes seemed to remain stationary despite the efforts of his hand-picked officers – clansmen of his personal guard, a Tymphaean loyal to him to death – commanding each embarkation point to move things along. Eventually the men manning the first of the craft to cast off started hauling on the rope, hand over hand, pulling themselves and their cargo of sixteen cavalrymen and their mounts east.

One by one the rest followed until the river was dotted with crafts at various points of the crossing. As the first craft touched the east bank Polyperchon urged the officer at that landing point to get the cavalry off at speed. 'Keep them moving, Ialysus; we need to go faster.'

'Yes, sir,' the officer responded, pulling at the bridle of the first horse, encouraging it and its rider into more haste.

Thank the gods I still have loyal clansmen to reply upon.

'Get pulling!' Ialysus shouted to the handlers as the last beast splashed through the shallows onto dry land. 'Get back to the other side as fast as you can, otherwise you'll all be on fatigues.'

The men glanced at him, taking the threat seriously, as they busied themselves with the guide rope attaching the vessel to the spanning rope, pulling it towards what would now become the stern as they returned. Grateful that he at least had the respect of the loyal core of his officers, Polyperchon jogged away as they heaved off, heading for the next craft to urge them into swifter action and then the next until the pace of the operation had picked up to what he considered acceptable.

By the time the sun appeared over the peaks to the east, the light cavalry had all been transported and were now setting off north, east and south, looking for signs of Crateuas' army as the remainder of the heavy infantry, not transported during the night, began to make the crossing. On through the morning the operation continued, exactly as Polyperchon had planned it, his lists and orders ensuring every unit knew where it had to wait on the west bank and where to go once it reached the east bank.

By midday half of the army was across, but, although this was the juncture that caused Polyperchon the most nerves, he found himself able to relax as the first of the scouts had come in from all three directions reporting there was no sight of any enemy activity within three leagues of the bridgehead, not even a stray scout.

To greater efforts he tried to urge his tired men, even as they once again changed shifts manning the craft, but all his shouting and cajoling were for nought as they were already working at the limits of their strength; his Tymphaean officers had seen to that.

On they came, crossing into Macedon, the infantry packed close on the craft, their shields slung on their backs and their pikes, unscrewed into halves, as two poles resting on their shoulders. In good humour did they splash through the shallows, the old hands joking about coming home using the rear entrance and getting as much ribald humour as possible from the situation as they moved with the ease of professionals to their muster points and the craft returned once more.

With the heavy infantry across, the heavy cavalry were next in line. The beasts were heaved and pulled onto the craft, their hooves stamping on the wooden decks, their riders holding their bridles firm and blowing into their nostrils whilst stroking their muzzles and speaking soft words in their ears. By mid-afternoon they were all across, Herakles among them, although Polyperchon did not see him land as he was busy at the other end of the bridgehead having the guide ropes supporting a bracing stake retied after the stake had come loose.

And then it was the turn of the light infantry to make the crossing, with the braver ones who had knowledge of swimming hanging onto the vessels as they were hauled across, their equipment being no threat to their buoyancy. Up and down the lines did Polyperchon jog, checking with his officers at each landing point, ever observant as to the state of each spanning rope, testing it remained secure to its stake, and that the two teams of four men manning each craft rotated their shifts every three crossings.

As the last of the light infantry jogged up the bank the first of the baggage carts was hauled off its transporter with others following over the breadth of the river. With mules braying in protest and oxen lowing in fear, the final part of the army, its stores and supplies, most dear to Polyperchon's heart, made its way into Macedon. All his sacks of grain, crates of spare boots, tunics and cloaks, the replacement shields, pikes, swords and javelins and all the other stores that kept an army in the field for a season were ferried over with haste and care; and it was with great relief that Polyperchon could tick off the last of his precious wagons as it rolled onto the east bank for, apart from the rear-guard now embarking in the fading light, the whole army, more than twenty thousand, plus the baggage had made it across the Haliacmon in a day; and it was, to Polyperchon's certain knowledge as he congratulated himself upon a job well done, down to meticulous planning and well-ordered lists. With the rear-guard now well on its way across, Polyperchon's mind turned to food for he had eaten nothing since before dawn, such had been his concentration on the smooth running of the crossing. But first he knew his duty was to report to his king.

'Very good,' Herakles said, not looking up from his trencher of grilled lamb, having heard Polyperchon's report.

Polyperchon stood in the entrance of the king's tent waiting for him to say something else; to expand upon his feelings for an operation that successfully got over twenty thousand men and their support across a fifty-pace-wide river with no casualties in one single day.

'Was there something else, Polyperchon?' Herakles asked, finally deigning to look up.

Polyperchon swallowed, feeling awkward. 'No, my lord king.'

Herakles waved him away. 'Then you can get back to your lists.'

Humiliated once again, Polyperchon walked the short distance to his tent; pushing aside his body-slave waiting within, he kicked over the table set with bread, cold meat and cheese, swearing in a manner that would normally have shocked him.

'I've a message for you, Polyperchon,' a voice said, causing him to start.

He turned to see a figure seated in the shadows and frowned. 'Who are you? How did you get in?'

'Don't blame your slave,' the man said. 'I told him I had a proposal that would be of great interest to you, and if he refused me entry then you would punish him for jeopardising a deal which could enrich you and get back the estates you've lost in the east of the country.'

Polyperchon was immediately interested. 'Whom do you represent?' he asked, already guessing the answer.

'Kassandros and Thessalonike wish to talk to you. They're waiting half a league downstream; I have a boat waiting on the fringe of the camp.'

It took but a moment for Polyperchon to make his decision.

*

'So, other than the title of general commanding the king's European army, Herakles has offered you nothing?'

The way Thessalonike put it made his part of the bargain sound very meagre indeed. 'He's promised reward when he takes the throne. Substantial reward.'

'But he's not going to take the throne,' Kassandros pointed out, 'is he?'

Polyperchon looked at the couple seated opposite him on boulders on the riverbank, their faces lit solely by the light of a half-moon. 'Our army outnumbers yours.'

'That's not what my husband was talking about,' Thessalonike said. 'What he means is Herakles isn't going to take the throne because you're here talking to us, implying that your loyalty to him is less than absolute.'

'He shows me no respect.'

'So our informants say.' Kassandros shook his head as if unable to believe how shoddily the ageing general was treated. 'It must be intolerable.'

'It is.'

'We can make it right for you and give you the respect you deserve. We would offer you this should you eliminate Herakles: restoration of the estates around Amphipolis which we confiscated when we came to power, plus a hundred talents in gold.'

Polyperchon considered the offer. 'That's all very well; but wealth and property is one thing, respect is another. I must have a position.'

'And so you shall, Polyperchon; of course you should have a position.' Thessalonike pulled her cloak tighter around her shoulders against the chilling mountain air. 'We thought military governor with autonomous command of the Peloponnese from the isthmus down, with your own army and fleet.'

'Military governor, eh? Autonomous, you say? That sounds very respectable. What about my daughter-in-law, Penelope? She still controls Corinth and Sykion.'

'You are free to deal with her as you will; you'll have the troops you need and the ability to land behind her wall. I think she'll be very happy to join you in your support of us.' Thessalonike leaned forward. 'There is one other thing my husband forgot to mention: Barsine is also part of the deal.'

'Dead?'

'Dead.'

Polyperchon looked from Thessalonike to Kassandros and back again. *They're offering me the opportunity to avenge the humiliations I've been subjected to and become a man of respect in my own right with my own army and fleet. And as yet I've had no such assurances from Herakles and Barsine.* 'What about Andronicus?'

'We've already spoken with him,' Kassandros said.

Polyperchon could not hide his shock. 'When?'

'Last night as soon as he crossed the river with the assault troops. We agreed to pull Crateuas' army back and he agreed to do nothing until we had spoken to you. You see, he sees the value of not having another king to fight over. Let the empire split into four or five kingdoms peacefully and all our lives will be far easier.'

'Andronicus is a pragmatic man,' Thessalonike put it, 'which incidentally is, I think, why Ptolemy sent him. He will help you control the army once you've had Herakles and his mother dealt with.'

That had been his final worry. 'Very well, I'll do it. Herakles has done nothing to earn my loyalty, despite me giving him respect as a king. He does nothing but laugh at me and make jokes at my expense.'

'Well, now the joke can be on him,' Thessalonike said, her voice soft and smooth.

'Yes, it can; and then we'll see who's laughing.' A thought then occurred to him. 'What about Artonis?'

Thessalonike's eyes hardened. 'She might not be a threat to us like Barsine and her bastard are, but she still supported them and would have gladly seen us dead. You can do what you like with her, so long as you kill her afterwards.'

ARTONIS.
THE WIDOW.

ALL SENSE OF urgency had evaporated from the invasion; for two days now, since the river crossing, the army had remained in its camp and Artonis could see no purpose for such inaction. It was no surprise to her that Polyperchon claimed the reason for the pause was to scout forward, seeking news of the enemy, whilst repairing equipment damaged in the crossing and taking stock – what of, he did not say. What Artonis did find surprising was that Andronicus did not dispute these pathetic excuses and would do nothing to hasten the move east along the river valley. Even when, that morning, she, Herakles and Barsine had confronted the two generals and ordered them to advance immediately, Andronicus had said they were not yet ready but they both promised the advance would commence at dawn the following day. Frustrated, they could do nothing but accept the situation for, between them, the two generals controlled the loyalty of most of the officers. The consequence of Herakles' calamitous error of spending so much time hunting during their march north rather than getting to know the men who would be fighting for him was now clear to Artonis and Barsine – if not to him: he was nothing more than a figurehead.

'But at least we're moving east tomorrow,' Artonis said to Barsine as they walked together that evening towards a large tent especially erected by the riverbank for a banquet to celebrate the commencement of the campaign proper.

'Perhaps, my dear,' Barsine said, 'but I find this new concord between Andronicus and Polyperchon disturbing. The fact Andronicus brazenly supported Polyperchon's pointless delay surely is a matter for concern; to me it smells of bribery. You don't think Kassandros and Thessalonike could have got to them, do you?'

It was the first time Artonis had given any thought to the subject. 'How would they benefit from going over to Kassandros?'

Barsine nodded to the guards standing either side of the entrance to the dining tent. 'Try looking at it from the other way around: how do they benefit staying with us? What have we actually promised Polyperchon?'

Artonis had to concede the point. 'Well, apart from an empty title, nothing.'

Barsine took her half-sister aside as they entered the dining area. 'Exactly; and Andronicus is, essentially, a mercenary: it's neither here nor there to him who wins this war, he'll just go back to Egypt and tell Ptolemy he did what he thought was best.'

Artonis understood the awful implication. 'And for Ptolemy it makes no difference if Kassandros or Herakles is in power in Macedon; it's far away from Egypt.'

Barsine looked at Artonis, her expression grave. 'Which means, in the final analysis, we can't trust either of our two generals as neither has a vested interest in Herakles becoming king.'

'But Polyperchon is so deferential to him; he calls him "my lord king" and boasts of being general of the king's European army.'

'Which, as we said, is an empty title. No, Artonis, I think we've been too complacent in assuming their loyalty was totally fixed on Herakles.'

She's right; I should have seen it, especially as I've no reason to trust either of them. I just made the assumption they would far rather see Herakles as king of Macedon than the odious Kassandros. 'We should watch them carefully. The trouble is: if we can't trust them then who can we trust in this army?'

'That's the problem I've been wrestling with since Andronicus started agreeing with Polyperchon.' Barsine turned and looked towards the assembling guests, mainly senior officers of Polyperchon's Companions along with a few of their wives. 'Come, my dear, this evening we should cultivate some new friends.'

'My lord king,' Polyperchon, said, rising, along with the rest of the guests, as Herakles entered the tent, impolitely late, 'you are welcome. I'm honoured that you've accepted my invitation.'

Herakles dismissed the welcome with a curt nod. 'I wouldn't have wanted to mess up your carefully compiled list as to who should recline next to whom. I know how much you pride yourself on your lists.'

Artonis saw the anger in Polyperchon's eyes at her nephew's demeaning of him and then looked around the assembled guests: none showed any surprise or shock in the way the king had just treated his senior general, and none

277

found it amusing. She whispered in Barsine's ear: 'We've been remiss in allowing Herakles to treat Polyperchon with such disrespect – see, no one is the slightest bit surprised by that insult and none are amused. Most are from Tymphaea and don't take kindly to their clan chieftain being treated thus.' *What does Andronicus make of it, I wonder?* But of him there was no sign.

Barsine walked towards her son, arms outstretched. 'Come and recline next to me, Herakles.'

Herakles took her hand. 'If that doesn't interfere with our host's lists.'

'Herakles, my darling,' Barsine said, lowering her voice as she ushered him to her couch, 'a man's loyalty doesn't survive such mocking. You should pay more respect to Polyperchon; he works very hard for your cause.'

'Mother, he's a finicky old woman who needs me more than I need him. I tried to respect him at first but then his pedantry began to grate on me and I realised why we found him where we did, hiding behind a wall. What would he be without me? A faded nonentity. No, Mother, I'll treat him as I wish.'

'And you expect him to fight for you?' Artonis asked as the three reclined with Herakles in the middle.

Herakles looked at his aunt in surprise. 'I'm his king; he'll do as he's told. Besides, he does the organising; Andronicus and I will do the fighting.'

Artonis glanced across to Barsine who gave a slight shake of her head, telling her to drop the subject. She turned away, looking around the assembled company, cursing the arrogance of youth that had blossomed so quick and strong in Herakles, since his claim to the throne became a reality backed by Polyperchon's army.

But as these thoughts drifted around her head, Artonis became aware of movement in the crowd, female move-ment, as one by one the gathered wives were leaving the tent, the final two making their way to the exit as Artonis registered the departure. She glanced over to Polyperchon; his eyes were hard and focused on Herakles. With panic rising within her, Artonis turned to see Andronicus entering the tent as the last two wives left; folding his arms he stood, legs astride, blocking the exit. 'Barsine, Herakles, run!' she shouted, jumping to her feet. But even as they both stared at her in astonishment, she knew it was too late.

The trap had been sprung.

Polyperchon got to his feet as six officers of his personal guard, Ialysus to the fore, approached Artonis, Barsine and Herakles.

Herakles stood, his face betraying concern. 'What's the meaning of this, Polyperchon?'

The wizened general's smile did not reach his hard eyes. 'The meaning of this, Herakles, is to teach you the price of mockery. It's been on my *list* of things to do for a while now.'

Herakles looked left and then right, but there was no escape as the officers approached from different angles and Andronicus still blocked the exit. 'Take your hands off your king,' he demanded as he was seized.

Artonis felt her shoulders gripped as she was pulled away, separated from her nephew and Barsine. She gasped as a noose was slipped over her head and secured around her neck.

Herakles' struggle was fierce as two men grappled with him but the third got the noose in place, with a wooden rod between it and the back of his neck. The would-be king was forced to his knees.

Barsine made no attempt to resist her fate and submitted to the garrotte, her eyes fixed on Polyperchon. 'How much did Kassandros and Thessalonike pay you for our lives, old man?'

'Their currency was respect, Barsine. Respect! Something your son didn't understand.'

Barsine nodded, looking with sad eyes down at Herakles as he continued to struggle against the inevitable. 'We've brought this upon ourselves.' She closed her eyes, muttering: 'Forgive me, Alexander, I've killed our son.'

'Do it!' Polyperchon ordered.

As Barsine voluntarily went down to her knees next to her son, Artonis felt irresistible pressure on her shoulder and her legs buckled.

'Not Artonis,' Andronicus shouted. 'She lives.'

'She dies, Andronicus,' Polyperchon snarled.

Andronicus strode forward. 'Ptolemy ordered me to protect her, Polyperchon. She is Eumenes' widow and Ptolemy's sister-in-law. I've served with Eumenes and I am now Ptolemy's man; I'll not stand here and see her harmed.' He pushed away the two men holding her down and raised her to her feet, slipping the noose back over her head.

'But Thessalonike and Kassandros want her dead!'

'It's not their decision.' Andronicus placed himself between Artonis and Polyperchon, his sword hilt gripped, his arm tense and ready to draw the weapon. 'Artonis lives.'

Polyperchon gritted his teeth, clenching his fists, but backed down in the face of the adamant Andronicus. 'Get on with it,' he ordered, his voice petulant.

And the rods began to turn, twisting the nooses, tightening them so they cut into the throats of Herakles and his mother. Up their hands came to attempt to drag the ropes away even as they bit deeper, constricting the airways as their eyes bulged and tongues quivered, swelling with the pressure.

Artonis stood rooted in horror, as the slow execution played out, the loosening of bladders and bowels adding a further, pungent, sense to its ghastly image, as their croaking was cut off with full constriction of the windpipe. It was almost with relief that she watched the executioners let go of the rods, allowing the bodies to slump to the floor into the puddle of their urine; faeces smeared Herakles' legs and stained Barsine's robe.

'Let the men know that tomorrow we will meet with Kassandros and swear to him,' Polyperchon said, his eyes resting on his two victims. 'There will be no war in Europe.'

'Come,' Andronicus said, pulling Artonis out of her frozen state. 'You need to get away from here; Polyperchon will never forgive you for running to Ptolemy and asking him for help. And Kassandros and Thessalonike will kill you if you were to fall into their hands. I've a boat and a reliable crew standing by; they'll take you downriver to the sea and then on to Pydna, but no further.' He handed her a weighty purse. 'It's up to you to get a ship over to Asia. If you have no luck there, take passage to Chalcis; if he's there, Ptolemaios should help you as he's rebelling against his uncle. If you want my advice, I would make for Halicarnassus – Ptolemy was there last I heard; tell him I shall leave Polyperchon as soon as I can and wait for him in Corinth as ordered.'

Down the great river the boat was swept by a swift current; shadowed hills given vague form by pale moonlight towered to either side. Not one of Artonis' three companions spoke as they glided east. One man on the steering oar and the other two there to handle the sweeps or the sail should either be required; but their pace was fast enough for the conditions, a swift-flowing river in dim moonlight is no place for indecent haste.

Artonis was grateful for the silence; her emotions frozen by her close brush with death, she needed time to reflect. That she had failed was obvious – she fought to banish the image of her half-sister and nephew lying at her feet in pools of their own urine, eyes bulging and tongues swollen in a final, agonised horror mask – but how she was going to redress that failure was now her concern. What were her options? How would she now gain revenge on Antigonos for the execution of her husband? She smiled to herself as even now Eumenes' saving hand had reached out from beyond the grave to protect her from Polyperchon's rage. She had not known Andronicus well when he had served with her husband, in fact she had barely remembered him when he had reminded her of their acquaintance, but the loyalty Eumenes had always inspired – with the exception of the traitor Peucestas – had been strong enough for him to step forward and demand her life be spared.

But what was she to do with the time her husband had just given her? To run to Ptolemy, as Andronicus had suggested, was not necessarily the best course she could take, as what could she do once with him? She had no influence over him; indeed, he had plenty of women all vying for his ear so her chances of getting his attention were slim to say the least. No, if it was not to Ptolemy she should head then to whom? Seleukos? Too far and she would have to cross Antigonos' territory. Lysimachus? Too disinterested. And then she saw where she should go. *Sardis. Of course. I'll go to Kleopatra and take counsel with her; she will have an idea how to unite all these men against the common enemy, Antigonos and his son.*

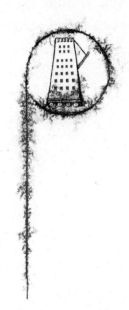

DEMETRIOS.
THE BESIEGER.

'**I**'M PROUD OF you, my boy,' Antigonos said upon Demetrios' arrival, ahead of his army, on the coast at Rhosos; he drew his eldest son into a manly embrace, swathing him in the fumes of resinated wine. After a couple of slaps on the back, Antigonos held Demetrios at arm's length. 'That was good, quick work.'

'The job's not done, Father; Seleukos has had some major success out in the east, beyond the Zagros Mountains.'

'Yes, but we hold Babylon.'

'Only seven thousand men hold Babylon. But as I said in my letters, holding Babylon means virtually nothing if there are no people there; it's like holding an empty seashell.'

'Which makes it less likely that Seleukos will bother to try to get it back.' Antigonos was not going to allow mere details to subdue the excellent mood he was in upon seeing his son again – and having had three jugs of wine. 'Let him keep the Zagros Mountains for the time being; we'll deal with him when we've finished here.' He attempted to stifle a burp but failed, and then thumped himself in the chest to clear some more excess wind.

'You've not been exercising enough, Father,' Demetrios observed, eyeing Antigonos' expanding frame up and down. 'You've got fatter since I've been away.'

Antigonos looked down at himself; his stained tunic bulged out, preventing a clear view of his feet. 'Nothing a good campaign won't get rid of. Playing politics with the petty kings of Cyprus is sedentary work.'

'And thirsty work.'

Antigonos' eye glared at his son. 'And what do you mean by that, my boy? I'll drink what I want, when I want; I always have.'

'And you always will, Father.' Demetrios smiled to defuse the situation.

A hearty slap on the shoulder showed there were no hard feelings. 'Come, my boy, we've much to discuss; summer is approaching and we need to use our time well.'

'It's Dioscurides who bothers me,' Antigonos said once they were ensconced in two wicker chairs beneath an awning outside his favourite tavern, overlooking the harbour crowded with transport ships; both had their own jug of resinated wine. 'He hasn't been heard of this year; he was wintering with the fleet on Lemnos and then nothing. All the messengers I've sent to the island return saying the fleet's gone but no one knows where it went. How can a fleet of over seventy ships just simply disappear? You tell me that.'

Demetrius sipped his drink as his father quaffed his. 'Perhaps he's gone up to the Euxine Sea.'

'What would he do up there?'

'Set himself and his lads up in some unsuspecting town and live off piracy.'

Antigonos considered the prospect for a few moments and then shook his head; he refilled his cup as the tavern-keeper placed a platter of fried squid and sardines on the table. 'No, I can't see it. A fleet doesn't simply go through the Hellespont and the Bosporus without someone noticing it. Besides, there would be rumours of a large pirate fleet from all the trading ships coming back from the Euxine Sea. Philippos is campaigning in Hellespontine Phrygia – he would have heard about it and would have written to me.'

'How is Philippos doing?'

'Very well, from all accounts according to Peucestas who's keeping an eye on him. He's got Phoinix bottled up on Cyzikos. The rest of the satrapy is ours again.' Antigonos paused for a squid ring. 'Once I've seen you off, I'm heading up there. I've decided it's time for me to start founding a few cities.'

Demetrios looked surprised. 'Already thinking about your legacy, Father? Mind you, if you carry on putting on weight like that then it's probably wise that you do.'

'Legacy, my arse!' He washed down his squid with the entire cup. 'No, it's my capital that I'm going to found, the place from where I shall rule over the whole empire.'

'The whole empire west of the Zagros Mountains, you mean.'

Antigonos growled and poured himself another drink, spilling much as his cup overflowed.

'And east of Greece, south of Thrace and north of Egypt.'

Antigonos hurled his cup, wine spiralling from it, to shatter against a stone wall. 'All right! Enough!'

'That's just my point, Father: we have enough. Do we really want to be chasing around, fighting Ptolemy's incursions here, a rebel satrap there and worrying about what Seleukos is getting up to leagues away? Do we really want all that bother – forever? Or should we just decide to be pragmatic about the situation?'

'Pragmatic, my arse.'

'Yes, Father, your arse *is* probably more pragmatic than you.'

'Don't give me your cheek, boy. I tried to be pragmatic by making peace with Ptolemy, Kassandros and Lysimachus and look where it got me.'

'That was temporary pragmatism in order to have time to deal with Seleukos. Once that was done you would have then taken each one of your new friends on one by one.'

'They were the ones who reneged on the deal.'

'You mean Ptolemy was the one who broke the peace.'

'He invaded Karia and Lycia.'

'Of course he did; he knew you were in Tyros making sure he didn't try to take Syria again. Philippos had taken another army to Hellespontine Phrygia; Ptolemaios was interested in what he could get for himself in Greece; and Dioscurides had turned up missing with a whole fleet; of course he broke the peace, he would have been a fool not to. And he timed it perfectly, knowing the only person you could call upon was me out in the east, meaning I had to leave the job I was sent to do half done. Don't you see, Father, we are in the middle and continually fighting on all fronts is draining and ultimately impossible.'

'We're not fighting on all fronts.'

'No? I've just brought my army back from fighting in the east.' Demetrios pointed to the transport ships in the harbour. 'I'm now going to embark it onto those ships to transport it west to Halicarnassus which is under siege by Ptolemy who claims sovereignty over Egypt in the south.

Meanwhile, my younger brother is fighting his first campaign in the north against a rebellious satrap who was put up to it by my cousin Ptolemaios, who's trying to make himself independent over in Greece. And I haven't even mentioned the Nabatean Arabs.'

Antigonos was downcast, his fit of temper subsiding into melancholy. He picked up his jug and took a swig from it in lieu of his cup.

Demetrios pressed on. 'And what are Kassandros and Thessalonike up to? Quiet at the moment, I'd have thought, otherwise you would have told me about their latest outrages already.'

Antigonos finished his jug in one long draught and then slammed it down upon the table. 'Kassandros was heading west to deal with Polyperchon and the bastard Herakles on the border with Epirus, the last I heard.'

'How many men does each of them have?'

Antigonos waved a hand. 'I don't know for sure; twenty, twenty-five thousand. Something around that number.'

'Each?'

'Each.'

'So, whoever wins could be sitting in the west with an army approaching forty thousand. What are they going to do with that? Have the lads sit around on full pay improving their cooking abilities?'

Antigonos' melancholy deepened; he reached for Demetrios' jug.

Demetrios grabbed his father's wrist. 'And Lysimachus to the north in Thrace, what about him? He spends a lot of his time fighting Scythians and keeping the Getae down whilst all the time building defences against this coming storm of giant savages with red hair that he's forever going on about. But that doesn't mean he doesn't dabble in Hellespontine Phrygia; he still has garrisons in Pergamum and several other towns. Do you imagine Phoenix would not have asked him for help? And after all the gold you sent to the Thracians to revolt against Lysimachus a few years back, do you imagine he refused? Even though he was still theoretically bound by your peace agreement.' He let go his grip. 'How are we ever going to subdue all of them? You fight one or two at a time and then another will wait his chance and take advantage of your absence from somewhere and before you know it…' Demetrios clicked his fingers.

Antigonos seized his son's jug, lifted it to his lips, paused and then threw it to join his shattered cup. 'I need more men.'

'There are no more men unless you take then from one of the others; the problem is whilst you're attempting to do so someone else attacks you from a different direction. We–are–in–the–middle, Father; the middle. This is as much territory as we're ever going to secure. Why don't we just recognise that, at least for a few years? No one can hold the entire empire; it's too late. We've got beyond that; now's the time to divide it up. We need to come to an agreement with everyone.'

'And what happened to the boy I brought up to seek glory at all costs, eh? The one who lost to Ptolemy at Gaza because he refused to listen to advice to fall back and stood his ground instead and got a drubbing; what happened to him?'

Demetrios closed his eyes and drew a deep breath. 'Father, he's still here. I want to be known as the greatest general since Alexander, but that's not going to happen if we're continually chasing our tails because each time we defeat a threat another pops up elsewhere. Let's call a halt, make a settlement that'll last so we can build up our strength until we're in the position to fight effectively on two, or even three, fronts at the same time.' Demetrios fixed Antigonos' eye with a beseeching look. 'Father, it really is time to—'

'Be pragmatic?'

'Yes, Father; be pragmatic. If we don't, we run the risk of looking weak.'

Antigonos got to his feet, none too steadily, and pointed a vicious forefinger at his son. 'Now you listen to me, boy. You say no one can hold the whole empire, meaning me; well, I'm not the only one who's trying.'

Demetrios could not hide his surprise.

Antigonos leered. 'That got you, didn't it? Well, I'm not. Ptolemy has been in negotiations with Kleopatra; he sent his eldest son, Lagus, to Sardis to speak to her. What could be the only reason for that? Simple. Kassandros has Thessalonike, but Ptolemy has the full sister, Kleopatra. But Kleopatra is too old to have children so she can be only of use to Ptolemy for one thing...'

Demetrios understood. 'To give him legitimacy to claim the whole empire. But I thought he was content with just Egypt and Cyrenaica.'

'Perhaps his beating you at Gaza has given him ideas above his station.'

Demetrios bristled but did not rise to the bait.

'So, you can take your pragmatism and shove it up your pragmatic arse and when you've finished wincing at the discomfort you can take your army and get it on those fucking ships I've provided and go and pragmatically kick Ptolemy out of my fucking satrapies before he manages to hook a dangerous, royal bitch.'

'And what are you going to do? Get drunk?'

Antigonos raised his hand but then stumbled, just catching his weight on the table enough to prevent himself falling, sending the seafood crashing to the ground. He breathed deeply, both fists supporting himself on the tabletop, and looked at Demetrios. 'No, now you're here, I'm going north to make sure Philippos has secured Phoinix and make an example of him. Then I shall found Antigoneia; in fact, two or three of them in Hellespontine Phrygia and fill them with my veterans to secure the satrapy once and for all; just like Kassandros has done with his new Thessalonike and Kassandreia and what Lysimachus is doing with Lysimachia on the Hellespont. And whilst I'm up there I shall take your suggestion to Kassandros and Lysimachus – as you will to Ptolemy as he leaves for Egypt – and if they all agree to a permanent settlement, which I'm sure they will, I'm going east to deal with Seleukos and take back the entire east. And with him gone and me as the most powerful man in the empire we shall see just how pragmatic everyone really is.'

Demetrios watched his father turn and weave away and shook his head. *He just doesn't see it; his ambition is blinding him.*

Antigonos turned over his shoulder. 'And on the way I'm going to stop off for a little chat with Kleopatra.'

'If he kills her, it will get out that he was responsible and it will be just like when Alcetas killed Cynane,' Demetrios said to Phila once the serious business of being reunited with his wife after several months had been accomplished.

'Worse,' Phila murmured, half asleep, 'Cynane was, like Thessalonike, just a half-sister. Kleopatra shares Alexander's blood. Your father would be risking a great deal killing her.

Kassandros blamed the young Alexander's death on him but nobody believed him really; but people might start to rethink that if he's seen to have killed the sister as well. That becomes a pattern emerging.'

Demetrios swung his legs off the bed and got to his feet. 'Well, I don't know about patterns but I do know my father's not thinking straight at the moment.'

Phila raised herself, supporting her weight on her elbows. 'That's what I was thinking. Why did he call you all the way back from Babylonia, leaving a job half done, so you can go and do something he was more than capable of doing himself, deal with Ptolemy, just so he can go and found his capital up in Hellespontine Phrygia before going back east to carry on what you were doing before he called you away? It's nonsense.'

'And it's given Seleukos enough time to re-establish himself.'

'Not if you deal with Ptolemy quickly.'

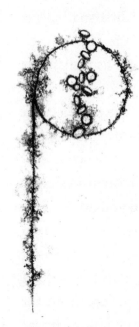

PTOLEMY.
THE BASTARD.

THERE WAS NO point in continuing the siege, Ptolemy could well see as he watched the dead being collected from beneath the smoke-swathed walls from the day's failed assault upon Halicarnassus. His spies had brought him warning of Demetrios' arrival at Rhosos and the embarkation of his army onto a fleet that would have them in Halicarnassus before the full moon and that orb was already almost a complete circle. Today's attack had been his final attempt to take the town and now it was time for pragmatism.

'Is everything prepared on Kos, Cleomones?' Ptolemy asked his siege commander, shading his eyes and looking across to the island a couple of leagues out to sea to where he planned to withdraw, rather than getting caught between Demetrios and his own siege lines.

'It is, my lord,' Cleomones replied. 'Timaeus reported the last of the supplies were ferried over this morning.'

'Then we should begin the evacuation at dawn. Have all the transport ships brought to the beach as the sun rises and the men waiting there ready for them. I'll make the crossing now.'

'Very good, my lord.' Cleomones did not dismiss.

'Was there something else, Cleomones?'

'Indeed, my lord, there is. Archias the Exile-Hunter wishes to see you when you have the time.'

Ptolemy's mood brightened. 'Good; let's hope he's come back with some good news. Tell him to join me on my ship.'

Cleomones sapped a salute and went about his orders.

Ptolemy turned and walked in the opposite direction in search of Thais, hoping that she had finished overseeing their packing; it was time to leave.

'We got as much out of it as we could, short of taking Halicarnassus,' Ptolemy said as he and Thais stood in the stern of the ship, watching the Exile-Hunter come aboard his great Five with his Thracian henchmen. 'Demetrios has been forced to return west, giving Seleukos time to secure the east and then to retake Babylon, which, my dearest,' he put an arm around Thais' waist, 'will be the catalyst that sends Antigonos back east with a good part of his army. And then we shall see.'

'What will we see, dearest?' Thais fluttered her eyelashes at him in the most vacant and naive fashion. 'A big battle?'

Ptolemy slapped her buttocks; his hand stayed in place, stroking. 'With luck the loser will be utterly defeated and the winner will be sufficiently weakened to have made the whole thing a very expensive exercise.'

'And you want Seleukos to be the victor, obviously.'

'I would prefer it to be Seleukos because I won't need to fight him – at least not for a good while – but if it's Antigonos, I'll have to consider a very swift campaign against him whilst he's still weak and before he benefits from the wealth and manpower of the east. But I'll have right on my side.'

'Because you will be married to Alexander's sister.'

'Was that jealousy I heard in your voice?'

Thais removed his hand from her backside. 'No, Ptolemy, it's exasperation. Although I understand you must prevent someone else having her, the more I think about it the more I realise that marrying Kleopatra is the wrong thing for you to do; but I'm going to let you find that out for yourself.'

'That's very kind of you.'

'You're welcome. Now let's go and talk to your favourite playmate, shall we? Other than me, that is.'

'He's waiting for me on Kos?' Ptolemy could not hide his surprise at Archias' report.

'Yes, he went to Pella to speak with Kassandros,' Archias said, leaning with one arm on the rail as a slave filled his goblet with wine. 'Whilst he did so I saw Cratesipolis in Corinth and then came back to Chalcis to await his return. Whatever Kassandros had offered was not enough, so I persuaded him to come and see you. I travelled with him and he ordered his ship to dock in Kos; there was nothing I could do. He insisted he would wait for you there. However, interestingly, I wasn't the only passenger on his ship.'

'Yes, you had your seven little friends with you.'

'Ah, but there was another passenger; this one was female. She'd taken passage on a trader from Pydna as far as Chalcis, Ptolemaios' main city, arriving just before we were going to leave. She begged him to bring her to Asia; he did, happy to help someone who was fleeing from Kassandros.' Archias halted as if that was the end of the tale and took a sip of wine, savouring its fullness.

'Go on.'

'It's very good,' Archias said, raising his goblet to Ptolemy. 'I take it that Lycortas isn't accompanying you, otherwise I wouldn't be treated to such a fine vintage.'

'Never mind the wine, what about the woman?'

'Oh, yes. Artonis disembarked at Ephesus, on her way to Kleopatra in Sardis.'

'Artonis? I thought she was with Polyperchon and her nephew causing Kassandros a lot of inconvenience.'

Archias' boyish face lit up with a delightful smile. 'Kassandros bribed Polyperchon to kill Herakles and his mother: a hundred talents in gold and a position as military governor of the Peloponnese south of the isthmus – or something along those lines.'

'He always loved a title, and the longer the better, the silly little man; it gave substance to his otherwise vacuous nature.' Ptolemy glanced over his shoulder as a whistle blew and the triarchos approached, bellowing orders to get the huge galley under way, and then turned back to Archias. 'What a shame for Herakles, though.' Ptolemy's face conveyed the exact opposite to that sentiment. 'Did Artonis say anything about Andronicus?'

'He saved her life and helped her to escape.'

'But didn't come with her?'

'She said to tell you he would wait in Corinth for your orders once the army had returned to the Peloponnese.'

'Good man.' The two steersmen nodded with deference at Ptolemy as they slipped past to take their steering oars. 'Come, let's move; we're disrupting a smooth naval manoeuvre,' he said, taking Thais by the arm and moving away from the realm of the triarchos, allowing him to take his place between the steering oars. 'And the redoubtable Cratesipolis? What did she have to say for herself?'

'She's open to negotiations as she can no longer trust her father-in-law.'

'I look forward to making the good lady's acquaintance.'

Archias grinned. 'She certainly merits closer inspection.'

Ptolemy glanced down at Thais, who gave him an innocent smile. 'Yes, well; I'm sure I'll make a full assessment of her qualities.'

'It would be very unlike you not to,' Thais observed.

Ptolemy cleared his throat and turned back to Archias. 'And what of Dioscurides and the missing fleet? Was there any sign?'

Archias shook his head as the ship edged away from the quay. 'No; Chalcis had no more ships in it than you would expect Ptolemaios to have and I looked into Oropos and Eretria and a couple of other ports and found nothing out of the ordinary; but there are many more smaller ports I couldn't investigate as I didn't travel north of Chalcis.'

'There're plenty of places to hide a fleet in the north of Euboea.' Ptolemy considered the thought and then dismissed the Exile-Hunter. 'Thank you, Archias; your remuneration will be waiting for you in Kos. Once you've picked it up, I want you to make a quick trip to Rhodos; I'll give you the details before you go as well as another fat fee.'

'"It is wise to pay the worker well,"' Archias quoted as he drained his goblet and, handing it to a waiting slave, made his way back across the deck to where his companions waited on the starboard rail..

'I sometimes think I pay you far too much,' Ptolemy observed as the Exile-Hunter left, before turning to Thais and rubbing his hands. 'Andronicus seems to have managed to do what I charged him with.'

'What, kill Herakles?'

'No, have Herakles killed by Polyperchon on Kassandros' orders thus putting the odium for spilling more of Alexander's blood on the two of them and not on me. I told him to marginalise and mock Polyperchon relentlessly, knowing the nonentity's misplaced pride in his soldiering would not stand for it and he would be ready to swop sides, if the right position were to be offered him. All Andronicus had to do once he'd achieved that was to make contact with Kassandros and suggest the plan to him. It seems to have worked, although I'm sorry about Barsine. I always liked her.'

'She should have known better than to try to set her son up above us,' Thais almost shouted against the rasping of scores of oars running out below as the great Five spread its wings.

'Quite. And now Artonis has gone running back to Kleopatra; that will be interesting.' Ptolemy slapped Thais' behind once more. 'Well, what started out as a terrible day, failing to take Halicarnassus, has just got much better with that news and it'll get better still when we reach Kos.'

'Really?'

'Yes, my dearest Thais, for waiting to see us on Kos is Ptolemaios and if anyone knows the whereabouts of Dioscurides and his missing fleet it will be his brother.' He ran a finger up the crease between her buttocks and motioned with his head towards his grand pavilion rigged on the foredeck. 'But we have a bit of time whilst we make the crossing which should not be wasted.'

The stroke-master's flute sounded and with a massed grunt of human exertion the beast of the sea was under way.

*

It was a refreshed Ptolemy, having put the time with Thais in his pavilion to extremely good use, who stepped off the gangway onto the quay in the port of Kos; Thais followed, with a contented smile on her face, looking unsurprisingly dishevelled. But his good mood did not last beyond his meeting with the man he had charged with setting up the military camp on the island. 'Where's Ptolemaios, Timaeus? Why's he not here to meet me?'

Timaeus grimaced as one does when the news about to be imparted is less than pleasing. 'He's waiting for you in the suite he made me give over to him.' Timaeus swallowed. 'He said to say he's expecting you as soon as you arrive.'

Ptolemy did a double-take, unsure that he had heard correctly. 'Say that again.'

Timaeus swallowed again. 'He said to say he's expecting you as soon as you arrive.'

'Yes, I thought that was what you said.'

'Yes, it was; I'm sorry, my lord.'

'No, no, don't be; I'm pleased you told me his exact words, it's helped me to get the measure of him.' Ptolemy strode by his local commander, with Thais speeding to keep up, his pace growing with his anger. 'The arrogance of the man! Summoning me when he's a guest in my own territory. What sort of way is that to open negotiations?'

'It would be bad enough if he considered himself your equal,' Thais said, her breath quick with the speed they were travelling, 'but to try to set himself over you is outrageous. What are you going to do?'

'Do? I'm going to do exactly as he says and see him immediately upon my arrival. I'm going to make him think I'm honoured that he should have deigned to visit me and how much I need his friendship. He won't suspect a thing.'

'Until you've got what you want and then he'll—'

'Meet Archias again? That's always a possibility. They know each other well already.'

'It's good of you to come, ' Ptolemaios said, getting up from his chair as Ptolemy was shown into the suite Antigonos' nephew had appropriated.

At least he has the decency to stand when greeting me. 'My dear Ptolemaios, it is an honour to welcome you to Kos.' He clasped the proffered forearm with a hearty grip. 'Let us hope we can be of good service to one another.'

'I'm sure we can. Please, be seated.' Ptolemaios indicated to a chair at an angle to the one he had been sitting in.

Bristling, but hiding it well, Ptolemy sat, affecting not to notice the slight difference in height. *What does he think he's going to achieve by all this?*

'So, I hear you're withdrawing from Halicarnassus,' Ptolemaios said in a tone that made it more of an accusation than a statement.

'It's not worth fighting Demetrios for; let him have it.'

Ptolemaios nodded in sympathy. 'Yes, you've beaten him once, no need to push your luck.'

Ptolemy's smile was warm. 'Quite. So, tell me, Ptolemaios, what did Kassandros say that gave me the good fortune of having you here?'

'Kassandros is an arrogant fool.'

And you're not?

'He seeks to make himself king of not only Macedon but of all Greece.'

'And, therefore, over you?'

Ptolemaios inclined his head a fraction. 'You see the problem in its entirety.'

'Well, I can assure you that I have no ambition to become king of Greece.'

'I'm pleased to hear it as I feel it's a position that, should it come to the taking of crowns by the foremost generals of the empire, I should be entitled to.'

It was a struggle for Ptolemy to keep his expression neutral, but with a gallant effort he managed.

'And it's for that reason I've travelled to see you.' Ptolemaios leaned forward, to add emphasis to his request. 'I want you to support me in my claim when the time comes. I would like us to be allies and, as such, we would take Athens together and remove Kassandros' creature, Demetrius of Phaleron.'

Ptolemy felt an eyebrow twitch but otherwise managed to retain control of his features. 'And why do you need my help to take Athens? Surely you have sufficient troops and, between you and your brother, you certainly have sufficient ships.'

Ptolemaios' facial control was not nearly as proficient as Ptolemy's; he could not cover his surprise. 'How did you know Dioscurides was with me?'

I didn't until just now. You're more foolish than I thought you were and far less clever than you think you are. 'I made an assumption that I was pleased to hear you confirm; I assume it was a sign of your good faith.'

Confusion flashed across Ptolemaios' face but he brought himself back under control. 'Yes, it is. Obviously, I was going to share my brother's whereabouts with you, should we come to an agreement, but then I thought it would help our mutual understanding if I were to vouchsafe that information.'

Ptolemy almost spluttered out a guffaw, but swallowed it and immediately felt a hiccup rise and get trapped in his throat; his chest jerked.

'Are you all right?' Ptolemaios asked.

'I'm fine; the midday meal repeating on me, that's all.' He reached for his cup and drank slowly from it, holding his breath. 'That's better,' he said as he felt the wind shift. 'So, Ptolemaios, if you have Dioscurides' fleet as well as your own and all your troops, what do you want from me?'

'Other than your public support for my claim to the crown of Greece?'

Bearing in mind there has never been such a thing. 'Yes, other than that; and I can assure you my support will be forthcoming and very enthusiastic.'

'You will find me very grateful; but what I'd really ask of you is your military support when I move against Cratesipolis and Polyperchon on the isthmus and further south. I have enough men and ships to take Athens but when Polyperchon brings his army back, now that he has come to an accommodation with Kassandros, I will need—'

'Men?'

'Yes.'

Ptolemy thumped his chest and released the final pocket of trapped wind with a satisfying burp. 'Men I can lend you, ships I can't spare, but that should not be a problem as you have your brother's.'

'I do,' Ptolemaios agreed.

'So where is Dioscurides now?'

'Skiathos; spread around the island.'

Clever; a few here and a few there and all able to see a beacon on the highest hill of the island to know when to muster in the port or wherever the designated assembly point is. And hardly anyone takes any notice of the island as they sail by as they're far more concerned with navigating the narrow strait between it and Magnesia so they don't become Poseidon's playthings. 'How many ships has he got?'

'Eighty-three.'

'Say a hundred men on each ship for the crossing to Greece, so I'll lend you eight thousand three hundred men, half Macedonians and half mercenaries. Would that be acceptable?'

Ptolemaios could not hide his relief and gratitude. 'That would be very acceptable, Ptolemy. A kind gesture from one equal to another.'

'Summon Dioscurides here with his fleet and I'll have the troops waiting when he arrives. In the meantime, please stay here as my honoured guest.'

'Are you really going to lend him the troops?' Thais asked as they prepared to dine with their new guest.

'Of course not. What advantage would I get with him defeating Polyperchon and Cratesipolis?'

'That's what I was wondering. Unless you want a strong power in Greece to counter Kassandros then I see nothing in it for you.'

'Exactly; but promising them to Ptolemaios will get Dioscurides and his fleet here and I don't intend it to leave again unless it's under my command.'

Thais reached up and held his chin as she raised herself on tiptoes to kiss his lips. 'You generally come up to expectations, Ptolemy.'

'Generally?'

'Yes, generally.'

'And when have I not?'

'With your ridiculous plan to marry Kleopatra.'

'You admitted it was best that I should have her rather than someone else.'

'You don't need to marry her to have control of her; just taking her to Egypt would suffice. You could say you were protecting her from Antigonos without threatening to replace the cyclops as the man who wishes to rule over the entire empire. Far safer, in my mind, as you won't unite everyone against you in the same way as we've all been united against Antigonos.'

'Well, it's settled and she will be arriving here very soon. In the meantime I'll consider your suggestion, although I can't see Kleopatra meekly accepting it. Lagus has gone back to Sardis to bring her to Kos. No doubt the formidable Artonis will be with her as she should be arriving in Sardis around now.' Ptolemy smiled at the thought. 'It'll give me an opportunity to commiserate with her about the unfortunate demise of her nephew.'

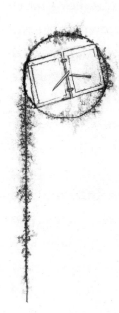

ARTONIS.
THE WIDOW.

ALMOST TWO MONTHS her journey had taken; almost two months since Artonis had watched her nephew and half-sister have the life throttled out of them by the slow twist of the executioner's garrotte. For three days after Andronicus had sent her to safety on a small river craft the vessel was swept down the swift-flowing Haliacmon to arrive at the coast between Pella and Pydna. Out to sea they passed and two days hugging the coast brought the little boat to Pydna with Artonis barely conscious through seasickness. Here, once she had recovered, her three escorts left her, their task complete. Unremarkable in her travel-stained clothes, she used the little money she had to buy passage on a ship headed south to Chalcis for she did not have sufficient to cover the huge fee the only trader bound for Asia was asking. But it had proven to be a fortunate lack of funds, for she had come across Archias in Chalcis and he had taken her to Ptolemaios. Once she had relayed her tale of betrayal by Polyperchon and her subsequent flight from Kassandros, Ptolemaios had agreed to deliver her to Ephesus on his way to meet with Ptolemy on Kos.

And now here she was, approaching Sardis to seek shelter with, and advice from Kleopatra, one of the few people she could trust to oppose Antigonos with all her being. Now that the final chance to place Alexander's blood on the throne had died with Herakles, and thus provide a focal point for resistance to the resinated cyclops' drive to bring the empire under his control, Artonis had decided to return to the original plan, the idea put forward by her husband at his death: to unite the main generals against Antigonos in coalition and defeat him in one grand campaign cumulating in a decisive battle to settle the issue once and for all and to finally sate Artonis' thirst for revenge.

But to bring the leading generals together so that personal interests would all be served at the same time had proven impossible, as had been made clear by Kassandros and Lysimachus making peace with Antigonos only to be followed by Ptolemy doing likewise. Ptolemy had then broken the treaty when it suited him, whereas Kassandros could now claim his subverting of Polyperchon's campaign and the subsequent execution of Herakles was in line with his agreement with Antigonos and thus was still at peace with him. As for Lysimachus, who could say what went on in his mind as he strove to keep the northern frontier of the empire secure from the growing pressures thrusting against it? But what was sure was Lysimachus had shown no interest in expanding his realm south of the Hellespont since losing most of Hellespontine Phrygia to Antigonos; although his founding of the new city of Lysimachia on the Thracian shore of the Hellespont did indicate a new willingness to look to the south. Artonis, therefore, needed a new rallying point to unite Kassandros, Lysimachus, Ptolemy and, perhaps, Seleukos. And Kleopatra was the one person left who could fulfil that role.

Thus it was that Artonis, similar to Kleopatra when she had entered Pergamum in disguise, came through the gates of Sardis, past the guards of Antigonos' garrison, looking like no more than the wife of a merchant down on his luck.

With no chance of getting into the palace without giving her name to the guards, and so revealing herself, Artonis sat down on the steps of the Temple of Artemis, across the Processional Way from the palace, to watch the comings and goings of the slaves and officials as they went about their duties, awaiting an opportunity to get a message to Kleopatra; for there was one person whom she knew could help her.

It was soon after dawn the following day that Thetima, Kleopatra's body-slave who had accompanied her to Pergamum, came out of the palace's gates and hurried away down the Processional Way towards the agora. With her cloak wrapped tightly around her, covering her head, Artonis followed, gradually gaining on her as the crowds heading for the market thickened.

'Thetima,' Artonis said, drawing level with the slave, 'it's me, Artonis. I was with Barsine when your mistress visited her in Pergamum.'

The slave slowed to look at Artonis, who pushed back her cloak to reveal her features more clearly, praying the woman was in possession of a reasonable memory.

'I remember you,' Thetima confirmed. 'What are you doing here?'

Artonis took her by the arm. 'I need to get into the palace to see Kleopatra. Can you get a message to her?'

Thetima thought for a few moments, assessing the potential dangers to herself before coming to a reluctant decision. 'What is it?'

307

'Tell her I'm waiting at the Temple of Artemis; I'll wait there until I hear from her. I have news she needs to hear.'

With an unconvincing nod, Thetima acquiesced. 'But first I have to buy herbs for my lady's bath.'

'Yes, of course; do whatever she has sent you out for. But please don't forget to pass on my message as soon as you get back, will you?'

'Of course I won't.' Thetima looked insulted by the reminder. 'I must get going.' Without another word she hurried forward to disappear into the crowd of morning market-goers heading for the agora.

There was nothing to do but wait. With her last few bronze coins, Artonis bought a loaf and some cheese and then returned to her vigil, sitting on the temple steps, half concealed by a column and the hawkers selling religious knick-knacks; tearing off small hunks of bread, she chewed methodically, her eyes never leaving the gate. Eventually, after what had seemed like most of the morning, she saw Thetima coming back from the market; with not a second glance, the guards let her through the gate. *And now my fortunes are in the hands of a portly slave.*

The day wore away and despair crept up on Artonis as the shadows lengthened. With gloom now falling and lamplight beginning to appear in widows opening onto the street, the gate opened; two silhouetted figures, soldiers, came through and, without pausing, headed straight to where Artonis sat. She tensed, one hand on a column, watching them approach. Panic rose. *It is me they're coming for.* The realisation of betrayal galvanised her into action. She pushed against the column, propelling herself to her feet, and sprinted away along the steps, her sandals clacking as they pounded the stone, barging a hawker out of the way, spilling his tray of crude statuettes.

But it was fit men who pursued her, men who sprinted every day in order to keep themselves at the peak of condition, and although she took the steps three at a time as she descended the other side of the temple, she only got less than a dozen paces away from it before a muscular arm wrapped around her waist, lifting her off her feet, her legs still working.

'Kleopatra wants to see you,' the man's voice growled in her ear, his breath made pungent by a rotting tooth, 'so quit your struggling.'

Such was the steel of his grip she could not squirm in his arms to better see his face in order to batter it, so she just pounded her small fists over her shoulder, striking wildly until she felt her wrists gripped by the second man and further resistance became impossible.

'That's better, my lady,' the man said, with another waft of foul air. 'It's much easier if you come quietly.'

'I'm sorry, Artonis,' Kleopatra said as they sat alone in her apartment looking out over a courtyard garden glowing in torchlight. 'There was no other way to get you in without using your name; those two guards still have loyalty to my brother. It's easy to get someone who has been arrested through the gates, far easier than getting someone not approved by Antigonos through.' She smiled at her guest. 'But you're here now and looking much better for your bath and clean clothes than when you arrived. I thought I was a sight when I came to Pergamum in disguise, but you, my dear, you didn't need a disguise; you were genuinely worn and torn from travel.'

'I've come all the way from the borders of Macedon and Epirus.'

'Then I can only assume it's with bad news.'

Artonis nodded, tears now welling in her eyes as the grief which she had not yet had time to express surged within her. 'Polyperchon betrayed us; he made a deal with Kassandros and Thessalonike and...' a series of sobs exploded from her, 'and executed Herakles and Barsine. He had them garrotted. Garrotted and I was forced to watch. I would have joined them had Andronicus not saved me. He wouldn't allow Polyperchon to order my death and got me away.' She collapsed into Kleopatra's arms as they folded around her, drawing her close, the pent-up grief now, finally, coming out in waves, her body shaking without control.

'It was always a risk we ran,' Kleopatra said. 'No one can ultimately be trusted as we will always do what is best for ourselves; but Polyperchon and Kassandros coming to a deal surprises me. Kassandros hates him because Antipatros gave the nonentity the Great Ring of Macedon thus passing his own son over. And Polyperchon has every right to fear Kassandros for his vengeance.'

'It was Herakles who drove them together; and mine and Barsine's fault for failing to see what was going on,' Artonis said. 'He constantly humiliated Polyperchon. I know he's a pedantic little marionette of a man, but he was trying to do his best for Herakles. At first Herakles took no interest in him as he spent his whole time hunting with his new friends; and then, after I had gone to Ptolemy to beg him to lend us a general with more dash, urgency and intelligence, and I came back with Andronicus, Herakles began taking more of an interest in the campaign and military matters. Andronicus spent all his time mocking Polyperchon's way of doing things and his priorities, encouraging others to do so too, and inevitably Herakles did the same. It got to the point when he couldn't speak to the old man without a snigger or sometimes outright laughter.'

Kleopatra rubbed Artonis' shoulders as she digested her news, frowning. 'Did Andronicus go out of his way to humiliate Polyperchon from the moment he arrived?'

Artonis heaved another sob, pulling herself together, ashamed at showing such frailty. 'He seemed to, yes, from the moment he...' Her eyes widened; she lifted her head and looked at Kleopatra. 'Do you mean to say?'

'With Ptolemy, who can ever say?'

'But why?'

'That's something I shall ask him if I marry him.'

'Marry him?'

'Yes.'

Artonis did not conceal her shock. 'Why?'

'We've been in negotiation on the subject for a while, but I've said neither yes nor no as I was waiting for news of Herakles' bid for the crown. Ptolemy's son, Lagus, was here yesterday to find out if I'd made up my mind; I sent him back saying I was still considering the matter. Had Herakles been successful I wouldn't need to marry Ptolemy. But now, well, now he won't be claiming the throne perhaps it's down to me to do so for the sake of my bloodline. Who else is there left who is worthy of me to be my consort?'

Artonis could see the point. 'You would be queen?'

'Am I to sit here for the rest of my days as an unclaimed prize or should I take what's there for the taking before Thessalonike claims it or Antigonos wins it?'

'And with the crown, you will take on Antigonos?'

'That'll be the price Ptolemy pays for my hand. Instead of playing with the cyclops, leading him around, stretching him this way and that, I will expect him to bring him to

311

battle and defeat him utterly with the help of Lysimachus, Seleukos and even Kassandros. And then, well, then we shall see.'

But what would happen then did not concern Artonis as then Antigonos would be dead and her vengeance done. She had never thought seriously about what would happen after she had spat in Antigonos' glazed, cyclopic eye.

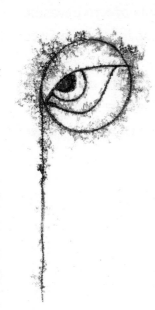

ANTIGONOS.
THE ONE-EYED.

ANTIGONOS KNEW WHEN he was being toyed with, and someone had been toying with him for the whole year; two even. Recently, however, he had become sure it had been Ptolemy behind the various moves, although how he had coordinated them, he knew not.

That Seleukos' retaking of Babylon had been with Ptolemy's troops was for certain; but had he also had a hand in Ptolemaios' bid for independence and Phoinix's rebellion in Hellespontine Phrygia? Antigonos had always shaken his head when he contemplated this point; he could not see how it was possible.

And then Ptolemy had invaded Lycia and Kyria at a time when Philippos was on his first campaign in the north against Phoinix, Demetrios was out east in Babylonia and Antigonos was afraid to leave Syria for fear Ptolemy's move north was a diversion for an invasion from Egypt allied with the Nabateans – who were still, despite the gift of camels, making a nuisance of themselves on his eastern border. With Ptolemaios in revolt and Dioscurides missing, he had had no option but to recall Demetrios. It was then he knew he was being toyed with, but what the final objective was he had not known, but he was sure it was more than just to annoy him.

With the latest news to come to his ears, however, it was all beginning to make sense: Ptolemaios had arrived in Kos to meet with Ptolemy. Ptolemy's general, Andronicus – the man who used to be loyal to him, Antigonos – had been sent to aid Herakles and had clearly done something to sabotage the endeavour. *A very sensible move, it has to be said, seeing as another king would have helped no one.* And now, with the final male of the Argead line dead, Ptolemy was in negotiation with Kleopatra for her hand. Now the mist was clearing; now he could see Ptolemy's goal. *He's making a bid for the whole empire; he wants to take what should be mine. He's in talks with Ptolemaios to help him against Kassandros in the west, whilst Seleukos will always support him against me in the east, leaving Lysimachus in the north as an unknown factor. Demetrios was right: we're in the middle – we always are, if we're not on the offensive.* These thoughts went around his head as he made his way north to Sardis, determined to face down Kleopatra and force her to stay, making her an actual prisoner if needs be, rather than just the 'well-looked-after guest' as he considered her to be at the moment.

And this well-looked-after guest was about to benefit from his thoughts on the matter, he mused as he stormed through the royal palace in Sardis, having growled orders that his arrival was not to be made known to Kleopatra. Working himself up into more of a rage with each step he took, he barrelled through the colonnaded main hall, with two burly companions in tow, then stormed up the stairs, two at a time, pushing his way past the guards at the bottom and top, indicating to them that they should follow him, before turning right along a high-ceilinged, lavishly painted, wide corridor, taking no notice of the nymphs and other mythical creatures gambolling and fornicating to either side.

'Antigonos!' Kleopatra exclaimed, getting to her feet, as he crashed through the door to her private apartments, leaving the two following guards on the door.

'Yes, Antigonos, the resinated cyclops! I'm sure you're thrilled to see me.' Movement caught the corner of his eye and he turned. 'Artonis! You too? Well, my precious, well-formed arse, it's my lucky day. Sit down.' Kleopatra looked over to Artonis and gave a barely perceivable shake of her head.

You thought I wouldn't notice that, bitch; what are you two up to? He turned to his two companions. 'Make sure neither of them makes a run for it.'

'To what do I owe the pleasure of this unexpected visit?' Kleopatra said, gathering her composure and sitting back down as the companions positioned themselves behind each of the women.

'I can assure you this visit will be far from pleasurable.' Antigonos took a seat without being asked.

'We shall see.' Kleopatra clapped her hands; Thetima stepped into the room. 'Call for sherbet, Thetima, and resinated wine.' She glanced at her guest, noting his red complexion. 'A lot of resinated wine, I should think; our guest has quite a thirst on him.'

'Don't you make fun of me,' Antigonos snarled as Thetima left the room with a fearful glance in his direction.

'I would never dream of it, general.'

'No? Then what do you mean by marrying Ptolemy?'

'Marrying Ptolemy? Really?'

315

Antigonos' eyes narrowed. *I knew the bitch would deny it. Fine, we'll play it her way.* 'Ptolemy's son, Lagus – who, incidentally, takes after his father in that he too is a bastard – has been here negotiating the terms of your union.'

'Whatever gave you that idea, Antigonos? Surely Ptolemy has enough wives as it is? What would he want with one more, especially one who is past child-bearing age?'

'Don't play innocent with me, Kleopatra; he doesn't want you for what may or may not slide out from between your legs – he's got enough brats of his own. He wants you because of what your blood can give him.'

'And what would that be, Antigonos?'

'Don't be obtuse; the crown of course.'

'But I thought that was what *you* wanted.'

'I'm the only one strong enough to hold the empire together and you know it. "To the strongest," Alexander said and that has proven to be me.'

'Really, I hadn't noticed. If you're the strongest then you have a very strange way of showing it, sending armies here, there and everywhere fighting all these insurrections by people who dispute your claim to be the strongest. Why, even your nephews disagree with you.'

'I wipe my arse with my nephews.'

'How very nice for you, Antigonos; and them, I'm sure.'

'Don't attempt wit with me, Kleopatra; you're in a far more dangerous position than you might think. My patience with you has just run out.'

Kleopatra stared him straight in the eye, unblinking. 'Is that a threat, general? And if so, what does it mean?'

'It means that should you try to go to Ptolemy – or should I even think you're trying to reach him – then I will have no alternative but to restrain you in any way

I deem appropriate to ensure you do not make the attempt again.'

'Are you threatening my life? Me, the sister of Alexander?'

'You think I should be afraid of you just for the blood flowing in your veins, do you? My arse, I should! Olympias used to play that trick and she ended up being executed, stone by stone, and no one so much as reprimanded Kassandros for engineering it. And what about when the pockmarked little toad had the young Alexander murdered and tried to blame it on me? Did anyone raise their voice against him? No. Did I protest very loudly that he was trying to blame me for something he'd done? No. Why not? Because everyone knew it was bollocks and he and Thessalonike were responsible, but no one really cared as it made life a lot simpler. And I've recently heard Kassandros has managed to rid us of Herakles; well, well.' He cupped a hand to his ear. 'Listen to the outrage.' Antigonos got to his feet, pushing his chair over. 'So don't try to hide behind your blood, Kleopatra; those days are over. Yes, it could help Ptolemy claim the crown, but no, it won't stop me from having you killed. There, is that blunt enough for you? Do you consider that to be fair warning? I do and I think it's more than generous of me.' His malevolent eye fixed Kleopatra, who stared back unmoved.

Antigonos glowered and grunted before turning his eye on Artonis. 'As for you and your vicious little scheme of trying to make Alexander's bastard king of Macedon in order to outmanoeuvre me, you've got exactly what you deserved: a dead nephew and a dead half-sister. Killed before your eyes, if all I hear is true. I've spared your life twice now because I don't make war on women and children but you've stretched that point.' He thrust his finger at her.

'Anything, Artonis, and I mean *anything* you do against me again will result in your demise. Even if I hear so much as a rumour from one of my spies in this household that you're encouraging Kleopatra to go against me, that'll be it for you.' *That's had the desired effect, judging by her eyes.* 'Of course I have spies in this household, Sardis is mine; everyone in it is mine.' The eye roved between the two women. 'You are mine.'

Antigonos did not look back as he kicked his fallen chair out of his way and stormed out the room with his men stamping after.

By the time he arrived at the site of the future Antigonea the following evening, Antigonos' mood had barely improved, despite Philippos presenting him with the head of Phoinix. 'It took you long enough,' he snarled at his youngest son, pulling the head up by the hair, grimacing at the stink and then letting it drop back into the bag.

'Is that all you can say, Father?' Philippos asked, annoyed more than hurt. 'I've put down a rebellion in Hellespontine Phrygia, garrisoned every major town, brought the rebel satrap to battle and defeated him thoroughly, taken his surviving troops into our army and brought you his head and all you can snarl at me is "it took you long enough"? That could be construed as ingratitude to say the least.'

Antigonos grunted and then looked at his son, putting a hand on his shoulder. 'You're right, my boy, you've done well.' He then looked at the sack again. 'But couldn't you have brought him to me alive?'

'Not really, Father; he was missing an arm and had an arrow in his chest so I don't think he would have survived the journey here.' Philippos looked around the low hill upon

318

which his father's tent stood and then down to the river at its base; all around hundreds of slaves dug deep foundation trenches under the watchful eyes and sharp whips of their overseers. 'Wherever here is.'

Antigonos smiled and dismissed the slave holding the foul-smelling sack with a wave. 'Here, my boy, is the site of my new capital in Anatolia. It'll bestride the river which is navigable all the way to the Propontis and it is only fifteen leagues to Sardis and the Royal Road, the same distance to Pergamum and then only another five leagues from there to the sea.' He drew a deep breath of satisfaction as he surveyed the industry going on all around. 'I'll fill it with my veterans and it'll become the main trading centre north of Tarsus and west of Halicarnassus.'

'But it's in the middle of nowhere. I should know because I've just fought a campaign throughout this country, and I can promise you, this place was never once considered to be of any strategic importance.' Philippos looked around again and shook his head. 'If it's not worth a drachma in military terms because, apart from the river – which at this point, is unfordable – there's nothing to be said for it, then how can you expect it to prosper as a centre for trade?'

'Don't ask stupid questions, boy. What do you know about it? You're seventeen and barely weaned from your mother's tit.'

'I know enough to tell a well-placed town when I see one; I've just spent the last few months taking them and leaving the other less well-placed ones because they were not worth the effort and would have to surrender anyway once the important ones had opened their gates to me. And I tell you: I wouldn't bother taking this when Sardis, Pergamum, Magnesia and Ipsus are all of far more strategic importance.'

'Ipsus! What's so important about Ipsus that would have it overshadow Antigonea once it's built?'

'It's at the junction of the Royal Road east and the branch leading south to Tarsus, thus controlling the route to and from the centre of Asia.'

'Yes, I know that; that's why I have a garrison there.'

'Well then, Father, what are we arguing about?'

'We're arguing about the fact that Ipsus is too far inland to be of great importance.'

'Father, if I had a choice between fighting to control Ipsus or here, it would be Ipsus because this place will never be of more strategic importance than Ipsus and so therefore it will never be suitable as your capital; nor will it be suitable as a trading centre.'

Antigonos' eye narrowed. 'It'll be suitable because I say it is; I will make Antigonea suitable.'

Philippos shrugged as he saw Antigonos' temper rising. 'If you say so, Father. It's just that I can't see people like Babrak the merchant diverting north off the Royal Road instead of carrying on to Sardis and Ephesus; why should he when the trade is all in those two cities? Which reminds me, did you see him on your way here?'

'Babrak? No. When did you see him?'

'Five days ago, on the Royal Road just before it crosses the River Hermus, heading to Sardis.'

Antigonos cursed. 'No, I came here across country; I would've just missed him. Did he have news from the east?'

'Not good, I'm afraid. Seleukos has defeated Nikanor somewhere beyond the Zagros Mountains; the rumour is that Nikanor escaped and Seleukos incorporated most of his army into his own. At the time Babrak left Media, Seleukos was making his way back to Babylon via Susa; apparently, he's made an alliance with the Cossaei and can travel through the mountains rather than having to go round. So, I would say he's there about now – Babylon, that is, not Susa.'

Antigonos spat another curse and then invoked his arse. 'What else did he say? Did he give any details of how large Seleukos' force is now?'

Philippos shook his head. I didn't ask, Father; it was only a brief meeting as I was following your instructions and hurrying to install a garrison at Ceramon and then get back here to meet you.'

'I need to speak to him personally. If Seleukos was on his way back to Babylon via Susa when Babrak left Media then he should definitely be at Babylon by now. The only question is, is he inside or outside the walls? And my guess would be if he's defeated Nikanor he'll easily have the numbers to overrun Demetrios' seven thousand-strong garrison, no matter how strongly they defend the two citadels.' Antigonos came to a decision. 'You stay here in the north; keep the work going and see if you can get news of what Lysimachus is doing; he has, no doubt, heard of Kassandros' success against Herakles and probably of Seleukos' victory. I want to know whether that will affect the treaty we have with him. Keep a quarter of your army with you and send Peucestas with the rest to Tarsus with orders to get provisions in for a long campaign; I'll meet him there. I'm going to head east with your men and mine so I've the strength to deal with Seleukos once and for all, once I've seen Babrak at Sardis and have found out as much as possible about Seleu—' He stopped mid-word. 'My arse!'

'What, Father?'

'Babrak is probably sitting having sherbets with Kleopatra and Artonis, telling them all about my setbacks in the east.'

'So?'

'So, Kleopatra and Ptolemy have been negotiating a marriage.'

'No! Surely not.'

'I'm afraid so. I stopped in Sardis and threatened her life should she even think about going through with it. If Babrak has given her the impression I've lost control of the east, she might well think the time has come to defy me. And if she is in two minds about it, I can guarantee Artonis will help her make the wrong decision.'

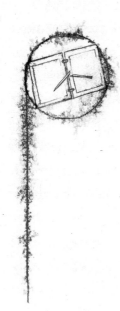

ARTONIS.
THE WIDOW.

ARTONIS GLANCED AT Kleopatra as Babrak finished recounting recent events in the east. *This is a life and death situation; if we make the wrong decision, Antigonos will triumph and Eumenes will go unavenged.* Kleopatra's expression, however, was inscrutable behind her veil, worn to put the Paktha at ease in the company of women.

'Are you certain Seleukos will be able to pass through the Zagros Mountains unmolested by the Cossaei, Babrak?' Kleopatra asked the merchant sitting opposite her, shaded from autumnal sun by a mature almond tree, laden with fruit ready to harvest. 'Antigonos almost lost his army trying the same route a few years back.'

Had he done so, Eumenes would still live.

Babrak's dark eyes twinkled. 'Gracious lady, the difference between Seleukos and Antigonos is as the difference between a boy and a goat...' He paused as he remembered to whom he was talking. 'I meant to say a camel and a donkey: one is...' He grimaced as he tried to get his thoughts in order to come up with the appropriate comparison. 'One is—'

'Babrak!' Kleopatra had had enough of the Paktha's indirect mode of speech. 'Just tell me what makes Seleukos different to Antigonos in your opinion with no mentions of animals – or boys, for that matter – they don't interest me, nor do they make things clearer.'

Babrak eyed the purse set on the table between them. 'Indeed, most gracious lady. Antigonos is a man of the west, with little or no understanding for – and certainly no interest in – the ways of the east. He refused to pay tribute to the Cossaei as he travelled through their lands after Eumenes,' he nodded to Artonis, 'may his name be ever honoured, defeated him at the Coprates River. Deeply offended by this insult, the tribe harried the army all through its transit of the Zagros Range; Antigonos lost far more in men and supplies than it would have cost him to come to an arrangement with the Cossaei – as we all do, who travel that road. In other words, he was saving a drachma to lose a talent. Seleukos, on the other hand, has a Sogdian wife, Apama, and she has instilled into him the need to respect the customs of the various peoples of the east and not just act like a conqueror with the right to do whatever pleases whenever it pleases. He therefore went to pay his respects to Spinates, the King of the Cossaei, and brought him a great gift of two chests – large chests – full of treasure as a show of respect with the promise of repeating the gift every year.

'Spinates was so moved by such a testament – as he put it – of Seleukos' regard for him, he immediately decreed that Seleukos, and anyone travelling in his name or on his business, had the right to cross Cossaei territory at any time.' Babrak extended his hands, palms up. 'And there you have it, gracious lady.' He inclined his head to Artonis. 'I should say: ladies. Seleukos understands the east, Antigonos does not.'

Kleopatra contemplated the assessment for a few moments. 'So, with the ten thousand or more he captured from Nikanor, Seleukos has an army numbering around forty thousand?'

'Indeed, gracious lady; and there is a rumour he'll receive – or might even have received by this time – a present of many elephants from King Porus in India. Although I stress it is but a rumour.'

Kleopatra indicated to the purse. 'Thank you, Babrak; you have, as usual, been most informative.'

'I am pleased to be of service, gracious lady.' The merchant stood, picking up his payment. 'If I can do anything else for you before I leave for Ephesus when my business here is complete, I shall be most honoured.' Touching his forehead and chest, Babrak bowed and reversed a few paces before turning to make his way back through the garden.

Kleopatra waited until he was out of earshot. 'Well?'

Artonis could sense the importance of the coming conversation. 'Well, I think Antigonos has no choice but to take an army east and have it out with Seleukos, much as he did with my husband; only this time I pray for a different result. The question is: will he pass through here on his way or will he travel to Ipsus and then take the Tarsus road?'

Kleopatra looked at the departing figure of Babrak. 'I think he's absolutely correct in his assessment of Seleukos.'

'Which makes him the most likely winner of the contest,' Artonis said, 'as he'll have more allies to call upon during the campaign who would rather be associated with the coming power than the old order. Antigonos, however, will only have what he takes with him.'

'Which means he'll lose a war of attrition.'

'A reasonable assumption. But Antigonos' defeat is unlikely to be fatal for him; he'll just come back west as a wounded beast.'

Kleopatra unclipped her veil and turned to Artonis. 'Why do you say that?'

'Because both Seleukos and Antigonos will retain the loyalty of their respective armies and therefore won't be betrayed and sold out as my husband was.'

'And we all know what a wounded beast is like.'

Artonis removed her veil to give herself time to choose her words carefully. 'Should Antigonos come here on his way east then he will take measures – shall we say – to ensure you don't flee to Ptolemy in his absence.'

'I agree. And if he goes directly east and is defeated, he'll do all he can to secure what remains to him upon his return.'

'And he would see you as a more potent threat than you are now, because he would be that much weaker.'

Kleopatra nodded to herself as she digested the information and revolved the different courses of action around her head. 'Seleukos' success has changed the weight of power in the empire away from the cyclops; he is now surrounded by forces he would struggle to defeat singularly, let alone if two or more of them should join together. He must have realised that by now and so, if he has any sense – which he does – he would come through Sardis to eliminate me on my way east to leave one less threat behind him.'

Artonis felt relief at not having to persuade Kleopatra to act now against her will. 'So, we go to Ptolemy?'

'Yes, we go.'

'Then we should leave immediately and not openly. Babrak may have to curtail his business here.'

'I shall make it worth his while.' Kleopatra clapped her hands. 'Thetima!'

In a covered wooden wagon, veiled and wearing clothes of little note, Artonis and Kleopatra passed under the west gate of Sardis in the midst of Babrak's caravan, moving at the speed of a camel's walk despite the downhill incline. Attended by Thetima and a younger slave, Laomini, the two women made themselves comfortable on deep cushions, trying to make cheerful conversation to disguise their nervousness at the slow pace of their flight.

'Once we're a couple of leagues from the city we'll take the horses and ride as fast as we can for Ephesus,' Kleopatra said, for the third or fourth time since they had passed through the gates. 'Thetima, look back to check there aren't any cavalry racing after us.'

'There's nothing on the road, my lady,' Thetima said, having peered out through the grille in the door.

'I wish Babrak would make his camels go faster. Perhaps this wasn't such a good idea after all.'

Artonis sighed, finding the air stifling. 'How else would we have got past Antigonos' guards on the gate? Had we been on our own the wagon would have been thoroughly searched. Babrak just earned his gold by insisting we were his property and that if they wanted to inspect us then they had to buy us first.'

Kleopatra laughed at the memory. 'Who would have ever thought I'd end up as being considered the property of a boy-loving Paktha?'

Artonis joined her mirth. 'And have him threaten to sell us rather than us be defiled by the removal of our veils; had I not been so concerned he would simply give into the guards, I think I would have giggled into my veil.'

'He did well not to attract attention by trying to bribe them more than the going rate; I'll be sure to reimburse him the eight drachmae.' Kleopatra lay back into the pillows with her hands behind her head and stared at the ceiling in silence as the wagon rumbled on down the hill. 'What's Egypt like?' she asked at length.

'Hot and dry, most of the year round. Alexandria is going to be beautiful once it is completed. It would be lovely now if it weren't for all the building sites and the dust rising from them. But that's a minor inconvenience compared to the jealousy of Eurydike in particular and probably Berenice as well.'

'I'm ready for that; they'll not be able to argue against my superior blood. I'll make sure we all understand one another straight away. But you've not mentioned Thais; will she not be jealous too?'

Artonis shook her head. 'She has no need to be as Ptolemy spends more time in her chamber than the other two put together. He also dines with her for pleasure and goes to her for advice. It wouldn't surprise me if this marriage were her idea. If the rumours are true, it was she who suggested Ptolemy marry Berenice.'

'Really? Well, then, I think Thais and I might get on extremely well.'

'Yes, I think you might.'

'My lady,' Thetima said with a degree of alarm.

Kleopatra lifted her head and pushed herself up onto her elbows. 'What is it?'

'Horsemen – a dozen or so have just come out the gate and are galloping after us.'

Kleopatra sprang to her knees, crawled to the grille and looked out. 'What do we do?'

Artonis felt the world disappear from beneath her feet; her stomach lurched. It took a few moments before she braced herself for positive action and pressed her eye to the grille; the horsemen, still small in the distance, were less than a quarter of a league away but moving fast. 'We're dead if we give up, and we're trapped if we stay in here. Out!' Artonis slid up the restraining bar and the doors fell open. 'Thetima and Laomini, you stay here; there's no need to share our danger.' Out she jumped and, unhitching one of the horses tethered to the side of wagon, swung her leg over the beast's back. 'Kleopatra, quick!'

The response was a scream, high and suddenly curtailed.

Artonis turned the mare and pulled it round to the back of the wagon. Her eyes widened in shock at what she saw. 'What are you doing, Thetima?'

'I can't let her live,' the slave shouted, tears in her eyes as she held a knife to her mistress's throat, her left arm clamped around her chest. Laomini lay with her throat slit next to her. 'Antigonos said he would blind me and leave me in the street if he caught me with her and she was still alive.' She tightened her grip around Kleopatra's chest and pressed the knife into her flesh.

'Why did you not say?' Kleopatra gasped, her chin high and throat taut.

'He said he would do the same if he found me in Sardis and you gone. I had no choice but to come with you and hope we made it.'

'Put the knife down, Thetima,' Artonis urged. 'We can

still escape all together.' But as she said it, she knew it was not true; the horsemen would follow Kleopatra and eventually they would overhaul them. She saw in Thetima's frightened eyes the same conclusion.

Kleopatra squirmed in her slave's grip, twisting left and pulling her hands down to be free of the arm, but Thetima was equal to the attempt and pulled them both back so Kleopatra lay on top of her, her legs kicking but her torso locked firm. 'You can't kill me, Thetima, I am the sister of Alexander.'

'And I am Thetima. I have as much right to life as you.'

It was abrupt, brutal and bloody. Kleopatra's eyes bulged as her last exhalation sprayed a red mist from her mouth; her weakening pulse spewed gore from her slit throat, soaking the dress of her killer, lying beneath her, screaming with the horror of what she had done.

It was pointless to stay. With no second glance, Artonis kicked her mount forward and accelerated away alongside the caravan to clear it and then race on down the hill to where the road bent to the south-west in the direction of Ephesus. Here, out of sight of the caravan, she turned south off the road, urging her horse uphill, climbing until she could look back. There was no one following her. The caravan was now stationary, shouts rising from it, sounding hollow as she looked down. Horsemen now surrounded the wagon; one, judging by his size, was Antigonos. He slid from his mount and pulled Thetima, screaming, to the ground, hauling her by her arm to the side of the road, still screaming. Her head spun in a circle and the screaming ceased; the body fell forward, slumped in the rough by the road. Antigonos kicked it in disgust and then turned to his men, shouting a couple of orders.

Laomini's body was hauled out and thrown down next to Thetima's and then the wagon was turned about and set off back up the hill, back to Sardis, with Antigonos and his men as its escort.

And yet he's allowed the caravan to move on unmolested and doesn't seem to be concerned about finding me. Artonis looked down at the bodies left by the side of the road and realised just what Antigonos planned. *He's going to blame her slaves for her murder and, no doubt, give her a magnificent funeral, his eye discharging tears of grief, proving to the world he was completely innocent of her murder. The hypocrite!* She turned her horse away and headed back down to the road; hitting it well ahead of the caravan, she waited until Babrak drew level.

'Did Antigonos say nothing about you smuggling us out of Sardis, Babrak? He just let you go?'

'Why, of course, my lady; what would the great one-eyed beast want with a poor Paktha merchant like me? How was I to know the woman who asked me for passage to Ephesus with her two slaves was none other than the great Kleopatra herself? I could not presume to ask the lady to take off her veil so as I could identify her, could I? No, of course not. We do enough business together to understand one another.'

'Wait; you said woman, not women.'

'There was only one woman and her two slaves; I was very clear on that point with Antigonos and he saw no reason to disbelieve me.'

'Thank you, Babrak; although I'm sure he's got more urgent things to do than chase around the country for me.'

Babrak nodded with an air of sage agreement. 'When a man has urgent need of his boy there is very little else that can distract him.'

'I'm sure you're right, Babrak,' Artonis said, glancing at the doe-eyed creature riding a mule just behind his master's camel. 'Where will you go when you get to Ephesus?'

'Ephesus is the end of the Royal Road, good lady; there I do whatever business needs to be done, trading my goods for wares from Greece and beyond, and then turn around and head home by the southern route, sometimes going via Egypt and then sometimes not and instead heading straight to Damascus and then on to Babylon.'

The idea of staying with the caravan was tempting to Artonis for it would take her back to her homeland on its way back to the limits of the empire and beyond. But she found the urge easy to resist, for whilst her husband remained unavenged, she could not return home. *But once I've spat into that eye, I'll wait for this caravan to come around and travel home with it. But first I have no choice now but to go back to Ptolemy.*

PTOLEMY.
THE BASTARD.

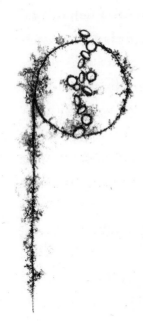

'WHILST, AS YOU know, I'm always pleased to see you, Lycortas,' Ptolemy said, looking at his newly arrived steward with a degree of puzzlement, 'I'm struggling to understand what you are doing here in Kos, so far from Alexandria where, if I remember rightly, I told you to stay in order to ensure that not too much blood results from Eurydike and Berenice fighting in my absence – especially as Eurydike is outraged that I've named Berenice's new son Ptolemy.'

'It was a brave decision, lord.' Lycortas inclined his head, his expression pained, as he stood in his long white robe before Ptolemy and Thais; they were seated in the shade of a walnut tree, overlooking the harbour of Kos, enjoying their midday meal of roasted meats, white cheese and green olives. 'Your forbearance in the matter of my deserting my post is greatly appreciated.'

Ptolemy struggled to mask a smile and glanced at Thais sitting next to him sipping pomegranate juice. 'I wasn't aware that I was being forbearing of anything.'

'But you're always going on about how forgiving you are,' Thais reminded him, squeezing his thigh.

'Indeed, lord,' Lycortas said, 'and I'm sure when you hear the reason for my making the most unpleasant eight-day voyage from Egypt to Kos, leaving your two wives unsupervised with claws sharpened, you'll deem your forbearance justified.'

'Will I? In which case you had better sit down and revive yourself with some unwatered wine.' He indicated the jug on the table and clapped his hands at a slave to bring another cup. 'You'll be pleased to know that Archias arrived here only the other day and so I broached the best vintage I had for him; you are most welcome to finish off what he left.' The look of disapproval on Lycortas' face at the thought of Archias being given wine of the best vintage, as always, amused Ptolemy, but his curiosity as to what had brought his steward so far to give him his news in person cut his enjoyment short. *I should brace myself for having my good mood broken.*

'It's not good,' Lycortas said as he sipped the vintage and found it to his liking. 'I mean the news is not good, the wine is superb; you didn't really give this to Archias, did you, lord? Please tell me that you only said that to annoy me.'

'I did give it to Archias and I told you just to annoy you.' Ptolemy chose a plump, green olive. 'Now, this bad news, please.'

Lycortas looked nervous and then downed the contents of his cup in one, steeling himself. 'It's Agathocles, lord. As you know, he landed in Africa and defeated the Carthaginians but failed to take Carthage itself. Well, he then turned his attention to smaller fare and took Thapsus and Hadrumetum, having made an alliance with King Aelymas of the Numidians.'

'Yes, yes, I know that; the last I heard was that they'd signed a treaty.'

'Well, he broke it.'

'That doesn't surprise me,' Ptolemy said, spitting out an olive stone into his hand and flicking it away over Lycortas' shoulder.

'No, I mean Aelymas broke it and turned on Agathocles, who defeated and killed him with considerable losses on both sides.'

'Well, that all seems to be good news.'

'Indeed, lord, would that were where the story ended.'

Ptolemy popped another olive into his mouth. 'Go on.'

'He now needs a new ally and so has made overtures to your governor of Cyrenaica.'

Ptolemy spat out his olive, unchewed. 'Ophellas?'

'Indeed, lord; I believe you only have one.'

'Ophellas didn't, did he?' Thais asked, holding her cup in both hands and leaning forward in alarm.

'I'm afraid he did. Eurydice, Ophellas' wife, is Athenian; her very wealthy family and Agathocles have ties of hospitality; Agathocles was their guest in Athens for almost a year after he was banished for attempting to overthrow Timoleon, his predecessor. They helped finance the army with which he took Syracuse. On the basis of that guest-friendship, Ophellas made an agreement with Agathocles that he would raise a mercenary army and aid him against Carthage; in return, he could keep all the gains in Africa when Agathocles returned to Sicilia.'

Ptolemy slammed his palm on the table, upsetting the olive bowl. 'The bastard's rebelled and declared himself independent?'

'He has.'

'How long ago did this happen?'

'Two months ago, or thereabouts.'

'He must assume that I'm too busy looking north and east to be able to police what he's doing in the west and has taken this chance.'

'But how's he going to afford it?' Thais asked, catching a couple of olives as they rolled off the table. 'Cyrenaica is rich from the silphium trade, but not rich enough to recruit a mercenary army.'

'Eurydice's family will help finance the venture. Nearly a thousand Athenians, democrats disenfranchised by Demetrius of Phaleron's oligarchy, have already made their way to Cyrene; I left Alexandria to travel here on the day I heard of their arrival. More Athenians and other Greek mercenaries will be coming – indeed, they might already have arrived. Add them to his mercenaries in his garrison and he could have four or five thousand before long.'

Ptolemy came to a decision. 'Then we send troops to stop him now, before he gets more men.'

'Indeed, lord; hence my presence.'

'Which is more welcome than usual, Lycortas.'

'You are most gracious and generous, lord. I need your permission to send troops to put an end to this act of foolishness by taking troops from the eastern defences at Pelusium. That's why I came in person; I can be back in Alexandria in eight days to give the order.'

Ptolemy leaned forward and took his steward's hand. 'You have done well, my friend. Two thousand cavalry and five thousand infantry is all I can spare from our border with Antigonos, but that should be enough to defeat the treacherous bastard. Use what's left of the fleet in Alexandria to transport them.'

'I've already given the order for the fleet to sail to Pelusium to stand by. I will sail directly there to supervise the embarkation. They could be in Cyrene in less than a month.'

'Make sure they are.'

'Of course, lord; but there is one piece of good news.'

'I doubt it, but try me.'

'Carthage has gone on the offensive, so Agathocles will not be able to risk turning back east to help his friend.'

Ptolemy's face brightened. 'You're right, that is good news. Agathocles might even have been defeated by the time—' Ptolemy stopped, raising his hand with his forefinger extended up. 'Wait!' He turned to Thais. 'Am I going too fast? Do I really want Carthage to beat Agathocles?'

Thais pursed her lips and frowned in thought. 'Not really, if the truth be told. If Agathocles defeats Carthage, they will lose their hold on Sicilia. Last time that happened it took them a generation to get it back.'

Ptolemy nodded. 'That's twenty years of them not threatening me.'

'That's a lot of years.'

Ptolemy chuckled. 'Unwittingly, Ophellas has just provided me with a golden opportunity.' He turned to his steward, smiling, his voice relaxed. 'I've a feeling we might be acting in haste; I think we should let Ophellas go with his mercenaries and help Agathocles defeat Carthage and only then, once he is on his way, bring our troops over from Pelusium to fill the gap. Then, to make sure our erstwhile governor of Cyrenaica can't come home, I'll supplement them with mercenaries from Greece which I'll have sent over directly to the new ports in Cyrenaica. Send the transport fleet over to the Taenarum peninsula on the southern Peloponnese; I'll have the mercenaries assembled there at the ports of Caenepolis and Psamathus. If my business here goes as expected, I should be back by the time Ophellas thinks of turning back our way; and then we shall see.'

Lycortas stood. 'There is one more thing, lord.'

'Yes?'

'It occurred to me that if I were to take the families of the officers and men who have gone with Ophellas into custody and bring them back to Alexandria, it might encourage their menfolk to rethink their positions.'

'A sound notion, Lycortas; see it done.'

'Yes, my lord. I'll leave for Egypt immediately.' With a brief inclination of the head, the steward turned and glided off.

'Who can you trust to replace Ophellas?' Thais asked, scooping up the rest of the olives and putting them back in the bowl.

Ptolemy considered the question for a few moments. 'It's going to take careful planning. For the next two seasons at least, my attention is going to be north and east; so, I need to just keep Cyrenaica defended until I have time to concentrate all my attention onto it. Andronicus should be able to do that, seeing as he's waiting for me in Corinth at the moment. I'll send to him to start signing on the mercenaries at the recruiting centres in the Peloponnese to bulk up Cyrenaica's defences. Then I need to write to Carthage and deny any responsibility for Ophellas' actions; whether they'll believe me, though, is another matter. After that, well, it will need a dynastic solution involving a diplomatic marriage to Agathocles.'

'Not our daughter, surely?'

'No, Eirene isn't, if you would forgive my saying, of sufficient status because we're not married. I'll need to put my mind to it. The trouble is Eurydike's daughter is only three and Berenice's two are eight and seven.'

'Arsinoe is seven and Philotera is six.'

'Well, I got one right.'

'But you've forgotten two.'

'Have I? I thought I only had four daughters at the moment.'

'Your step-daughters. Antigone is coming up fourteen and Theoxena is twelve.'

'My step-daughters, of course.' Ptolemy smiled, slow and calculating. 'Yes, but Berenice will need some careful but firm handling.'

'I thought handling women firmly was your speciality; at least, it is in my experience.'

'Oh, it is; and she does have the new baby to distract her. Perhaps if I were to promise her son, Magas, will become my governor of Cyrenaica when he's old enough... That might do the trick.' He poured himself another cup of wine, leaned back in his seat and looked out over the sea, pleased with life. 'And now all I need is for Dioscurides to show his face.'

A fleet in full sail with oars spread was a sight always to stir Ptolemy's heart but the vision of Dioscurides' fleet, of eighty-plus vessels gliding towards Kos, as Lycortas' ship sailed south, was even more of a thrill, for he planned to make it his – although, naturally, he did not mention that to Ptolemaios, standing next to him in the island's harbour. 'We'll give Dioscurides a couple of days to do any necessary refitting and provision the fleet,' Ptolemy said, shading his eyes against the glare of the sun glinting off a still, bronze sea, 'and then embark the troops. With luck you should be on your way in three or four days. Athens and the isthmus should be yours by the new moon.'

Ptolemaios grinned and gave Ptolemy a hearty slap on the back. 'We make an excellent team, you and I, Ptolemy.'

That's just where you're wrong, you patronising mediocrity. 'We do indeed, my dear Ptolemaios. Between us we'll take both east and west.'

'My uncle will regret easing me and Dioscurides out of independent commands in favour of his sons.'

'Gaza showed him what a mistake that was. Had you been on the other side of the field instead of Demetrios it might have been a very different result.'

'Undoubtedly.'

Ptolemy could barely conceal his astonishment at this latest piece of unthinking arrogance. 'Yes, I'm sure I'd still be back in Egypt licking my wounds.'

'More than likely; and Seleukos would never have been in a position to retake Babylon. Yes, Antigonos only has himself to blame for his present predicament.'

'His loss is my gain.'

'Indeed.'

Outrageous; he just doesn't see it. Even if I were his best friend, I'd certainly be reviewing my opinion of him now, seeing as he so obviously considers himself my superior. 'I thought to celebrate our alliance and to welcome your brother we would have a feast tomorrow to which I intend to invite all the triarchoi of his fleet.'

'That would be a most appreciated gesture.'

Oh, it'll be much more than a gesture; be in no doubt about that.

'When I left Sardis, five days ago, Father,' Lagus said, having just arrived back in Kos soon after the great fleet had docked, 'Kleopatra told me she was still considering the matter.'

Ptolemy thumped the arm of his chair. 'Considering the matter? What more is there to consider?'

'Whether you're to be trusted, for one thing,' Thais suggested.

'Trusted? What reason would she have not to trust me?'

'The fact you're in an alliance with Ptolemaios, for a start.'

'But I'm not.'

'Well, you might know that and I know that and Lagus knows that, but Ptolemaios certainly doesn't, otherwise he wouldn't have got Dioscurides here with his fleet. So, as far as Kleopatra sees it, you *are* allied with one of Antigonos' nephews. It may be she considers Ptolemaios to be a surprising choice of chum.'

'Well, she'll find out the truth of the matter very soon, I can assure you.'

Thais smiled with faux sweetness. 'I'm sure she will. Personally, I think she's being very sensible in holding back; I've always maintained the marriage would be a mistake. Perhaps she shares my caution and is anxious not to goad the resinated cyclops and draw Kassandros and Lysimachus into an alliance with him against the pair of you.'

Ptolemy turned his attention back to his son. 'Did she give an indication as to which direction her thoughts were heading?'

'No, Father. When I arrived, she saw me immediately and then sent me straight back to you with her message.'

Ptolemy shook his head. 'Women!'

'Annoyed that we don't automatically bow to your will, my dearest?' Thais asked with an innocent expression. 'Personally, I think now you've achieved your aims with this excursion we should head back to Egypt and forget all about Kleopatra and stop being jealous of Kassandros having

Alexander's half-sister and trying to outdo him by marrying his full sister. It's a "mine are bigger than yours" sort of thing and you're better than that, Ptolemy.'

'It's nothing to do with the size of my balls; it's about power and leverage.'

'Who has the biggest balls, in other words.'

Ptolemy was about to refute the statement. *It's pointless arguing with her; she'll never admit she's wrong – and, if I'm honest, the chances are, she isn't.* He looked at Lagus and paused in thought. 'Five days ago, you said you left Sardis?'

'Yes, Father; I was delayed for a couple of days in Ephesus. Ever since Demetrios arrived in Halicarnassus, Ephesus has been keen not to upset him; I think they would have handed me over to him had they caught me in the town. They're keeping a tight watch on the port. My ship had to sneak out at night and pick me up from a beach to the south of the city.'

'Which means Kleopatra will have problems sailing from there should she eventually deign to be my wife; in fact, it'll probably be nigh on impossible. Miletus to the south will undoubtedly pose the same problem so where will she go?' Ptolemy came to a decision; he reached across and squeezed Thais' hand. 'I think you might be right after all, my love: I should forget Kleopatra – at least for the time being – finish my business here and then head back to Egypt. There's nothing more to achieve in the north, other than, perhaps, an understanding with Cratesipolis.'

'At least you're just thinking of *understanding* her and not of marrying her.'

Ptolemy's eyes glinted with mischief. 'She doesn't currently have a husband.'

Thais removed his hand from hers. 'Impossible man!' She stood and beckoned her son. 'Come, Lagus. Let's leave your father; he's far too busy with his scheming and plotting to have time for the likes of us.'

'Now that Archias has returned from Rhodos with such excellent news, I'm done with scheming and plotting for the moment,' Ptolemy said, sitting back in his chair.

Thais looked over her shoulder as she headed for the door. 'Really? And what about your lovely surprise scheme tomorrow evening? Have you finished plotting that?'

'Ah, yes.' Ptolemy smiled to himself. 'That's something I'm so looking forward to.'

And it was with high expectations of enjoying himself more than usual that Ptolemy welcomed the eighty-plus triarchoi of Dioscurides' fleet the following evening. Having spent the past year on the island of Skiathos, with little in the way of entertainment, the men were only too pleased to enjoy Ptolemy's more than generous hospitality. The feasting hall of the palace filled with ever increasing good cheer as toasts were drunk and wine flowed freely to wash down the roasted lamb and pork served with side dishes of both eastern and western origin. Ptolemy, reclining next to Thais, with Ptolemaios and Dioscurides on a couch to his right and Lagus and Archias to his left, had kept up a lively conversation with the cousins as the meal progressed – at least as lively as was possible with members of Antigonos' family who, like their uncle, showed little interest in anything other than military prowess, wine and women. Fortunately, Ptolemy was an expert on all those subjects.

'How did you keep the men fit whilst you were on Skiathos?' Ptolemy asked as his goblet was filled once again.

Dioscurides spat out a mouthful of gristle into his hand and then discarded it onto the floor. 'Each ship went out for a couple of hours every day but not all at the same time and never together, always separately. I only allowed then to go east out to sea, never west towards the mainland, or north and south so as to avoid the shipping lanes. Obviously, I had to send the occasional ship to pick up supplies from my cousin on Euboea; there wasn't nearly enough on the island to feed us all, but they were always traders, never warships. In all the time not one ship came to have a look at the island. Had they done so they would've found two or three ships on every beach or in every cove.' He smiled at Ptolemy. 'I'm surprised you didn't send a squadron out to look for me.'

Ptolemy shrugged. 'I thought you'd gone up to the Euxine Sea; but to be honest, I didn't care where you were so long as you weren't with Antigonos. Your keeping the fleet from him greatly restricted his movements and made my life easier.' He raised his goblet. 'I'm much in your debt, Dioscurides.'

'I'm sure you'll find a way to repay it.' Dioscurides returned the toast, taking a large swig and then wiping his mouth with the back of his hand.

I'm sure I will. Ptolemy drained his goblet and then glanced at Archias as he held it out for another refill.

The Exile-Hunter smiled his broad, boyish smile, lighting up his face. 'About now, then?'

'Yes, Archias, now is as good a time as any.'

'Very well.' Archias swung his feet off the couch and stood, adjusting his dress so the hem of his tunic was level, before sauntering around the table as if heading outside to relieve himself. Passing behind the two brothers, he looked across to the open double doors, where his seven Thracian companions stood, fox-fur hats pulled down on their heads, blending with their ginger beards of varying shades. Catching the eye of their leader, Sitalces, Archias nodded and then crouched down to adjust the strapping of his knee-length boots. With a fluid motion, blurred to vision, he pulled the blade from the confines of his right boot and plunged it from behind into Dioscurides' chest, forcing it between ribs, through sinew and on into the heart, bursting it open. For a moment, Dioscurides remained motionless, his cup raised near his lips; his eyes lowered and widened at the sight of the dagger wedged in his chest. He dropped his wine and tried to move his hand to grip the handle but his strength faded. He was dead before he rolled from the couch as Archias took his shocked brother in an iron grip, both arms forced up behind his back with one hand and his throat constricted by a muscled forearm. Through the door came Sitalces and his six associates, rhomphaia hefted in both hands, the sleek curved blades reflecting the light from many lamps. Behind them, two files of Ptolemy's guards jogged, double time, one group heading around the room to the left, the other to the right, surrounding the guests.

'What have you done?' Ptolemaios shouted, struggling against the Exile-Hunter's lock.

'Me?' Ptolemy looked surprised. 'I've done nothing. Archias is the one who's been busy. He's just killed your brother.' He looked down at the corpse on the floor. 'But I'm sure you noticed, Ptolemaios; or were you too busy feeling pleased with yourself, thinking you'd completely outwitted me?' Not giving Ptolemaios time to answer, Ptolemy got to his feet, raised his hands above his head and clapped. 'Silence! Silence!'

Gradually the consternation died away; the triarchoi sank back down onto their couches, looking around with nervous glances at the soldiers surrounding them and then at the seven outlandish Thracians standing in their midst.

'That's better,' Ptolemy said once he could be heard without having to shout; for now was not the time to raise his voice, now was the time for reasoned argument. 'Gentlemen, there's about to be a realignment of allegiances. Dioscurides, your erstwhile commander, is lying dead on the floor.' He pointed to the body. 'I'm sure those closest can see him.' He then gestured to the Exile-Hunter. 'And here, as you will notice, my good friend Archias is currently restraining Ptolemaios. Now, you might well be asking yourselves why I have taken these steps when we were meant to be in an alliance all together. Well, the answer is simple: I want your fleet to come south with me to Egypt: I want to concentrate all the sea power possible in one place and then take on Antigonos in one great naval battle. Now, Ptolemaios and Dioscurides would never have countenanced that strategy as they wanted to forge themselves a kingdom in Greece strong enough to eventually threaten Kassandros. That's of no use to me in my long-term goal of defeating Antigonos. And so, gentlemen, I make you this offer: join me and be well paid in my service, or,' he pointed down to Dioscurides, 'join him. It's up to you, but I'll have your answers before you leave this room.'

Before Ptolemy had sat back down, there was a clamour of support for his proposition as Sitalces and his Thracians roamed through the tables glowering at anyone they deemed to be insufficiently enthusiastic.

'I think they like your idea,' Thais observed as more and more of the triarchoi got to their feet, shouting Ptolemy's name.

'Yes,' Ptolemy agreed, 'they do seem to be very keen.' He turned to Ptolemaios, still restrained in an arm lock by Archias. 'Which leaves you with a problem, my friend: you have nothing.'

Ptolemaios spat. 'You bastard; we had a deal. Why are you doing this?'

Ptolemy sighed as if his patience were sorely tried. 'Ever since you arrived here, Ptolemaios, you have attempted to lord it over me: summoning me to your presence; implying you would have bested me at Gaza; making it clear you consider yourself to be at least my equal, if not my superior. Well, Ptolemaios, I would find that to be unacceptable even had I wanted an alliance with you. But seeing as I just wanted to use you to find Dioscurides' fleet and take it off his hands, I find it intolerable.' He gestured around the cheering triarchoi. 'Now I have the fleet, you are of no further use to me. But I am of a forgiving nature, as I'm sure you've heard, so I'll give you a choice: either Archias can aid you on your way to the Ferryman in much the same way as he did your brother, or...' He turned to Thais. 'Do you have it, my dear?'

Thais produced a small glass vial from within the folds of her dress and handed it to Ptolemy. 'It's fast acting and pain-less – at least, so I'm told.'

He held the vial to a lamp and admired the clarity of the liquid within. 'Or you may take your own life with this.' He offered the poison to Ptolemaios. 'Either way, you're a dead man.'

'I don't deserve this.'

'No?' Ptolemy shook his head, disappointed. 'Ptolemaios, I hold Egypt, Cyrenaica and Cyprus; Seleukos has the east, Kassandros Macedon and Lysimachus Thrace, and Antigonos wants to take the lot but in practice has only Anatolia and Syria. Where do you fit in if you are not allied with your uncle? There's no room for another contender; there are too many as it is. You're nothing without your uncle and you should have taken his promotion of his own sons as a natural course of events and not as a grave insult. Your arrogance has killed you. Now choose.'

The light went out of Ptolemaios' eyes as he saw nothing but death ahead of him. 'I'll take matters into my own hands,' he said, reaching for the vial. He looked at it with regret and then raised his eyes to Ptolemy. 'I thought I could be a part of the new order.'

'But not by yourself, Ptolemaios. Kassandros, for all his faults, is the son of Antipatros, Alexander's regent in Macedon. Lysimachus and I were two of Alexander's seven bodyguards; Seleukos was educated with us and we all served with Alexander on his conquest of the empire; we have legitimacy as far as the troops are concerned. You, however, are nothing without your uncle; a man we had all but forgotten as we went east leaving him languishing in Anatolia to complete its conquest. But then you know that because you were there with him; you should have stayed loyal to Antigonos and seen what scraps he might have thrown you.' He nodded at the vial. 'You've chosen well. Now, get on with it.'

Ptolemaios looked down at his dead brother and pulled out the stopper. 'We chose badly, Dioscurides; both in our enemies and our friends.'

'Good,' Ptolemy said with evident satisfaction. 'If I were you, I'd lie back on the couch and let it creep up on you slowly. Archias here will watch over you as you go. I'll ensure that both you and your brother receive an honourable funeral.' With a brief nod, he turned. 'Come, Thais, Lagus, let's leave Ptolemaios to rue his decisions and actions as he makes his last journey.'

Upon reaching the double doors, Ptolemy turned to address his guests. 'Gentlemen, you will all be sworn into my service before you leave this room; until then, please, enjoy the feast.' Putting an arm around Thais, he led her away. 'Well, I think that went exceedingly well: I'm up one fleet and down two potential political problems.'

'Yes,' Thais agreed, 'I'd say you have good reason to feel pleased with yourself. I just hope this woman won't spoil the evening.'

'What?'

Thais pointed to a figure standing in the middle of the great hall.

Ptolemy focused on her and felt his heart sink. 'Artonis is rarely a bringer of good news.'

'Murdered by her slave under threat of death from Antigonos should her mistress try to come to me?' Ptolemy did not find it difficult to believe. *It's probably how I would have set things up. Well, that finally settles that question; Thais must be over-joyed.* A sideways glance at his mistress revealed nothing, one way or the other.

'Yes,' Artonis said, tears still flowing from her recounting of recent events sitting in the evening warmth of a torchlit courtyard garden. 'And then he executed the woman by the side of the road so the truth would never come out.'

Quite right too. 'Appalling.' He received a sharp elbow in the ribs from Thais.

'And now, with Kleopatra dead, where am I to go to pursue my vengeance against the one-eyed monstrosity?

Kassandros and Thessalonike wanted Polyperchon to kill me for aiding Barsine and Herakles; and you, Ptolemy, you give with one hand and take with the other.'

Ptolemy frowned. 'What do you mean by that, Artonis?'

Artonis wiped away her tears with her forefinger. 'You know perfectly well, I believe. Kleopatra suspected it and the more I think about it the more I realise Herakles' death was far more convenient for you than his defeating Kassandros and taking Macedon. He would have been our legitimate king and it wouldn't have been just Antigonos who would have had to bow to him or be branded a traitor. No, Ptolemy, it would have been you as well, would it not? You told Andronicus to encourage Herakles to humiliate Polyperchon; I see it now but at the time I was too blind to notice what was going on. You tricked me, Ptolemy.'

Ptolemy could see no advantage in denying the matter. 'I did, Artonis; no one wanted another king; Polyperchon was too puffed up with the promise of a position to see that. I had to sabotage it somehow; frankly, I think it went rather well – although I'm sorry for Barsine, I always liked her, but that's what comes of being too ambitious for an undeserving child.'

'Her blood is on your hands.'

Ptolemy dismissed the suggestion with a flick of his wrist. 'Not really; but I did save your life, Artonis, by instructing Andronicus to keep you safe from Kassandros. So now we really are equal.'

Artonis' red eyes burned into Ptolemy's. 'You are a wicked man.'

Ptolemy affected a look of surprise. 'Wicked? I don't think I've ever been called that. Forgiving, yes, as I've proven by overlooking your desire to see me dead and keep you alive; something I didn't have to do.' He held her gaze in a test of wills.

Thais broke the impasse, smiling at Artonis. 'My dear, seeing as you cannot go to Macedon and you quite evidently don't wish to come back with us to Egypt, so, short of trying to cross Antigonos' territory to get to Seleukos, wherever he might be at the moment, I would suggest Lysimachus is the best man to give you sanctuary.'

'Yes,' Ptolemy agreed, glad to find a way out of the staring match by turning to Thais. 'I think that's an excellent idea. Who knows, she might even be able to persuade him into looking south instead of forever obsessing about the tribes to the north.' He turned back to Artonis. 'If you wish, I'll lend you a ship to take you to Thrace.' *Seeing as I seem to have a surfeit now; and, besides, now I come to think of it, she could prove very useful to me.*

'What about Cratesipolis in Corinth?' Artonis asked.

'Corinth?' Ptolemy pursed his lips and raised his eyebrows as if thinking the idea to be of merit. 'Yes, you could go to her; in fact, you would be more than welcome to join me as I intended to pay the good lady a visit before I head back south.' *And I also need to get Andronicus started on raising the mercenaries to defend Cyrenaica whilst I'm there.*

Artonis backed away from the idea. 'I think I'll try my luck with Lysimachus in Thrace, after all.'

Perfect; it's your decision. 'Then you may leave in the morning. In fact, I will even supply you with an escort at my expense; Archias and his savoury friends will go with you.'

'Very well,' Artonis said, without a hint of gratitude. 'But don't think that puts me in your debt, Ptolemy.'

'You aren't in my debt, Artonis; but you could do me a great favour which would put *me* into *your* debt.'

Artonis' eyes narrowed. 'Why should I do you a favour?'

'Because it would be in your interest to do so.'

Artonis' narrowed eyes filled with suspicion. 'What do you want?'

'I would like you to act as my ambassador to Lysimachus. I want an alliance with him against Antigonos; a proper alliance, not one which Antigonos can buy off with meaningless peace treaties, as he did the last time.'

'Why me?'

'Apart from the fact that you're going to him anyway? Well, I think he'll be receptive to the idea, whoever I send; but that is no guarantee that he would finally agree and take the field against the cyclops. Thus, I need another level of persuasion: you, my dear, can persuade his wife, Nicaea. I would send her sister, my wife Eurydike, but she's so contrary and liable to do more harm than good; my other wife, Berenice, is Nicaea's cousin and far more diplomatic; unfortunately – or fortunately, I should say – she's just given birth to another Ptolemy.'

'And I cannot go,' Thais said. 'Nicaea is haughty and is all too aware that her father was Alexander's regent in Macedon. As I'm an unmarried woman, a mere mistress, a courtesan, even, she would, necessarily, expect me to defer to her and would not listen to my argument. You, on the other hand, Artonis, are Eumenes' widow and therefore have an equal status with her; you can reason with her without causing offence and she can be convinced by you – and will be, I'm sure – without losing face. Get her to work on her husband; stiffen his resolve, as it were. In sending you, we stand a greater chance of bringing this alliance together and then expanding it. And that is what you want, after all; is it not? That is the route to your vengeance.'

Artonis paused to consider the proposition.

Ptolemy squeezed his mistress's arm in gratitude. *Thais, where would I be without your ability to persuade?*

'What about Kassandros and Thessalonike?' Artonis asked, frowning, after a few moments. 'They want me dead. I would be an obstacle to them joining any alliance.'

'I will write you a letter to give to Thessalonike, suggesting pragmatism when it comes to dealing with you. Nicaea is Kassandros' sister; she can talk him round, I'm sure.'

'And once she has,' Ptolemy said, 'the only person missing would be Seleukos.'

'Assuming he can regain Babylon,' Artonis pointed out.

'Oh, now that Antigonos has recalled Demetrios, leaving a relatively small garrison there, I've no doubt he will.'

Artonis took a couple of moments in thought and then set her jaw, a decision made. 'Then, if he does, I shall bring him into the alliance as well.'

'You could try, but the question is, once he has retaken Babylon, would he want to bring an army west or would he prefer to sit back, build his strength and let us deal with Antigonos?'

'Apama is a good friend of mine, she'll help me convince him.'

There was, Ptolemy could see, a new-found determination emanating from Artonis; he smiled. 'Yes, Artonis, you're right: Apama is the way to Seleukos' heart and because of your long friendship with her you are one of the few people who could get her to persuade her husband to march west.'

SELEUKOS.
THE BULL-ELEPHANT.

TWO HOLLOW THUMPS and corresponding jolts, straining his left arm, as a couple of arrows juddered into his shield and three more hissing over its rim were enough for Seleukos to withdraw around the corner as another flight whooshed by, unseen in drifting smoke. He leaned on his javelin and turned to Azanes, crouched close behind Seleukos' sixteen dismounted Companion Cavalrymen, the main strike-force of the unit. 'I'd say they're on the roof on the other side of the road; at least five of them.'

The Sogdian chieftain grinned. 'Then we had better join them on their level.' He looked to his seven kinsmen accompanying him, bows at the ready and arrows nocked into place, and issued an order in his own language. Once more, his men readied themselves as four pioneers came forward at the crouch, past the two units of peltasts, one used for house-clearing and the other covering the rear of the party, and set up their ladders as they had done almost every time Seleukos and his unit had turned from one street into the next.

And this is how it had been ever since breaking down the Marduk Gate, in the eastern section of the triple wall, and entering the old city of Babylon the previous day: dozens of assault groups like his, struggling for every pace of ground, fighting house to house, street to street, neighbourhood to neighbourhood, clearing one area at a time and then securing it with a ring of medium-quality mercenaries whilst he and his senior officers, once again, led their elite troops into the next occupied quarter.

It had been a hard, bloody slog and many a good man had been left behind in the gutter for the burial parties to pick up later, to take them back, along with the wounded, to the sprawling military camp beyond the outer city wall. It was not a form of fighting Seleukos had had much experience in; a couple of cities out in India had been taken by storm and then cleared with bitter hand-to-hand combat in confined and foul-smelling alleys but they had not been on such a scale as this; for Babylon was indeed a huge city.

With the four ladders set up against the two-storey building and the pioneers footing the bottom rung of each, Azanes clambered onto the lower rungs of his with a comrade standing ready behind him; he glanced across to the other three ladders, similarly manned, and nodded. All four leading Sogdians drew their bows, looking up their ladder's length; as one, with their hands occupied with their weapons, they pumped they legs, rising up the ladders as if they were taking a shallow set of steps two at a time. Up they leaped as they reached the top, their backups surging behind them. Four bowstrings thrummed; Azanes and his men rolled forward, disappearing from view; four more bowstrings thrummed. 'Now!' Seleukos hissed, leaping around the corner; his Companions followed, each hefting a javelin. Out into the open they ran, locking shields together as they turned the corner, right arms back, ready to release as they searched the skyline for the enemy. Movement to the left; Seleukos hurled his sleek shaft true, into the arm of an archer as he raised himself over the parapet, drawing his bow. Back with a cry he fell; his missile just about sprang skywards, impotent, as the men behind Seleukos launched their weapons an instant before two more archers appeared. Luck in war is a crucial commodity and the archers' had expired: each received two javelins in their chests as a volley of arrows from Azanes' men slammed into them from close range, twisting their bodies as they collapsed limp, out of sight.

Forward, Seleukos led his men, one steady pace at a time so as not to blunder blind into a trap; each door they passed kicked down by the peltasts following, and the rooms within searched, as above, Azanes and his men sent the occasional well-aimed shaft across the rooftops, into any face or limb presenting itself as a target. To their rear the other unit of peltasts guarded the junction to ensure nothing came down the street to take them from behind. And this pattern was being replicated in each of the streets parallel as thousands of men, in tight units, zigzagged their way into Babylon.

On they pressed, Seleukos breathing heavily, smoke stinging his throat and eyes, crouching low behind his shield as his second ranker held his over both their heads; eyes darting left and right, alert ever to lethal threat. And threats had been many and often, for Demetrios' garrison of seven thousand men, less than a fifth of the size of the army Seleukos had brought back from the east, had decided that the best use of their numbers was to fight for every narrow street and alleyway where a superior force is of no advantage other than the weight its depth can bring to a close-quarters melee. But of these there had been few for the defenders had found ambush and archery to be the most effective tactics.

And so, Seleukos had no choice but to fight for each street, for if he were to take Babylon for the third – and, he hoped, final – time, then that was what was required.

From the street to the left it came: as sudden as it was brutal, the bolt slammed through the shield of the outside man of the front rank, passing through him and on into and out of the second man of the second rank, to fall spent and bloodied with a clatter on the paved street behind, tripping a couple of peltasts as it entangled their legs. Back they all stepped, leaving the dead slumped upon the ground as a second bolt, as long as a man's arm, whipped past Seleukos' nose to crack into the wall beyond with an explosion of stone splinters. He ran to the corner, pushing himself flat against it; he eased his head forward to peer along the street. At the next major junction, a hundred paces away, men worked a couple of bolt-shooters with furious efficiency, shoulders rolling as they wound the ratchets, pulling the cords back so the projectiles could slot into the grooved housings, ready for their deadly flight; in the background the Temple of Bel Marduk rose in splendour. To either side of the artillery pieces hoplites stood, formed up two or three deep, from what Seleukos could make out before a swiftly growing, blurred dot forced him to jerk his head back; with a shower of sparks the arrow cracked into the brickwork next to where his eye had been a moment before. 'Azanes!' he shouted up to the Sogdian, still at his station on the roof. 'Can you get a clear shot at them?' He indicated around the corner with his finger.

The Sogdian crept to the edge of his roof and risked a look; it was the briefest as a flight of arrows fizzed past, one through his hat, forcing him back immediately. 'Not from here.' He indicated to the low roofs behind him. 'We'd stand out on the skyline as easy targets.'

Seleukos cursed. *This is taking far too long.* 'Azanes, take the peltasts covering our rear, up the parallel street; get on the roof halfway up and get a clear line of sight down to the bolt-shooter. Send up a couple of fire arrows to signal when you're ready. I'll draw the shots and then… well, and then we kill the bastards.'

Azanes grinned. 'I like the last part the best.'

'Just get on with it, you eastern horse-botherer.'

The Sogdian grinned even wider and led his men back to the ladders; soon they flitted across the road to the peltasts stationed at the corner and, after a brief discussion with the officer, disappeared up the road parallel to the bolt-shooters.

'Keep your eyes on the sky,' Seleukos told his Companions, 'I don't want to miss those fire arrows.' He leaned back against the wall and allowed himself a few moments' respite, exhaustion creeping up on him.

Since his defeat of Nikanor it had been a non-stop rush to get his army back to Babylon, leaving garrisons at Ecbatana and Susa and other major centres to secure himself from any rebellion fomented by the annoyingly alive Nikanor in the east, as well as against the possibility that Antigonos, when he came – and come he would – might choose to cross over to the Tigris and take that route, thus putting himself between Seleukos and his eastern allies, thereby tempting them to change allegiance – again. Therefore, speed had been of the essence for he had to be ready when Antigonos brought his army as he had no illusions: it would be a campaign as large in scope as the one in which Eumenes had been defeated; a hundred thousand men in the field and the whole of Babylonia and Mesopotamia in which to fight. And Seleukos smiled to himself as he rested his head on the wall, his eyes closing, for he meant Mesopotamia, to the north of Babylonia, as he intended to take the fight to Antigonos and use ground he had already seen to his advantage. And to do that it was imperative Babylon should be secured in his rear and repopulated so his supply line would be as short as that of the resinated cyclops would be long.

Thus, Seleukos was a man in a hurry.

'There, sir!' a trooper shouted, pointing at the sky.

As he opened his eyes, Seleukos caught the tails of two fire arrows, flashing side by side through the thin haze of smoke veiling the sky. 'All right, lads, we draw the bolt and then it's a straight hundred-pace dash, praying to Bel Marduk that Azanes and his boys have a good line of sight and can disrupt them reloading.' He picked up the shields of the two dead men and handed them to a comrade. 'Molon, I'm going to sprint across the road. When I'm clear just push one out from the corner a fraction and then lob them both over to me, one after the other in quick succession; got that?'

Understanding the ruse, Molon nodded, smiling. 'Yes, lord.'

Seleukos steeled himself for putting his life on the line. Holding his shield to his side, he pelted the ten paces across the street to the opposite corner, a volley of arrows passing behind him. He pressed his back against the wall, breathing heavily, and looked to the man with the spare shield. 'Ready, Molon?'

'Yes, lord.'

'Go.'

For a couple of heartbeats a shield was pushed a quarter of the way out into the open and then withdrawn before it was hurled across with the next one close behind; but they never made it, disappearing instead with a sudden crack as if an invisible rope had yanked them both away in an accelerating blur, one spinning like a top, as the two bolts smashed through them.

'Now!' Seleukos shouted as he charged around the corner, his shield up, head down and legs pumping; his comrades were but a couple of paces behind him. Three mighty hits to his shield knocked some pace off him and for a moment he thought Azanes was not in position to offer cover and the fire arrows had been a coincidence. Another missile slammed into his shield but still he kept on, glancing behind him to see one of his Companions fall clutching at a shaft protruding from his calf. And still he sprinted, his chest heaving and thighs aching as his boots clattered on the stone slabs, knowing the hoplites facing him would be covering the artillery crew with their hoplons as they desperately reloaded. The vision of the shields being snatched away came to his mind. *That will not be me; not now; not when I've come so far and am so close.* Now that the archers seemed occupied with bringing down the threat to them on the roofs, Seleukos risked a look forward: forty paces, thirty. He braced himself for impact knowing there was no time to ensure they went in as one line; this would be messy and unsupported.

The whump of wood onto leather-bound restraining-arms came at the same time as the neighbouring man's head disappeared; his legs ran on as gore surged from his open neck, his heart still pounding, unaware the brain had gone; two, three and then four steps the headless cadaver ran towards the enemy, shield held firm, sword outstretched, before plunging forward, death finally catching up with it, to slide into the horrified defenders, disgorging its contents over their feet. Transfixed for a moment they stared at the thing that had lived on after death should have taken it; for a few, it was the last image they saw as Seleukos and his Companions, all very much alive, crunched in, exploding their shields forward and out and ramming the tips of the blades ahead in repeated pumps in a frenzy of violence, as much self-defence as vicious assault. Through the mercenary hoplites Seleukos ripped, his blood rushing in his head and his sword arm working without conscious thought, frantic, moving purely by the instinct born of an adult life spent in the grim harvest of lives that was war; war, where the best chance of survival was to offer violence more extreme than the man standing before you.

And extreme violence it was, using every weapon to hand: blade, fist, elbow, shield, rim, forehead, knee and foot; each wielded at the utmost of his strength to inflict maximum damage and intense pain. Through the hoplites he carved a path of ruin, twisting and sidestepping, for this was individual combat, not shoulder to shoulder, like a regimented killing machine; alone he fought, pushing himself to his farthest limits in the twenty or so racing heartbeats of the action.

He was through; none stood before him. The foe were either dead or writhing at his feet or racing away, west, down towards the Temple of Bel Marduk; there to turn right along the Processional Way and head to the comparative safety of the Second Citadel, still in the hands of the defending garrison.

'Azanes!' Seleukos called over his shoulder. 'Let two go; kill the rest.'

The Sogdians warmed to their task, releasing, nocking and drawing at a speed few could match, sending shaft after shaft into the backs of the fleeing surviving mercenaries, slamming into them to punch them off their feet, arms flying, to crash onto and slide along the smooth stone, worn through years of continuous usage. As quickly as chaos had come to the street so did peace return, with just the retreating sound of two men's racing footsteps, beating west, and the low moans of the fatally wounded writhing beneath Seleukos' men's feet.

Seleukos drew breath; it rasped in his smoke-raw throat. He fell to his haunches, looking around. 'How many did we lose?'

'Three dead, lord,' Molon replied, 'Diokles and Sagarios to the first bolt and then Neon in the fight. A couple are too wounded to carry on and will be taken back to the camp; they've arrows in the legs but they should be fine with a bit of strapping.'

Seleukos shook his head. *This is costing far more men than it should. What have the bastards got to gain by holding out when they know I'll win in the end? The arithmetic should tell them that, especially once my garrison still in the Main Citadel manages to get through the Ishtar Gate.* 'Well, hopefully the two we let go will tell their mates that if they want to live they'd do well to join us because they won't beat us, not with the lads from the Main Citadel ready to link up with us.'

And that was the sentiment he hoped would soon sweep through the opposition as he waited for the progress reports from the units to his left and right. Once they had come in, he gave orders for the perimeter ring of security to be brought forward to encompass the new territory gained as his men gulped down food and watered wine brought up from the rear by the men who would carry back the dead and the wounded.

Refreshed and with their minor wounds bound and their numbers replenished by replacements, Seleukos' men bestirred themselves for another effort. 'Two more pushes and we shall be at the Processional Way, lads,' Seleukos shouted. 'Once there, the city is as good as ours for they'll be caught between us and our boys still holding out in the Main Citadel; the garrison will have no choice but to surrender or retreat to the Southern Citadel. We'll lock them up and wait until seven thousand men realise that life is much better with food and pay, and they'll know where they can find it. The Southern Citadel will fall this time without us shedding a drop of our blood.'

A cheer greeted this statement, for the men knew it to be true: with the city empty and the farmland for leagues around abandoned, it would have been impossible to collect enough supplies to last the men in the Southern Citadel for more than two or three months. His garrison in the Main Citadel, however, had been provisioned to withstand a very long siege, and they had. Seleukos punched his sword in the air and then swept it forward. 'To the next junction, boys!'

And his men followed willingly, sure in the knowledge their work was nearly done. Seleukos led them forward with growing optimism that all would be set by the time Antigonos came east.

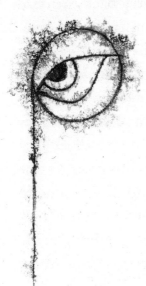

ANTIGONOS.
THE ONE-EYED.

S LIM-FINGERED AND long-nailed, the *kitharodes* plucked two strings of his instrument repeatedly, one high, one low, a mournful tone, almost discordant, before bringing in his voice, pitched between the two notes, navigating a quavering melody. 'While you live, shine, have no grief at all; life exists only for a short while and Time demands his due.' Although all knew the funerary song, such was the occasion and so deep was the mourning, few remained unmoved by this perfect rendition; by the time the singer had repeated the words for the third time, all in the great crowd in the agora of Sardis were weeping. After the fourth repetition the kitharodes brought the tune to an end and the crowd was still; silence fell. But within four heartbeats it was broken by a wail, low then rising to a highly pitched shriek before being joined by a multitude of voices in the same vein, rising and falling in a dissonance of grief as Kleopatra's women led the funeral procession, tearing at their hair and raiment, striking their torsos and pummelling their breasts as they preceded the body of their murdered mistress, carried on a lavish bier. And lavish it was, carved from cedar from Tyros and inlaid with ivory and gold, for Antigonos had spared no expense, determined to squeeze as much political capital as possible for being the man to bury the sister of Alexander – that he was also her killer had been long forgotten by the very few who knew. Walking behind the bier with Demetrios and Philippos to either side of him, he forced tears from his one eye and beat his chest at regular intervals with his fist as the procession threaded through the agora and then on down the Processional Way and out the gates towards the city of the dead, beyond Sardis' walls.

Here the pyre awaited, for like most of her house, she was to be burned; but unlike all her house, her ashes were not to be taken to Aegina, but, rather, kept in Asia, for Antigonos intended to inter her at his new capital of Antigonea to add legitimacy to his position.

Through the ceremony, Antigonos stood, his head bowed in grief as the priests of Apollo made their sacrifices and the priestesses of Demeter chanted the dirges proscribed for one so great as Kleopatra.

And as the bier was placed upon the pyre, Antigonos stepped forward, raising his arms, silencing the crowd. 'Today we mourn a daughter of Macedon whom you, the people of Sardis, had taken to your heart. Ripped from us by treacherous slaves, she will be remembered as a woman who dedicated herself to the wellbeing of Macedon and its empire, conquered by her brother Alexander; an empire that I, Antigonos, strive to keep whole in order to preserve his great achievement and his name. And it is I who take the lead in paying our respects to this great lady; it is I who lavish upon her the funeral she deserves; as it was I who punished her murderous slaves quickly and without hesitation at the scene of their crime. And it is I, Antigonos, who mourns for Kleopatra as I would for my own daughter.'

On he went, praising first Kleopatra's memory and then himself for being an integral part of it, shameless and open; but with nothing to lose and everything to gain by associating himself with the sister of the man he sought to replace, he felt no compunction to be modest – or truthful.

By the time the pyre's smoke rose to the sun, at its zenith, and the body gave up its fats to sizzle and sputter on red-hot fuel, the crowd were shouting thanks to Antigonos for his generosity and decency in ensuring the adopted daughter of their city had been shown honour in death according to her station in life; they cheered him as he, Demetrios and Philippos made their way back towards the city gates, his duty done and his position in the hearts of the citizens of Sardis assured. And through the town they followed him, singing his praises and turning the day from one of sorrow to one of joy for the man who ruled over them had proven to be of the highest quality.

'And if they believed all that then we shouldn't have trouble creating a heartland here in Anatolia should I not be successful out in the east,' Antigonos said as the palace doors closed behind him and his two sons.

Demetrios frowned. 'What do you mean: not successful, Father?'

'Exactly as it sounds. You see, I've been thinking on what you were saying about us always being in the middle, and you're right. If I'm not successful in taking it all then the part we will be left with, the major part, is surrounded by men who would wish us harm. So, we will need the goodwill of the people if we want to survive. Not that I'm giving up already, far from it; however, today was too good an opportunity to miss as insurance should the worst come to the worst. This will spread to Halicarnassus, Ephesus, Miletus and all along the coast as well as inland and I'll be feted for what I did today. Whilst I'm gone, I want you and Aristodemus to work on our relationship with the cities; spread some silver and gold around; build things they need. I want them to consider us as their natural overlords so that whether I come back with Seleukos' head pickled in a jar or leaving him secure in Babylonia, Anatolia and Syria will be our natural heartland which we will always control.'

Demetrios shrugged. 'If you say so; but isn't it defeatist thinking?'

'Father won't lose,' Philippos assured his brother.

'No, Son,' Antigonos corrected him, 'you don't *expect* me to lose; there's a big difference and I should prepare for both eventualities. It's my new pragmatism because, dare I say it, I listened to your older brother for once. As you said, Demetrios, we'll always be surrounded unless we're on the offensive, so whatever happens out east, when I return we'll have to decide whether to go north, south or west, and to do that we want a stable base.' He clapped his hands on both his sons' shoulders. 'But don't you worry, lads, I will defeat Seleukos, and when I get back we'll have the wealth of the east behind us. I'll sail to Tarsus tomorrow to rendezvous with the army. Peucestas was in charge of provisioning it; he should have finished by now.' He grimaced more than grinned at his younger son. 'I've decided to take you with me. We're going to take the army east as fast as possible and hopefully catch Seleukos before he recaptures Babylon.'

Thapsacus on the Euphrates was where Alexander had crossed the river twenty-two years previously as he chased the Great King, Darius, east, catching and defeating him eventually at a place known as The Camel's House, or Gaugamela, beyond the Tigris. Antigonos himself had crossed at the same point, sixteen years after Alexander, as he had chased Eumenes east, and now, for the third time, another huge Macedonian army waited on the west bank to be ferried across in an armada of countless river craft of all sizes. Forty thousand men under arms he had brought with him and they, in turn, had brought half as many camp-followers with them. And all had to be rowed or sailed across.

'Four days?' Antigonos fumed. 'Four days, is that the quickest we can manage?'

'If we work day and night, then yes,' Nearchos replied. 'It's a question of arithmetic: sixty thousand people, twenty thousand horses, mules and oxen and seven thousand wagons and carts, divided by five hundred and twenty-three boats, each averaging a capacity of—'

'Bugger your arithmetic!'

Nearchos shrugged. 'Buggering it won't change it, Antigonos; it will still say four days after you've finished, however hard you've buggered it. Now, shall I get on or do you want to shout at me for a while longer?'

'My arse!' Antigonos looked around the vast encampment, on the banks of the mighty river, that Nearchos had been entrusted with preparing in advance to ease the endeavour. 'And what's that Persian-loving disgrace Peucestas doing? Where is he? I haven't seen him.'

'I've put him in charge of the cavalry and transport jetties. He's also seeing to the elephant transports.'

'No wonder it's going to take so long.'

'If anything, he's speeding things up by sharing my load.'

Antigonos grunted into his beard and waved his hand in dismissal. 'Get on with it then. And see if between you, you can surprise both yourself and your arithmetic by doing it quicker.'

'Unless you can think of some sort of device that would propel the boats at a greater speed, I don't think we'll be in for any surprises.'

Antigonos growled at the Cretan, the man Alexander had delegated all his nautical operations to such was his ability on water, and dismissed him with a petulant wave of the hand, knowing Nearchos would do his best and none could do better. But would his best be good enough, for time was now of the essence?

It had been almost a month since Antigonos had left Tarsus at the head of his huge army to march the seventy leagues to the Euphrates. During that time, he had sent out a succession of scouts and spies into Babylonia and what he had learned disquieted him: Seleukos had retaken Babylon and was now laying siege to the garrisons in the Second Citadel; that in itself was bad enough but what was worse was, according to reports, his army now matched Antigonos' in numbers. Granted, it did not contain such a large core of Macedonians and Greeks, being composed of many eastern troops – some newly trained now to fight in the Macedonian fashion – but that aside, it was still a formidable force and Antigonos wished to confront it sooner rather than later, before Seleukos had time to meld this mishmash of an army into a homogenised unit and before the Southern Citadel, garrisoned with the remains of Demetrios' troops, fell, as it eventually had to. To compel Seleukos into battle while the siege was still ongoing would deprive him of a good five thousand men from his field army as they neutralised the similar number in the overcrowded garrison.

Despite his precautions against failure in the coming war with Seleukos, by securing a heartland in Anatolia and Syria that would prove loyal to him and his successors, Antigonos had no intention of coming back west with anything short of complete victory, for not only was he still in the thrall of his ambition but also he was concerned – worried even – by his geographical vulnerability should he fail. He cursed himself for this state of affairs for he knew he had no one to blame but himself, as he had been so concentrated on dominating the entire empire, he had allowed himself to become encircled. He should have secured the east when he had defeated Eumenes, leaving far greater garrisons in cities, and then Seleukos would never have been able to regain such a footing and he, Antigonos, would not now be in this situation of retracing his steps of seven years ago.

Thus, with a growing sense of frustration, he settled down on the riverbank, in the shade of an awning, with a pitcher of resinated wine, to watch the crossing, knowing his preferred tactic of running around, kicking arses to speed matters along, would only serve to hinder, not help, on this occasion.

Throughout the day the operation continued with lines of men queuing at one of the hundred jetties, originally constructed by Nearchos for the previous invasion of the east, now repaired or rebuilt, fit for purpose. Constant was the flow of vessels back and forth across the slow-moving river, more than a hundred paces wide, one docking as soon as another cast off from a jetty; file-leaders marshalled their men onto the arriving boats as quickly as possible – especially those close to the cyclopic gaze of their commander

370

– so they could be away and room left for another. Towards the northern end of the manoeuvre the last twenty jetties, under Peucestas' command, were reserved, first for the cavalry mounts, then livestock and the baggage train and finally the elephants, two dozen of them, the last in Antigonos' possession. Larger and higher were these jetties, in order to accommodate the heavier transport ships required for the safe passage of so many beasts. Along gangplanks they were guided, blindfolded, their riders speaking soothing words into their ears as they stepped down into the belly of the boat to be tethered with two dozen others, sometimes more. Throughout the crossing, their riders stayed with their mounts, calming them, knowing the speed in which terror could spread through the cargo of one ship and what that would result in.

As the sun fell towards the west, behind him, and the trumpet calls of the elephants now being loaded onto the transports rent the air, Antigonos downed the last of his wine, belched, and made his way to the nearest jetty, pushing to the front of the queue embarking on an eight-oared boat with room for a file of sixteen passengers.

'You're crossing with the best in the army, sir,' an old sweat in his mid-forties said with a grin as he seated himself next to Antigonos in the bow with a waft of garlic and onion breath. 'Don't you worry, sir, we've done this twice before, once with you and once with Alexander; you'll be fine with us, won't he, lads?'

With good-humoured joshing, as if they were teasing a new recruit, his mates assured Antigonos of their intention to watch out for him.

'Thanks, lads, I don't know what I'd have done without you,' Antigonos replied, entering into the spirit of the repartee. 'There was me wondering how I'd know when it was time to disembark, and now I've got a complete file looking out for me.' He looked at the veteran, frowning, for a few moments. 'I know you; Adrastos, isn't it?'

'It is, sir; good of you to remember.'

'You and your lads were with me when we beat Eumenes and then chased him to the fortress at Nora, weren't you?'

'That's correct, sir; we'd joined you after the sly little Greek had killed our man Krateros who we'd been with ever since Alexander sent him back west. After the battle we surrendered to Eumenes and then scarpered to you the first chance we got; we weren't going to take orders from no Greek, were we, lads?' The growling from his mates made it quite clear what they thought of Greeks giving Macedonians orders. 'And we've been with you ever since: Coprates River, Paraetacene, Gabiene and then back to the west.'

'And now east again,' Antigonos said as the river boat cast off, its dockside oarsmen pushing it away from the jetty before all eight pulled together with a concerted heave.

'Yes, sir, and now back east again,' Adrastos replied, gripping the gunwales to steady himself as the boat surged forward. 'The only difference this time is we'll be facing different lads. Seleukos has, from all accounts, got a right mixture in his army: some lads who were with Ptolemy who he lent him, some who were with us who he captured when he retook Babylon, and some who were with Nikanor. It'll be interesting to see who's out here still. It could be that I've a couple of cousins with Seleukos; it'll be nice to see them again, it's been four or five years now.'

Antigonos did not question Adrastos as to how he would get to see his kinsmen: he knew perfectly well how much coming and going there was between the camps when out on campaign; so long as it did not impair their willingness to fight each other, he tolerated it – indeed, sometimes it could prove useful. 'I hope you find them, Adrastos.'

'If they're still alive, sir, no doubt I will. I just hope we don't end up facing each other in a toe to toe. It wouldn't be the first time that's happened, though.'

Antigonos had heard of a few instances of that occurring. 'Has it happened to you?'

'No, sir, not me personally; but I remember Gabiene, when we stood opposite the Silver Shields and one of their officers came forward asking why we were standing against our fathers and, in some cases, grandfathers, forcing them to kill their own progeny. And he was right, a lot of the lads did have fathers in the Silver Shields – I didn't, my dad got his at Gaugamela, poor bastard. Anyway, some of the lads really were killed by their fathers, and one of my mates, since deceased, killed his dad; you should have seen the state of him afterwards. But that was the turning point for many of us because we realised if we wanted to earn our keep in the army and not take the bounty and slope off to rot on some farm in the arse-end of nowhere, then we just had to accept it would happen from time to time. It's an occupational hazard, so to speak, sir.' Adrastos paused, looking at the approaching east bank. 'But you know how it is, sir, now, since then: we try not to kill too many of our own – at least, not after the first contact. It's different for the cavalry, they've got no choice with the way they fight; but in the infantry, we can just raise our pikes a bit and then push against each other. It comes to the same thing in the end except fewer of us end up dead, and they're mostly crushed. It ain't like when we were fighting barbarians where the object was to do for as many of the bastards as possible.'

And Antigonos knew that to be the truth: his son's whole phalanx had surrendered at Gaza without even coming into contact. *He's made a very good point without realising it: the way to defeat Seleukos is to neutralise his better-class Macedonians and Greeks with my less good units, hoping it'll turn into a shoving match as Adrastos says, and then use my elite Macedonians against his newly trained Asian phalanx and thrash him there.* He slapped the veteran on the shoulder and rose to his feet as the boat slid alongside a jetty. 'Thank you, Adrastos, I'll make sure I take your advice.'

'Advice, sir? What advice?'

'Good advice; you and your lads and the rest of the veteran phalanx and mercenary hoplites are going to be the key to the coming battle. I'll make sure you'll have barbarian blood to spill when we face Seleukos.'

SELEUKOS.
THE BULL-ELEPHANT.

I T HAD STARTED as a trickle but now it was a flood; every hour more of the population of Babylon returned to the city. To the east, beyond the great military camp around which the army was now mustering for the coming campaign, the road was packed as far as the eye could see – and, no doubt, further, as the line of humanity and livestock paled into the distance – for Seleukos had ordered the end to the Babylonians' exile and, now, a month since the taking of every quarter of the city bar the Southern Citadel, all were anxious to return to salvage what they could of their belongings after more than a year's absence.

'You've done well, Patrokles,' Seleukos said to the general who had masterminded the exodus and return as well as maintaining the guerrilla warfare resistance during the occupation. 'I shall see you handsomely rewarded.'

'It was revenge for the four years I spent in a cell below the Southern Citadel whilst you were in the west, lord.'

'Nevertheless, once it's settled you can come to me and ask what you will.'

Patrokles bowed his head. 'I will, lord; but first we have

to finish the matter. I'll go back to see how your son's doing with the muster of the army.'

'Make sure he feels he's in command, even though he isn't.'

'I do, lord.'

'Good; tell him I want to march in two days, whether or not the Southern Citadel has fallen.'

'He'll be ready, lord.'

'But, with luck,' Seleukos glanced at the Babylonian priest next to Patrokles, 'the Southern Citadel will have surrendered by then. What news, Naramsin?'

'As you requested when inspecting the scythed chariots, I sent a couple of my brethren in by the secret way, lord, disguised as slaves,' said Naramsin, the chief priest of Bel Marduk, bowing his head. 'That was five days ago. They've come back and reported major unrest within the garrison; they're hungry and ripe for mutiny. All they have left is grain and not much of that; rats are already selling at a premium.'

'That's most welcome news; again, I find myself in your debt, Naramsin. First, your priesthood was instrumental in persuading the people from their homes and going into exile.'

'It was a sacred duty.'

'Indeed, it was.' Seleukos admired the priest's ability to act as if his order had not received large financial incentive to terrorise the population with the threat of the great god's displeasure in the form of plagues of boils, locusts and the deaths of first-born. 'And then you trained the slaves to drive the chariots.'

'It wasn't me personally, lord; it was a couple of the brethren.'

'At your instigation, Naramsin; and a fine job they made of it, giving me an offensive weapon to spread terror for all

376

who face it. And now I owe you personally again, Naramsin, and it shall be paid. But first we need to defeat Antigonos; therefore we must get the population back to work as soon as possible, especially on the land. Supplies have to be brought in for an army of forty thousand, both food and equipment; this, again, is where your order can help. Tell the people it's the god's will that they should strive for victory against Antigonos.'

'But it is, lord. Antigonos gave up all right to Babylon when Demetrios stripped it as if it were a conquest; that was how he saw it. A man with a right to rule this city would never have done that; he would have nurtured it as you do. The way you treat Babylon shows you have the moral right to rule. Bel Marduk knows this and so it *is* the religious duty of every Babylonian to strive towards your victory; they will work to keep the army supplied. My brethren and I will need to do little reminding as to who has their best interests at heart.'

'I wonder for how long that attitude will last when the people find out I intend to move the whole city to Seleukia,' Seleukos said as he and Apama walked, once again, in the gardens of the summer palace; the beauty of the place enhanced by so long an enforced absence.

'But that won't be for a long time yet, Seleukos,' Apama said, bending down to pluck a bloom from a flowering shrub. 'I'm no expert but I imagine it'll take at least ten years before there's anything worth inhabiting over there on the Tigris. Look at Alexandria, for example, that's still not finished after twenty-five years.'

'But people were living there after five.'

Apama fixed the flower into her hair. 'Yes, but how many? And anyway, they came from all different places. No,

Seleukos, if you want to transport the whole population of a city to another location, you should do it in one go, not bit by bit. Have Seleukia completed before you attempt to do such a large-scale move. If the population of this stinking old place moved into a brand-new city, with clean air and all the modern facilities they could wish for, there won't be any unrest. And if you make it grand enough then they'll see it as the work of the god without your priests having to drop their unsubtle hints.'

'That could take fifteen to twenty years.'

'Then you'd better hurry up and beat Antigonos and get started.'

Seleukos bent down to kiss his wife. 'I seem always to be a man in a hurry.'

And his sense of urgency did not diminish the following day as he watched the carcasses of pigs, sheep and oxen, suspended over red-hot coals, rotate, dripping their fat sizzling into the fires below them, just beyond effective arrow range along the walls of the Southern Citadel. But the defenders were not interested in taking shots at the men so tormenting them as they lined the walls, looking with longing at the feast roasting before their eyes; salivating at the aromas.

It was a simple ruse, Seleukos prided himself, but an effective one as eventually his troops began to slice tender cuts from the joints and, with fresh, soft bread, settle down to enjoy their meals as more men crowded onto the defences.

Judging the time right, he walked forward under a branch of truce and stood before the walls with his arms spread wide. 'Men of Macedon and Greece, and I say men of Macedon and Greece, rather than men of Antigonos' garrison, for we are all men of Macedon and Greece here and as such we're brothers. You have done all honour demands of you in the discharge of your duty to Antigonos and his son Demetrios, and now it is time to be pragmatic. I know you didn't have the opportunity to stock your supplies because I'd stripped the entire area before you arrived. My garrison in the Main Citadel lasted for more than a year under your siege and yet you, after little more than a month, come to drool over my men taking their midday meal. Why wait any longer? Why put yourselves through this unnecessary torment? You'll have to surrender at some point, if you wish to live, so why not today and join our meal rather than wait till tomorrow when it'll be nothing but a pile of bones?' He looked back at the many fires, more than a hundred, each topped with mouth-watering crisp roasted meat. 'Come; share our meal.'

There was an audible groan of unsated hunger from all along the wall. 'Get back, back to your posts!' came a cry, soon repeated, as the garrison commander and his senior officers tried to regain control. 'Back, I say! Back!' But with each repeat of the order, the confidence in the voice dwindled and soon silence fell over the Southern Citadel as they watched the men surrounding them eat their fill, holding up their wooden trenchers piled with meat and sucking the juice from their fingers, making popping noises to exaggerate the pleasure.

The first clash of arms was sudden and soon drowned by the howls of two or three men in abject pain, their cries swiftly and abruptly curtailed.

Seleukos watched the gate with eager anticipation for, if it were to open, it was in the nick of time as Antiochus, now aged fifteen, was approaching from the Ishtar Gate, ready to give his report.

And it was slow and with the grind of metal upon metal, at first, that the double gates of the Southern Citadel eased open, but their momentum grew to soon reveal the defenders packed in the entrance and crowded in the courtyard beyond.

Seleukos stood opposite them, the branch of truce still raised over his head. 'Do you surrender?'

The answer came in the form of three heads lobbed out to roll in the dust leaving a bloody trail and then the decapitated corpses flopping to the ground behind them. 'We yield,' one man shouted and then stepped forward with the rest of the garrison following.

Seleukos opened his arms to them. 'You will be fed and then sworn into my service. How many are you?'

'Four and a half thousand, give or take,' the man replied, 'minus Archelaos and two of his officers who seemed to think we could hold out until Antigonos gets here.'

'He'll never get here again.'

'That's what we tried to tell Archelaos but he wouldn't listen.'

'You're all welcome in my army.'

'That makes a grand total of thirty-six and a half thousand, Father,' Antiochus said as the besieged garrison began to shuffle out, throwing down their weapons, to the cheers of their former foes.

'So, you're ready then?'

'Yes; every man is fully equipped except for this rabble,' Demetrios said, watching the defenders shamble out of the citadel, 'but I'm sure we can have them split up and integrated into other units by the time we leave at dawn tomorrow; they can pick up their weapons after they've sworn to you.'

Seleukos looked down at his son, now almost at the height of his chin and still growing. 'Well done, Antiochus; that was your first major task and from all accounts you completed it well.'

The youth smiled. 'Come on, Father, you know perfectly well that all the senior officers did the work and then delegated the tasks down to their juniors; I did next to nothing.'

'Not so; not so at all. You were the focus; your officers reported to you and that's the first step to overall command. In just a few days you got a grasp of the structure of the army and how it is supplied. You learned who reports to whom and who is in charge of what supply chains.'

Antiochus contemplated his father's words. 'I suppose so.'

'You suppose so? You know so. Tell me, if you want to know the current active number of the Sogdian horse-archers, who do you summon?'

'Azanes.'

'Correct. And if you want to know the status of the Leukaraspedes phalanx, who do you ask?'

'Patrokles.'

'Exactly, because both Azanes and Patrokles command their men in battle. And if you wanted to know how many days' rations each of those two units have been issued with, would you ask Azanes and Patrokles?'

'Yes.'

'Of course you would because it's something they both need to know. But if you wanted to know how many days' rations remained in reserve that could be issued to those two units if it were necessary, would you still ask Azanes and Patrokles?'

Antiochus paused to consider the question. 'Ah, that's differ- ent. No, I would not ask Patrokles, I would ask Nikodemos.'

'Why?'

'Because he is the quartermaster for the whole army.'

'And he would be able to tell you the answer for both units?'

'No, Father; he could give me an accurate number for the phalanx, but for the Sogdians I would still have to ask Azanes because his lads are irregulars and therefore a law unto themselves when it comes to supplies.'

'And even then, Azanes would only be able to give you a rough estimation.'

'If I was lucky.'

'You see; you're learning. Once you know all these things, every little detail about how the army functions, then you'll be ready to wield it as an offensive tool; you've just taken your first steps.'

Antiochus beamed at his father, visibly swelling with pride. 'So, I can be of real help to you now, can I?'

'You won't leave my side throughout the campaign.'

And so, with his son at his side, Seleukos bid farewell to his wife as he set out on the defining campaign of his life. 'You command here now, Apama. If I fail, take the desert path through the land of the Nabateans, to Ptolemy.'

She rose up on her toes to kiss him. 'You won't fail, Seleukos; this is the moment that your whole life has been building up to. And besides,' she took the helmet from the crook of Antiochus' arm and raised it above his head, 'you have your eldest son with you.' She lowered the helmet into place and admired it on her first-born. Bronze, inlaid with silver depictions of horses, with a red horse-hair plume flanked by an eagle feather on either side, it transformed Antiochus, in her eyes, from a youth to a man; tears welled as she stroked his cheek. 'Go with your father and take what's ours.'

'I will, Mother.'

With the memory of the exchange, Seleukos mounted his stallion, feeling pride in what he had achieved since returning to Babylon. Apama was right: this was what his life had been building to and it was now down to him, with his son at his side, to go and take what would belong to him and his family forever. He raised his fist above his head and pumped it in the air; horns bellowed and drums boomed. With a sense of history in the making, Seleukos looked at Antiochus and, with a smile, kicked his horse forward.

For five days the army marched north, following the same route Seleukos had taken a couple of years previously when he had ridden to confront Nikanor. Through mainly depopulated country they rode, although signs of the people's return grew the further they got from the city, with women working in the fields and men repairing fences and farm buildings whilst children saw to sheep and other livestock. It was mid-morning of the sixth day that the walls of Sittace came into view on the mud-brown course of the Tigris, its fertile fields to either side supporting so much life. 'This is it, Antiochus, this is where Seleukia will be. Smell the air compared to Babylon; this is the site of a city that'll prosper.' He looked around, pleased that on the second time of seeing the place it still felt as perfect as before. 'And just to the north of here is where we start the defence of our land. We go forward to the canal.'

In truth it was more of a reed-filled stream now, rather than a canal, thirty paces wide with the water at the bed not more than a third of that across, but it was deep enough to still just be navigable by small craft, thus providing a valuable link between the two great rivers. It was not, however, its mercantile benefits that appealed to Seleukos at this time – although, dredging it and widening it would be a priority at a later date – but, rather, its obvious benefits as an obstacle for an advancing army. What was also of interest was the wall Nebuchadnezzar had caused to be built, not half a league to the north of it. Crossing the canal with Antiochus, Patrokles, Polyarchos, Azanes and a dozen other of his senior commanders, Seleukos rode hard to the wall. The height of two men and still intact along much of its length, it was constructed of baked brick secured with bitumen around an earthen centre; it ran, south-west to north-east, straight as a spear shaft, twenty leagues from one river to the other.

'Are you thinking of defending this, Father?' Antiochus asked as they stood on its summit, gazing north whence the enemy would come.

'Defending it? No; I'm going to use this as a fishing net.' He turned to his assembled officers. 'Gentlemen, I want this wall repaired so it is at least the height of a man, almost all the way to the Euphrates; it doesn't have to be pretty, just a bastard to climb over. The last part to the banks of the Euphrates, I want levelled; the gap between the end and the river should be three hundred paces less than the distance between the canal and the wall, which is the frontage we will fight with. Patrokles, I'll let you organise that. Polyarchos, whilst Patrokles busies himself here I want you to use the rubble from the wall to construct two fords across the canal, each one wide enough for twenty horses; the first, towards the Euphrates, half a league from the new end of the wall and the second another half a league after that. They're to be invisible, so mark them with reeds and make them two hands' breadths deep so horses can get across them at a canter at least. When you've done that, start levelling the ground on the northern side of the forward ford; don't make it obvious, just remove any big stones and fill in any holes.' He looked to his son. 'Antiochus, bring up the army and get it across the canal. Have the pioneers throw up temporary bridges but do not, on any account, use the fords; I don't want hoof marks and footprints giving away their location.'

'Yes, Father,' Antiochus replied, his eyes sparkling with excitement at the importance of the task.

'Good lad. Set up camp two leagues from the new end of the wall; infantry closest to the canal, cavalry to the north of them.' He turned to Azanes. 'And you and I, my friend, are going to take most of the cavalry north of the wall, find Antigonos and then draw him south, tempting him with the possibility of an easy victory.' He indicated to the land between wall and canal. 'This, gentlemen, is where we shall trap our resinated cyclops; here where his superior numbers make little difference.'

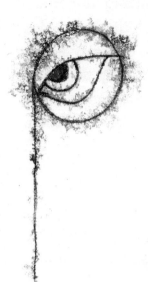

ANTIGONOS.
THE ONE-EYED.

HEAT AND DUST were taking their toll on the army as it marched south. Many in the ranks were recent recruits, not old sweats like Adrastos and his mates, and had never yet been so far south and east and suffered in the baked lands between the two great rivers.

'At least water isn't a problem,' Antigonos observed to Nearchos and Philippos as they followed the line of the Euphrates south for the tenth day since the crossing. He pulled his horse out of the column and turned to watch the demeanour of his men as they marched under a burning sun, heads covered with improvised hats or pieces of cloth. He took his straw sunhat off and wiped his balding pate with a rag. 'If there wasn't so much wealth to be had out here, no one in their right mind would bother with the place.'

'This is nothing compared to the Gedrosian Desert over towards India,' Nearchos replied, he too wiping the sweat from his forehead. 'I brought the fleet back from the east along that shore and I can tell you it is a barren, waterless furnace. Alexander lost more men crossing that than he did in India itself; the ridiculous thing is he didn't need to come back that way, he could have stayed north and gone the same route he'd sent Krateros on.'

'Why did he split the army?' Philippos asked.

Nearchos shook his head. 'I'll never understand that decision.'

'It was for his vanity, Son,' Antigonos said. 'So he could claim to have conquered one of the most inhospitable places anywhere and fuck everyone with him if they died of thirst.' Antigonos shook his head, replacing his sunhat. 'My arse, Alexander makes your brother, Demetrios, seem like a modest lad with little ambition and a strong desire for others to achieve well. I think Alexander knew I thought him to be an arrogant puppy, which is why he left me behind in Phrygia. It was just as well, really, as I wouldn't have put up with his treating barbarians as if they were the equal to Macedonians; and then as for wanting to make us all abase ourselves before him as if we were a conquered people by performing full proskynesis, well, my arse, he wouldn't have got far with me.'

Nearchos sighed and shook his head at the memory. 'He didn't get very far with anyone; yes, we did it but no one liked it, and if the fever hadn't taken him, or Kassandros' potion, if you believe that version, then I think it's fair to say he wouldn't have lasted another year before someone decided their honour could take no more. Krateros was having problems towards the end, which is why Alexander sent him back to Macedon, ostensibly to replace Antipatros as regent. Men of your generation were finding it increasingly hard to respect what Alexander was doing: making us bow to him and mixing easterners into Macedonian units and then creating a purely eastern phalanx. Us younger ones, especially those of us who were brought up with him, found it slightly easier but even then we weren't happy about it.'

'And you're a Cretan.'

'But raised in Macedon with Alexander as one of his pages. Anyway, I felt the same way as most of the others; I think that, had he lived and the conquest of the Arabian peninsula was successful, matters would have come to a head before we headed west to Carthage.'

Antigonos shrugged. 'Well, I've never shed a tear over his demise and I've even been in alliances with his alleged assassin, which goes to show just how much I care about his death.'

Nearchos smiled and pulled at his beard. 'So have Ptolemy, Lysimachus, Polyperchon and Seleukos. I think that clearly shows no one is much concerned about Alexander's death now it's safely in the past and we're concentrating on taking the best for ourselves.'

'Yes, we've got a lot to be grateful to Kassandros for.'

'If it really was him,' Philippos cautioned.

Antigonos had no doubts. 'Oh, it was him all right; Archias the Exile-Hunter admitted getting the poison for him in Tarsus.'

'Ptolemy could have paid him to say that,' Nearchos pointed out.

'Think what you like, old friend; the fact is the empire without Alexander has a lot more opportunity than with him.'

'That, I'd say, is something we can all agree on.'

'Adrastos!' Antigonos shouted, spotting the veteran as he passed. 'Any more good advice for me?'

'Yes, sir; turn the fucking column around and send us somewhere cold; we ain't fucking camels!' This raised a lot of good-humoured joshing from his mates around him and brought a smile to Antigonos.

'That's exactly what I'll do once we've kicked Seleukos' arse using your plan.'

'I'm still none the wiser as to how I helped, sir,' Adrastos called back over his shoulder, 'but if it gets us back quickly to regions where you don't singe your arse every time you take a shit then I'm a happy man.'

'What advice?' Philippos asked.

'Oh, I crossed the river with him and he was going on about how he might have a couple of cousins with Seleukos and how they try not to kill too many of the enemy if they're fighting fellow Macedonians or Greeks even.'

'Yes,' Nearchos said, 'well, we've known that for a while.'

'Ah, but we've not done anything about it because there is very little we could do. Now, I've got a lot of Anatolians in my army serving in the phalanx, but most of them have some Greek heritage and, when you look at them, they all seem to be reasonably normal, dressing in tunics like decent men. But we're now going east to where Alexander recruited his eastern phalanx. Seleukos has them in his army, I'm sure of it; he would have reformed them when he was short of troops. A phalanx of Persians, all wearing trousers!' Antigonos chuckled at the mental image. 'Imagine it? Our boys won't like that at all.'

Nearchos grinned as he caught on. 'That'll be one fight they won't hold back on.'

'Yes, so all I've got to do is to get my hardened veterans, Adrastos and his mates in the White Shields, facing the Persians and we break them there. That's how I'm going to win.'

A shout caught their attention; they turned to see a unit of a hundred or so mounted men, heavy cavalry, not light scouts as he would have expected, coming in from the south. 'Well?' Antigonos asked their officer as he pulled up his mount to report. 'Who are you?'

The officer wiped the dust from his face as best he could, but his beard remained the colour of the desert. 'It's me, lord, Nikanor.'

'Nikanor! You've got a nerve to show your face here after letting Seleukos beat you and take your entire army. My sweaty arse, if you had done your fucking job I wouldn't have to be out here. I should have you executed on the spot. It's only for old time's sake that I don't.'

Nikanor lowered his head. 'Allow me to try to make amends, lord.'

'Amends? How are you going to make amends?'

'Whilst we were looking for you, we made contact with the enemy, lord; there's a very large group of cavalry about two leagues to the south, heading this way.'

'How large?'

Nikanor risked raising his eyes. 'Five or six thousand, lord.'

'Five or six thousand? Any infantry?'

'No, lord, just cavalry. If you look carefully at the horizon, you can just make out their dust.'

Antigonos shaded his eye, staring into the distance, and then looked at Nearchos and Philippos, excitement rising within him. 'That's probably three quarters of his cavalry strength. If I can catch them, I'll have won the war without having to risk a battle. Nikanor, you might be in the process of saving your life; find Peucestas and tell him to form a flying column as fast as if his Persian-loving arse depended on it. Which it does.'

*

390

It took less than an hour for Peucestas to form up the Thracian, Thessalian, Greek and Macedonian cavalry into a flying column; seven thousand of them, both loose-order skirmishers and the close-order heavies, including three thousand Macedonian Companion Cavalry lancers, the main weapon that Alexander used to crush all before him. South, Antigonos, Philippos and Peucestas led them, south through Mesopotamia towards the Babylonian border; south past the river port of Is over on the western bank; south past the entrance of the Pallacopas canal, also on the western bank of the river, leaving Nearchos to follow with the rest of the army as fast as possible. And all the time the dust of Seleukos' cavalry could be seen on the horizon, never coming any closer.

'He's leading us on,' Antigonos said to Philippos as they stopped to water their horses on the afternoon of the second day of the chase.

'Which means he has a place in mind to lead us to,' Philippos replied, surprising Antigonos.

'Good lad to make the connection; that's what's been worrying me since this morning.' Antigonos adjusted his horse's bridle. 'He must have known we were coming and so has prepared a battle site to his advantage. I did the same at Gabiene: I had the salted earth loosened and raked over so the whole place became a dust bowl and used it as cover to get around Eumenes' flank. We need to be careful, Son; it was too good to be true Seleukos sending his cavalry into my arms. He's not stupid but neither am I. We'll wait here for the rest of the army to catch up and go on together. In the meantime, I'll send out scouts to see if we can find out what sort of a surprise he's preparing for us.'

*

'A wall, you say?' Antigonos was astonished. 'Stretching from a league beyond the Euphrates all the way to the Tigris?'

'Yes, sir,' the scout commander said. 'It's the height of two men; but the last part, the last league to the Euphrates, has been recently dismantled.'

'It's the Median wall,' Peucestas said. 'You must have passed it last time you came east.'

'Last time I travelled by river to Babylon, ahead of the army in order to negotiate Seleukos' surrender; I was racing after Eumenes and not on a sightseeing tour.'

'Then you would've missed the wall and the canal to the south of it.'

Antigonos looked in alarm at Peucestas. 'Canal? To the south? How far to the south?'

'Half a league or so, linking the two rivers at their narrowest point.'

'How wide is it?'

'Wide enough to be a serious obstacle.'

'So that's it; that's what he plans to do: draw us into an enclosed space at the narrowest point between the rivers and then press us against the wall. He'll have an escape route across the canal to fall back over should he not be successful, bridges, no doubt, destroying them as he goes to prevent me from following up. Very clever of our Titanesque friend.'

Peucestas looked at the Euphrates, now almost a hundred and fifty paces wide. 'We need to cross back over in order to avoid his trap.'

'But then we either have to re-cross in which case he'll be waiting for us, or take the western half of Babylon and try to fight our way over the bridge into the old city.'

Peucestas took the point immediately. 'Both would end in failure, if not disaster.' He looked to the east. 'Crossing the Tigris won't do us any good either as we'll still have to cross back if we want to get to Babylon or we'll end up in Susa. So, we've two options, I would say.'

Antigonos grunted. 'My arse; I should have seen this coming. Why would he just hide behind Babylon's walls when he has an army of forty thousand? No, Peucestas, surprisingly, you're almost right: we either go forward or forget about the whole thing and slink home to the west, so actually we only have a single option. We go on. Send the scouts back out; I want to know every aspect of this trap that Seleukos has set for us.'

SELEUKOS.
THE BULL-ELEPHANT.

THE BUSINESS OF getting the army across the canal was ongoing when Seleukos led his cavalry past the wall, veering to the left, eastwards, to where his camp was being set, two leagues away, next to the canal. Sending Azanes with the cavalry to the northern side of the camp where he had ordered the horse-lines to be set, he headed south, towards the crossing point. As he drew close, the first of the twenty scythed chariots rattled across one of the temporary bridges, its four horses with scale armour protecting their chests and backs and with high red plumes attached to their harnesses, high-stepping and tossing their heads; the others followed one by one. 'Get yourselves over to the north of the camp,' Seleukos ordered the driver of the lead vehicle. 'You'll be on the right flank tomorrow; then we shall see how you do. Who knows, perhaps you'll be free by this time tomorrow.'

'Free or dead, lord.' The driver grinned and shook the reins, accelerating his chariot away, its scythes hanging safely inboard in their leather sheaths waiting to be fitted into deadly position, the rest of the unit rumbling after it.

'How's it going, Antiochus?' Seleukos asked, flinging a

leg over his mount's rump and jumping to the ground by the awning under which his son sat; a couple of scribes took notes as officers reported in, having seen their units across the canal and settled in their rightful position in the camp.

'We'll be finished by nightfall, Father,' Antiochus replied, taking a scroll from one of the scribes. 'The remaining eastern cavalry that weren't with you are all across as well as the chariots, as you've just seen; all the phalanx, both local and Macedonian, are setting up camp; and the Greek mercenary hoplites and peltasts are waiting for the last of the Persian and Arab light infantry units to clear the bridges before they come over. Three hours at the most.'

'Excellent.' Seleukos looked north-east along the length of the canal. 'How many bridges did the pioneers build?'

'A dozen, all together.'

'Good; don't dismantle them. I want Antigonos to see them.'

Antiochus frowned. 'Very well, Father.'

Seleukos could see the question in his son's eyes. 'I'm keeping him focused on one hand whilst I do my magic with the other.' He turned to gaze the other way down the canal; it was now his turn to frown. 'How's Polyarchos doing with the fords?'

'Can't you see anything?'

'No.'

'That's your answer, then; he's finished and made a fine job of it. Both are marked with reeds but you'll not see them unless you're very close.'

And it was true: where he estimated the two fords to be, he could see nothing untoward in the water or on the banks; it was as if nothing had been touched. *That is most satisfying. Now all I can do is wait and hope that Antigonos sees just what I want him to see and is satisfied with that.* He took his horse by the bridle and began to walk to the centre of the camp where he would find his tent. 'Have all the senior officers report to me as soon as the crossing is complete, Antiochus.' He walked on a couple of paces before turning back over his shoulder. 'Oh, well done, by the way; that was good work.' He didn't need to see his son's face to know just how much the compliment would have meant to him.

The evening was warm and still; behind the swathe of smoke hovering over the camp, an almost full moon, directly to the south, gave the night sky an eerie quality as if a frail, silver gossamer net had been held up to it. Seleukos sat outside his tent in a high-backed wicker chair, with his bare feet up on a stool; a slave washed and massaged them as all about him the chatter of tens of thousands of men at their evening meal continued in a drone that was soon ignored by one so experienced on campaign. A cup of wine in his hand and a plan in his head, he was in the finest of moods as the senior officers began to assemble. He indicated to the stools and chairs already set around his. 'Sit down, gentlemen, and make yourself comfortable.' He indicated to the slave. 'As you can see, I won't be getting up for a while.'

With good humour fuelled by the excellent wine, Patrokles, Polyarchos, Azanes and the half dozen others relaxed as slaves passed amongst them with trays of grilled meat on sticks and fillets of fried river perch and other fish.

'I'm sorry I'm late, gentlemen,' Antiochus said as he appeared out of the shadows of the camp.

396

'Well, my boy, all across?'

'Yes, Father; except for the artillery train.'

Seleukos raised his eyebrows at his son. 'Really? And why's that? They're not too heavy for the bridges, are they?'

'No; I just thought they would be better left on the other side where they could be of use.'

'You mean they won't be of use here, do you?'

'Well, no; there's no hill or knoll to put them on and so they'll be useless once the army begins to advance.'

'Advance, eh? Who said we're going to advance?'

'Well... surely...'

'Surely what?'

'Well, the scythed chariots for example: they have to charge to be effective.'

'There's a big difference between charging and advancing. You don't have to advance before you charge.'

Antiochus looked abashed that so obvious a thing should be pointed out to him in public. 'Yes, I take your point, Father.'

'Now, what did you have in mind for the artillery on the other side of the canal?'

Antiochus looked around at the assembled staff all evidently keen to hear a young man's wisdom concerning artillery. 'Well, you had two fords constructed, didn't you? Both of which you wish to remain a secret. That being the case, I can only assume that one will be behind our line, and our line will be far enough away from the other ford to ensure it is behind Antigonos' line.'

The boy has seen what I intend to do; good lad. 'Hold it there, Son; we'll keep the rest of the details for the morning. So, what do you plan for the artillery?'

'I think they should be placed along the bank by the second ford because there they could take Antigonos in the flank as he comes forward.'

'But won't it just attract attention to the ford?'

'He won't know it's there and, besides, if you place them to one side of the ford, either close to our line or further away, anyone who tries to cross the canal to get at them will just flounder.'

Seleukos' face lit up. 'Brilliant! Absolute brilliance, my boy; again, show him something with your right hand whilst doing your magic with the left. I'd say you've left the artillery train in exactly the right place.' He looked around his officers as his son glowed with the praise. 'Now, Azanes, what have the scouts reported?'

The Sogdian's dark eyes glinted in the firelight. 'He'll be here by tomorrow, soon after midday; I've left men out there to make sure he doesn't try to steal a night march.'

'Soon after midday, eh? That gives us all morning to get into position; excellent. I think we should concentrate on eating and drinking for the rest of the evening.'

'Out of interest, lord,' Azanes asked, 'what will the disposition be?'

Seleukos wagged a finger side to side at him and then took a mighty swig from his goblet, covering his face.

'At the rear, behind the phalanx! But that is the place of least honour, lord.' Azanes was indignant as were those of the Sogdian clan leaders with him who could understand Greek. Nor did the commanders of the Bactrian, Arachosian and Parthian horse-archers look best pleased having heard the news; as for the Median and Persian heavy cavalry officers, they held their heads high, looking down their noses at Seleukos with their eyes half closed, exhibiting their disdain for their positioning on the field.

'Believe me, all of you, it will be the place of the most honour,' Seleukos said, the thickness of his head after a late night's carousing not helping his mood.

Azanes' dark eyes showed deep disappointment. 'But how can we get to the enemy if we're stuck behind the phalanx whose left flank is hard on the canal?'

Seleukos sighed. 'You will go where you're told: all the eastern cavalry will be stationed behind the phalanx – and if you will let me finish my sentence this time – half the horse-archers on the northern side of the ford and then half on the southern side; the heavy cavalry will be on the northern bank behind the horse-archers. It's imperative that all three units keep your flanks as close to the canal as possible so that from a distance and behind a large formation of infantry you will look like one unit.' He paused, allowing the implication to sink in.

Azanes' face brightened. 'Ah, I see; one unit on this side of the ford.'

'Exactly. That's what I want Antigonos to think when he looks at our line of battle.'

ANTIGONOS.
THE ONE-EYED.

'I CAN ONLY SEE cavalry on his right wing,' Antigonos said as he, Nearchos and Philippos sat on their horses at the end of the wall, looking south-east towards the Seleucid line. 'He must have more than that.'

Philippos pointed to the top of the wall. 'Shall I, Father?'

'Yes, your two eyes are better than my one; see what you can see up there.'

Philippos drew his horse next to the broken end of the wall and, standing on the beast's back, clasped hold of jagged brick; scrabbling with his feet, dislodging loose shards, he pulled himself up, gaining the summit to stand, shielding his eyes from the noonday sun with one hand.

'Well, what do you see?'

'Cavalry behind the light infantry screen on his right. Mercenary Greek lights and then what looks to be Asiatic infantry – they're wearing trousers – and then more cavalry – wait, they're not cavalry, they're chariots.'

'Chariots!' Antigonos bellowed a laugh. 'Who does he think he is? Achilles at Troy? Chariots! What's he going to do with chariots? Drag Hector's body around the city walls? How many?'

'Twenty, perhaps two dozen, with other cavalry behind them and some more Asiatic infantry. Then come his Macedonian Companions – I should imagine he's with them – and then the phalanx all the way to the canal: Macedonians, then the Persians who you want to target and finally the mercenary hoplites up to the canal. Ah! The rest of his cavalry is behind the phalanx; a couple of small units of Macedonians and then a large mass of easterners by the looks of them.'

'Right behind the phalanx?'

'Yes.'

'My arse; what are they doing there, I wonder? Has he got bridges across the canal?'

Philippos scanned the line of the waterway from directly ahead of them back past the enemy formation and then onto Seleukos' camp and beyond. 'I can see a dozen or so, but right back at the camp and then further away.'

'Nothing up this way? What are those artillery pieces protecting just in front of the mercenary hoplites?'

'Nothing that I can see; they're on the other side of the canal ready to take us in the flank as we advance, I suppose. There are a lot of eastern archers with them.'

'I'll place our light infantry over there to draw their attention from our heavy troops. But that still doesn't explain what he's doing with his horse-archers.'

'They're mainly behind the hoplites, which are formed up only eight deep.'

Antigonos considered this for a few moments. 'He's either thinking of pulling the hoplites into a sixteen-deep formation and creating a gap for them to come through, or he's going to have them come around the right of his phalanx once the rest of his cavalry advance far enough forward to leave a gap.'

'Or he's going to get them across the canal,' Nearchos said.

'What good are they on that side? All the bridges are behind him; how would he get them back? They'd have to wade across through water up to their necks whilst we enjoyed the target practice. No, I'll put the elephants behind the phalanx at the midpoint. The lads are trained in opening ranks to let the beasts back through; this time they can open ranks to let them out and counter the easterners whichever way they come.' His mind made up, he looked back up to his son. 'Anything else worth reporting?'

'No, Father; don't you want to look?'

Antigonos patted his ever-expanding girth. 'I don't think I'll make it up there. No, my boy, I've seen enough. Down you come. Let's get back; we've got a battle to win.'

'Our phalanx will overlap his; we get the Chalkeraspedes opposite the Persians – Adastros and his lads will appreciate that – and have the Hypaspists on our extreme right to deal with the mercenary hoplites, whilst the Macedonians will, no doubt, just shove against one another, exchanging family news with long-lost cousins until those two battles are decided,' Antigonos explained to his senior commanders, pointing with a stick to the formations scratched into the dirt between two straight lines, one representing the canal, the other the wall. All around the meeting, the army readied itself for the advance having taken a cold midday meal. 'The light troops will screen the phalanx; then the Greek and Thracian peltasts and a small detachment of our mercenary hoplites will support it. The cavalry will take up position opposite here, on our left wing, lancers opposite his char-iots; let them have a bit of fun; in fact, I think I'll join them. Nearchos, you take the right of the phalanx and Peucestas, you have the left. Philippos, you'll command the reserves in the second line—'

'But, Father—'

'Enough! Don't look disappointed; your command will include the elephants so it's down to you to keep an eye on those easterners.' He stared down Philippos until the young man agreed. 'Good. Now the main problem we have, gentlemen, is that Seleukos has positioned himself at an angle with his left flank on the canal, much more in advance than his right which almost reaches the wall. This means as we advance in line past the break between the wall and the river we'll have to wheel left; however, as the gap is not quite as wide as the space between the wall and the canal, we will also have to expand our frontage as we make that manoeuvre. Seleukos has set this up well, so let's not begrudge him our respect. Therefore, the cavalry will be in a deep formation and expand its frontage, turning to face the enemy, as the phalanx marches forward three hundred paces before beginning its wheel. As that happens, the light infantry on the right must concentrate their attentions on the bolt-shooters and archers, on the other side of the canal, to allow the manoeuvre to take place without too much loss from volleys coming in on our unshielded flank. Nearchos and Peucestas, do you understand?'

The two commanders looked at each other and then back to Antigonos in agreement. 'Excellent. So, gentlemen, once the wheel is complete and we're facing the enemy, four things need to happen: first, we need to engage Seleukos' Persian phalanx as soon as possible. Peucestas, that's your job seeing as you're so keen on Persians.'

The former satrap of Persis scowled at his new master, not sharing his humour.

Antigonos shrugged and pressed on. 'Second, Nearchos, I want the Hypaspists getting toe to toe with the hoplites; whilst that's happening, I'll take our superior strength in cavalry on our left to push back his right wing and shatter those ridiculous chariots. Finally, as all this is going on, Philippos, keep an eye open for any weak points developing in the line and plug them double quick with our hoplites whilst all the time having your elephant commander keeping watch on the movements of those eastern archers and then having his command counter them.' He looked to the commander of the elephants. 'If you don't spot them from where you're sitting, no one will.' The cyclopic eye roved around his commanders. 'Is that all clear?'

There was a general bark of agreement.

'Good.'

'What do you want of me, lord?' Nikanor asked.

'You? Yes, you. I want you with me, and if I get so much as a scratch, you are a dead man.'

Nikanor grinned. 'Thank you, lord.'

Antigonos rubbed his hands together with great vigour, savouring the moment. *Gods, this'll be good; the first proper battle since Gabiene; and I outnumber Seleukos by a good seven or eight thousand.* His mouth split into what passed for a grin, his eye attempting to convey pleasure to the men around him but not getting much past hunger for battle. 'Gentlemen, we form line.' He looked up at the sun. 'Once we're ready we should have four hours to settle this thing. Remember: we'll win if we allow nothing to get behind us because we'll push Seleukos back and catch him on the bottleneck of his bridges.'

*

I really need to lose some of this weight. Antigonos looked down at the flab bulging out from under his breastplate – the fourth he had had in as many years, each one bigger than the last – *I need to start fighting and training on foot again; I've been getting lazy just sitting on a horse or in a chair all day.* He looked at his Companion Cavalry to either side of him, all at the trot as they approached the enemy out of view beyond the wall; none were less than twenty years younger than him but all were in trim condition, even those in their fifties who had been fighting on horseback for over thirty years without putting on weight. He shook his head, putting such an irrelevant matter from his mind, and concentrated on the gap before him. *This is going to take very careful timing.*

Advancing in line of battle, with the Hypaspists on the extreme right, hard up next to the east bank of the Euphrates, and then the various units of the pike-armed phalanx streaming along from them in one dense pack of soldiery, weapons held upright over their shoulders, as they stamped forward. Most of the hoplites, grim and bearded, marched next to them taking the left-hand place of least honour in the huge formation of eighteen thousand infantry, screened by Cretan and Thracian archers, Rhodian slingers and light javelin men from Thessaly and the uplands of Greece and Anatolia. Behind it, his twenty-four elephants, the last of his herd, lumbered, swishing their trunks, their tusks and the crowns of their heads sheathed in bronze as the mahouts, sitting astride their necks, kept up an endless chatter of encouragement with their charges. To either side of the great beasts came the peltasts, both Thracian and Greek, and a small detachment of mercenary hoplites, there to support their close-formation counterparts on the flanks or, in the hoplites' case, by filling a gap should the formation fracture.

And then came the cavalry, comprising all of the left wing, not yet completely in battle formation for it had contracted its frontage to pass by the end of the wall onto the field that would decide Babylon and the east's future. Macedonian, Greek, Thessalian and Thracian, all races from the west, it struck Antigonos; and then he looked again across his army and realised that the only easterners present were the elephants. Casting his mind back to what he had seen as he surveyed Seleukos' formation he recollected that the vast proportion of them were from the east. *It really is a battle between east and west this time; not Macedonians following one general with assorted allies, versus another army of Macedonians with the same assortment of allies. This is pure east versus west, something not seen since Alexander. Gods, this is going to be good. Seleukos, I'm almost grateful to you.*

SELEUKOS.
THE BULL-ELEPHANT.

SILENCE HAD DESCENDED along the whole line as the crunch of tens of thousands of footsteps drew closer. Sitting on his stallion at the head of his Companions, already formed into a wedge, Seleukos could see the dust cloud raised by the advancing enemy rising over the wall, coming ever nearer. His stomach tightened for he knew that by the end of the day he would either have a kingdom in the making or be lying dead not far from where he now sat; surrender was not an option after what Antigonos had done to Eumenes. As if sensing his anxiety, his horse tossed its head, snorting, and stamped a foreleg; Seleukos patted the beast's neck and leaned forward. 'Easy, boy, easy; we'll be charging them soon enough.'

Now the sound intensified as the first ghostly figures, emerging from swirling dust, cleared the line of the wall; too far away to discern their exact nature, being right on the banks of the Euphrates, Seleukos breathed a sigh of relief, for they were infantry, which implied Antigonos had not guessed his strategy for the battle. On they came, the noise of the advance growing, as each new unit cleared the baffle of the wall. Light infantry followed by the dense mass of the phalanx dominated the right flank from the river; and then the cavalry appeared, all stacked on the left of the army, exactly where Seleukos wanted them, as far away from the ford as possible. But his joy was short-lived for now the reserve line came through the gap and his heart sank. *Elephants! Elephants behind the phalanx; gods below, of all the worst possible luck that is it. What made him put his elephants there?* But there was nothing he could do to change it; he now had to work with what he had been given. *How do I distract those beasts?*

Straight towards the canal the infantry continued, the sun glinting dim on their bronze helmets and the tips of their raised pikes through the dust, whilst the cavalry spilled from the edge of the wall, fanning out to face Seleukos' obliquely angled formation. More and more cantered forward to extend their line, the pace of their deployment ensuring they never lost contact with the left flank of their phalanx as it continued its march across the field.

Any moment now. Seleukos looked left and then right to check for the sixth or seventh time that he still had a line of sight with the banners of Antiochus, Azanes, Patrokles and Polyarchos; all were in view. He turned his concentration back to the enemy. A lone horn sounded, followed by the raised shouts of officers; the cavalry halted. Another horn, this time higher, and the left-hand unit of the phalanx, mercenary hoplites, began to wheel, the first man turning slowly on the spot as his comrades kept in line, passing the movement onto the pikemen next to them and so on all along the length of the great formation, each unit having to pace a fraction faster than the last so that by the time the extreme right was wheeling they were at a brisk jog, the screening light infantry running before them. Around they came, standards fluttering in their midst, the straightness of the line never compromised, such was the discipline of some of the finest soldiers in the world.

Now! Seleukos thought when the manoeuvre was almost halfway through. He pointed at his signaller. Raising his horn to his lips, the man squealed out three piercing notes whilst Seleukos' standard was raised and lowered in time. The call was repeated by the signallers and standard-bearers of his generals. Seleukos punched a fist into the air and led his Companions forward as the cavalry line and their covering light infantry, taking their pace from his unit, followed, the extreme left staying rooted on the phalanx whilst the extreme right came forward to be level with the hoplites over on the canal. Seleukos' army had now become a shallow V shape.

Were you watching my right hand, Antigonos? I hope so. Seleukos looked to his left; Azanes had led the rest of the horse-archers over the ford and the heavy Medes and Persians were just emerging from it. His eastern cavalry was now where he wanted it, the move made whilst Antigonos and all his officers were puzzling what his Macedonian cavalry were about moving forward as they had.

On came Antigonos' phalanx, continuing their wheel, as their light infantry hurtled towards the canal; the first volley rose from them to fly high into the air and plunge down amongst the bolt-shooters beyond as their arms thumped and their cords twanged, sending bolts the length of a man's arm into the skirmishers. Back men flew, off-feet, doubled over as the projectiles passed through them in sprays of blood, and then on through the next man to lodge in a third, such was their velocity; over the top of the artillery pieces came the volleys of the eastern archers, stationed behind to cover the time spent reloading the machines. Seleukos smiled, grim, as the first men died to protect their close-formation comrades as their manoeuvre came to a halt and they faced the enemy full square, copying their oblique angle; over on the left flank the cavalry wing came forward to mirror Seleukos' own. Apart from the ongoing duel between the light infantry and the artillery, the field became still as both sides paused to muster the courage for the fight, staring at each other two hundred paces apart.

It was Seleukos who moved first. *Watch my right hand, Antigonos.* 'Chariots, attack!' he shouted. Another clear call rent the air and the slingers and archers, Persians, screening the chariots, streamed away to either side leaving the four-horsed, mobile butchering machines a clear view of the enemy. The drivers, all slaves with nothing to lose and everything to gain should they survive their one and only charge, braced themselves for what would in all probability be the last few moments of life. Raising their many-tailed whips above their heads they cracked them over their teams, shaking the reins as they did. Forward the beasts strained, pulling on the yoke, turning the wheels so that the curved blades, now protruding from the hubs, rotated, glinting in the sun with deadly intent. More blades, two on either side, fixed one above the other into the ends of the yoke spanning all four beasts' withers, protruded at neck and face height; the final horror were spears thrusting out from between the beasts ready to collect those not fortunate enough to be trampled under their hooves. Gradually the chariots gained in speed, the whips working hard on the haunches of the beasts as they built up into a gallop, straight at the enemy line; straight, for there was no manoeuvring, else they would fall foul of one another and become victims of their own honed blades.

I'll be interested to see how you deal with those, Antigonos.

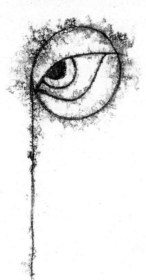

ANTIGONOS.
THE ONE-EYED.

STILL PUZZLING OVER the purpose of Seleukos moving his right wing forward at an angle, Antigonos watched the chariots emerge from behind their screen of light infantry, heading directly towards him. *He threatens me with those ancient engines? My arse, he must be suffering from staying out too long in the eastern sun.* A quick glance over to his right told him that his phalanx, to a chorus of horns, had begun to advance, Nearchos and Peucestas obeying his orders to engage the enemy as briskly as possible. *Let's get this done quickly; gods, this will be good; break those lumbering chariots and we'll almost be through his line.* He signalled to the commanders of the heavy lancer units to either side of him. 'Prepare to advance!' All around him his Companions made last adjustments to their equipment, tightening chin straps and bridles, loosening their swords in their scabbards and then taking up their lances clenched between their knees and the bellies of their mounts in order to keep their hands free.

Antigonos felt the weight of his lance as he gripped the haft, raising it above his head, pulling on his mount's reins to rear its forelegs up. 'Advance!' At his command over six hundred cavalrymen urged their horses on to stream forward. To his left and right, half a length back, Antigonos' cover-men and Nikanor took their positions as their comrades fanned out behind them, each rank wider than the last to create the wedge that Macedon's cavalry had always favoured. To either side the units did the same so that three sharp teeth gradually built up speed to canter towards the chariots, now a hundred paces distant.

The thunder of hooves filled Antigonos' senses, the thrill of the charge surging through him and every man and beast involved; war-cries were raised and accompanied by equine calls of excitement. On they surged, Antigonos at the centre of the formation, cloak billowing out behind him as over on the right wing the phalanx thudded across the field towards opponents who had, so far, remained stationary. But that mystery had barely entered his consciousness when it was abruptly smothered by a reflection, or, rather, many reflections of the sun westering behind him glinting from between the wheels of the vehicles hurtling towards him. Even as he urged his mount into greater speed, Antigonos squinted his one eye, trying to ascertain just exactly what might be the cause of the phenomena. Fast the reflections blinked, one instant there, the next not, but each one different with different timing; it was then he realised there were two separate glints between neighbouring chariots. *Two! My arse, they must be attached to the wheels.* And then he knew the full horror of what was approaching: a weapon he had only heard rumours of. *Scythed chariots! They'll slaughter us.* 'Turn! Turn!' He raised both arms in the air and slowed his horse, the weight of those behind pressing against the beast's rump as, by degrees, the message was transmitted through the formation. Slowing, with the line of lethal revolving

413

blades under fifty paces away, Antigonos yanked his horse about, his cover-men following his lead and then so on back through the ranks as the order to turn and evade spread. Jostling as they did, the bulk of the unit turned and kicked their horses back whence they had come, looking over their shoulders at what it was that had so scared their fearless general into ordering their flight for the first time ever. And what they saw terrified: a line of horses, harnessed in fours, nearly a hundred and fifty paces across, each beast frothing and rolling its eyes as it pounded forward dragging wheeled death behind. Now Antigonos could see the blades spinning on every hub whilst more protruded from the yokes and in between the semi-armoured beasts; now he felt genuine terror, a sensation he had never before encountered, as he urged his mount away from the oncoming slicing-machines of war. With less than ten paces now between him and the lead chariot, Antigonos felt his horse kick forward as it found space through the untangling unit with more and more having turned to flee; on he pushed the beast, on until the distance between him and the terror behind grew, the weight of the chariots hampering their teams' speed.

But as the cavalry pulled away they exposed the very thing Antigonos had placed them in that position to protect: the phalanx, still heading forward. Away the cavalry raced, away from the spinning blades as the chariots risked a very small alteration of their course, a couple of degrees, to head at the hoplites on the right-hand flank of the phalanx. It was the very man who had been the pivot of the wheel not so long ago who was the first to be alert to the incoming danger; shouting to his comrades, he turned, others following him, to present a shield wall, just eight across, to the chariots. Behind

414

them, the peltasts protecting the flank pulled back out of the line of charge.

Just two of the twenty chariots hit the hoplites, literally scything through them, throwing pieces of soldiery up into the air, with gouts of blood exploding from new-carved stumps, as the rotating blades cleaved their path through flesh and bone; the now-rampant beasts fuelled by fear, crushing broken men beneath their hooves as others hung as grotesque displays from the spears between them. Those trying to jump the blades lost their head, whole or in part, to the blades in the yokes and those who tried to duck the higher blade were relieved of their legs by the lower. Over twenty files were butchered in this fashion until the two chariots ground to a halt, choked in carnage of their own making, the drivers leaping from them in an attempt make it back to their own lines and freedom. But the rest of the machines travelled on, behind the hoplite formation, two running straight into the flank of the sixteen-man-deep phalanx now turning to face, presenting a hedge of pikes. In they tore, snapping pike hafts as if they were kindling as the weapons' points cracked into the scale armour covering the horses' chests. And then the blades bit, heads at first and then legs, as the machines sliced their way into the unit. But, again, the impetus was checked by the weight of men before and under them, both whole and in part, as the rest of the chariots which had failed to make contact passed on behind the phalanx, blades reaping the legs and heads of the hind-most, straight at the elephants, turning to face them.

With tusks swaying back and forth, the great beasts of war rumbled towards the deadly engines, neither blinking nor showing any signs of backing down. But horses unused to the scent of a pachyderm are spooked by them, and the sight and smell of the brutes charging towards them, tusks sheathed in bronze, proved too much for beasts already exhausted from a long gallop pulling a heavy object over rough ground. Left and right did they shy, their drivers bailing out as the honed blades of the neighbours bit into their team's legs, bringing them crashing to the ground in shortened-limbed torment, screeching high and bestial as they dealt butchery upon themselves to then disappear, crushed, beneath the huge feet of the elephants whilst their fleeing drivers were picked off by the archers mounted high on the beasts' backs.

Clear of the path of the chariots, Antigonos turned to rally his cavalry, as the elephants made short but bloody work of the maimed horses trapped in their wreckage. To the right of the elephants, the remaining units of the phalanx, untouched by the flank attack, pushed on towards the enemy, whilst to Antigonos' left between him and the wall, his light cavalry probed forward to skirmish with the opposite numbers as both sides tried but failed to find a route around the flank. *By standing between the wall and the canal, Seleukos has effectively nullified my superiority in numbers.* Antigonos looked back to the phalanx as it approached the end of its charge, its pace increasing to maximise the shock of impact. *Now, lads, it's down to you. Break the monstrosity that is a phalanx comprised of trouser-wearing barbarians. Make Seleukos regret his sacrilege of thinking Persians could be trained to fight in the Macedonian manner and beat actual Macedonians.*

Seleukos.
The Bull-Elephant.

Now! *Move, Patrokles.* And as he thought it, so did his phalanx finally move forward to counter the heavy mass of infantry, picking up speed for the last twenty paces of their charge. Now was the time. He looked across the river to where the eastern cavalry waited, with Azanes at their head, formed up facing west ready to carry out their orders, a thousand paces away.

Timing was everything: the phalanx had to be fully engaged, its officers concentrating on the task before them and not what was going on around them. With the massed groans of exertion and the cries of belligerence of more than twenty thousand men, the two great formations collided, each bristling with a thick hedge of sharpened, pointed iron. Almost physical was the sound of the collision of two such weights; visceral were the screams of the dying and wounded, spitted and slashed in the first contact. And then came the chorus of war as man strove against man, each in their own microcosms of deadly endeavour, now locked in a struggle that would be decided by who could push and stab for the longest.

Seleukos glanced ahead: covered by a unit of Greek mercenary horse, Antigonos had rallied his cavalry, two hundred paces away, beyond what was left of the chariots – virtually nothing – and was now forming his men into line. *Thinking of charging again, are you? Good, watch my right hand.* He looked back at the battle between the phalanxes to gauge its intensity. 'Give Azanes the signal!' he shouted at his standard-bearer once satisfied the phalanxes could not break away from one another without mutual agreement.

Up the bearer raised the pole flying a square flag with the sixteen-point star-burst of Macedon flying from a crossbar at the top; he faced it south towards Azanes' eagle-wing standard. Back and forth it was waved, slow and deliberate, raised high in two hands so it had maximum movement from side to side.

See it, Azanes; see it. But Seleukos was confident the Sogdian would be looking out for the signal as he had been told it would come soon after the clash of the phalanxes; he was soon rewarded with the response from the Sogdian's banner, raised and waved. Within a few moments there was movement on the far side of the field, beyond the canal; the eastern horse-archers and their heavier support moved forward.

Now the trap was set. *Just keep looking at my right hand, Antigonos.* And that hand, clutching his lance, he raised in the air and looked back over his shoulder at his Companions. 'Forward!' And then repeated the gesture to Antiochus' Companions supporting him on his left with Antiochus protected in the middle of the third rank to keep him relatively safe in his first cavalry charge.

With the jangle of tack and the snorting of beasts, the lancers moved forward, still in wedge formation as the light cavalry on his right wing continued to skirmish with their opposite numbers, swarming in and out to hurl their javelins but rarely coming into full contact. Behind them a unit of Thessalian medium cavalry waited, along with infantry support, to counter any breakthrough. Seleukos dug his heels into his mount's flanks and urged the beast into a trot, towards the Greeks covering Antigonos' rally. *I'm coming for you, Antigonos.*

But first the Greeks had to be swept aside; tough fighters and proud, Seleukos knew from experience, but, as with all mercenaries, not profligate with their lives if fighting for a losing cause; what was more, they did not fight in a wedge.

And so it was with extreme violence in mind that Seleukos thrust his lance forward, pointing direct at the enemy, and bellowed his battle-cry, inchoate and hoarse as his stallion opened its legs, stretching its neck, bursting into full gallop. Head down, arm extended, roaring, Seleukos felt the power of the beast beneath him as it surged towards the enemy, horses of equal stature streaming in its wake, the riders bawling their defiance at the mercenaries ahead of them. A quick glance over his shoulder told him that Antiochus' men were just a few dozen paces behind. *A double-wedge impact; that should do it.*

But the Greeks were no cowards; javelins hefted, they counter-charged, dark-bearded and wild-eyed, unarmoured and unshielded but unafraid.

In slammed the first volley of fine-pointed missiles, thrown at an almost flat trajectory, to punch rider and horse back to disappear in a shrieking mess of limbs beneath crushing hooves.

A sharp ding on his helmet and a jolt to his neck as a javelin glanced off it momentarily deafened Seleukos, wiping out the thunder of hoof-beats so it was as if he were surging forward in silence, his movements slow and his heart thudding, deep, in his ear as time's chariot took a more leisurely pace; but it was only for a few booming heartbeats before the thunder returned and the pace accelerated again, the Greeks approaching at reckless speed.

Jarring his shoulder back, the lance tip sliced into a howling man, punching him back, his helmet spinning up as blood sprayed from his mouth; along the haft of the lance did the man slide, to crunch into Seleukos' outstretched fist, their faces coming within a pace of each other, the Greek's eyes wide in shock, staring into his. With an upwards jerk, Seleukos hauled on the lance, the weight of the writhing man pulling in the opposite direction and snapping the wood as he disappeared below. Spinning the remnant so the weighted butt-spike became a mace, Seleukos slashed it across to the right, hitting flesh – what he knew not – and then repeated the action to the left as his mount, snapping and snorting, pushed on into the gap between two horses. With an upward block above his head he caught the blade of a sword, swooping down on him; he twisted his wrist, forcing the weapon away, as, letting go of the redundant reins, he leaned over to drive his fist into a screaming mouth, taking the teeth from it and the flesh from his knuckles. A lance tip slid past his shoulder and on into the Greek's throat; his grip faded on his sword. Seleukos pulled the remnants of his improvised mace up and twisted the embedded sword from it; now with a weapon in both hands he slashed and bludgeoned his way through the press of death as his cover-men stabbed at anyone who managed to avoid his multitude of strokes.

Once again time slowed as Seleukos worked his arms, each at a different pace according to the threat from either side. Sensing danger, rather than seeing it, before it threatened, he cut and blocked and thrust, cleaving his way through the mercenaries as the wedge behind him widened the gap, breaking the cohesion. A physical shock to his left briefly registered. *Antiochus' charge has hit home.* But with no more than a fleeting acknowledgement of the event before returning his full concentration onto his work, Seleukos felt no concern for his son.

For how long he forced his body to the very edge of its strength, dealing out violence that would haunt the dreams of most men, he had little idea, for he just slew and slew until there was none before him requiring slaying. Out he emerged from the rear of the Greeks, bloody and weary, as his erstwhile enemies, the survivors at least, fled the field, heading towards the gap between the wall and the river. Away they streamed, grateful to get clear with their lives but knowing they had done all that honour required of them for they had plugged a hole in the line that had been left by their general when he had evaded the scythed chariots. And as they streamed away, it was their general and his newly rallied Companions whom they exposed to Seleukos, not more than a hundred paces towards the river.

There you are, you one-eyed monster. Now I shall crush you in my trap. Seleukos looked left, over towards the ford closest to the Euphrates. There the duel between the artillery and the light infantry still raged as a sideshow, the outcome deciding nothing, but its existence an important distraction. *Good lad, Antiochus; placing the artillery near the ford was excellent thinking.* He turned and with relief saw his son at the head of his men, his cover-men far bloodier than him in testimony to the effort they had put in keeping him safe. Waving to Antiochus, Seleukos gestured to him to come over. His son shouted something lost in the surrounding cacophony, but nodded his head in an exaggerated fashion and urged his horse across the gap, his cover-men to either side. Pulling up next to his father, he pointed to Antigonos' cavalry. 'Do we charge them, Father?'

'No, Son, we rally back.'

'Back?'

'Trust me.'

Now, again, it was a question of timing: Antigonos was ready before him; the elephants were extracting themselves from the remains of the chariots and, uneasy at having cavalry behind their flank, would no doubt pick Seleukos' and Antiochus' units as targets. Over to the right the light cavalry swirled all the way to the wall. Staying put, Seleukos gave his men time to regroup, the wounded still able to ride turning away towards the rear. Another glance, past the elephants, over to the ford gave him the answer he wanted as Antigonos raised his arm and ordered his advance. Seleukos was ready for the final move. 'Rally back!' *Now, come on, Antigonos, do what I want and follow up; let's finish it here.* And as the thought went through his head he was distracted by a familiar face next to the cyclops. *Nikanor! Oh, that really does make the prospect of defeating Antigonos even sweeter.*

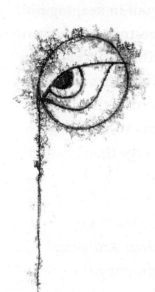

ANTIGONOS.
THE ONE-EYED.

HE'S PULLING BACK! *My arse;
why's he doing that?* Antigonos
glanced left and then right as
his mount walked forward. *It must be
the elephants; he's afraid they'll take him in the flank if he
engages me. And they will if I have my way as some small
recompense for the scythed chariot trick. But, on the other
hand, is he trying to lure me into a trap? Should I pause?*
Another glance to his right told him that the majority of
his phalanx, unscathed by the chariots, had had the best of
the first contact, pushing back the enemy by at least a
dozen paces before stability ensued. The remnants of the
mauled hoplites, however, had broken and were now
fleeing across the path of the advancing elephants leaving
many of their comrades screaming in lost-limbed agony
behind them. It was a small unit of Seleukos' peltasts
attacking the more numerous and much heavier pikemen,
next to the fleeing hoplites, that made up Antigonos'
mind. *They're demoralised by the hideous injuries caused by
the scythes and are wavering; they aren't even counter-
charging mere peltasts. If I don't charge Seleukos' cavalry next
to them, they'll break.* To do nothing was to see the left

flank of his phalanx crumble, undoing the advantage of the initial charge and not allowing his Macedonians enough time to break their Persian counterparts; and besides, Seleukos was less than a hundred paces away. He kicked his stallion into a trot; his men followed his lead, anxious now to make up for their ignominious evasion of the chariots.

It was as Antigonos was about to order the charge and accelerate into a canter that a change occurred in the ambient din of the field. It was from behind him to the south towards the canal: ululations; but there was no unit in his army who would make such a noise. He looked over his shoulder; his heart juddered. Where before he had a clear line of sight to the canal and his light infantry protecting the flank of his phalanx from the bolt-shooters and archers on the far bank, now all he could see were horsemen. Eastern horsemen; horse-archers, riding rampant behind his army, releasing volleys as they came swarming over the canal. *He made a ford! But they were behind his phalanx on this side of the canal; Philippos saw them.* But as he had the thought, he saw what had happened. *My arse; the bastard made two fords!*

Antigonos then saw the elephants, lumbering towards Seleukos, facing in the opposite direction to the threat they were meant to counter. *And then he distracted my elephants. My putrid arse, he's completely played me.* The sickening realisation hit him. 'Halt!' If he went forward all would be lost; it was a trap. 'Right wheel!' He had to contain the easterners in order to give Nearchos and Peucestas enough time to form square with the phalanx and withdraw from the field. He looked over to Philippos' command behind the phalanx: they had already turned to face the danger. *Good lad; but you've not nearly enough men.* He looked to his cover-man to his left. 'Get those elephants facing the right way!' Without waiting to see the man off, he turned to the cover on the right and pointed at the fleeing hoplites, now changing direction away from the new threat. 'Ride and rally them. They don't need to advance, just get them to hold their ground. Go!' As the rider sped away Antigonos looked back to Nikanor behind him, his eye glaring with urgency. 'Get two of the light cavalry units holding the wall and bring them to me here, now! And the Thracian peltasts; there'll be rhomphaia work.'

Nikanor's eyes blazed with the opportunity to make amends and turned his mount without a word.

Antigonos focused his attention back to the oncoming horde as it split in two: the lead section heading straight on towards him and then the rest of the horse-archers and the heavy cavalry swooping around to their right, straight at Philippos' fragile command, barely a quarter of their number, as the phalanx, as yet unaware of the danger it was in, heaved forward, trampling Persian dead beneath its feet.

So close! Antigonos could have cried had he had the time. 'Forward!'

And forward he and his Companions went towards the ululating easterners now halfway between the canal and Antigonos; vastly outnumbered and with no long-range weapons there was very little he could do other than charge them straight on and hope that enough of his men would get through the arrow hail to bring their lances to bear to kill sufficient to at least stem the tide until the reinforcements arrived. *I'm dead anyway if I don't try.* 'Form a single wedge!'

And as the formation change was made and the three units combined into one great spearhead, the easterners spotted them and their ululations intensified; they kicked their ponies on, right hands nocking arrows as they raised their bows with the left. Closing fast, Antigonos knew his only chance was to accelerate as he saw the first volley rise and pray that he could run underneath it. *After, it's in the hands of the gods.* At the apex of the wedge he remained at a canter, watching the mass of man and beast thunder towards him, their expanse filling the width of his one-eyed vision. It was at two hundred paces that the release came. 'Charge!' The bellow was lost in the din but his hand gesture with his lance was not and he and his Companions surged forward. On they rushed, for their lives depended on speed. High did the volley climb, a dark sheet of swift-moving cloud blown on a storm wind, high above him as he craned his neck to watch; and then it seemed to pause before it fell, down, down, hurtling to the ground. On he and his men kicked their horses, on and under the volley that clipped the last two or three ranks, bringing casualties down but in dozens and not scores and causing no carnage behind them as they rolled.

But it was the next volley, striking mere heartbeats after the first, that inflicted the damage as it culled fifty or more and they in turn triggering further casualties amongst those whose mounts' reactions were not fleet enough to hurdle the obstacles. Antigonos braced himself for the last lethal volley, released flat and at almost point blank, squinting his eye half closed and turning his head away as if it would help. It did not: the impact exploded the wind from his frame, punching him back and almost raising him from his seat had not his girth provided ballast enough to keep him in place. Back he floundered, arrow protruding from his left shoulder, arms flopping out and chin falling to his chest; he raised his fading eye to see a maelstrom of snarling, wild faces engulfing him. A hand grabbed his neck; his eye closed. *Seleukos has won.*

SELEUKOS.
THE BULL-ELEPHANT.

I T WAS AS the elephants turned and charged the horse-archers' flank at the same moment that Antigonos' lancers swept into them, the wedge driving deep, that Seleukos knew his victory could not be complete. Yes, he would camp on the field of battle, but no, Antigonos' army would not be entirely destroyed or captured; the great beasts of war and the suicidal attack by the resinated cyclops would be enough to prevent the phalanx from being completely surrounded. Thracian light cavalry had thundered in from Antigonos' left to plug the gap, along with the peltasts who had rallied after evading the chariots, between the elephants and Antigonos' companions, still cutting their slow way through the Sogdians, Bactrians and other assorted easterners. Averse to close combat, they swirled around the lancers but were unable to release too many shafts for fear of hitting their own. Round they went, hacking at the edges of the enemy until the elephants waded into them, causing them to turn and flee like a flock of starlings, dark and twisting, first this way, then that.

Over towards the canal the eastern heavy cavalry were locked in a fierce combat with the reserve Macedonian cavalry and hoplites, with the Hypaspists now bulking their numbers having put Seleukos' Greek mercenaries to flight. And that battle and defeat for Seleukos' mercenaries had gone unremarked at the far side of the field on the bank of the canal, but, Seleukos reflected, it, along with his Persian pikemen being pushed back, had enabled Antigonos' phalanx to extract itself. Now it was managing to turn its rear eight ranks and face both ways and begin to edge north towards the wall, all the while expanding its width as the southernmost ranks fed into its centre. With meticulous – and life-saving – discipline, the officers, under Nearchos and Peucestas, called the pace and, as one being, the great square, pikes bristling on all sides, began to pick up speed and withdraw. With the elephants and reserves shielding their western flank and with just Seleukos' mauled Persian phalanx and his insufficiently large Macedonian one, plus a few cavalry to threaten the eastern flank, it could only be down to him to try to prevent the escape by charging the massed formation with his cavalry. But he knew full well the impossibility of that, for horses would shy before throwing themselves upon a hedge of sharpened iron.

And as the phalanx tramped on, the men on its west and east flanks stepping sideways and those to the south walking backwards in order to remain facing the enemy, Seleukos could see they had no need to surrender; he realised, therefore, he had a choice. *Either I let them go or I become known as the man who murdered fifteen thousand Macedonians as they retreated.* Had they still been in contact all the way along their line and unable to disengage, there would have been a chance to get them to surrender; but it was not to be. Thus, the retreating infantry square slowly made its way towards the wall and on to its camp beyond. With the sun now on the horizon, Seleukos gave the order to fall back from the defeated army and let it pass out of the trap that he had set between the wall and the canal.

'But why, Father?' Antiochus asked, his voice tight with emotion, as he heard the orders to fall back sound up and down the line.

Seleukos looked at his son, bloody and dishevelled, and smiled, wiping a globule of gore from the corner of his eye. 'Because night is falling and I have a better idea.'

'The men are to stay in their kit,' Seleukos said to his assembled commanders, briefing them just to the east of where the chariots had met their end. 'No one, and I mean no one, is to take off so much as a greave. They are to eat sitting in rough formation. And don't let them have too much wine.'

'What do you plan?' Patrokles asked. 'The lads are shattered, what more can you ask of them tonight?'

'One more effort.' Seleukos looked to the silhouettes of the mangled chariots, backed by the last glow of the day in the western sky. 'Did any of the drivers make it back?'

'Two,' Polyarchos replied. 'I've got them under guard until you've time to see them.'

'Two? That's not bad; that's a one in ten chance of survival. With odds like that I think we'll have no shortage of volunteer slaves. I want a hundred of those chariots; just the thought of them being opposite will make men weak with terror; they're a wonderful weapon until they meet elephants.' He kicked a severed foot, lying on the ground. 'Although, I doubt the man who used to own this thinks so.'

The macabre humour sent a wave of relief through exhausted men relieved and amazed that they were still alive.

'Get some rest, all of you, and make sure your men do too. I want them ready two hours after midnight. We've done it before and it's worked, so we'll do it again. We'll take their camp just before dawn and I want the cyclops alive.'

The moon had at last set and all was ready. Seleukos sat on his stallion at the head of his army, waiting for the return of the scouts. In column, with all the cavalry as the van along with the light infantry, and with the heavy infantry following behind, Seleukos had brought them up from their camp to their present position just before the end of the wall. With only a few brief hours' rest, perhaps even some sleep, and a meal inside them, Seleukos knew that his men would be good for one final, but brief, effort; again speed was of the essence, for it was vital that the enemy would have no time to organise.

The beat of hooves announced the arrival of the scouts long before they materialised in the thick gloom of the now moonless night.

'Well?' Seleukos asked Azanes as he brought his horse to a halt.

The teeth showed in the Sogdian's beard as he grinned. 'He stood them down!'

'The whole army?'

'Yes. Some of my men crept through their lines; they reported that the army has disarmed and, having eaten and drunk, most of them have fallen asleep – passed out is probably a better way of putting it.'

Seleukos suddenly felt much calmer. 'I can't believe Antigonos has allowed that to happen.' *But I won't be complaining.* He turned to Patrokles and Polyarchos. 'It's half a league to their camp. Azanes and I will take the cavalry and light infantry; we'll form line as we approach and then just ride through causing panic – but not too many deaths – as the light infantry fan round either side to the east and west. You bring the infantry behind, at a jog, and form up along the southern perimeter. Once the cavalry are through, we'll cover the north, surrounding the whole camp. And then we'll parley. Any questions?'

There were none; it was a simple plan and a plan made all the easier by the astonishing lack of watchfulness displayed by Antigonos' army. Unopposed, Seleukos and Azanes led their cavalry out of the night and into the camp as the light infantry raced to secure either side. Through they went, in line but spread out so they could avoid the recumbent forms, now stirring, groggy with sleep. With the occasional shout and ringing of weapons drawn, followed by the twang of bows and the death cries of those foolish enough to attempt resistance when so thoroughly infiltrated, the operation began with surprising calm. But as they progressed so did the warning of their arrival run before them and it was towards the middle of the camp that resistance began to be more than sporadic as awaking men quickly formed into centres of resistance. 'Advance!' Seleukos cried, urging his stallion on into a canter for now there was no time to observe any niceties: if men were crushed, so be it. *At least I can point to the fact that I intended to be as merciful as possible*, he mused, readying his lance to thrust down into the next man to try to oppose him as the noise of mild resistance grew into the rage of battle as more and more men appeared in the dim light of dying fires to provide targets for his eastern horse-archers and his lancers. On they went at pace, pushing through the camp, driving men before them or cutting them down with shaft or lance if they did not kneel in surrender.

On towards the centre of the camp, Seleukos led his cavalry, striking out if he needed to but trying to keep the blood clinging to his arm to a minimum, all the time waiting for the defiant figure of Antigonos to appear.

ANTIGONOS.
THE ONE-EYED.

I T WAS THROUGH a haze Antigonos came to the surface, as consciousness slowly opened his mind. The maelstrom of snarling, wild faces engulfing him melded into a blurred vision of the soft light of lamps flickering on the ceiling of his leather tent. Then the pain hit him and in his mind's eye he saw the feathered shaft protruding from his left shoulder. With tentative movement, he brought his right hand to where the arrow had hit him. *Gone. Bandaged. How long have I been here?*

'Don't move, lord. I don't wish the stitches to tear.'

Antigonos turned his head to see his physician, grey-bearded and sitting looking down at him with deep-set, concerned eyes. 'Move? My arse, I can barely breathe.' He frowned as yet more of the haze slipped away, and then cocked an ear. 'What's that?'

'Fighting, my lord.'

'Fighting?'

'Yes, lord, I fear that the camp is under attack.'

'Under attack? I must get up.' He pushed himself onto his elbows and immediately regretted it and slumped back down, panting.

'Hold still, lord, or it will start bleeding again. You've already lost a great deal of blood.'

'Father!' Philippos shouted, rushing into the tent. 'We must move you; we've got to get you away.'

'Why have you got to get me away?'

Philippos ran to Antigonos' side, looking down at him. 'Because if we don't, you'll be captured.'

'Why?'

'Because the enemy are in the camp.'

'And that is exactly my question: why are they in the camp? If they weren't in the camp, you wouldn't have to move me for fear of my being captured, would you?'

'But they *are* in.'

Antigonos' hand clamped around his son's wrist, causing a flash of pain deep within his shoulder; he gritted his teeth. 'Where were the scouts? Where were the pickets, sentries? Was the camp secured?'

Philippos' face gave him the answer; the sound of fighting grew ever nearer.

'You did nothing, did you?'

'Father, I—'

'You what? You thought that because we had just lost the battle – and I assume we lost as we certainly weren't winning the last I can remember – that we can all go and have a quiet sit down and a skin of wine before falling into a drunken sleep.'

'Well, the men were exhausted and I assumed Seleukos' men would be the same.'

'You assumed? You fool; you've just assumed us into Seleukos' hands. What did Nearchos and Peucestas advise?'

'I'm your son! When you were carried from the field, I took charge. The phalanx withdrew in good order and then I disengaged the cavalry and we withdrew to the camp.'

'Meanwhile, Seleukos just sat there and let you do all this, did he?'

'Well, the battle was over.'

'No, it wasn't; I can still hear it. Seleukos' victory was not complete so for him the battle was not over. Didn't you think about how he beat Nikanor? Remember that, do you?'

Philippos had suddenly found the ground between his feet very interesting.

Antigonos struggled to keep his temper; each breath came with pain. 'Do you remember how Seleukos beat him?'

'Yes, Father.'

'Tell me.

'It was a night attack.'

'And what do we find ourselves in the middle of at the moment, eh?'

'A night attack.' Philippos' voice was small.

'My arse; where is Nikanor? Didn't he have something to say on the matter?'

'He warned me to make sure I set pickets.'

'And you ignored him.'

Philippos had nothing to say as the eye, weak as it was, blazed at him.

'And you want me to be carried away from a mess of your making like the invalid I am on the day when I've already ordered my cavalry to evade a charge for the first time ever? Ever! My arse, I will. I'll not run twice in one day. I'll stay here and wait for Seleukos; let him do to me what he wants; he deserves it for the way he used his army. No, Philippos, we could have retrieved something from the situation, but it's too late now. Go and tell our men to lay down their arms and kneel. It's over for us in the east and it may well be over for me altogether for I'll not beg Seleukos for my life. My precious arse, I won't.'

'Your precious arse is about all you've got left,' Seleukos said, standing in the entrance to the tent.

Philippos spun around, drawing his sword.

Seleukos put his hand on his hilt. 'Put it back, boy; there's been enough Macedonian blood shed today without adding yours.'

'Do as he says, Son,' Antigonos said, closing his eye and letting his head fall back onto the pillow.

Philippos looked between his father and their enemy and then did as he was told.

'Good lad,' Seleukos said, stepping into the tent. 'Well, that answers my question: you're wounded, Antigonos, which explains why I was able to walk into your camp.' Seleukos pushed past Philippos and glared down at his foe.

Antigonos looked back up. 'The arrogance of youth.'

'Ah, yes; I have that problem sometimes with Antiochus.'

Antigonos winced again at another spasm of pain. 'What do you want with me, Seleukos?'

'By rights, I could execute you, since you foolishly set that precedent with Eumenes and threw Antigenes alive into a fire-pit. Perhaps that should be your fate.'

'Do your worst.'

'That's exactly what I'm going to do.'

'Before you do, I've got a question: why did you move your right flank forward?'

Seleukos grinned. 'To keep you looking at it whilst my eastern cavalry crossed the ford. I was always going to do it, but when I saw where you had placed your elephants, I moved it even further than I originally intended, so that the scythed chariots would be angled to hit them and the flank of your phalanx once you evaded with your cavalry. I needed the elephants distracted until all the cavalry were over the second ford and behind you.'

Antigonos chortled deep in his throat and then winced again. 'Scythed chariots! Where did you find them?'

'The priests of Bel Marduk.'

Antigonos nodded. 'Go on, get it over with, then – quickly.'

'Oh, no, Antigonos; I'm not going to execute you. No, it's worse than that: I'm going to put you in front of the army assembly.'

For four days Antigonos had lain in his tent, regaining his strength, cursing his luck and marvelling that he had not been summarily executed in equal measure; now he sat on a dais next to Seleukos, before the army assembly, all Macedonians by birth and thus made up mainly of men from his own army. He had been wondering how Seleukos would win them over to his cause and get them to condemn him to death but now that Seleukos had begun to address the thirty-five thousand Macedonians present, Antigonos realised that his execution was not his intention.

'None of you here today who fought against me for Antigonos can say I did not let you go. I could have surrounded your phalanx with horse-archers and pounded you all the way back to your camp, if there were any left alive by then. But I didn't because that would have been close to murder; instead, I defeated you by a night attack killing as few of you as I could before Antigonos ordered you to surrender.' Seleukos paused as his words were relayed back through the assembly. 'I have tried to kill as few Macedonians as possible in fighting for my rights.'

Again, he paused; he looked down at Antigonos next to him and raised an accusatory finger. 'My rights! The rights Antigonos tried to take from me. Since I was appointed satrap of Babylonia by Antipatros, Alexander's regent of Macedon, I have been forced to retake it three times. Three times, brothers! Thrice! And why? Because Antigonos keeps on taking it for himself; but each time I come back. And this time I was again victorious. It is my right, as the victor, to put my prisoner in front of the army assembly and ask for his death; it is my right!'

There were dark mutterings throughout the crowd as those who had fought for Antigonos over many years thought they would be asked to condemn him. Seleukos heard them with pleasure for it made his task easier. 'But I will not ask that of you, my brothers; I will forgo my right in that respect.' The relief was audible. 'I will only ask what I think is just. I ask that I be allowed to remain in Babylonia as is my right. I ask that Antigonos and his sons, Demetrios and Philippos, refrain from continually attacking me and causing the deaths of many of our brothers. What I ask, soldiers of Macedon, what I ask is peace. I ask for peace! I say to you that those who wish to remain here in the east will be welcomed into my service; those who do not are free to go and escort Antigonos to the west having sworn an oath recognising my lawful right to Babylonia and my authority over the satrapies of the east, and then, my brothers, we can live in peace. What say you, the army assembly? What say you?'

The answer was unambiguous. 'Peace!'

Antigonos concealed a wry smile. *The clever bastard has made it so that I can never put claim to the east. But, what's more, instead of killing me and joining in the fight for my territory, he's sending me back west so he can build on his power here knowing I'm a buffer between him and the rest of the kingdoms. For that surely is where we now are: five separate kingdoms. The question is: who will take a kingly diadem first – Seleukos, me, Ptolemy, Lysimachus or Kassandros?* And as he sat, pretending to look pleased at the outbreak of peace between himself and Seleukos who was working the crowd, orchestrating their cheers, Antigonos' mind turned to what he would have to do if he wished to crown himself king. *Demetrios is right: we're in the middle and Seleukos has just confirmed that by making it impossible to come east again. Now the question is: do I now go south to take Ptolemy or north to break Lysimachus?*

Lysimachus.
The Cruel.

DARK HAD BEEN Lysimachus' thoughts of late; dark and troubling, for he could see no end to the struggle to keep the northern border free from barbarians and yet he had urgent business in the south. And there were many barbarians of many kinds; this, Lysimachus knew all too well after almost fifteen years fighting them. But the man who had continually made war against him was Dromichaetes, the King of the Getae, a Thracian tribe with Scythian influences – not least being the wearing of trousers and the use of massed horse-archers in support of the rhomphaia-wielding infantry. The cause of contention between himself and the Getic king was the ownership of the southern bank of the Istros, the great river flowing into the Euxine Sea. For Lysimachus it was a matter of security, crucial for his self-appointed role in keeping the empire safe from the horror lurking in the north; it was a horror that he was certain would soon be coming south, just as it had done over eighty years previously, further west, in Italia: the Keltoi were innumerable giants from the deep forests of the northern interior, forever on the move, but for the last fifteen to twenty years they had

441

been pressing on the Getae's northern flank, heading in the direction of the Istros.

In preparation for the inevitable invasion, Lysimachus had built fortresses – many fortresses – in strategic places. One of the greatest was guarding the entrance to the Succi pass, through the Haemus Mountains, the range bisecting, from east to west, his kingdom – as he had come to think of it. Although he considered himself king of his domain, he had not, as yet, taken to wearing a diadem nor did he refer to himself as king; that he would do once either Ptolemy, Kassandros or Antigonos claimed the title. Even Seleukos, from what he had heard, might elevate himself to the lofty heights of king if he was successful against Antigonos' latest incursion. But at the moment that was a distraction from the task in hand.

The Haemus Mountains might form a formidable barrier across his kingdom but they were within his realm, not on the border. The border was the Istros, whatever Dromichaetes might think; and all along the Istros, Lysimachus had built fortifications, the grandest of which was now all but complete. It was with great pride that Lysimachus looked upon the fortress of Axiopolis on the southern bank of the great river, just as it turns north for its final seventy-league flow to its delta. Tall towers with artillery platforms had been constructed along its river wall to control the shipping and force traders to pay a toll. To the east of the fortress the construction of a wall that would eventually reach to the Euxine Sea, at the port of Tomis, ten leagues away, had just begun. *Dromichaetes is welcome to the land north of the wall, but everything south of it and the river is mine. How dare the barbarian pretend otherwise?*

Lysimachus turned to the Getic delegation waiting upon him, surrounded by his bodyguards, as he surveyed his new line of defence. Reeking far worse than the Thracians from the south – a feat in itself – since they rarely took off their clothes, let alone changed them, the six men, with wild red beards, had come with an offer from their king. 'So Dromichaetes suggests that he marry my daughter and in return he gives me what is already mine!' *The arrogance of the barbarian.* 'You shall have my answer. Who will take it?'

'We are all together, lord,' the eldest of the group said, his red beard diluted by grey.

'But you are the leader, I assume.'

'I am the king's cousin.'

'Then you will bear my answer.' Lysimachus turned to the officer of his bodyguards. 'Take the heads of the other five.' He looked at the horrified leader of the delegation as his comrades were grabbed and, struggling, forced to their knees with their hands clamped behind their backs. The first head tumbled; blood slopped onto Lysimachus' sandal as the four kneeling men cried out, pleading for their lives. 'That is my answer.' Two more heads fell; the last men screamed in horror; their eyes transfixed on their decapitated comrades for the final few moments of their lives.

'But we are an embassy.'

'You're not any more; you lost that right when you insulted me and my daughter. Your master knows what I want; I've set out my terms and I don't bargain.' Lysimachus stepped to the right to avoid another gush of blood spurting from a newly hewn neck as the fourth and fifth heads rolled along the ground. He indicated to the five ghastly specimens. 'Now take these and be gone, thankful that I've left you with hands to carry them.' He paused and scratched at his two-day stubble looking at the man's hands, which slowly balled into fists and disappeared behind his back. 'Come to think of it, you only need one hand to hold a sack.'

'Lord, no, I beg you.'

Lysimachus threw his head back and laughed with little mirth. 'I've always enjoyed a good joke.' He turned on his heel and left the man rubbing his wrist and looking at the heads of his erstwhile friends. Swinging up onto his stallion and feeling much better within himself, Lysimachus kicked the beast forward and galloped towards his new fortress.

High on an artillery platform, Lysimachus looked north at the lone figure of the delegation leader making his way along the riverbank as it curved away from its eastward path, a bulging sack hung across his horse's rump. *An alliance against the Scythians is my price for peace, Dromichaetes, as I've already told you. I never make the same request twice; I just emphasise it with gestures. Perhaps you'll see things a little clearer now.* And indeed, it was a genuine hope, for Lysimachus desired to make an alliance with his old enemy, as once again the Scythian threat was massing in the northeast and the last time that occurred, four years previously, Dromichaetes had joined with them. Lysimachus had thrown the combined armies back across the river but at great expense and considerable loss of life. This time he would rather have the Getae fight alongside him and not against him, for they were formidable warriors; an alliance at this stage against a common enemy would also make it easier to negotiate the same arrangement when the real enemy, the Keltoi, appeared on the horizon. But, more than that, Lysimachus was tired of always having to concentrate upon the north when an equal threat to his existence also lurked in the south.

444

He turned to gaze over the grasslands running to the Haemus Mountains, just visible as a grey shadow in the distance; yes, it was time for him to go back south to oversee the construction of his newly founded capital of Lysimachia on the Hellespont and the forced transfer of its new population. It was to be peopled with the citizens of nearby Kardia; indeed, it was to be built with Kardia as Lysimachus had ordered the destruction of that city for its stone, thus earning the enmity of its erstwhile tyrant, Hecataeus, who had sworn to kill him and had fled, with a good part of a fortune amassed over twenty-five years, into exile in Sardis.

But that could not be helped as the man had stood in his way; Lysimachus had no doubt he would find a way to deal with Hecataeus. What was important, indeed crucial, was that Lysimachus should have his own capital named after him, and the city obviously needed citizens. It was a vital part of his preparations for taking the crown, for the city would look to the south and it was now time for him to secure his southern borders against Antigonos.

This he planned to do by expanding his dominion into northern Anatolia, pushing back the resinated cyclops before he, once again, attempted to get an army across the Hellespont into Thrace; for that was what Antigonos must surely do, should he not wish to be constantly surrounded by enemies now it was obvious to all that one man would not hold the entire empire. To Lysimachus it was clear this would be Antigonos' logical move if he were to fail in the east – and, as yet, he had no news one way or the other of his struggle against Seleukos. To try to take Egypt was fraught with difficulty, not least as there was no ally to attack on a second front; with Kassandros as a neighbour, Lysimachus could never be too vigilant. Thus, to pre-empt the move before Antigonos came back west, victorious or not, Lysimachus planned to rebuild himself a buffer zone in Anatolia, stretching as far south as Sardis; but to do so he needed first to be sure of his northern border for at least a year. As he contemplated his situation, movement on the plain below caught his eye: a small group of horsemen, half a dozen or so, were making their way towards the fortress; as he watched them approach it became clear that there were nine in all and in the midst of the group was a woman; a veiled woman. *What's she doing back here?*

'Archias, it's always a dubious pleasure,' Lysimachus said as the Exile-Hunter led his seven Thracian companions – disarmed and heavily guarded – and the woman into the audience chamber. *In fact, the timing could hardly be better; you can do me a great service.*

'"There is no pleasure like a glad surprise,"' Archias said, his boyish face beaming at Lysimachus. 'And I too am always pleased by your cheerful company.'

Lysimachus looked at the woman. 'Artonis, what strange travelling companions you have.'

Artonis' eyes, the only part of her veiled face visible, were cold. 'Ptolemy paid for Archias to escort me to you.'

Lysimachus' smile was grim. 'To slit my throat, eh? Although I fail to see how that would benefit Ptolemy.'

'Even so, I think you've made sure that won't be the case, Lysimachus,' Artonis said, gesturing to the bodyguards surrounding him and the guards encircling her and her companions.

'I'm a cautious man; and a curious one.' Lysimachus studied his unexpected visitor for a few moments. 'I assume you're here to, once again, ask for my help.'

Artonis lowered her gaze and made no reply.

'The last time you asked for that, I refused you; why should you think I would change my mind this time? Especially as since then you've been conspiring with that fool Barsine to put her bastard on the throne and cause everybody a lot of inconvenience.'

'For the past two months I've been a guest of your wife whilst I was waiting for you to return from the north; I've had long talks with Nicaea and she thinks you will help me.'

'Does she, indeed?'

'May we talk alone?'

Lysimachus looked at Archias and nodded at the door. 'You've fulfilled your task, you can go; she'll be safe with me. I'll see you before you leave; I have some work for you in Sardis as you make your way back to Ptolemy.'

Archias bestowed his most radiant smile upon Lysimachus. '"Seek your fortunes by hard work."'

'As much as you may like Euripides' advice, Archias, it won't necessarily be applying to you; you'll be doing hard work, yes, but for free as far as I'm concerned.'

Archias' smile died. 'What makes you think that I would consider that?'

'Because, my friend, it would be in your interest to do so as the target is very wealthy and has gone into exile taking a lot of that wealth with him. It seems to me, after all the inconvenience he's caused me, only right that he should pay for his own assassination rather than me – provided you can find his gold. Now go, I'll brief you once I have spoken to Artonis.'

'I now realise that it was a mistake to support Herakles' claim to the throne; it has deflected me from my purpose and has annoyed everyone who I could consider to be allies,'

Artonis said, coming straight to the point once she was alone with Lysimachus in his study, high over the slow-flowing Istros, speckled with small fishing boats, each one crowned with gulls; she had not been invited to sit in the vacant chair on the other side of the desk from her host.

'Annoyed is one way of putting it,' Lysimachus said, leaning forward in his seat, baring his teeth. 'Massively fucked off is the way I would describe how most of the people who count felt.' He held Artonis' gaze until she bowed her head. 'So, this great realisation came to you before or after Polyperchon had Herakles and Barsine garrotted?'

Artonis' eyes remained downturned. 'I thought that if Herakles were king – the true Argead heir – then Antigonos' pride would have forced him into rebellion and he would have been crushed by an alliance of all those loyal to the king.'

'You mean me, Ptolemy and Seleukos – if Antigonos hasn't already defeated him, that is – as Kassandros would have been dead in your scheme?'

'Yes,' Artonis said in a small voice.

Lysimachus gave a hollow laugh. 'I take it by the lack of confidence in your tone that you can see now just how unlikely it would have been for any of us to bend the knee to the bastard.'

'Yes.'

'Another king would have just complicated matters. The empire will never be reunited.'

'I know that now.' Artonis raised her eyes. 'But does Antigonos?'

'If he's sensible, he will.'

'But he's not sensible, is he? His position means that he can never be sensible.'

Lysimachus frowned. 'Meaning?'

'Meaning that he's surrounded by people he perceives to be enemies. He will always be lashing out one way or the other. At the moment he's in the east campaigning against Seleukos; do you think there will be a difference in him if he comes back victorious compared to coming back defeated?' Artonis laid her hands on the back of the vacant chair, leaning forward, her intensity growing. 'Of course there won't be; either way it will be the same power-hungry Antigonos. If he beats Seleukos and wins the east, he'll want to take the rest of the empire, starting with either Egypt or Thrace; but if he loses, he will find himself surrounded and therefore will try to take either Egypt or Thrace in order to break out. Unless he is killed, whatever the result, his reaction will be the same.' Artonis pulled the chair back and sat. 'My guess is he will consider Thrace an easier target than Egypt so he'll come this way; whatever happens against Seleukos, he *will* come this way.'

'I've already anticipated that, which is why I intend to move into northern Anatolia to form a buffer.'

'He'll come at you whether you have a buffer or not.'

'Most probably.'

'But first he will have to secure Cyprus and make an alliance with Rhodos in order that he can control the sea to prevent Ptolemy invading Syria and southern Anatolia in his absence as he did the previous time, which cost Antigonos most of his navy. Failing to sign an agreement with Rhodos and tempt them out of neutrality, he will be forced to invade the island and lay siege to the city.'

Lysimachus considered this for a few moments. 'If the Rhodians decide not to ally themselves with him, then yes, that's very plausible; but time consuming.'

'Exactly; which gives us time.'

'Us?'

'Yes, us.'

'Time for what?'

'Time to build an alliance.'

Lysimachus waved the idea away. 'Again? It didn't work too well last time, did it? We were completely uncoordinated and then Antigonos made peace offers that none of us could refuse.'

'Yes, and look what happened. We're now in the same situation as we were before that peace treaty: Antigonos is attacking whoever he wants. Finish it, Lysimachus; finish it for once and for all with a strong alliance. An alliance in which all the members swear there will be no peace until Antigonos is dead. Do this for yourself, Lysimachus, for your security as much as I do it through my desire to avenge Eumenes, and, within a few years, we'll all be able to spit in the glazed eye of the cyclops.'

The mental image pleased him as much as the idea Artonis put forward, for it fitted with the time-scale of his plans. *She's right; if Seleukos doesn't capture and kill the cyclops, the war will just go on and on until someone does. Therefore, it would be best to do it sooner rather than later.* He studied the small frame of Eumenes' widow and saw the determination in her bearing and the fire in her eyes. 'I'll say this for you, Artonis: you are persistent and constant in your hatred for Antigonos. Very well; what do you want of me?'

'I need to borrow your wife.'

Lysimachus sat back in surprise. 'Nicaea? What do you need her for?'

'Kassandros and Thessalonike want me dead for what I did; for what I tried to do to them. I need Nicaea to come with me to Macedon to intercede with her brother and his wife on my behalf. I need them to put aside personal animosity and allow me to forge an alliance. Thais has already written a letter for me to give to Thessaloniki, urging a pragmatic attitude to my mistake.'

'They might just kill you anyway even if Nicaea is with you.'

'That is the risk I'll have to take. I will throw myself at their mercy; even if they just spare me until I see my husband avenged. After that they can do what they will.'

They might agree to that with Nicaea's persuasion. 'And if they agree to the alliance, what then? What about Ptolemy and Seleukos?'

'It's Ptolemy's idea; I'm here as his ambassador. He understands the need to act now.'

He understands the need for others to act is, I think, closer to the truth. 'And Seleukos?'

'I'll make no plans for him until we know the outcome in the east. But if he survives his war with Antigonos and his army is intact, Apama is my friend, she'll help me convince him. We women will secure the alliances, Lysimachus; you men will do the fighting. This will work, I know it; Eumenes foresaw it just before he died. He knew that one day he would have his revenge from beyond the grave.'

Author's Note

Once again, this work of fiction is based mainly upon the writings of Diodorus, Plutarch and fragments of Arrian, all of whom wrote some considerable time after the events and used the lost history of Hieronymus as one of their sources. As always, I have kept to what are the accepted facts. Again, I have blurred things in the timeline; the High and Low timelines differ by a year and so I have created an amalgamation of the two to best suit the narrative. The actual timeframe of the book is almost three and a half years, so – much as in *Babylon* and *An Empty Throne* which have similar timescales – I felt that some obfuscation of the passing of time was necessary in order to avoid continually saying how much time has passed. Once more, this led to a few little round-ups of what had been occurring elsewhere for which, again, I ask your forgiveness, as I am writing historical fiction and not straight history.

Most of what is portrayed in the book is reported to have happened, whether it be Cilles' unguarded march north against Demetrios and the latter's surprise night attack or Polyperchon's betrayal of Herakles and his mother; the ill-fated expedition against the Nabateans and Demetrios' subsequent foray and his receipt of seven hundred camels; or Seleukos emptying Babylon so that it would be a value-less prize; they, and much else in the book, all happened roughly as I have shown so I will point out the parts of the narrative that are my fiction instead.

We know next to nothing about Antigonos' campaign against Seleukos and the subsequent battle other than from a reference in Polyaenus' *Stratagems of War* written in the second century AD:

> In an engagement between Seleukos and Antigonos, the evening put an end to the undecided action; and both armies retreated to their respective camps, determined to renew the conflict the next day. The soldiers of Antigonos in the meantime put off their arms, and relaxed in their tents. But Seleukos ordered his men to eat, and sleep in their arms, and lie down in order of battle: that they might be ready for action, whenever the charge was sounded. At break of day the army of Seleukos rose up, already armed and in order. They immediately advanced against Antigonos, whose troops were unarmed and disordered, and therefore afforded an early victory to the enemy.

This gives no context other than an otherwise unheard-of battle, so it is reasonable to suppose that it was the final conflict in that particular campaign – it also fitted in with the night/dawn attack theme of the battles in the book! With just that snippet to work on, the rest of the battle is my fiction and I had great fun doing it, using my collection of 25mm lead soldiers. I decided to set it close to where Seleukos founded Seleukia, as the area where the Tigris and the Euphrates come closest to each other was a traditional point of defence for Babylonia – hence the wall and the canal constructed by the ancient Babylonians. Taking over the dining room table, I recreated Seleukos' and Antigonos' armies using about 400 figures on either side and worked out the tactics using the wall and the canal. It was a most enjoyable few days and I have the pictures to prove it!

Artonis' travels are all my fiction; there is nothing to say that she was a part of Herakles' attempt to gain the throne of Macedon although she was Barsine's half-sister and so, therefore, it is not beyond the realms of possibility. Ptolemy sending Andronicus to sabotage the attempt is likewise fictitious. There is also nothing to place Artonis with Kleopatra when she was murdered by her slaves at Antigonos' behest, but her being there meant that we could witness the events at first hand.

Kassandros' forced heroics at the siege of Bylazora are imaginary, although he did campaign in that area at around that time. He did also order the deaths of Alexander and Roxanna; however, the circumstances I've described and Thessalonike's direct participation in them are my fiction.

I am indebted to many modern histories of the time, especially *Dividing the Spoils* by Robin Waterfield, *Antigonos the One-Eyed* by Jeff Champion, *Antigonos the One-Eyed and the Creation of the Hellenistic State* by Richard A. Bellows, *The Rise of the Seleukid Empire, Antipater's Dynasty* and *The Ptolemies – Rise of a Dynasty*, all by John D. Grainger, both volumes of *The Wars of Alexander's Successors* by Bob Bennett and Mike Roberts, *The Rise of the Hellenistic Kingdoms* by Philip Matyszak and *The Macedonian War Machine* by David Karunanithy.

My thanks, as always, go to my agent, Ian Drury at Shiel Land Associates, and Gaia Banks and Alba Arnau in the foreign rights department.

Many thanks to my editor, Sarah de Souza, for her invaluable input, vastly improving the narrative by her inciteful comments and suggestions; and also to Tamsin Shelton for another thorough and excellent copy-edit.

And finally, once again, my thanks and love to my beautiful wife, Anja, especially for her understanding attitude to my commandeering of the dining room table for so long.

Alexander's Legacy will conclude in *Beyond the Grave*.

LIST OF CHARACTERS

(Those in italics are fictional.)

Aeacides	The former King of Epirus.
Agathocles	Tyrant of Syracuse.
Alexander	The cause of all the trouble.
Alexander	Alexander's posthumously born son by Roxanna.
Alexandros	Polyperchon's son. Now deceased.
Andronicus	One of Ptolemy's generals, formally with Eumenes and Antigonos.
Antigenes	Veteran commander of the Silver Shields. Now deceased.
Antigonos	Satrap of Phrygia appointed by Alexander.
Antiochus	Son of Seleukos and Apama.
Antipatros	Regent of Macedon in Alexander's absence. Father of Kassandros and Philip. Now deceased.
Apama	Seleukos' Persian wife.
Archias	A one-time tragic actor turned assassin.
Aristodemus	Antigonos' chief agent.
Artakama	Ptolemy's first wife, from Persia. Sister of Artonis and half-sister of Barsine. Now deceased.
Artonis	Eumenes' Persian widow. Sister of Artakama and half-sister of Barsine.

Asander	Satrap of Caria. Now deceased.
Atarrhias	A Macedonian general.
Athenaios	*A Macedonian officer in Antigonos' pay.*
Azanes	*A Sogdian chieftain.*
Babrak	*A Paktha merchant.*
Barsine	Alexander's half-Persian mistress and mother of his bastard, Herakles. Half-sister of Artakama and Artonis.
Berenice	Antipatros' niece and cousin to Eurydike. Ptolemy's third wife.
Cilles	One of Ptolemy's generals.
Crateuas	A Macedonian general.
Demetrios	Son of Antigonos.
Demetrius of Phaleron	De facto Tyrant of Athens.
Dioscurides	Antigonos' nephew and brother of Ptolemaios.
Eumenes	First Philip's and then Alexander's secretary, a Greek from Kardia. Now deceased.
Eurydike	One of Antipatros' daughters, married to Ptolemy.
Gelon	*Kassandros' ambassador.*
Glaucias	Macedonian soldier and gaoler of Roxanna and her son Alexander.
Herakles	Alexander's bastard by Barsine.
Hieronymus	A soldier turned historian; a compatriot of Eumenes.
Kassandros	Antipatros' eldest son.
Kleopatra	Daughter of Philip II and Olympias, Alexander's full sister.
Krateros	The great Macedonian general killed in battle with Eumenes.
Lagus	Eldest son of Ptolemy and his mistress Thais.
Lycortas	*Steward to Ptolemy.*

Lysimachus	One of Alexander's seven bodyguards. Satrap of Thrace.
Malichus	King of the Nabateans.
Menelaus	Governor of Cyprus. Brother of Ptolemy.
Naramsin	*Priest of Bel Marduk and Seleukos' architect.*
Nearchos	A Cretan, Alexander's chief admiral, now in Antigonos' pay.
Nicaea	One of Antipatros' daughters, married to Lysimachus.
Nikanor	Antigonos' satrap of Media.
Olympias	One of Philip II's wives, mother to Alexander and Kleopatra. Now deceased.
Ophellas	Governor of Cyrenaica.
Oxyartes	Satrap of Paropamisadae. Father of Roxanna.
Patrokles	Governor of Babylon.
Penelope	Alexandros' wife, known as Cratesipolis.
Perdikkas	One of Alexander's seven bodyguards. Now deceased.
Peucestas	One of Alexander's seven bodyguards. Former satrap of Persis, now serving Antigonos.
Phila	Antipatros' daughter, widow of Krateros, now married to Demetrios.
Philip	Son of Antipatros and Hyperia, twin brother of Pleistarchos, half-brother of Kassandros.
Philip – formerly Arrhidaeus	The mentally challenged half-brother of Alexander. Now deceased.
Philotas	Friend of Antigonos. Executed by Eumenes.
Phoinix	Satrap of Hellespontine Phrygia.
Pleistarchos	Son of Antipatros and Hyperia, twin brother of Philip, half-brother of Kassandros.
Polyarchos	A Macedonian officer loyal to Seleukos.
Polyperchon	Former regent of Macedon. Father of Alexandros.
Ptolemaios	Antigonos' nephew and brother of Dioscurides.

Ptolemy	One of Alexander's seven bodyguards, perhaps Philip II's bastard. Satrap of Egypt.
Pyrrhus	Son of Aeacides, King of Epirus.
Pythan	Antigonos' nominee as Seleukos' replacement as satrap of Babylonia. Now deceased.
Roxanna	A Bactrian princess, widow of Alexander and mother to his son Alexander.
Seleukos	Satrap of Babylonia.
Stratonice	Daughter of Demetrios and Phila, grand-daughter of Antigonos and Stratonice.
Stratonice	Wife of Antigonos and mother to Demetrios.
Telesphorus	One of Antigonos' nephews and senior officers.
Teutamus	A Macedonian officer loyal to Antigonos, commander of the Babylon garrison. Now deceased.
Thais	Long-time mistress of Ptolemy.
Thessalonike	Alexander's half-sister and wife of Kassandros.
Xenophilus	Warden of the royal treasury in Susa.